# The Scabbed Wings Of Abaddon
*by Sean Kennedy*

First Printing April 2007

Written By: Sean Kennedy

Illustrated By: Sean Kennedy

Edited By: Corinne Durocher

Formatted By: James O'Brien

Sean Kennedy:
www.darkatlas.com

RantMedia:
www.rantmedia.ca

ISBN: 978-1-4303-1620-6

First Printing
10 9 8 7 6 5 4 3 2 1

**Thoughts On Editing Scabbed Wings Of Abaddon**

I read and re-read this book so many times as one reads a beloved novel. I would have to repeatedly remind myself that I was EDITING it! It was difficult to omit anything, because Sean's vision was so pervasive, with each word so carefully and thoughtfully picked to seep into the readers' subconscious. It was like clearly hearing his voice in my head. That sensation, that shift in perception- I've never read any fiction that rocked my relationship with reality so violently.

I had that eerie sense of Déjà vu, as one does when a book is written about one's hometown, but I had not prepared myself for the fact that reading this book as I did, (many, many times), it would change forever the way I viewed our little meager society, the paranormal and spirituality (organized religions) at large.

We exist in a society that reinforces material needs; we all understand the struggle to pay bills and the overwhelming desire to buy toys and those boots and the need to try and better ourselves with the superficial ideal of "success". An overwhelming contempt for these stupid things haunted me as I continued reading, knowing that some of the things that I value, such as my passion for performing can not only haunt me in my afterlife but also will serve as my everlasting brutal penance. I am a dancer and always have craved attention, "essence". I love to entertain people and have been training since I was five years old and devoted my whole life to ballet jazz, tap, flamenco, salsa etc. and theatre. That's exactly why the 'thespians,' which populate Abaddon along with the other ghoulish creatures, freaked me out so thoroughly.

I was reading about the Virto-Verax Feline symbol and I glanced at my cat Stella who was drowsing beside me on the couch. I looked in disbelief at the M shape that was scrawled on the page and it looked identical to Stella's markings. The cat looked at me with her glassy beady eyes at that exact moment and glared. I half expected her to open her mouth and say ominously, "Now you know too much". That's when I felt slightly sick and thought "okay there is something to this. This other plane of existence... the "paranormal"... and (take a breath) get a... a hold of yourself...you're not crazy".

I have always been a person open to suggestions, theories and conspiracies. I am well aware that the "truth" is what is printed by our lording Media conglomerate and drug manufacturers and "history" is a blithe representation of what the dictators and winners of wars want depicted.

That being said, the content of this book gives a subversive glimpse into some of the real truth and history as envisioned by SKTFM. Namely those spiritual elements that give us the creeps and reassure us that when a beloved dies they can see and watch us as we grind away at our pathetic lives here in the living. The afterlife has always fascinated me, and I often wonder what truly awaits the dead. Those images of angels with harps, airy clouds and some white bearded guy who looks an awful lot like Santa Claus just don't fly with me. Neither does Hieronymus Bosch's concept of Hell as seen in "The Garden of Earthly Delights- Hell" with its writhing, swirling orgies and gruesome, tortured agonies.

I think Sean's concept of Hell/Heaven as demonstrated in this book, is a lot more likely though it is way more twisted.

I hope you enjoy your perception altering experience as much as I did.

C. Durocher
*January 14, 2007*

The god or gods that created the universe look in on us from time to time, and witnesses all the worlds' suffering. Seeing this, they weep tears of despair that fall to the Earth and become people. These people fight the worlds suffering by spreading joy and love with their every motion and thought.

This is for my wife.

She's a teardrop from God.

**Abaddon** (e bad'n) *vt* {Heb, destruction, abyss} *bible*

/

**1** place of the dead; neither world: Job 26:6
**2** in Revelation 9:11, the angel of the abyss; [*Gr. Apollyon*].

## Chapter 1

"Demons are angels reflected in the eyes of judgment."

*-Professor. Scott Harker*

As a member of the Klu Klux Klan you have certain responsibilities.

Scott Bartlet stood in his rancher gazing at the uniform donned by the man in the mirror. The white cloak, the scarlet crest of The Klan and his hood, gave him a feeling of nobility. Outside, the days' sticky humidity was fading under the Alabama night sky, but another dampness would drench him soon.

Tonight the Klan had unfinished business. It started just after their last ride, almost a month ago now. Young Sandra Pinto was seen kissing a nigger just beyond the edge of Shantytown. Now, it's all well and good if a woman, who had no business being out that late, wound up having too much fun with some of the boys, but when little Sandra was pawed by one of those filthy creatures, steps had to be taken.

This sort of thing had to be nipped in the bud. After all, in 1937 a man had enough problems without having to worry about his family. Those niggers only understood one thing, force; and a message had to be sent. They had to remember their place.

And so it was that the Klan rallied twenty five good God-fearing men, strong and true. They donned their honored hoods and called that filthy monkey out of his pathetic shack and into the street. Three families lived in that hole, and when the cloak called his name, they all knew the masters' voice. That bastard child came slinking out onto the porch like a crippled dog.

They heard the young boy's mother screaming restrained, other cowards were holding her back. It wouldn't have mattered if his family or neighbors did put up a fight, the Klan killed niggers, and it was their God given duty. Whether it was one hanging from a tree that night or three families of six, it made no difference to them.

Scott had always been good with a bullwhip and the boy's stringy neck was an easy target for the oiled leather lash. Even in the low glow of the torchlight the whip found its mark, and with a quick twist around the saddle horn, they gave him the final ride.

They dragged him through the dirt. Excited yells, choked screams, beating hooves, the strain of flesh torn asunder drifted past the cricket whispers. The sounds of hate and fear filled the night. The young man was found hanging in a tree the next morning, broken and bloody amidst the buzz of the morning flies.

Scott smiled thinking of the fear those savages must have felt, but they couldn't just take their medicine like men. No, they had to use the cowardice of their people. Through the perversion of their rituals, they called something from the festering pits of their homeland.

No one knew where he came from, or when he had arrived, but it wasn't long after the hanging. The blacks called him a Houngan. They said he was a priest sent by their tribal Gods to punish the Klan for what they had done. They called him the Skatman, and though their Gods had sent him, he was the embodiment of their most ancient fears.

People started to die.

Bob Deegan was the first. A family man with three children, he was torn awake one night so terrified he couldn't stop screaming. He thrashed wildly in his bed, waking everyone in the house. He was raving about the beasts beyond the veil, and how they were all damned. His wife tried to comfort him, but he rammed his bedside shotgun under his chin and pulled the trigger.

Another man on that fateful night ride was Jim Sedbanks. He was found trampled to death in his horse barn. Later, the sheriff mumbled the tale of how Jim's horse was found eating his intestines, whinnying through gurgling bloody bubbles.

A bizarre rotting sickness took Mark Hawthorn. Within three days, he went from the picture of health to a festering corpse. Near the end, he watched his flesh dropped off in splatters over the sounds of his screaming children.

Luke was torn apart by wild dogs.

Jacob choked to death on his own chitlins, and they still hadn't found Old Man Rogers, the Grand Wizard of that night.

The good minister spoke of God working through man to purge this evil from the town. He may as well have asked the Klan to ride, by means of a formal letter, and Scott wasn't about to let the good people of this town down.

Distant thunder roared in the night.

Scott walked out from the rancher. The night air was cool and wet on his face as he mounted his horse. He could see Tommy, his four year old son, from the side of the house watching with wide eyes of wonder. Tommy was too young to understand

The Klan, but knew his father rode for him, and the rest of the white children.

Scott made sure his bullwhip was fastened and was off amongst a savage flurry of hooves.

Old Man Rogers had hand picked young Scott for Grand Wizard in case something should have happened to him. Barely twenty five, Scott had the sense of duty and cold conviction needed by a Grand Wizard in order to keep the race clean and pure. He had been the grand wizard, the master of the local Klan for only the short time since Old Man Rogers' strange disappearance.

The night opened her arms to Scott. She barked forth a stuttered wink of lightning; lighting the path before him for eternal moments. Ahead, he saw his torch-lit brothers waiting by the edge of the wood. Thirty klansmen, all waiting anxiously for their master. Scott slowed as he approached while several voices called a greeting in awkward unison.

"Hail and well met, Grand Wizard!"

"Hail and well met Brothers." This was the proper response. Scott paused, catching breath before the initiatory rite.

"Is there any man here who is not pure of body, mind, blood, and soul?"

Silence ran through the twisted ghosts.

"Then we have work to do brothers!"

The words brought the formality of the meeting, but now they could all speak clearly to assess the matters at hand. Scott cleared his throat.

"Y'all know what we got to do tonight. That filth outside of Shantytown is attacking our loved ones, and has to be put down. Do we know where his den is?"

A single voice answered. "The far side of Shantytown, just by the riverbank"

Scott's commands seeped dark authority, like a surgeons' death sentence. "Then know that the method of cleansing we'll use tonight will be the same used on black witches in the past. We'll take him for the ride, lash him to a tree, and burn him. Brother Elkson, Brother Donald, is the cleansing site ready where we discussed?"

A chant of voices from the crowd, "Yes, Grand Wizard."

"Aw'ight, any questions?"

An uneasy, expectant murmur went through the sheeted posse.

"Then let's go kill us some niggers!"

A hoof beat choir sang into the night. The thrill of the hunt, intoxicating sadistic

3

dreams that made these men grunt a little louder when they fucked their smiling southern wives. The darkness swirled around their torchlight as they rode. A thousand tiny eyes watched, what a thousand tiny tongues would whisper to those who could hear them.

The area where the blacks were allowed to live was nothing more than a garbage dump. They had been forced to settle there by the Klan's constant threat. In Shantytown, everyone took shelter at the unmistakable sound of Klan hooves.

The Klan was riding, and this was to be a night of pain.

The light from candles came into view from the tendrils of darkness. Small shacks built from stolen fence-boards loomed out of the night. The candlelight slipped through the awkward branches and rag curtains. The warning of the Klan's approach had long since been heeded. Whole families were in the shelter of darkness, anticipating each approaching hoof beat of hate. The buildings of Shantytown watched the Klan's approach, like a child watching his father coming home drunk yelling for his mother again. It was a silent dignity that promised: *Someday...someday.*

The Skatman lived on the outskirts of town. These people knew the dark power he held, that power brought fear and respect in equal serving. Some said he didn't even exist and was only a ghost to frighten the children in the night. Old women said he was the spirit of a sacrificed goat, rejected by the voodoo god Dambala, only to return and become a vengeful spirit of death. Now he and the massive rooster familiar he kept traveled throughout the world as dark mercenaries. He was a legend amongst these people, a myth, until he appeared plying his trade, called by the scent of vengeance to the victim's door. His work would come to pass, and the Skatman would vanish back into the darkness from which he came. Of course, there was always the matter of his fee, which most assuredly would be paid.

Death by trade, evil by virtue, and his currency was the pain of others.

The Klan rode onwards through the village. Scott thought of how the niggers would shake seeing their witch-priest dragged through these streets. The Klan feared no pagan god of the black man.

The horse's hooves beat harder and faster against the soil, and each of the hooded men could feel the anxiety's tightening grip as they approached the hollow darkness where the Skatman's shack stood. As they approached the forbidden place, the orange glow from the torches threw shadows of madness singing into the trees. This place did not have the pride of Shantytown. Instead there was the feeling of abandonment, like an electric chair thrown into the prison trash.

Scott saw the twisted sticks of his hovel, sitting like the nest of some great river rat on the banks. It was a mass of strangely warped branches intertwining impossibly together. Their torchlight fell on the gaping entrance of the stick hut, but no light was permitted inside this night. Scott called the traditional challenge of the Klan.

"This is your master's voice, boy! You come on out here!"

The other's horses slowed and filed into a wide crescent beside their leader. Crickets dared not whisper, this was the world created by hatred come home. The confidence that had flowed as a raging river within the Klansmen, slowed to a sickening trickle. The silence continued.

"Skatman!"

Silence.

Guillotine silence.

Through the slight filter of hoods, the acridly sweet scent of rotting flesh began to fill the air. The horses became more uneasy with each breath of the horrid stench. Tossing their heads and whining as they staggered. Above them in the darkness, the source of the scent shifted its weight and positioned itself for an attack. Eyes neither living nor dead looked upon these men of hate, preparing to show them what hate really was.

The howl of a slaughtered infant came from the branches above them. A massive frenzy of flesh and feathers crashed down into the circle of Klansmen, tearing one white cloak from his horse. No time to scream, the claws bit into the back of his neck and slipped into his spine. He felt no pain as he fell, nor was he aware that he had cast his torch into another horses' face.

In an instant, the horses were bucking, and screaming in blind fear. Over half of the Klan was thrown and trampled by their horses as they fled. The very air now tasted of madness.

Scott had his own mount twist, throwing him to the ground. The force of impact stunned him for a moment and with the screaming and sudden darkness he wondered if he was even conscious. His hood came off and he searched frantically in the night for any source of light. The sounds of horses, only a few with riders screeching commands, could be heard drifting into the distance. Some had run straight into the creek and were swept off by the current that silently waited. Scott found his torch still partially lit only a few feet away. He swept it up and held it high. As the flame took hold, its glow was cast on the carnage around him.

Many cloaks had been thrown down hard, some wouldn't get back up. Unfortunate were the ones who went down first. Five horse trampled blood soaked cloaks lay broken, still, scattered and seeping in mud. Five more were in agony from broken bones, but seven had stayed on their horses as they bolted in a mad panic. This left thirteen men to draw themselves up from the muddy clay. Others found their torches and took the flame from Scott. Their light fell upon the beast that had attack them.

This was Babayan, the hideous rooster familiar kept by the Skatman, and it knew the deed for which the Klan had come. It squat, hanging its head low to fight, but still stood three feet to the shoulder. Each claw was larger than a man's hand, and gripped the earth with each barbed step. It skulked back and forth growling its foul voice. The sick stench of rot permeated through every pore, making each breath vile.

The shadows thrown by the torches seemed to mould around the bird, making it shift with the darkness and hard to focus on. Several Klansmen now stood by Scott. A few had drawn guns from beneath their cloaks now trained at the massive rooster a few yards in front of them. The horrible thing lumbering mockingly from side to side, becoming larger with its wings cocked to the side in its own war dance.

A cloak to Scott's left raised his pistol and fired a shot into the massive rooster. The roar of the blast was deafening, as though the trees themselves rejected the sound. It was a clean shot, easy to make from the twelve foot distance between the shooter and the foul thing, yet the bullet missed. It must have, for the blast only made the creature fly into a hideous rage.

Almost as fast as the bullet came at Babayan, the rooster now came at its attacker. With a single flap of its gigantic wings it was upon the Klansman, catching his wrist easily in its beak. A wet popping and a loud scream came as Babayan sheared his pistol hand away.

As fast as it attacked, the rooster leapt away, leaving great gashes of blood in the cloak's torso where taloned feet had found purchase. The rooster leapt sideways to another cloak who had turned to assist his brother.

The Klansmen couldn't fire their weapons now, the creature was too close. They would only kill each other in a frenzied crossfire. In the sedated moments of combat, they helplessly clutched impudent pistols like teddy bears as this monster came through the darkness.

As the throat of a second Klansman was torn away by Babayan's bloody beak, the shock spell was broken on the remaining men. The rooster tried to leap to yet another cloak, but they took their pistols and began beating the bird in wide swinging strikes. Babayan was twice as strong as he was fast, but the steel swings of the cloaked figures knocked him down into the mud. The rooster landed on its side and the Klansmen now had a clean shot at the filthy thing.

Another figure emerged from the darkness in a furious lunge of shambling color. As the pistols of three Klansmen blasted smashing lead balls and blue smoke down into the form of the rooster, two Klansman's heads were severed and fell into the circle they fired in.

Scott turned with his brothers as another heartbeat passed to face their attacker. In the stretched seconds of bloodshed, the night shifted and the dark Houngan came into view. He stood tall and proud with a wicked sickle fresh with blood held by his side.

A mountain of a coat stretched down his 6'5" frame, made of small patches stitched together and overlapping each other in colorful chaos. The patches were all manner of fabrics, shambling in a comical array. Some were dirty and rotting, while others were bright, new, seemingly untouched.

From under the coat, his bare black chest showed stretched leathery skin over the sinewy muscles that covered his torso. Around his neck lay amassed trinkets and charms that sounded a rattling brush with his every step. His pants, striped in all the colors of a circus tent, clung around his waist and frayed just above the ankles from travel. His feet looked callous and scarred, as though he had never worn shoes. His hands, long and powerful like great spidery hooks trailed at the side of his frame. Only the palms of his hands had a slightly lighter pigmentation, seen as he nimbly flexed his fingers.

His face betrayed his age. The hard tight skin cracked and wrinkled with the constant beating of time. High cheek bones accented a sharp nose, giving him an elfish expression. Massive twisted dreadlocks hung down to his waist in tattered links. Each dreadlock weaved a different charm into its matting.

The most bizarre feature about him wasn't his height or his hair, but his eyes. There was no iris to be seen at all, only large white fields showing like death camp searchlights against his dark skin. Only the most powerful Houngan priests were touched in such a way to see the dreams and fears of the common man, and the light of madness shone from within them.

The Skatman's low hoarse whisper slashed the night. "Da bullets not kill Babayan. Dey only make him go away for awhile."

As he spoke, he casually swung the sickle up from his side and caught another clansman under the chin and lifted him in the air as the sickle bit into him like a great hook. With the Klansman struggling on the end of his blade, each jerk of his body drove the blade further up into his brain. The Skatman's muscled corded arm lashed out and grabbed Scott by the throat.

He effortlessly pulled Scott close to his death camp eyes. "Da gran' wizard bringin' da watcha's, I-Ya!"

As the Skatman spoke he threw the impaled Klansman like a rag doll, off his blade and into the other cloaks nearby. The body knocked three of them down and created a gap of a few meters between the cloaks and the dark priest. Still jerking from his severed consciousness, the white robed figure smeared a putrid mix of mud and blood onto his white form as he twitched.

Scott could feel his own consciousness slipping away in the dark Houngan steel grip, but still he had the strength to draw his pistol from its holster beneath his cloak.

The Colt Walker was an old gun for this day and age, but Scott carried it with him on these rides to honor his grandfather, who held it in the Mexican war. It was a 44 black powder pistol that had enough power at close range to drop a bull in full charge. Scott brought the pistol only inches from the Skatman's side and pulled the trigger.

The hollow blast and white smoke of black powder filled the air. Scott was dropped, gasping for air into the bloody mud beneath him. As he struck the mud the hideous scream of a burning child came from the smoking pile of feathers.

Half a razors flash of time had passed since the rooster had been shot, the slowed time of combat had made the Klansmen forget the abomination they had just shot, yet now, with three new gaping wounds in its feathers and flesh, the demon familiar Babayan was impossibly alive and in full flesh frenzy.

With a jerk of its head the bird severed a Klansmen's leg below the knee as keenly as a broadsword strike; the force of its wings knocked two more cloaks to the ground. The rooster fought to clear the circle of Klansmen and return to its master's side. As the three cloaks fell, the mass of blood and feathers emerged from them and came to the Skatman's defense.

From under his smoking coat a trickle of blood came from the Skatman's side like urine, yet still he stood vacantly staring at the crowd of Klansmen. The cries of the maimed and wounded became the background, the sound of each of their beating hearts.

Scott scrambled to his feet and past the rooster, stumbling back to the line of white cloaks that pointed the pistols like crosses at the unholy duo. He chased the remaining darkness of suffocation away from his eyes and brought the massive Walker pistol to bear on the dark priest. He should be dead, that blast should have thrown him from his feet and into the form of a broken carcass, yet still the dark priest stood with the smoke from the gun blast still clinging to his coat.

Babayan stood between them now, wings cocked out showing light though impossible wounds for a living being to sustain. Louder still, the sound of returning horses came from behind, and the seven Klansmen returned fresh with anger and hate.

Bleeding from a gaping wound in his side, the Skatman watched them form a loose circle around him, holding their torches as he had seen so many do before. He had been clumsy and had let himself be wounded. For hundreds of years he only had to worry about the bite of a blade, but now he could feel the gaping hole the hot ball of lead had punched through his chest. A modern firearm would have little effect on the Sorcerer, but this pistol was old, with too much time and essence spent in careful polishing and loading. Now the essence spent had saved Scott, but damned the Skatman.

The Skatman knew what the Klan had planned for him. Casting his eyes through the bloodied sheets, he could see their hatred spilling out. He knew what they planned to do, so he had to do what must be done.

His voice came, whispered and hypnotic. "Ja come all dis way to kill da Skatman. Ja come to burn away his soul."

The Klansmen could have fired, but they didn't. These things before them were unnatural, evil in a way that holy priests could never fathom. He had a lethal wound, and yet stood staring, never moving his death camp gaze from Scott.

The beating hearts, breathing, and screams of the injured mixed into a storm around the Klansmen. Frozen in their horror, they watched the impossible. The

Skatman made his hand like a great claw and held it over his rooster familiars head. Babayan made a sound like a man vomiting and collapsed in a heap. The force of life was drawn from the dead thing back into its master.

As the blood soaked into the ground from his slain familiar, the Skatman brought the sickle up to his shoulder on his wounded side, tapping it lightly. He spoke again, never taking his eyes from Scott.

"No burnin' dis day Klans-mon, no burnin' da Skatman. But don' ja worry Scott Bartlet, Da Skatman be seein' ja again soon."

His searchlight eyes widened. "Skatman go now, keep Babayan. Skatman go down to Abaddon."

With one fluid motion the Skatman drew the blade across his shoulders. The sickle cut deep and clean, snapping the tendons and severing veins. It slid between the vertebrae in his neck, severing the spinal cord and through the flesh on the other side. He didn't cut his head completely off, before the fountain of blood erupted thrusting his body down into a collapsed pile.

## Chapter 2

Diary entry #66571
Anywhen in the Neverwhere.

Dear Mr. Diary,

I'm not exactly sure where I am right now, but I'm quite certain that I don't like it very much.

It was Aug. 11, 1812 this morning, but I'm not quite certain it's the same day now. It seems I'm not quite certain of a lot today.

Today has been a very strange day, a very strange day indeed. This morning I arose to have my tea and toast and spoke with my dear cat, who will be quite concerned about what happened to me I must say. Then, as usual, I came to the library and started to hide.

Normally, I would come to work and begin tending to the books. But this morning, I really did not want to work, no, not at all. So I said good morning to that loathsome chief librarian Mr. Beasley, and ran quite cleverly to hide in book restoration and ancient texts.

I find it makes much more sense when you run cleverly, because if you run stupidly you're bound to draw attention. People in the library would look and say, "Oh, there goes Clarence Winker. He's not running very cleverly, he must be going to hide."

That would certainly not do.

In any case, anyone at all, I don't feel a man in my position should have to hide. If they would only see how important my work is to the library, I wouldn't have reason to hide. I'd be able to stride right into Her Majesty's library and say "Good morning everyone." And they would say to me, "Good morning Mr. Winker. You don't have to hide, you can just walk straight back to your old books, and we'll be certain not to bother you, not even a little bit."

But they don't.

So after I hid with my books for a while, I realized it was time to go home. That's the beauty of my place in the library. I have a slower sense of time than anyone else. I'll simply be working away and if I'm not careful I'll miss all my meals. But I'm usually not that bad, especially after diary entry #51334 when I happened to get locked in the building. I had to wait until the next morning. That was ghastly I must say!

I knew it was time to go home because of the usual pain in my tummy. It's my own personal clock that lets me know the sun has gone down. It is very rarely wrong, a rather good alarm tummy I must say! So I gathered up all my papers that I couldn't possibly leave, and yourself of course Mr. Diary, and walked out and into the library's entrance which of course was now the library exit due to the fact that I was leaving.

When I got outside, that would seem when things got more than just a little bit peculiar.

There was nothing peculiar about the street, or the way the lamps were burning. There was a fog, but it was slight for a London fog, and there wasn't all that much peculiar about it anyway. So, I started back to my little home in the most un-peculiar way that I knew how.

When I passed by the alley just off Muldoon Street, I felt a sharp sting on the back of my head. Well, to be honest, it wasn't really a sting, more it was a whump but I'm not entirely sure that one can feel a whump, perhaps a wallop, but I think the whump is by far more accurate. My head hurt to say the very least, and I fell to my knees immediately. When I started to get up, which was when I felt the crunch.

This was definitely not a whump, or even a wallop, this was a crunch, a rather loud one at that. I felt it on the crown of my head. I don't feel sounds that often, but this one I most definitely did feel, after which I blacked out and wound up...here.

This is when my day turned from only slightly peculiar to very peculiar. It is important to remember these milestones, don't you think?

My first feeling was that I was cold. Not particularly biting cold mind you, but an annoying cold that slipped under my clothes and lay next to my skin. I don't remember actually opening my eyes, just realizing that all at once I was aware. It was as though my eyes had been staring for quite some time, and then I just became aware that my eyes were watching something. I recognized the alley I was in, but I couldn't be sure of anything else.

The cobbled streets had changed and were going in directions they shouldn't for that particular area of London. This of course led me to the conclusion that this was not that particular area of London, or any particular area of London for that matter. I seem to be getting ahead of myself. I should start with the more personal peculiarities first and move on from there.

I think I was attacked by some kind of a retrieval thief. A thief who not only took the papers I was heading home with, he replaced it with my favorite waistcoat from home. It's a good thing that I was already wearing my favorite pants, shirt and coat or no doubt he would have got them for me as well. He got my waistcoat though, and my top hat. So I sat there, on the ground, looking about, pondering for quite some time. At least I thought it was quite some time, but I couldn't be certain since the watch I had just bought (see diary entry #59878) was taken by said retrieval thief.

Where I am now, this odd place that is most certainly not London seems to be in an awful state of decay, and as well, it's made up of the most peculiar buildings. Everything is either a church, theater, or house that must well be over 300 years old. The streets twist and turn like mad serpents going nowhere, and the people here dress in the most astounding way. Not only that, but all my efforts to find anything even remotely normal have turned up somewhat dry.

Everyone and I mean everyone, including me, is quite afraid. Mind you, we have good reason to be. You see after I had wandered not very far at all, I called out to a couple of fellows that I saw dressed in a rather ratty garb, but they were running and screaming an awful lot, and I don't think that they were very happy about being here either. They ignored me quite entirely, and went about their rather odd running-and-screaming business.

That was when I saw the spider. Now I promise you, Mr. Diary, I have not been drinking. He was much larger than an average spider. Not "larger" as in the size of a dinner plate, but "larger" as in the size of a rhinoceros. It came out of a space between buildings and grabbed one of the men outright, catching him up with its jaws.

He, the spider that is, seemed very upset. This was very peculiar because you would think that a spider the size of the rhinoceros would be more good-natured. But he wasn't, he was very cross indeed. While his friend continued the screaming and running business with renewed vigor, the rhinoceros spider dragged the poor fellow into the shadows.

I imagine the spider is probably a lot more good-natured now that he has eaten. Nevertheless, I made a mental note of where that alley was, in case that big fellow should happen to fall into a rather foul mood again. I think rhinoceros spiders are rather moody.

But I'm getting ahead of myself again. I should probably describe the other peculiar things that are about in this city. But of course, you can understand that that was one of the more significant moments, and I couldn't keep it all to myself too much longer. Rhinoceros spiders are quite impressive.

When I say the fellow was dragged off into the shadows, I imagine it would be quite important for you to realize exactly what it is that I mean. You see, there is not the usual sort of light here, from either the sun or the moon. Now that I look about in this twilight, I can see no stars, or clouds. All the light for this city comes from the city itself.

There are these glowing patches on buildings; I imagine the light is quite like that of a firefly, I've never seen a firefly so I couldn't say for sure, or perhaps a candle. There is enough light to see by, but not much more. These patches glow with just enough light as to illuminate the areas close to them. It reminds me of when it has just stopped raining, but very different. To be the same, the rain would have to be glowing, and the puddles that would form would have to be on the vertical parts of the world rather than the horizontal.

Never mind, it's a bad comparison, I'll try to do a better one later.

I have seen no lamps anywhere in this place, or coal stoves, or any kind of steam power. Only the buildings and streets give off their powerless glow. As you can no doubt sympathize, it's rather difficult to write in this light, but even still I still feel a sense of duty to you my dear Mr. Diary, I am so very glad that you are here.

You must forgive me for being fragmented, no one can tell me what is going on. Even though I have seen many people wandering about, no one seems to live in these buildings. All of the buildings that I ventured inside, a total of seven, including this one, have no one living in them. All except for that dreadful building No. 4. When I went inside, I heard the most unpleasant sound, and decided it would be best to leave.

As you can guess, this whole thing was entirely stressful. As a matter-of-fact, most of my journeys from buildings one through seven were not because I was exploring, more so that I was screaming and running in a nonsense manner.

It seems, to be truthful, that the rhinoceros spider was a rather horribly un-delightful sight to behold, and I didn't handle it very well. I didn't want to tell you about it because I didn't want you to think me a coward.

I've gotten ahead of myself again. Sorry, where was I? Oh yes the candle!

I was sitting in house number seven, on the second floor. I don't know for certain that was in fact the house number; none of the houses here have any kind of numbers at all. I would wonder how one would get around; I imagine they knock on doors quite an amount. But this was the seventh house that I was in, and I was on the second floor; that much is certain.

So there I was, trying to look small and unpeculiar behind a rather ratty old chair. I suppose now would be a bad time to tell you that there's furniture inside buildings. Well, it has been a very peculiar day; please forgive me for not doing so. Yes indeed there is furniture inside these buildings and now that I look outside the window I can see that there is furniture outside the buildings as well. This is a rather good vantage point I must say. Whether it is an advantage point or a disadvantage point I have yet to see, but I doubt that I'll see much of anything by these horrible light conditions.

So I thought I should talk to you about it. I imagine I'll be making quite a number of these entries in the next little while, or the next large while for that matter. I don't imagine it will be hard to keep you fed; there is a great abundance of paper blowing about on the streets not totally unlike leaves. A greater concern would be for a pen. Luckily I have my favorite quill in my vest along with my lucky inkbottle. I knew it would come in handy someday.

But then again, since there is no sun or moon, there is no day or night. So this isn't someday, this isn't any day, or any night, or anytime. I'm starting to get scared again, and I don't like it. I'm rambling, however, and probably shouldn't waste the ink. It doesn't seem to have gone down any in the bottle, but no one ever knows. It is entirely possible that I may look again and the bottle would be empty.

Yes I think I'm quite certain I don't like it here.

Your Friend,

*Clarence Winker*

**Chapter 3**

"Distant memories often come home to roost."

*-Voodoo proverb*

The day was over.

*Thank God.*

Sasha Edwards got into her small red Civic and pulled with all her might to close the door. The daily routine of the fabric store could drain more energy than anyone could possibly have. Now, with the sun in the right place and enough seconds spent, she could return home to her family and be a mom, and a wife.

Often she would look at her customers at the store to gauge the future. It was funny the difference in people. Some women would come in like nothing in the world could bring them down. They would hum, or sing through a smile, using expressions like "Deary" and "Sweetheart". Yet at the same time, there would be women filled with a misery you could feel just by coming close to them. There was no pleasing those ones. No matter how quickly she moved, or how much the discount was, there would always be something to complain about. Wherever they went, it was like they cursed under their breath.

She slumped forward gently resting her head on the steering wheel. She toyed with the idea of not driving home, but just go to sleep right there. She would only have to be back.....

Friday. A ray of hope. The breath of life was upon her. There wasn't going to be a tomorrow, not as far as Fancy Fabrics was concerned. Monday's prophesy of the weekend had been fulfilled, and so, salvation! With renewed vigor she pushed herself back and turned the key.

As the car was warming up, she glanced at the damage Fancy Fabrics had done in eight hours of beating her. The lipstick was long gone, but her mascara had somehow survived. Once upon a distant morning she cared, but not right now. Her auburn hair was still perfect. She had heard of the bad hair day, but it never happened to her, her mid-back locks always fell straight, causing many a hairdresser to turn rainbows of envy.

She had a natural beauty about her, a wholesome purity. The makeup she did wear was usually limited to eyeliner and lipstick. Quite often she'd be so busy running around after Daphne that she'd forget eating and make-up altogether. But whenever Luke found out about missed meals, it was speech time in full force.

Sasha was 5'8 ft. tall and only 130 pounds, but she told her husband she was 135. It was a way to spare her the pain of his harping. It wasn't that she watched what she ate, or even tried to stay slim, it was just that it was near impossible for her to gain weight. Having a full-time job, and a five-year-old daughter will keep you quite trim indeed, no matter what Luke said.

Sasha had grown up in Fort Langley, a small community about an hour and a half outside Vancouver city. Her family was Christian, and instilled certain rigid values into their little girl. Being an only child let her have the full attention of her parents, yet still she was never spoiled. Instead it was in her nature to be gentle, tolerant and giving, with few relapses when she felt it absolutely necessary.

Her husband Luke had grown up in slightly different circumstances. Although his family also held Christian values, he rebelled early in his teens and took to the pleasures of the time. While Sasha was at choir practice, Luke was breaking windows and getting stoned.

After an adolescence spent in a chemical haze, Luke cleaned himself up and became an electrician. The trades were more his style than book work. He was hands on all the way, with a natural gift for figuring out the kinds of problems the real world could throw at him.

His instincts served him well in college and when graduation came, Luke found himself at the top of the class, a point which his friends seemed more pleased about than he was. In keeping with the tried and true male tradition, to celebrate Luke's good work his friends tried to kill him.

The weapons of choice were Jack Daniels, some very strong Russian vodka, and an unholy home brew from someone's uncle that could do double duty as an aerospace fuel. The battle raged from a Friday night, though Saturday and finally terminated on an undisclosed Sunday AM timing. The unfortunate but understandable mistake of Luke's was that he went home.

The rule in the Edwards household was that if you're in the house on Sunday morning, you have to get up for church. So one nasty Sunday morning after only three hours of sleep, young Luke Edwards found himself still twisted, in a loud car, going down a loud road, to a loud church, while he tried maintaining control of his intestines. A task he was managing not too badly, as long as his own personal body movement was at a minimum.

The service was a holy torture spent standing, sitting, hoping and praying that the world would stop spinning. He did commendably, right up until the service ended. On the way out of the chapel his guts had enough and there was no stopping it.

Luke puked. Hard. So hard in fact that it sprayed almost three feet ahead, onto the back of a pretty girl in a bright blue dress. A dress that was brand-new and gorgeous, but all at once ruined. This was when he met Sasha.

Sasha turned and stood aghast at the moron who had defiled her precious dress. It was an eternal moment where everyone stopped and stared accordingly. The stench of alcohol was unmistakable so the cause and culprit were known. Luke was speechless, Sasha was livid, and the preacher did a sermon on the evils of alcohol the very next Sunday. Sasha turned with the dignity of a vomit-covered queen and walked out of the church.

Luke's parents informed him that if he wanted to stay a member of the Edwards family he had better make the situation right. So Luke phoned the preacher at home later that day to find out who the victim of his vomit attack was. It took no small amount of suffering at his end of the phone before he got an address. He promptly sent a hundred dollars for the dress, a large bouquet of flowers, and a letter of apology.

Sasha didn't go for it. She took the money, threw away the flowers, and sent back a letter so scathing Luke felt bad touching it. It was only after several more pleading letters that she agreed to have an apology dinner paid for by the offending Luke. They dated, fell in love, married and became mother and father to beautiful baby girl named Daphne Stephanie Edwards.

The rest was history.

Sasha pulled the car out of the resting place outside the fabric store and began her voyage home. Any Friday in any city at five o'clock was destined to be an extended exercise in tolerance. The esprit of mutual suffering known to all motorists in North America, with only skill to spare some of the traveling turmoil.

The trick to getting around any city is knowing how the city works. What streets were good, what streets were bad, and what time their status changed. Sasha was by no means an aggressive driver, but in her own sly and subtle way she knew how to get around Vancouver in a timely fashion.

Driving through the back streets gave her glimpses into other people's lives through bay windows. Old couples watching television, an asexual trench coat cleaning the yard, dogs fiercely declaring that cars had no right to drive by while cats sat on the warm car hoods of those lucky enough to already be home.

Sasha lived downtown, so the small mercy was that she was going against the majority of the rush on the main roads until she got closer to the city core. Their apartment was a semi loft, just off Pender Street, near the old district known as Gas Town.

That type of apartment was a prized commodity in the Gas Town district. Gas Town was Vancouver's answer to the artistic problem. Cobble stone streets and stylized antique streetlights were waging a war against the encroaching tourist market, yet still the ambience of architecture gave the atmosphere a gothic feel.

To find a loft available in that section of town was akin to stumbling on the Holy Grail, yet through a friend of a friend's friend, they became aware at just the right time of an impending sale, and signed the paperwork three hours later.

When they first took possession of the loft, it was so overrun by dust and grime it seemed man would never be able to take it back, but take it back they did. Through massive cleaning, and exceptional deals from the local antique shops, it was transformed into an old world island in the urban hustle.

The building had been modernized with the paranoid additions for the twentieth century. Underground parking, steel mesh gates and reinforced concrete had all been added for no small sum of money, but in the end it was worth it for all parties involved.

Turning off Pender Street, she saw her looming apartment building like some knurled grandfather waiting to greet her. When she first saw the place she thought it was cold, morbid, and perhaps slightly creepy. Now after living there for the last eight years, its menace had given way to charm, and the feeling of foreboding became dark character.

Sasha pulled into the underground parking and let the familiar concrete corridors guide her to the car's final resting place. Rationally, she often thought it odd how people felt a kind of dread from underground places, dark corridors and the like. Most animals have a kind of security in dark places, the comfort of the subterranean ground, but humans never do. It was deep enough that she could scream forever and no one would hear. The only comfort being that it was rather brightly lit, and the great steel front gate to keep out undesirables. She tried not to think about it while locking the car and walking briskly with her purse.

She let the heavy industrial steel door swing shut behind her and began her climb up the stairs. No elevator, the price of high-vaulted ceilings. Four flights up, a short walk down the brick hallway, her key entered the lock and the door swung open.

Darkness.

She expected to swing open the door and have the resounding "Mommy's home!" echo throughout. Sasha wouldn't have it any other way, but sometimes the greeting ritual could be hard on a weary body. She stepped inside and closed the door, half wondering if Luke had taken Daphne to Stanley Park again and left her to come home to an empty loft. The sound of approaching footsteps told her different.

"You home baby?"

Luke rounded the corner with a waft of fresh cologne, something he only wore with purpose.

"Where's Daphne?" She asked as she slipped off her shoes, forgetting what Luke just asked.

From out of the darkness, Luke had her in his arms. He had such strength about him; she could always fall into his arms and let them squeeze the troubles of the day away. Her stress drifted away as he stroked her hair.

"Daphne is at Nana's tonight." He said tilting his head, speaking more into her neck. The sides of Sasha's face gave way to a smile, this was just about perfect. She heard the soft music drifting in from the living room and the scent of cooked meat. Despite the shelter of his arms, she felt it best to keep him able to romance her.

"Is something cooking?"

"Oh yeah, thanks." He let her go and hustled back into the dark apartment to tend to the stove.

Luke tried to be romantic, and came up with some excellent scenarios, but he had to be kept in sight or he would destroy something. He was a man with whom cooking should not be mixed.

Hanging her coat in the closet, Sasha ventured deeper into the apartment to see what was in store. Luke had lit candles all over the loft giving it a warm orange glow.

Their home had changed a lot in the last eight years. Although the walls had stayed in place, the paint scheme was subject to Sasha's will once every couple of years.

The loft was not a true loft as any Vancouverite artistic refugee would be quick to point out. From the front door, a hall led off to the immediate left to three rooms and a bathroom that was not nearly as big as Sasha would have liked.

She could stand the small bathroom because of the sixteen foot ceilings and floors, both finished in the original antique maple that had turned black with age. If it wasn't for the massive floor-to-ceiling windows facing the street, the entire place would be bleak, but with Sasha's decorative skill it became less dungeon, more Victorian.

Down the hall, the rooms became a master bedroom, Daphne's room, and a study where they kept various clutter, mostly books. Just after Daphne was born, Sasha developed a green thumb and bought 12 small creeping ivy plants. By now the creeping ivy had taken over the pillar beams by the windows and were assaulting the walls in their gradual dominion. With the green leaves over the dark wood, it lent a fantasy feel to the place. It became their pagan oasis in the desert of modernization.

The final member to the family was Sebastian; a large white Persian cat that once belonged to Steve Naylor, a high school buddy of Luke's. Steve went away to university in Twillingate, so the beautiful white monster Persian found himself a new home in the city. Tonight however, the Persian was an unwanted guest in his own home.

To keep the cat hair and interruptions out of their night, Luke had thrown Sebastian out onto the fire escape to go play on the rooftops. Whenever Luke would throw the cat outside, Sebastian's best friend Daphne would protest. But with his champion at Grandma's, he was out of luck and outside. Quite often there was a contest between Luke and Sebastian for Sasha's affection, but opposable thumbs and greater upper body strength clearly gave Luke the advantage.

"Don't do anything. Just sit down at the table, dinner is about ready!" Luke hollered from the kitchen. Sasha thought about getting changed, but the effort seemed too much. Instead she wandered into the candlelit loft, letting the surprisingly sweet smell of Luke's cooking bring her to a dining chair.

Luke had prepared a chicken dinner. He had videotaped a cooking show earlier in the day and watched it in slow motion as he prepared the meal. Time and God were on his side, and the meal seemed to be turning out just fine. He even picked up the red wine the all knowing television chef prescribed to serve with the meal. Of course, he placed it in the fridge to make certain it was good and cold by the time Sasha got home, and didn't understand why she laughed when he served it.

They sat, talking and listening, gently prodding each other to confess their sins of the work day. Luke had far less to atone for; he had taken the Friday off to prepare their evening. He loved her more than anything else in his universe, and at these times she knew it.

When the meal was over Luke took her plate into the kitchen. Sasha slid over to the couch and looked out the long windows onto the street, contently sipping her second glass of chilled wine. Luke returned from the kitchen, drying his hands on his shirt he came to sit beside his wife.

He wanted to say something clever, like how beautiful she was, but somehow it got lost. The washing gold of the candle flame mixed with the soft music, and took thoughts away.

"Well...?" She said.

Luke broke from his trance. "Well what?"

"You're staring at me." She said, placing her wine on a side table.

"Ah, yes, this is that portion of the evening. We've had the wine, and the dinner, we did the small talk, now it's time for the maniac to subdue his innocent unknowing victim."

Sasha sarcastically cocked her brow; she was beginning to feel the wine. "Is this a role-playing thing?"

"It could be." Luke said as he slid closer.

Sasha changed her voice to the higher pitch. "Wow! It was sure nice of you to pick me up from cheerleading practice. I've never been alone with a man before."

"Oh yeah?" Luke slid his hand along the cushion and pinched her ass. She led out of squeak and tried to grab his fingers, surging her body wildly as she fought. In seconds, Luke had pinned her down on the couch. She could have fought harder, but it felt good to surrender. He stopped to let Sasha catch her breath and watch her hair fall in a perfect mess about her face.

"You're a big loser." She said and punched him in the chest.

Luke outweighed her by almost a hundred pounds. He was deathly afraid of hurting his angel because of this. Once she scared him, jumped out from behind a closet. He spun and accidentally caught her in the side of the head with his elbow. It

22

was an accident, she got knocked to the floor and was laughing, but Luke almost died.

It took almost ten minutes of her telling him it was okay before he would change the horrible self-loathing expression on his face. Luke would rather die than hurt her, and Sasha knew it. Since then she always played down any injury she had. She wasn't made of glass, but Luke seemed to think she was.

After a few moments of gazing at each other in the comfortable warmth Luke spoke. "Do you ever think about having another baby?"

It caught her off guard. "What? Are you serious?"

"Yeah, I mean why not? We're making good money, and Daphne would be crazy about having a little brother to torment."

"Or little sister."

"Or little sister…you know what I mean."

Sasha smiled. "You're not the one who has to carry this thing around for nine months and go through hell at the end of it, Mister!"

"No, but I am the one who would have to put up with your constant whining, weird cravings, and all at other fun stuff and still say I love you in a believable way."

Sasha ignored him and thought about the idea.

"I wonder if it would be a boy or girl?" She wondered aloud,

"Oh hell, I wouldn't care as long as it was healthy." He said. "But I wonder if it would be right for us. I mean, could we handle the strain of another little one on an emotional level?"

"Oh, I think we'd be okay." She smiled. He was already trying to talk himself out of it.

The two lay on the couch for a few long moments lost in the thought another child. Luke had an idea; he slid off the couch with a newfound energy and made straight for his study.

"Now where are you going?"

"To get some advice!" He hollered back.

After a few seconds, and the sounds of distant rustling, he returned with a small square piece of wood tucked under his arm.

"I just pick this up today! More for my collection of strangeness and antiquity." Luke said as he placed a piece of pressed board down on the floor in front of the couch, sitting cross-legged beside it.

It was a piece of pressboard, about eighteen inches by twenty four inches with the complete alphabet printed across the top. The numbers one through ten were printed along the bottom, and the words YES, NO, HELLO and GOODBYE placed in strategic locations near the corners. Its paper finish was made like antique oak, but was scratched and faded making it appear even cheaper.

"What is that?" She said, feeling the romance of the evening starting to give way.

Luke was beaming with pride. "This is an original Parker Brothers Special Ouija board. I got it down at the Sally-Ann for five bucks! Not bad eh?"

"Wow." She said clearly under-thrilled.

Being brought up in a conservative Christian family, she never had the chance to learn about the Occult or New Age spiritualism but Luke had always been into it. He had built quite a collection in his office study. It was mostly books, but there are a few crystals along with a deck of faded tarot cards. Most of it he found at thrift stores and picked up for under a dollar, a throwback to his days of *House of Mystery* comic books.

"What exactly does this thing do?" She tried to sound interested. Sasha wasn't sure that she liked it, but would suffer for Luke; after all he did feed her.

"Well, it talks." Luke said as he placed a kind of pointer down on the board. The word, *Planchete*, was printed in faded fancy script across the top.

"Talks?"

"You bet. When you use it, you can speak with the spirits and ghosts in the spirit world and get advice for all sorts of things."

"All from Parker Brothers, how useful." She replied, her voice heavy with sarcasm. Luke was unfazed.

"Sure, check it out! It's kind of neat. Some say it's your subconscious playing games with you, but nevertheless you can ask questions and sometimes get correct answers."

Sasha's curiosity was not flowing as well as her sarcasm. This was the same kind of forbidden fruit she had to deal with when she was growing up. If her parents heard that she was doing this kind of thing, that she even had an Ouija Board inside her house, they would have had kittens. The echoed rules of her parents had no effect after two glasses of wine. After all it was good to rebel against the past now and then.

She slid down onto the floor sitting opposite to Luke. The music had stopped when the CD ran out, and now the silent candlelight provided a perfect séance setting. If she allowed herself to feel creeped-out, she thought it could be fun.

"How does this thing work exactly?" She asked.

"You put your hands on the planchete..."

"That's the little slidey thing right?"

"Yeah, it's French for pointer I think. Anyway, you put your hands onto it, ask a question and it answers."

"It answers?"

"Well, the board itself doesn't answer, the spirit on the other side does. It's like a telephone that lets you talk to another world."

She tried not to sound too patronizing. "What you think we should ask it?" She knew this was hog wash, like every other metaphysical thing Luke brought home, but she'd never tell him. It was cute to see him so excited over nothing, like a child finding bits of string.

"Well we should try to contact something first, it would be rude to start shouting questions into the spirit world."

"Oh yes, where are my manners." She smiled. "What do I do?"

"You just rest your hands lightly on the planchete, and I'll ask some questions."

Sasha hesitated but didn't know why. It was more than her parents' echo, this was something deeper within that told her not to. There was deeper dread there, the kind of dread that comes from forgotten scares. She could see how silly the piece of trash before her was, yet she could feel something hidden within the faded paper and ink

In an act of rebellion against herself, she laid her fingers gently on the Planchete next to Luke's, and sat quietly waiting. The cheap plastic felt cool and smooth beneath her fingers.

Luke sat very still, resting his fingers on the pointer. This was his idea but still he felt unsure and almost a little silly about the whole idea.

Feeling rather sheepish he spoke out. "Is there anybody there?"

Sasha tried unsuccessfully to stifle the giggle from within her.

"Hey c'mon!"

"I'm sorry." She said.

This whole thing was silly but she had to be careful not hurt Luke's feelings, so she resumed a serious posture to continue the game. Luke sat quietly for a few moments waiting for response.

"Maybe there's no one home, or they might not be there right now." Sasha said, trying to give him any easy out. He wasn't going for it.

"Sometimes these things take a couple of minutes, like someone has to answer the phone."

"Ah, I see."

The small plastic pointer lurched and slid into motion pointing towards the YES phrase on the board.

"You're pushing it!" She broke out.

"No, are you?"

"No!" Sasha had the urge to take her hands from the board. She already had enough of this game. Her guts were telling her to stop, but her mind knew this was impossible. Luke was pushing it. He had to be. He was trying to freak her out. She wasn't going to make it easy.

The Planchete was resting on the YES sign. Luke was excited that he made this thing work or at least that was how it appeared.

He looked to her with a fire in his eyes. "What should we ask it?"

*He's doing a good performance,* she thought to herself. "Well I suppose we should introduce ourselves, remember your manners."

Luke nodded. "Oh yeah."

He cleared his throat and said "Hello, my name is Luke Edwards, and this is my wife Sasha..." Before he could finish the Planchete began moving again over top the word HELLO. Luke look back to Sasha for ideas, she decided to test her husbands creativity.

"Ask their name Luke."

Luke opened his mouth to speak, but the Planchete was already in motion. As it slowly slid across the board, Luke called out each letter.

"J --O --S --H --U --A. Joshua. Well hello Joshua, we're pleased to meet you." Luke was starting to get the hang of this thing.

"How old are you Joshua?" He asked.

The plastic pointer moved to the Numbers one and three.

"You're thirteen?"

The Planchete moved again. "YES"

Sasha thought Luke was a little sick making it a child. She felt the words come out all at once.

"Are you dead?"

Luke looked, amazed to hear that kind of question come from his wife.

"YES"

He felt a chill as the pointer moved but tried to keep the mood going.

"How did you die?"

"MOMMY AND DADDY"

"Your Mommy and Daddy killed you?"

"YES"

This was rapidly losing its appeal to Sasha. The night had already taken a sharp turn out of the romantic and into the weird. If Luke thought this was her idea of fun he was sorely mistaken. She was growing more uncomfortable by the second and Luke could feel it. He changed the line questioning.

"Do you have a message for us Joshua?"

"YES"

"Could you tell us please?"

The planchete slid across the board spelling out words. Luke followed along saying the words as they were spelled.

"CAT RUN AWAY OTHERS COMING"

Sasha looked at her husband for signs of recognition. He looked back and shrugged his shoulders. She wasn't so sure this was all fake. Her guts were twisting up.

"Luke, I don't like this, let's stop."

"YES"

"Hang up on Josh? I just want to find out what this means okay?" He smiled gently. "It's only a game."

"NO" The board spelled out.

Sasha made a silent promise to herself to never touch one of these things again after this night. She sat quietly resting her hands on the planchete watching while Luke resumed the questions. She vowed not to let him win. He was pushing it, he had to be.

"What do you mean, 'Runaway cat'? 'Others'?

"RUN"

"Cat ran away. Is our cat going to run away?"

"NO"

Luke was acting confused now. "Are others there? Is there another spirit who wants to talk to us?"

There was a dropped phone pause. Sasha's imagination was playing tricks on her. It felt like there was nothing on the other end now, the absence of presence. She shook her head realizing how worked up she was getting over the stupid piece of plastic and paper.

"Hello, is anybody there? We seem to be experiencing technical difficulties?" She said smiling at Luke. He was glad she did. He was starting to feel that playing this wasn't such a hot idea. He was about to move is hands from planchete when another swift movement came.

"YES"

The Planchete moved with a sudden strong jerk.

Luke let out a small chuckle. "Whoa! Easy Joshua, we seem to have a real good connection now."

"NO"

"I don't think that this is Joshua anymore Luke." *I didn't just say that did I?* She thought.

He knew she was probably right and let out a small sigh. "Okay, who are we talking to now?"

The pointer flew across the surface of the Ouija Board with such force that it almost flew out of their hands. It barley paused on each letter before speeding to the next.

"ABADDON FOUND YOU"

"This is Abaddon?" Luke asked slightly more intrigued.

"NO"

"What happened to Joshua?" Sasha asked.

"GONE"

Luke tried to keep the mood light. "So, Mr. Stranger, you have a message for us this evening?"

The planchete zipped above the board spelling out the message. "SASHA IS ABADDON"

28

Luke laughed as he spoke. "Well buddy I think you got my wife confused with someone else."

"DEAD"

From the sudden movements of the planchete on the board, Sasha was beginning to get a feeling of something raw. Deep within her a feeling of danger was swelling. Luke was laughing and having fun with the idea of the board, but when he glanced up and met his wife' eyes and saw the fear; he made his decision in a microsecond.

"We got to go now, thanks for talking with us…"

"NO"

"Yes, yes I'm afraid we do."

The Planchete began to slide back and forth rapidly over the word "NO" so quickly that small flecks of paper were beginning to tear up. Luke scooped up the board up off the floor and threw it under the couch.

"Well that was a whole lot of fun!" He said with a mock smile.

Sasha didn't look so good. She sat silently in the candlelit darkness. This wasn't real, and yet this stupid game had touched her, grabbing something long forgotten and bringing it to the surface.

"One would think a spirit would have better manners! I have a good mind to report him to the Ouija police!" Luke said still trying to lighten the mood.

Sasha smiled and laughed a little, but it was forced. She felt numb, slightly dazed. The warm candles sent shadows through the room. It looked so much darker now.

Luke walked to the stereo and turned the CD player back on, letting the soft jazz fill the room again.

"Come to think of it, if I could suddenly know what kind of problems or wonderful things that might happen with a baby, I don't think I would want to know. I mean where would the fun be in that?"

Not much for conversation at that moment, Sasha still stayed silent. Luke slipped behind her on the couch and brought her back against his knees. Sasha's silence was starting to unnerve him. She felt his powerful hands slip down by her sides and pull her up onto the couch.

"How's my girl?" He whispered into her ear.

She waited a few moments before answering, she wasn't too sure herself. It was weird to start with, and then the feeling built up to what it was now. Whatever just happened, it stirred something from a forgotten past, a distant memory that had somehow found its way back, but still wasn't clear. A dream forgotten upon waking.

"I'm okay." She said, turning out of his grasp and curling onto his lap, putting her head against his chest. She could hear his heartbeat and the steady rhythm of breathing. She closed her eyes and lost herself in being surrounded by him.

Luke spoke softly into her ear. "Baby I'm sorry, I didn't mean to scare you. I just thought it might be fun to play around with. I won't ask you do it again."

"It's not that." She felt silly now, after all this was just a stupid parlor game. "Oh I don't know, I'm just being stupid I guess, but it just felt weird."

Luke's immediate laughter washed away the uneasiness that she felt. She sat up and looked deep into his blue eyes. "I thought you liked weird." He said "I thought that sort of thing turned you on."

"Luke!" She said pounding her fist into his chest. It was solid, firm muscle, and felt good under her hands. The two of them wrestled on the couch only long enough to get their blood flowing. Then, effortlessly, Luke scooped his wife into his arms.

"It seems that this battle should be fought on a different field my dear." He said with a grin and started for the bedroom. Sasha wrapped her arms around him and felt a wash of warmth through her body. This was her best friend, her lover, and her comfort all in one.

## Chapter 4

Sasha sat quietly on her kitchen stool, basking in the morning sunlight as it crept into the apartment. The candles, like the darkness, had burned away leaving the morning fresh and alive. She had woken before Luke and just lay beside him, drifting in and out of morning twilight sleep until reality took hold. She slipped out of bed and began her favorite ritual.

It was a ritual she'd practice every Saturday, while the rest of family slept, she would put on her bathrobe and make herbal tea to ease into the morning. While waiting for the kettle to boil, she would water all the plants and share a quiet word with them. She would offer encouragement and praise for growth, something she noticed in both the plant and herself in these times.

The white Persian cat Sebastian sat and observed his green mortal enemies being tended to. Sebastian was never one to complain, he had a more somber tone than most cats. He watched and waited, his turn would come, he knew the ritual.

He would not often try to destroy the plants with anyone watching, but if he was left inside without the family or overnight, the next morning would be witness to carnage. Until his time to strike out at them again, he would lurk in the corner, waiting to be fed.

Now with all watering done and growing words spoken, it was the quiet pleasant part of the morning. If she tried, Sasha could hear the noise of city traffic drifting through the windows. People coming or going from their Saturday. Some working, some shopping, but all in a great rush.

Living in Vancouver had its own unique way about it. People who visited always complained about the rain, and it was true that the majority of mornings were spent watching a gray sky through window drops. But when the morning sky was calm, when the sun did shine, that was when it was all worthwhile.

People in Vancouver weren't familiar enough with the sun to be contemptuous of it. Vancouverites threw open their drapes and greeted with sudden surprise that old and dear friend the sun. Then everyone would rush out into the city to make the most of the day.

Today was one such day. Outside the scent of wet concrete was in the air as the birds were admiring each other. The calling blue sky stretched from over the neighboring buildings, uninterrupted by clouds. Even the rage in traffic or the tensions that came from city life would be smoothed over by the phrase "Oh well, at least it's a nice day."

Sasha sat for more than half an hour, relaxing in her bathrobe and half reading the paper and sipping peppermint tea. The misgivings and obstacles of the week didn't seem so bad now; her perspective had been rejuvenated by her practiced Saturday faith.

An electronic buzz filled comfortable stillness. Getting up and slipper sliding across the floor to the intercom, Sasha already knew who it was.

"Good morning." She said cheerfully into the receiver.

"Good mornMUMMY!!" The receiver called back. An excited Daphne cannot be contained.

She put down the receiver and pressed the red button allowing her mother and daughter entrance to the building. Daphne would be excited after the night at Nana's house, so she spent the last few moments preparing for Hurricane Daphne now ascending the stairs. She put the kettle on for another cup of tea, and noticed the door to the bedroom still open. She thought for a moment she should close it, but the thought of Luke being awkwardly awakened by his daughter was delicious. The bedroom door was fine just the way it was.

With a quick wrap of the bathrobe, she swung open the door and was attacked.

"Mummy!" Daphne cried as she ran like a micro-juggernaut into her mother's legs making her fight for balance.

"Mummy." The elderly woman behind mimicked the excited tone. Gwen Nufeld was the perfect grandmother, always smiling and never a bad thing to say, almost to the point of being annoying.

Sasha's father had passed away two years previous. It was hard on Sasha, but harder on Gwen. She turned to the sanctity of her family. Luke, Sasha and Daphne became her entire world.

Luke came to love Gwen as a second mother. As far as Daphne was concerned, if Mom said "no", just ask Nana was a way of life. Usually Gwen would say no as well, but she had a nicer way of saying it. It's the understanding between the very old and the very young.

Sasha staggered back for a moment, steadying herself against the wall. A wide-eyed overwhelmed look to Gwen was returned by kind eyes and a gentle smile.

Daphne began spilling words everywhere. "Mommy! We went down to a magic store that had special paper an' crayons an' glue an' Magic sparkles an' we made pictures! See?"

Her bright green eyes continued talking after her mouth had stopped. Long golden curls vibrated with energy. Her faded blue denim cover-alls and tiny blue t-shirt contained the micro-nova of her four foot frame. In her hand, she held a crinkled sheet of construction paper that no doubt had to be magical. Scribbled on it was a cluster of wax crayon and glittering glued foil dust that didn't look totally unlike an explosion.

"It's a chicken."

"Oh my! It's a very pretty chicken. We should put that in the special place on the refrigerator so we can look at it every day!" Sasha could see the light in Daphne's eyes. On the right kind of day, it would show her the wonders of the world.

"I want to show Daddy!"

"Well Daddy's sleeping right now. Maybe you should..."

Gwen crouched beside Daphne. "Maybe you should go and wake him up!" She whispered into the child's ear.

"Yeah!" Daphne said and was off like a wobbling gunshot to the open bedroom door.

Before Sasha could issue a warning, the shrill cry of "Daddy!" was heard. Sasha gave a disapproving glare to her mother for using her granddaughter as such an instrument of torture.

"Not very nice, Mom." She said with a scolding smile.

"What? Luke doesn't want to see his daughter?"

Gwen dropped Daphne's overnight bag and followed Sasha to the counter to sit on a side stool.

"So I guess it all went well last night?" Sasha asked as she finished pouring two cups of peppermint tea.

Gwen took one. "Oh yes, we went out to that magic shop down on Main. I picked up a few things and we sat around having a gay old time."

Sasha took the sip from her cup. It tasted better now that she was sharing it with her mother. Gwen had the same mischievous spirit that often got Sasha into trouble. Daphne already had the same traits but at least she came by it naturally. Like mother, like daughter, right down the line.

"Thanks for taking her, Mom."

"Oh no problem! Luke phoned me yesterday saying he wanted some time alone. Anything I should know about?"

Gwen was an expert at walking the treacherous pitch between gentle inquiry and over-stepped concern. Sasha smiled, lowering her cup. "Everything's fine. He just wanted to spend some time with me."

The sound of the wobbling juggernaut was heard again as Daphne came back in full charge to the kitchen. Behind her, Luke staggered into the light of day looking torn from slumber by his daughter's onslaught and forced into his own bathrobe.

Daphne ran up to Nana. "Dad said that you an' Mommy would take me down to the park!"

Sasha looked over at Luke's stayed position with a raised brow. Luke returned a vengeful smile. What an unwitting weapon Daphne had become in the parental dual. Just as Sasha was about to speak Gwen cut in. "Sure we will, Mommy will go and get dressed and we'll take you there right now!"

"Oh Mom." Sasha whispered and dropped her head as though her life had been sucked away. Daphne was already wobbling off to her room with a resounding cry of "Yaaaaaay!"

"Off you go then Mom. You'd better go get dressed, the playground lies waiting." Gwen was looking as innocent as she could. Sasha threw her mother a look of contempt that would have made any wet cat proud.

Luke was still smiling and Sasha brushed past him towards to the bedroom. With her mother behind her, she licked her lips and let the bath robe slip open to show the curve of her breast, knowing full well Luke couldn't follow. He entertained the notion anyway, it was a sure way to teach her the dangers of teasing him. After all, that's what doors are for.

"What you smiling about?" Gwen asked.

"My face hasn't woken up yet." He replied, shaking off his thoughts. He took Sasha's place at the counter and poured himself the last of the tea.

"I hope Daphne wasn't too much for you?"

"Not at all, she was a perfect princess. It's good to have little ones tearing around the house from time to time."

He slurped his tea with a sloppy gulp. "Thanks Gwen for taking her like that, you're a real gem. Daphne always raves and raves about how much fun she has with Nana. Sometimes we think she'd rather live with you!"

"So did she show you her magical chicken picture?" Gwen asked.

"Mmmmmmm." Luke nodded as he took another gulp. "She did, and she told me that I had to keep it with me always. Made me promise as a matter-of-fact."

"Will you?" Gwen asked.

"Of course I will. I already have the spot in my wallet picked out. A promise to one of my girls is sacred."

"Any promise to a child is sacred." She agreed.

Daphne came thundering back into the room having dressed herself in a fresh white T-shirt and pants.

"Mommy, are you ready?" She called.

Sasha let out an undecipherable mumble from the bedroom and emerged wearing her trusty blue jeans and a green t-shirt. Her hair was in a ponytail for the sake of ease, and her face was void of makeup. Luke smiled from the comfort of his bathrobe. He did feel the slightest twinge of guilt for making her leave, besides, *it was such a nice day!*

Sasha was a wonder to him, even without effort she was radiant. It wasn't an artificial poise or store-bought glamour, she had a pure beauty within her core that radiated out like a star. Luke made a mental note to take her for a "nap" after she got back.

Gwen sipped the last of her tea and headed for the door. She looked back at Luke with a mischievous face. "Maybe Daddy should come with us!" She announced in a loud and coercing tone.

Daphne paused at the door with a puzzled look of disbelief. "But Daddy's not ready, Nana."

At once the room was filled with laughter. Luke extorted a victorious "That's my girl! Come give Daddy a big hug!" He crouched just in time to have his daughter reach him. Sasha followed not far behind.

"You be a good girl now and come home when Nana and Mom want to, okay?"

"Okay." Daphne replied, then turned and scuttled back to the door.

"Yeah, like to that's going to happen." Sasha said as he got to his feet. She threw her arms around him in a sloppy hug.

" We should have a nap after you get back." He whispered.

"Well I guess I better make sure she's tuckered out, hadn't I?" Sasha whispered back.

She broke the embrace and planted a kiss on his cheek. Gwen was already standing at the open door, holding Daphne's hand. As they exited Sasha gave him a final wink.

"I'll see you in a bit....Sebastian! Stop eating the plants!" Sasha yelled, freezing the Persian in mid chew. She rolled her eyes, smiled at Luke, and walked down the hall.

"Bye Daddy!" Daphne called.

"Goodbye, Baby." Luke said, and then heard the click of the door as it shut

Outside, Vancouver was clean. The rain washed away the smog and scum, leaving the sun to dry the streets. Everyone felt the blues when the rain came, but perhaps that was the price for the Sun's appreciation. If so, it was a fair price.

Stanley Park was where nature made its last stand against the claws of man. The city's bustle had pushed the wilderness out to the edges of the water. It was created by the sane few who decided to keep a large portion of nature safe from the tyranny of concrete. It was the spiritual sanctuary for artists and lovers who had to escape the fluorescent lighting.

In the park was a long since retired zoo, and an aquarium. Neither were necessary since there were enough raccoons, squirrels, and skunks to accompany the thousands of birds that littered the trails. It wasn't wild nature, but it was a reasonable facsimile.

The park was an expansive place, with a solid stone wall running the circumference of the peninsula, separating the park from the sea. A favorite Vancouver pastime was to travel the five mile Seawall, smiling and talking to the plethora of other walkers, joggers, and cyclists.

Daphne didn't care for the Seawall much, which suited Sasha and Gwen just fine. Her entire case for the parks existence was the squirrels, birds, and the artists.

Today was a Saturday. This meant that on the initial stretch of concrete pathways, artists would have set up their easels to do portraits for passers by. The cost was negligible, only about twenty dollars, but these masters would turn out the divine in about twenty minutes.

It wasn't that Daphne liked the pictures, they were fine, but it was the act of creation that brought her close. The magic of watching a white void slowly transforming, forced to take shape from rough grinding strokes, forms carved by a shaft of charcoal and the artist's will.

Daphne would watch them for hours, all the while holding a healthy supply of bread crumbs to dole out to the constantly shifting crowds of animals. She was such a common sight in the park that the artists would often draw pictures for her amusement in their slow times, just to see her face explode into a smile.

They had taken Gwen's boxy beige Volvo to avoid the hassles of taking two cars, but the traffic was bad enough to walk. It became apparent that they were going to Stanley Park on a Saturday. Traffic on a Saturday in Vancouver can often be difficult, when it was sunny it was worse, but in a more tolerable way.

What should have been a fifteen minute drive was stretched into a forty five minute game of go-stop and a route traveled in microscopic bursts of speed. Inside the car the three opened all the windows and were thinking of Walt Disney songs they hadn't sung yet. During a rousing round of 'Be Our Guest' they entered the parks domain.

After the initial trip, the next impossible task was to find a parking space. There is a spider web of tiny little parking lots connected by serpentine roads amongst patches of wild growth in Stanley Park. The Volvo found its way onto a lesser known offshoot road and slid behind a small red compact, a green van followed.

The road to lot 35D was harder to see than the rest. It was just past an ancient stump that stood like a wall in the road, a testament to giants that used to be. On the other side of this stump partially obscured by trees was the way to lot 35D. Unless familiar with the park, one would be more likely to blow past it, not noticing the entrance at all.

Gwen expertly zipped around the stump and slid into the lane, the low hanging trees brushing the sides of the Volvo. The green van was the only vehicle to follow, leaving the other cars to search for rest elsewhere.

They broke out from under the canopy of trees to reveal the lot, which of course looked full. A non-event for everyone in the car, their secret lot wasn't a secret at all. Nevertheless, they searched for a space that might have been missed. The van was content to let them keep the lead, following two car lengths behind them

"There's one!" Daphne cried out pointing ahead.

With a careful swerve, the Volvo seized the yellow lined space with its four tires.

Gwen turned the ignition off and let out a sigh. "There now! That wasn't such a chore now was it? Daphne dear, pass me my purse please."

SMA-SMASH!

The cars driver and passenger side windows exploded inwards, showering all three with shards of safety glass.

Sasha was checking her purse in her lap when it happened. She looked up in time to see a black hand grab a fistful of her hair and throw her face into the dashboard. Stunned and half conscious, she could hear Daphne screaming in the backseat. Sasha dropped back into her seat just in time to see the long blade being tucked under her mothers chin.

A powerful shove, and the knife cut through to the middle of Gwen's throat. The killer pushed the blade back and fourth, sawing until it hit her spine. Blood erupted into the car, coating everything in crimson. Another scream from the backseat.

Again, Sasha's head was twisted and thrown into the dashboard. She heard a loud crunch as her nose broke against the black vinyl dash. The iron taste of her blood was replaced by the sting of broken teeth. She realized that she must have bitten off a piece of her tongue in the last blow.

Her mouth fell open letting blood spill out as she fell out of consciousness. Darkness and the distant screams of her daughter fought for possession of her mind. The screams were keeping her here, but the darkness was forcing its way through.

She felt herself being pulled from the car.

"Don't kill her.... Hold... tight." Voices said fading against the void.

Muffled screaming came again as powerful hands jerked her body. She was being dragged across the ground. Another scream from her daughter faded against the blurring pain. The demon roar of a van's sliding slurred thunder through her head. She was thrown into a vehicle and could hear a distant crash as her head hit a metal wall.

"... Mustn't die..." The voices said.

Sasha was on her stomach. Something cold and cutting held her hands behind her back. Sound, motion, visions and pain were blurring together, numbing against the black. Fading screams of her daughter mixed with throatless visions of her mother. Gaping eyes, blood fountains and the thunder of a door sliding shut all spiraled into the void.

Outside in the park, people went about their business. Squirrels were rushing about fighting for attention, artists were well underway to a rather profitable day and the carcass of Gwen Newfield spilled out of her car, her head twisted at an impossible angle. The blood from the draining body shone a brilliant red as it trickled across the parking lot. It weaved and crept lazily, until it reached one of the many rusted drain grills, splashing down into the darkness.

It was a bright, beautiful, sunny day.

## Chapter 5

Sasha drifted into aching as she became aware of her surroundings. Hard cold stone stretched out along her now naked body while drafts like the breath of a beast drifted over her. She was finally slipping from the euphoric bonds of chemically induced tranquility and back into a world of pain. She'd been drugged a number of times since the first strike, the itching of hypodermic stings were all over her legs. A lot of time spent in slurred darkness.

The pain came next. Her face had an invisible weight pressing down with echoes of trauma. As she tried to move her arms, new cutting sensations came. Her hands and feet were both held by chains that knew no mercy. The tortured visions from the needles had made her struggle in her sleep and the steel of her binds bit deep. She could feel the dried blood from her wrists flaking like sand against her raw flesh as she twisted her hands.

Crashing waves of realization came as the drugs receded.

*Blood!*

*Mother!*

*Daphne!*

The panic began to swell as her mind battled back the artificial numbness. Sasha's first instinct was to open her eyes, but survival overpowered it. *They don't know I'm awake*, she thought. They could be watching her, but she didn't know. All she had right now was the knowledge that she was wasn't being touched. Keeping her eyes closed, she strained her other senses to gather information before sending her eyes in for the main assault.

Silence coupled with the scent of damp musk, this was an old place, unused and abandoned. She could hear only the slightest whisper over the stillness, lurking just beyond her eyelids. She opened her eyes a tiny slash, the crust of dried blood had caked around them, grating in protest as motion came.

The whisper beneath a whisper came again from her right but turning her head produced a whole new level of agony. At first, past her eyelids there was only golden blur but the room came into focus as the drugs released their grip.

The whispers were candles in ornate strands hissing and winking at her as they burned. The darkness here was thicker, barely cut by the dim golden stars of flame. She made out theatre seats. She was in an old Playhouse.

A large space on the floor had been cleared away, the seats piled against the walls. Faces and forms of angels and gargoyles glared down from the edges of flickering darkness, despairing and cheering, oblivious to her tragedy. She was higher than the moldy cushions, on a stage, spread eagle and naked, strapped to a table.

No, *an altar.*

Something was painted on the floor of the cleared space. Through the glaze of candles the stark shapes and patterns of a ritual circle became visible. She had seen similar symbols in Luke's books, but nothing as large or complex as this one. Symbols had been artfully spilled out in powder, while others were some tar-like paint. Placed amongst the intricacies, various copper bowls and metal chalices held rotting things.

It was a horror that would have sent any sane woman into a shrieking fit, but there was more than herself to worry about. The instinct of protection was stronger than her fear, and thoughts of her daughter came to the surface of her mind. She had to find Daphne, she couldn't afford the luxury of panic.

Sasha strained against the chains, but their grip was strong and held fast. Over the pain she searched for any possible means of escape. There was too much here to grasp at once. It was only moments ago it seemed that she was in a park with her daughter and mother.

*Blades cutting into the throat of her mother as blood pumped against a windshield.*

Her mind began screaming again, she shut her eyes and shook before the visions could attack her. No matter where Daphne was or what she was doing, at least she wasn't chained to an altar before a symbol of madness.

*Or was she?*

Sasha thrashed again, opening a wound in her wrist. An involuntary cry escaped her, and was amplified into an operatic bellow by the theaters' acoustics. She froze, her pulse pounding like war drums in her ears.

*Are they here? Did they hear her?*

Sasha gazed into the blackness that existed beyond the candle light. There was enough darkness here to shield an entire regiment of dark souls. Visions of robed figures watching her out of the darkness came into her mind. She could see them touching themselves under their ritualistic garb, whipping themselves into a frenzy while they watch her naked blood-smeared form on the altar.

Sasha gave another effort against the bonds that held her. The pain in her body was easy to focus on, it helped force the vision away. As promised, the pain came again and with it came the realization of futility.

The chance of flight was fading fast, she would have to battle with whatever came upon her on an internal level. It would be the kind of battle fought wherein a rape was inevitable, rape of the body, mind, or soul. She called upon her strength from within, fortifying herself and trying to prepare an escape route for her mind, some kind of buffer. The feelings of fear and desperation dulled, replaced by anger and hate.

She could take the pain that these monsters could give, the agony of whatever they had. She held onto the knowledge that her daughter wasn't with her. Daphne had to be safe for now, even if not for long. Daphne was strong, she had her mother's blood, she would survive no matter where she was.

Time passed. Time is measured differently for those in distress. It is measured by meals for those imprisoned, in hours by the desperate, and the tortured measure time in breaths.

After many breaths, a mechanical explosion echoed from beyond the candle flame rings of darkness. A door latch faltered followed by the scream of the hinges. There was no chanting, no percussion of candle-holding satanic monks, instead only a *swish* of fabric, barely whispering louder than the candles.

From the side of the theater, shapes revealed themselves from the darkness. Thirteen figures, all wearing long white robes. The line was led by one who wore a blasphemous symbol stitched in red on his robe. *This was their leader*, Sasha thought to herself, this is the man who killed her mother and now would harm her child. She felt the power of her hatred growing stronger.

The thirteen gathered inside the profane symbols drawn on the clearing, being cautious not to disturb the soiled sacred markings with their steps. Twelve stood quiet, waiting for the moment, whatever that moment might be. With slow reverence, the red stitched leader broke away and ascended the small flight of stairs at the front of the stage. In his hand, Sasha saw a bundle of strange skins emerge from the robe. She was shaking now, not from the fear or the cold, but the rage that was within her.

The leader took his place behind the altar looking out onto his congregation. He drew back his hood and looked out as the others in the flock mirrored his actions, drawing their own cowls down to their shoulders. Sasha looked about trying to see the faces of the twelve who watched, feeling for a single strand of humanity but found nothing. She looked up to see the face of this priest now about to begin his sermon.

He was in his early thirties with smooth skin and sharp features. Those features were strong and stern, like a soldier, accented by his high cheekbones. His hair was black, clean cut, and caught the whispering candlelight with an enticing shine. He was beautiful. The kind of beauty that called to people, lured them, beat them and subdued others to the will of the one. This was the tall, slender, attractive man that had slaughtered her mother.

The priest never took his eyes away from the congregation. Even as he placed the bundle of skins on Sasha's stomach, his eyes constantly wandered among the faces in the darkness. His hands moved slowly as he stared, unraveling the rough cord that held the bundle together and let it fall open. As it unraveled, she heard the faint clanking of metal brushing together. He held the open skin aloft, showing the congregation.

"Shandara!"

The congregation rumbled, repeating the word.

"Shandara Abaddon! Shandara Centodd!" He continued.

*Abaddon.*

Sasha's mind reeled at the word. *It couldn't be, it made no sense.* The confusion and frustration within her welled into hateful tears running down her cheeks. She watched as the fiend above her lay the skins back upon her stomach. A dark chorus chant filled the candlelit theater.

*"G'fawn myleh xantahedra dandrathu, dandrathus selohim Abaddon!"*

Sasha turned her head through the pain to see all of their faces staring at her, eyes wide, expectant. She could begin screaming, but she knew perhaps this was what they wanted. She would give these fiends nothing of her free will. She felt the priest reach within the leather on her stomach.

*"G'fawn myleh xantahedra dandrathu, dandrathus selohim Abaddon!"*

In one demonic tone, the congregation continued the chant. A deep rumbling like the Geyoto monks as they sat in harmonic meditation. It was more than prayer, it was more than some kind of reverence, this was precise. This was something practiced labouringly in dark corners and forbidden places when no other ears could hear. This was the hateful chant that the church hunted in their days of righteousness.

*"G'fawn myleh xantahedra dandrathu, dandrathus selohim Abaddon!"*

He spoke no words as he drew the first long blade from the skins on her stomach and held it aloft. The knife was like a spike, slender and sharply grooved to allow for easy passage through sinew and bone. It was the first blade, but there would be many more to follow.

"Shadrachalactu!" He called as the priest drove the finely edged blade through Sasha's ankle. It slid through, cracking the cartilage and immediately dislocating her foot with a hollow pop.

*"G'fawn myleh xantahedra dandrathu, dandrathus selohim Abaddon!"* The congregation chanted again.

Sasha was screaming now, she couldn't remember when she started. It felt as though pain was all she had ever known. The pain was fulfilling, washing her with bloody waves in a sea of agony.

*"G'fawn myleh xantahedra dandrathu, dandrathus selohim Abaddon!"*

A second blade was in the dark one's hands. It slid through her other ankle producing a slither of twisting tendons snapping up into her calf. There was no hope now in Sasha's mind. There was nothing left now except the blissful agony, cleansing her mind from the expectations of the future. Now, everything was the breath between cries.

*"G'fawn myleh xantahedra dandrathu, dandrathus selohim Abaddon!"*

The third and fourth blades were driven through her wrists dislocating them with a sickening snap. Next were the knees, broken inwards as the knives were driven home. The last four blades went through each hip and each shoulder.

Sasha *was* pain. She felt each part of her die under the steel spikes driven by this evil.

As the thirteenth and final blade was held over her chest. The muscle spasms of her body's shock caused her to convulse, twitching like a child's toy. The chanting had continued throughout with the same passion and purpose as it had in the beginning, only now with the final blade poised did they raise their voices.

*"G'fawn myleh xantahedra dandrathu, dandrathus selohim Abaddon!"*

Only now as they stood within the intricately drawn abomination did they show signs of an ancient nightmare coming to a climax. Waiting only for the sacrifice to be completed, to open the gateway for their Lord and Master.

*"G'fawn myleh xantahedra dandrathu, dandrathus selohim Abaddon!"*

As the handsome killer dropped the blade into Sasha's chest, the doors to the theater exploded. The room became bathed in the cutting beams of police ERT tactical flashlights. Sasha was too deep in the world of pain, transcending into death. She couldn't hear the sounds of gunfire as the cultists rushed the team. A single bullet spun through the air punching through the priest's chest above her, letting him gasp as blood filled his lungs.

Even with the blade piercing her chest, Sasha lived for a few seconds longer, watching but unaware of the sensation of the priest falling over her body. Staring but not seeing the swat team, rushing forward and smearing the lines of the Virtomic Matrix on the floor.

Then Sasha died.

**Chapter 6**

"We can never die when we want to."

*-The Truth*

Terror came for Luke Edwards on a bright beautiful sunny day. Terror was wearing the uniform of a Royal Canadian Mounted Police Officer. Terror buzzed up, knocked on his door, and destroyed his life. It was hard to know when Luke stopped feeling anything. It was probably after he identified Gwen's body, but the moment of total emotional severance came when they pulled out that second slab.

They tried not to show much of the body, but seeing the dried blood caked in her hair was enough. Every thing was automatic after that.

*"When did you last see your wife?"*

*"Did you make any calls?"*

*"How long have you been interested in the occult?"*

And so on. Each question asked twice before Luke would stumble out a distracted answer.

The police questioning room provided all the warmth of chalk and all the comfort of a car wreck. Luke stared down into the wood grains of the table. He watched the fluid flowing lines travel back and forth in their calming, hypnotic pattern. The stained veins wrapped around his mind comforting him in a strange way. Luke didn't know how long he had been there. He came into the room after identifying the body of the most wonderful woman he had ever known, and her mother.

It was best not to think about anything, so for the time being he took shelter within the fine wood grain lines of the table. Shock is the little mercy for the destroyed.

Instants, moments, seconds and years passed, then the door opened. Had he looked up, he would have seen three people walk into the room. Two of them were plain-clothed cops, the third was a woman in her 40's and short dark hair. The cops had the suffered features etched into their flesh.

Suffered features can be seen on those who have witnessed too much. You can tell by the eyes, distant and faded, while their facial expressions changed by choice rather than reaction. Too many bodies will do that. The woman was different though, she had wise eyes. Those eyes could learn secrets with just a glance and hold them safe forever. She had kept the jewel of compassion that the two officers had left in a blood soaked alley somewhere.

The taller of the two cops sat across from Luke, the shorter, heavier one sat to his left and opened a well-worn file folder. The woman sat to Luke's right and pulled her chair closer to him. He didn't notice until he felt her hand cradling his under the table. There was nothing sexual, it was the maternal soft, warm hands of shared grief. Luke felt himself begin to surface from within the sanctuary of the wood grain. For the first time in over an hour, he looked up from the table and into her eyes.

He was about to say something, he was about to throw his arms around her neck and fall into heaving sobs of despair, he was about to die when the taller police officer spoke.

"Mr. Edwards, I realize that this must be a difficult time for you but we have just a few more questions."

Luke felt the glorious numb return. The unfeeling shield covered his voice as he spoke. "Who are you again?" They had questioned him before but their names kept slurring in his mind.

The tall cop rolled his eyes, exhausted with repeating his name, but trying not to show it.

"My name is Detective Kluczinski, this is Detective Todd." He gestured to his short fat partner.

The older woman spoke in a voice like a summer fan, Luke hadn't seen her when he was questioned before. "My name is Susan Francis. I'm not with the police, I'm a consultant in these types of crimes…"

*Noise.*

They were speaking to him and he was answering them, but he had no idea what he was saying. The volume of his life had been over powered by mental agony, shock pulsed through him. Three lifetimes passed before he realized Susan was holding his hand and gently speaking to him, coaxing him out of his shock

The two detectives weren't in the room any longer. Luke was useless to them right now, deep in shock and drifting in and out of coherency. They had left and left the councilor to nurse this shattered man into movement.

"You should go home." She was saying to him.

The sound got through to him.. He nodded and rose from the table, hardly more than a compliant child. Susan was leading him outside by the arm, past the muffled chaos in the station and to the front exit. She released him momentarily to speak with the desk sergeant, and Luke continued his drift through the front doors.

Outside, the rain returned from the brief passage of the day's sun. It was the kind of rain that couldn't and wouldn't, let up for days. From inside his shocked shell, Luke knew the rain was striking his face. He could feel the gnaw of the wind as it sucked his body heat away, but inside of his shell it was only an itch.

The doors to the station opened and closed from their steady traffic. On the latest swing Susan Francis came outside with the surge. She produced an umbrella and held it above him. Two oceans of raindrops had washed over Luke since he stood there, but nothing could dilute the pain. Luke was only vaguely aware of the umbrellas' shelter.

"Mr. Edwards?" Susan coaxed him again.

Luke turned to see her and found himself in her arms crying. Fierce sobs wracked his body as the rain drum of the umbrella continued. As he wept, tears mixed with the rain on her coat and the wracked sobs with his own shivering.

When she thought he was strong enough, she led him to the door of a waiting cab that had appeared out of the night. Luke looked again into the face of this stranger, this woman he had known for mere moments but now found himself so desperately needing. He was angry, sorry, confused and in shock, with tears blurring his vision. He opened his mouth to speak, but only strange sounds came out.

"I...I...am...ah...."

"Mr. Edwards it's alright. You've been through a lot, more than anything else right now you need to get some rest." She said, sliding something into his shirt pocket.

"My office is in New Westminster. When you feel strong enough, call me and we'll talk about this."

Luke was lost. "I ...don't....."

"Victim services pays for this. They're paying for the cab ride as well as any sessions we have. There's no cost to you, and you're going to need to talk about this. We may be able to find some answers." She spoke with a certainty, with the conviction of crisis.

Luke couldn't manage much more than a nod, as she shuffled him into the waiting black vinyl of his coach He watched his new found savior say something to the cab driver, close the door, and the vehicle lurched into motion.

The rain pounded sadness into the roof of the cab. Inside, the devastating loss he felt was only beginning to set in. He wanted to die, and he probably would if not for the spark of hope that was Daphne.

The spark that said she might still be alive.

**Chapter 7**

Cold.

Damp, corpse cold.

Sasha became aware that she was curled up on a hard surface. It wasn't an act of waking up, she just became aware of her surroundings, as though her whole life was a daydream and the schoolmaster had just wrapped her knuckles.

The pain hit. Deep aching pain, more fulfilling than any she had ever known. Her muscles had been torn into little bits and then clumsily stitched together by an eyeless seamstress. Sasha let a sound escape before she took a breath. A half cough, half scream, echoed for a small infinity about her. Through the pain, a room came into focus.

Tinted green light came from green patches that pooled like glowing stains on the walls, ceiling and floor. They offered minimal light and no heat. More light came from pooled green patches along the deteriorating stage she was lying on now, the same stage. Memories of pain came flooding back, memories of her mother, memories of her child. She unfolded her body with gritted teeth, despite the deep ache from each movement.

Green illumination was everywhere. Pain and confusion clouded her vision, but she recognized the theatre. Where the clearing and symbol had been on the floor, only destroyed theater seats now existed. A thick scent of mildew and rot hung thick in the air. The confusion began to build, no one could dream that much pain.

*Nightgown.*

She was wearing her favorite nightgown, a black micro weave negligee. Luke had bought it from one of the best lingerie stores in the city and given it to her as a birthday present when they were just married. She wore it the first time they were together, and whenever she needed to feel safe or remember her husband's love. Now she was wearing it on this broken and shattered stage. Cold, confused and alone.

She struggled to her feet, unbound and free to escape. Confusion was transforming quickly into fear as the pain within her body faded giving birth to pain in her mind. The theatre, the nightgown, green glowing lights, the rot.....

She strained to remember the night's events. She was in the theatre, this theatre, but not this theatre. She had been strapped down.

*The knives!*
*The pain!*

"GUUUUUAHAAAAA...."

It came out of the shadows from the left wing of the stage, echoing out across the open theatre sending whispering repetitions back from each dark crevice. Hateful, bouncing replies that spoke of hunger.

It came.

Human-like, but not human, giant gray dead arms were pulling the upper torso of a corpse across the stage. Each arm was extended, more than six feet long ending in wide spidery hands. Putrid flesh hung in shreds barely covering the rotting muscles and dark shards that must have been bones.

Where the legs and lower abdomen of this creature had been, long spilled entrails trailed behind gathering dust and filth as it pulled itself along the stage. It wore no clothing, but its face was the epitome of all that it was, and ever had been.

Perhaps, at one time this thing had long flowing hair and a beautiful shapely face. At one time, but that time had past. The hair had fallen away and the flesh of the face had dried, leaving only tight stretched skin torn in places over the skull leaving tattered tissue clinging. What had been eyes were now worn away sockets, holding clouded orbs of tainted white, wide and gaping, filled with hunger and agony.

The vision came at her with the speed of lust, she barely made out its features before screaming. Sasha had never screamed like this before. It was a howl, an involuntary reaction, an instinctive motion she couldn't stop. This was the scream of fear, hatred, confusion, desperation and anger, but there was more.

It was a *Soul Scream.*

The scream ripped through the air, as if carrying a fine mist of acid, and struck the creature like an atomic wave. It was paused in the mid stride of a crawl as the scream took effect. The creature began dissolving away into the very air that surrounded it. Chunks of gray rotted flesh fell away and were disintegrated before hitting the floor like ash. In mere moments, there was only the skeleton and internal organs twitching, and then they too fell away into crumbling sand and evaporated.

One breath, and then another, with her scream still ringing in her ears as the last remnants of dust faded away. She began to shake furiously, shallow gasps of air inhaled and never left. She curled into a ball closing her eyes. She ran away, far away into her lidded darkness.

This wasn't real, this was some strange twisted death fantasy. This was the last throw of her life, a dream, a horrible dream brought on by the pain. As she shook in her little ball at the center of the stage, she knew the galloping hooves of madness were approaching.

A clear but timid British voice cut through her thoughts.

"Excuse me?"

Whether it was in response to the voice or if it was her body's involuntary twitching, her eyes opened.

"Excuse me miss," He said again. "I Say, I should quite like to talk to you, but I do want to be totally certain you won't attack me. I usually find it best to ask these things, what?"."

Sasha's eyes searched the theatre floor until she found him. A man was crouching behind some ratty theatre seats.

His hiding spot revealed, he slowly began to stand. "I imagine you have all the standard questions, about where you are, and how you got here, and I should quite like to help you if you wouldn't mind speaking with me. Would that be all right?"

He blended well with the dismal appearance of the theatre. He was tall and bordering on gaunt, wearing black slacks and coattails. His face was wrinkled with age, with high cheekbones and sunken features all came to a point on his long cliffhanger nose. Sasha could see a sparkle in his beady eyes from across the distance. In his hands, he nervously turned a tall top hat like a shy ringmaster unsure of how to approach the lion.

Over his shoulder he had slung a massive book, held in a makeshift harness by various mismatched belts. Loose pages sprouted from the binding, as though trying to escape. He turned his hat a few more times and began a careful walk down the theatre aisle. Sasha was past the point of comprehension, now she only shook and stared.

"I do hope you speak English, it could be painfully difficult if you don't, and then this would be a rather dangerous venture on my part, don't you know."

His voice was more nervous at the base of the stage stairs, talking more to himself as though trying to remember small details. "I don't quite know what you are, but you do seem to have the Madness. It's perfectly normal you know, when you first arrive that is."

Sasha's shaking slowed. Despite everything that was happening, the strong British accent in his voice gave a sense of comfort, it was familiar, human. He climbed the stairs but stopped just at the edge of the stage.

"Despite what you may think my good lady, you have me at a disadvantage. Clarence Winker, Abaddon researcher and traveler at your service." He made a wide bow with his hat in hand that could be mistaken for graceful.

"I say, that was smashing how you handled that Thespian and thank you very much for doing so! They can be somewhat nasty to deal with, and I was rather put off by having it for a neighbor." Clarence paused, silence rushed to fill in the void. He wasn't quite sure what he should say next.

Sasha managed a sound, a word. "..Where..?"

Winkers face lit up like a child with a book of matches. "Ah! So you do speak English after all! Splendid! This will make talking with you ever so much easier. Wonderful! Now, as to where you are, that question goes along with your undoubtedly next question, how you got here, what?"

Clarence stood for a moment with a funny pensive look on his face. After that moment, he took three strides towards Sasha and sat down cross-legged on the stage. He was only eight feet from her now and sitting at her level as she curled up on the floor. She could hear him mumbling under his breath, something about 'hating this part'.

Sasha was feeling more secure as each moment passed. This odd fellow was comforting. Clarence thought for a moment longer, still turning his hat in the green-lit darkness.

"You see, it's like this. There are two conditions, which will happen to you in the next little bit, they're like stages if you will. I've seen them thousands of times before and I'll tell you about them, so you can be ready alright?"

He didn't wait for her reply. "The two stages are '*The Sickness*' and '*The Madness*', or rather appropriately and in order, the madness and the sickness. The madness is the furious denial of the obvious truth, and the Sickness occurs when you accept it; the truth that is. You become dreadfully despondent about the situation. So be aware of that alright?"

Sasha kept staring. Clarence took that as a yes.

"You see, you have in fact, been killed by someone or something that didn't consume you utterly, so now you're here, in this place. It's called Abaddon, and there's no way out and no way back. I don't mean to come at you quite so hard with this, but it's the nature of humans to deny this particular fact to themselves. The sooner you can accept it, the sooner the madness will pass. It's rather dreadful business really, but there it is."

Sasha sat blinking for a few moments, his words sinking in . She remembered the theatre, the pain, she remembered...Daphne.

"My daughter..."

Clarence shook his head. "Please believe me good lady, you would do well to forget any friends and family. They are most certainly not here, not if they're lucky in any case. It really is unpleasant, but trust me, it's in your best interest. Honest."

Sasha blinked hard. Frustration and confusion were circling. "Who...Who are you?" She asked.

Winker broke into a wide smile, pleased with the dialogue and a chance to show off his knowledge.

"Clarence Winker, Abaddon researcher, formally of the Royal Library of England at your service madam. However, I believe what you are actually asking me, is what am I? That is to say; if you, and in fact I, are both dead, then what are we? I say! I'm glad you asked!"

Winker stood up with a twirl and spun his top hat like a showman high into the air, catching it again as it fell. He looked as though he might burst into a song here on the stage. Sasha could only sit and watch as he went off on his tangent, pacing back and forth, slashing his top hat about like some manic university professor.

"You see in life, we all had a certain amount of energy. Then as we go through life we either burn it off, or it gets stolen from us."

He stopped in mid motion and looked at Sasha, concern heavy on his face. "I know that this seems like a lot to accept right now, but I'm giving you the short version. I'll let you read my research notes later if you like." He spun on his heel then continuing on his monologue.

"In any case, what has happened to us, well me anyway, is that I was killed by a rather nasty crunching on my noggin, and here I am in the land of the dead. Abaddon, in all its unnatural nastiness. Now myself, I'm a common wraith, which is what most inhabitants in this place are. Yet usually between the madness and the hunters here, most wraiths never get the chance to realize where, or what they are."

Sasha was becoming rational again. Clarence's voice was resuscitating her.

"That rather unpleasant fellow you blasted there was a Thespian. They prey on wraiths and were once living themselves, but because of the energy that they absorbed during...."

"I'm not dead, I'm not a ghost!" Sasha cut him off. The tone in her voice betrayed her fear and denial, a mental survival instinct. Winker caught the tone in her voice immediately and began to shrink away remembering the effect she had on the Thespian.

" Ah, no. Not exactly, you're something else. A ghost or a common wraith such as myself can't do what you just did to that Thespian. That's why I was rather pleased to see you because I've never met anyone that could do that, so for my research it's...."

"I'm not dead!" Sasha got to her feet. She could feel the strength to run beginning to well up within her. Winker was shrinking back, looking smaller and smaller as Sasha's denial grew.

"Ah, now you see...that's the madness talking now. You're having a rather difficult time accepting the facts. Now, if you want to...ah.... calm yourself a little bit, I can help you through this bit of a rough spot...."

Sasha wasn't listening anymore. This man was crazy, he was evil and she had to get away. She bolted, jumping off the stage and landing barefoot amongst the littered clothing and papers about the theatre floor.

"Miss, please! You don't know what you're doing! You'll do yourself harm! Please stop!" Clarence was calling after her, but it was too late. Sasha had already run up the isle and out the broken doors of her dark birth chamber.

**Chapter 8**

"When your reality becomes too horrible to comprehend,
madness is a rather soft option."

*-Dr. Hans Verruckt*

Sasha expected many things as she ran out onto the street. She expected the cultists from the van to be hiding, to jump out and restrain her. She expected doors to be locked. If she made it out onto the street, she expected to find someone to help her. She expected to be in her own world.

None of her expectations were met.

Just yesterday she was in a place where the sun shone, painting shadows while birds and squirrels frolicked about. She stood now outside the theatre, in the center of the decaying cobblestone street, looking about at a world. The same green light that lit the theatre within had spilled out and infected the rest of the world. It was a twisted opposite of the world she had known.

The light came not from the sky but from the ground, from the roads and the city itself. The green light mixed together through a luminescent fog, creating a shallow horizon against the infernal black void that hovered above a mass of spires and steeples.

This city is where all nightmares are born, the keeping place of dread and the birthing matrix of so called "irrational" fears that haunt the land of mortal men.

Most boarding houses and decaying hotels were graced with creatures looking out from dark corners. Some were sculpted in stone, others breathed and moved. Through the iridescence of the fog, the shadows met, danced, and whispered in time to the constant chorus of rotting that echoed through the streets.

Cobblestone streets were covered with strange clutter. Dolls, furniture, old clothes and random holy pages littered everything. The smell brought her memories of bible camp and how she found a mildewed copy of the King James under her bunk.

Sasha's mind switched into the primal, she ran. As the dank, musty air filled her lungs, she pumped her legs ever harder against the papers and clutter under her feet. Through the darkness she could hear all the screams and wails of hell, coming from far off in every direction.

The madness was upon her.

From the sides of the streets, she saw dark human shapes shuffling about and picking through the various litter, raising their heads only far enough to determine she was no threat. There was no help for her here. To them she was just another wraith lost in the madness, another thing that didn't realize their own death.

The buildings that made up this strange place were the bearers of dread to the living world; the creepy places. Old houses and hotels mismatched together, with charcoal dirt between them, leered over the archaic cobble stone street. The shifting eyes of the dead that watched from the roof tops, windows and alleys, saw her run in the mocking green glow of the city.

Harder and harder, Sasha ran. The streets were never straight, always curving and warped in ways that no human could design. The street she was on doubled back, but another joined it off to the side. Sasha ran around the various valuables and furniture and bolted down this new street, panting hard.

This was the nature of the madness, the reason for its name. There were no thoughts now, no logic, no reason to where or why she was running. She had no concept of what was happening, there was only fear and panic, only the desire to flee; terror building on terror.

The road snaked into a wicked curve when pain in her chest forced her to slow to a jog, then a walk. She saw more wraiths watching her with mild interest from the sides of the street. Tears stung her eyes, then pain forced her walk into a stumble through the piles of loose clothing and debris. Nothing made sense, there was nothing to cling to, just this horrible place and the strange light coming from all around her.

*What if the man in the theatre was right?*

*What if I am dead?*

*Where am I now?*

*Can I get back?*

*How?*

*Why?*

Her body shook uncontrollably in the cool damp. Her nightgown provided little protection and even less security. She found herself rooting thought the clothing on the street for something to put around her.

The clothes lying about in loose piles were not things that anyone would throw away. Even through the dim green glow, she could tell they were all of the best quality. The coats were leather or expensive tweed, and the pants were of similar quality. The women's cloths were fancy dresses from spanning time periods and an odd array of lingerie.

She looked through the collage of lacy teddies and stockings cabled amongst broken toys, art canvases and torn biblical pages. This wasn't litter, these were the prized possessions of the living lost in an iridescent hell and left to rot.

The dresses were useless, but Sasha found a smaller leather jacket laying under in a heap of love letters. It was a biker style, with chains and metal buckles hanging off it, and too big for her, but at the moment she didn't care. Sliding it onto her body was like rubbing cold butter on bare skin. It was musty and just above damp, but the feeling of something around her helped her feel less vulnerable.

Her whole sense of reality had become shattered, now the instinct of survival was in charge, right now it told her to hide. When Sasha was five her mother would take her to visit her grand parents, but when it came time to leave, Sasha would hide in order to stay longer. It often took over three hours and a lot of anger to find her. She would be safe. She would hide again using that childhood skill.

A pile of furniture was at the side of the street. The light wasn't so strong there, a couple of tables and a tangle of chairs had clothing strewn over it in a heap. Sasha crawled and began pushing herself into the center of the dark wood. She pulled her feet into the tangled wreck and stared out the hole that she had crawled in. Through the childlike fort of clothing and furniture she could see down the street a ways before the buildings snaked across her vision. Sasha curled into a small ball, closed her eyes and began to rock.

Time passed.

From somewhere deep within her being, a switch was thrown and her rational mind came into play. She wasn't running and the warmth was gone, now she was aware of how cold her legs had become. She looked around her tight little space for a something to cover them.

What she had first thought was the sleeve of a large leather jacket turned out to be a pant leg. She pulled it down into her hollow and could see it was more motorcycle garb, but there was no way to get a good look at it from in here. She looked out to make sure it was safe, with no idea of what exactly she was looking for. She pushed her way back onto the street, dragging the pants behind her.

The coat had warmed up, providing a layer of comfort against this world, but the pants reintroduced the cold sensation to her body. They were designed for a sportier bike, with elastic sewn into the legs and hips to ensure a snug fit. They were men's small and they fit. She tucked her negligee around her crotch for makeshift underwear, and all she had left were her feet.

She wandered up the street, sifting through the clothing piles for footwear. There were many highly polished combat boots and cowboy boots as well, but never a pair of anything, always singles.

Since the combat boots were the most common, she opted for those. After finding a left one that fit, it was two blocks further before she found a suitable companion. It was identical in every way except not so highly polished. She pulled them over her bare feet lacing them as tight as she could. It wasn't the best feeling in the world when she stood back up, but it was feeling.

The brief search for clothing had given her mind something to occupy its time with. Now the search was over and the confusion was creeping back in with inevitable foreboding. She could feel the tension growing inside her.

Screaming.

Someone was screaming in the distance. Sasha knew she had to hide. It didn't matter what the voice said, or whom it belonged to.

A set of stairs led up to a shattered building to her right. It had been a gothic hotel, now in horrid state of decay. The shadows cast by the light pools would provide safe cover. Sasha slipped into them, wrapped herself in the shadow. Only her head peeked over the stone steps to watch the dim, littered street.

The call echoed again. It was a man's voice. A frantic, confused man calling a woman's name.

"Tanya!!" He cried as he came into view, running down the center of the street. He was wearing a business suit with a white shirt, but no tie, running as hard as his legs could carry him.

"Tanya!" he cried again.

The madness had him. Sasha could feel the desperation in his voice. He hadn't been here very long either, he was just as scared as she was, his eyes were wide and gaping.

She stepped out onto the street allowing herself to be seen. If someone asked her why she stepped out, she wouldn't have been able to say, but it seemed like the only thing to do.

"Tanya!" his eyes fell on to Sasha's form, he waved his hands to signal her. "HEY!" He shouted and began running towards her. Now Sasha wasn't so sure if she should have stepped out.

*What can I say to him?*

He came at her full bore, running until he was about twenty feet from Sasha. As he got closer, she could make out his features from the fog. He stood about 5'5" with short well-kept hair. He was in his work clothing wearing a nametag on his vest saying "Barry" etched in brass. He was puffing so hard that he could barely speak. His eyes had the frantic fury of a crashing pilot. The madness of Abaddon had taken a far heavier toll on him than it had on Sasha.

"Have you seen my wife? She was just with me in the car..." He was hyperventilating staring down, talking to Sasha's left knee. " We were driving…" His voice trailed off as his face betrayed the strain of memory. Accidents can happen in the blink of an eye, he didn't know what had happened.

"Do you know where she is?" He was pleading with her now, she had never heard desperation like this before. "You must tell me if you know please!! Do you know?! Have you seen her?" Sasha had tears in her eyes. She could only shake her head. The wind began to blow through the streets, rustling papers like the hush of a thousand children.

He looked anxiously from his left to his right and then back at Sasha's knee. She wanted to say something but wasn't quick enough, he was already moving past her.

"Tanya!" His forlorn cry echoed.

"TAN.." His cry was crushed as he ran past the alleyway only fifteen feet behind Sasha. He was running, screaming, drawing the attention of the horror, and the horror came for him.

Sasha remembered once, when she was a little girl, a huge spider crawled up the drain to wait for her in the tub. She never had a particular fear of spiders, but this one was almost two inches across. Her father had told her it was a wolf spider, the kind who hunt rather than spin webs.

She remembered the look in her father's eyes as he descended upon this tiny creature. It was trapped with little or no chance of escape, but still her father crushed it with a fervor that he himself didn't really understand. For a split second her father had the shadow of merciless in his eyes. But now the tables had turned.

Barry was running, calling his wife's name when a mountain of legs lashed out from of the alley engulfing him. Huge fanged jaws took his head, left arm, and his shoulder in one bite, severing his cry. He was dropped, dead and in a heap as the form shifted to face Sasha. In one crystal moment she saw it.

It wasn't a spider, spiders were small insects that caught flies. This was something else, some demon in a spider's guise. It had eight legs, each hunched for wide support of the massive body making the leg joints sit high in the air. Each monstrous leg was more than thirty feet long and covered with a coarse hair. The front legs were the longest, with huge gray barbed claws at its feet.

It had three body segments. The back one was the largest, like a garden spiders', next was the smaller torso where the legs all joined. The whole body was covered with the same coarse fur, but a weird pattern of gray hair was mixed in, like a zebra's pattern, but twisting and spiraling hypnotically. Then, there was its head.

It had multiple eyes, two huge orbs on top, four more wrapping around the sides, and two more situated at the front of the creatures head. A living spider has black unfeeling eyes, open and starring. On this creature, each eye had its own black pupil moving independently. Red eyelids blinked without pattern, constantly scanning its surroundings. Beneath the eyes were the fang-ridden jaws that dripped a milky fluid. There was no symmetry in those jaws, none of the balance found in nature, just a mass of fang tusks that tangled out, row after row, spilling from it's four foot wide gaping maw.

The creature opened that great gaping maw and unleashed its call. She stood frozen, watching as the teeth flexed outwards like a blossom. If one of those terrible hooks caught flesh, the mouth would drag its victim to hell. The howl was a guttural scream, reverberating and carrying through the streets. It wasn't a battle cry, it was a calling.

Its young, five-miniature creatures, each the size of a German Shepard tumbled over each other from the alleyway and began tearing Barry's body.

A good mother always provides.

Another form emerged in the alley. A second massive creature like the first, only this one seemed more concerned with the actions of the young, carefully watching with mad blinking eyes. The mother fixed her eyes on Sasha. The eternal moment hung as the hideous thing beheld its prey.

It would be hard to say what happened first, if it was Sasha bolting back down the street, or if the creature launched itself to where she had stood. The result however, was the creature thundering into the stone stairway with enough force to shake chunks of stone off the building.

Sasha ran faster after death than she ever had in life. Dodging the debris in the street while the sound of wood crashing into stone behind her. There were far more wraiths here than she first saw on the street, and none of them would help her now. She was new to this place, new to this terror. Doors shut, and sloppy barricades were pressed up against the windows as wraiths trembled in hiding.

She hurdled over a broken chair and kept running, each stride trying to be faster than the last. An instant later, she heard the splintering of wood as the thing gained speed in it's pursuit. She glanced over her shoulder to see the monster closing fast, almost upon her. A shadow to the left caught her eye. An alley, perhaps too small for the creature to follow.

Thoughts taunted. *What if there's one down this alley as well?*

She shifted, almost losing her footing on the littered pages in the street. The alleyway was darker than the street, less patches glowing from the walls, barely enough to see by. A splintering crash from behind made her look back. The creature spilled into the alley, turning itself sideways and running down the wall without losing speed, filling her view.

The soft clothing in the alley was absorbing her steps like mud. Ahead, she could see furniture and various litter was piled in the narrow space as a barricade. In the street she could run around it but here she had to climb over the piles costing her valuable seconds she didn't have. The end of alleyway was close, but the sounds of claws on stone were closer still. A pile of clothing shifted ahead, another horror emerged from under the mass.

Not another Spider, this was something else. A bald man, seven feet tall, his gaunt gray naked body was emaciated with skin barely covering his bones. Even In this darkness, she could see the deep dry rot sockets where eyes should have been. A lipless mouth showing human teeth in an eternal grin opened with a hiss.

Long arms, stretched out towards her, and a whispered gasp of breath came from his jaws. Sasha glanced back and could see the beast in pursuit, then ahead to the fiend in front of her. She felt the rage well up within her again, primal, hateful, and strong.

She grabbed a broken table leg that stuck up from the wreckage. An oak bar, knurled and molded into shapely curves, shattered at one end where it had been broken away. She swung it up as she closed with this gray thing and just as its long arms came at her, she brought the leg down crushing the top of its skull.

There was a brittle crunch like a stale eggshell. The table leg became stuck in the creatures now shattered head. She left it, and used the creature's shoulders as a step to throw herself over the barricade. The corpse slid down, still grasping at her with blind hunger. Sasha cleared the alleyway and turned to back just in time to catch a scorched moment.

The broken creature was trying to hold its head together as the massive spider closed. The zombie was away from the sanctuary of its clothing pile. It had exposed itself feeling Sasha's vibrations as she ran. But because the spider hadn't touched the clothing, it had no way of knowing of her pursuer.

Only for a moment, the creature clawed at its smashed pulp head. Only for a moment, the massive hooked spider hung in the air above it's crumpled form. That instant lasted just long enough for the moment to begin rotting, and then dissolved into the flow of time.

The giant arachnid landed with the muffled sound of crushing bones like dishes breaking underwater. The creature wasn't after Sasha, it was after a meal and this kill was easiest. If Sasha watched, she would have witnessed its proficient rending of flesh, tearing with its front legs and tusks, pulling the body apart. But she didn't stay, she ran and kept running. She was turning in the madness, afraid to stop, afraid to scream, until she saw it.

Then she stood very still for a very long time.

**Chapter 9**

"Hope is only a gentle lie."

*-The Truth*

It was her apartment building. She wasn't more certain of anything in her life, or death. With the luminous patches against the black sky, it was clear. She stood staring while disbelief, anxiety, pain, confusion, all stood with her arguing about who had the greatest right to her mind. She could feel herself shake in a passing shudder that came to stay. Sweat and tears mixed as her chest heaved. Her already shattered psyche was being ground into dust.

One strange eon passed, then another, still here home-but-not stood before her. The paint and renovations that had been applied in recent years weren't present here, instead the old stone front like a skull glared down. There was no comfort in its character now, only the silent mocking of stone.

She found herself walking towards the front steps in the homeward instinct of shock. Her logical and rational mind told her that there would be nothing familiar here, that this was a shadow, a ghost of what was, but her body had taken over. Her muscle memory had become muscle consciousness, and it was taking her home.

The massive oak doorway that was on the building when it was first built loomed at the top of the stairs. One of the doors' bottom half had been torn away, removed by some unseen force. Two symbols had been carved on the intact door, like a runic knocker etched deep in the wood. A jagged line, and a sideways oval with a line through it, both hacked out by desperate hands like runes against some untold evil.

Sasha placed her hand on the shattered door and felt the bitter damp of this world crawl across her palm. She didn't want to go in, but she had to. There was no way to know if she could to find this place again. Even if she was destroyed, at least she would perish in what could be her home.

The creak of hinges echoed forever, then vanished. Holy pages rustled as the door's movement pushed them out of the way. The door swung shut behind her with a firm latch snap. Inside, the light dimmed. The musty smell was vaguely familiar, it was far stronger here inside the building than in the outside dead realms.

Her combat boot footsteps were louder than she liked as she climbed through the torn clothing and toys that littered the hall. The old tiles on the floor were cracked and weathered between the luminous pools of light that drifted down from the walls. The doorway to the stairs remained empty, as though some great beast had torn away the barrier to the upper regions.

The stairs were cluttered with the toys and clothing as if snowdrifts, gathered by the spiraling winds of the dammed. Sasha stepped over these relics cautiously, avoiding each doll and wedding gown like it was child's grave. On the second floor landing, the doorway to her apartment's hall was half open, letting a mildewed draft drift into spiraling stairs.

She pushed open the door the rest of the way. It swung partially open, and then with a splintering crash, dropped off its hinges to the floor. The air pushed the pages up like so many leaves, only to have them float softly back down again. The dim glowing patches, ever present, scattered on without end. As she squinted, the bricks at the far end of the hall came into view. This wasn't hallway to her apartment, yet it was. She stepped though the doorway.

The apartments on this floor had lost their doors, not even splinters remained from where they once stood. She could see though the open portholes to the shattered furniture and clutter of emotional waste from human lives. Down this hall was her life, corrupted by this transition.

Her legs carried her over the broken toys, slabs of rotted fabric, and wood fragments. Another empty doorway, then another, and another. Soon, she was standing in front of what would be her own dwelling, her home on this side of the glass. There were too many thoughts going all at once. Any single one of them would have been crippling enough on its own.

She peered through her own open doorway. It was similar, with shards of furniture, but in this she also found some things that weren't so alien. She saw her plants, looking almost exactly as they had before, entwining up and around the open window frame facing over the street. The whole apartment had the green ambient lighting, but there was something else.

A burning light from behind a shattered couch. It wasn't the same green tint that came from the patches elsewhere, this was a far brighter, whiter light that hid from view. She rushed into the room without looking around, her focus was the light. A glimmer, a flashing prayer of hope passed through Sasha. She ran around the litter to see what the light was. A bright glowing rectangle came into view.

It could have been anything, she didn't know what she would find on the other side of that couch, but someone did. A hateful friend was watching her from the darkness of the room.

It took her a moment to recognize it, and a moment longer for realization. There was only the horrible truth, the hideous honesty of the thing that rested on the floor in front of her. It became the mortar, cementing the fragmented bricks of brutal reality in her mind.

The Ouija Board.

That same Ouija board she used with Luke a short lifetime ago. It was true, it had to be true, all the things that the weird British fellow said. She was dead, this was hell or perhaps worse.

With the pulse of muscle, the darkness moved. The fear returned to Sasha's mind and began screaming. Frantically searching the darkness, she waited for her eyes to adjust. The bright light of the Ouija board had taken away her vision, but slowly the shapes were revealing themselves to her again .

There was a thing before her blocking the doorway, a tiger like beast. It's massive muscled frame was hairless, with sickly pale skin and exaggerated claws flexing as it stood in its low crouch. The look of a cave creature, almost luminous with color forgotten.

She could see the muscles and organs shifting underneath the skin. Its wide-eyed predator head had over sized jaws perpetually snarling and showing jagged uneven teeth. A black marking of what looked like a great "M" crowned its head like war paint. A low, loud hissing growl came, but it seemed hesitant to cross the large vines sprawled on the floor.

*Were they there a moment ago?*

There was nothing to stop this monster from leaping the few meters and be on her, yet it didn't. Over the fear, there was something familiar in this monster. A recognition like a childhood bully years later.

The great beast lifted its clawed foot taking a step towards her, shattering her paralysis. Sasha began to back away. She was too high from the street to jump through the glassless windows. She had to get out of the apartment but the only path had been blocked by the beast.

*Trapped.*

She tried not to think of pain, death, torn meat or rending talons, but it was no use. It took another step towards her, and another closer still. She could smell it's acrid breath as it opened its mouth, and then the beast froze. Something happened

The vines, her vines, the vines that she had labored in the apartment over, came to life. Like lashing snakes, they moved around the catlike thing. With lightning speed, the thick cords of the plant moved, wrapping the cat's taloned feet in place. There weren't enough vines to completely bind the thing, but enough to distract it, and that distraction was all that Sasha needed.

She ran past the creature, careening wide around the broken bits of life. Now her legs were driving with all the force they could muster. The howl of the vine lashed beast was deafening, she could hear the hungry rage and it only served to make her legs work harder.

Down the hall, down the stairs, out the door, and down the center of the street she ran just as she had done moments before. Whenever she stopped running, things would come for her. The Madness whipping her mind; *Run Sasha, run!*

A wrong step brought her down into the papers on the street and terrible pain gripped her body. She could still hear faint howling of the thing in the distance. At some point she had started to cry again, maybe she never stopped. She crawled into pile of broken garbage in the street, covering herself with the holy pages and clothing as best she could.

She buried herself in the wreckage of life. She swept up holy pages and piled them across her legs. She pulled numbly at clothing and toys, propping the dreadful gaze of dolls out around her as sentries against the beasts.

Wraiths cannot sleep and there is nothing to dream of. Instead Sasha shut her eyes under the clothes, willing the world away as she curled into a ball. There was only screaming in her head amidst the rain of tears. Ever so gently, she sobbed under the waste of the living. She was the mad bag lady of a damned city.

## Chapter 10

"We are all in cults."

*-Graffiti suggestion*

"Sebastian!" Stop eating the plants!"

Luke grabbed the cat rougher than he should have, and dropped him out the window onto the fire escape just beyond. Sebastian had a hate-on for those plants, especially in the last few hours. Cats do that sometimes, they just decide that they hate houseplants, for no apparent reason.

Luke stood there, wearing his bathrobe, looking at an angry feline through the window. He had already torn up the apartment and cleaned it again… sort of. He had stubbed his toe on the couch and he became the powder keg after the match. The frustration and helplessness got the better of him. There was nothing to attack, no one he could blame.

Between trying to mess with the plants Sebastian had been especially affectionate. Luke wondered how cats always know when people are in pain. They always come by and try to soak some of it up. He forgot to eat again. He lost 15 pounds over the last nine days. It was easier than shooting himself, and easier to pretend it wasn't suicide. More than that, he simply didn't care.

It had been nine days since he was at the police station, nine days since his life ended, nine days since he started wanting to die. His life went into the crematorium, along with Sasha. Suicide was a seriously considered option, but he couldn't because of the chance, that one chance that Daphne was alive.

*Maybe.*

Maybe she would escape, run away somehow, or maybe she would be found by the police. At any moment maybe that phone would ring and bring Luke back from the dead. Then again, maybe not.

*Damn the maybe's.*

In lieu of suicide, he spent some time in a glass. When that glass became too much effort, he moved up to a bottle. A time tested mistake assisting grieving.

The usual things happened, friends tried to be there for him, other family members showed up out of the woodwork only to find him drunk and naked in his apartment. They should have expected it, but they didn't, and most of them who called really didn't know what to say.

*Sorry.*

Like that word meant a god damn thing. They were sorry, he was sorry, everyone was so fucking sorry but his wife was still….. Maybe it would be a good idea to start drinking again, reality was knocking at his door.

Doug Martin was the only one who made any worthwhile impact. His was a different kind of visit. Doug was a boyhood friend but they had drifted over the last couple of years. Usual reasons, time and what not, but they would give each other a call once every three or four months. Doug's girlfriend had died a few years back in a car wreck, they were fairly serious and everyone did the exact same thing to him.

Luke was more impressed by Doug than anyone else who had come by. They all spoke of caring and wanting to help, but only Doug knew. When Doug stopped by unannounced, Luke answered the door with the rehearsed "I just need time" speech in his head, already getting ready to chase whoever it was away. When he opened the door Doug showed no interest in coming in what so ever. He said hello, handed him about an ounce of the best BC Grass he had ever seen, and said to call him if he needed more, or someone to smoke up with. One strong hug, and Doug walked away.

There was nothing anyone could do. This was a war that he would have to fight on his own. This was a war where the enemy was within and you learned how to live with hidden torture.

He returned from Sebastian's window to his beaten armchair, the sentry post he maintained for the last week. Ma Bell on one side table, and Southern Comfort on the other. The phone had rang a lot in the first few days, then it tapered off. Work had called to say take all the time he needed, apparently others had informed them.

Pink Floyd's album "Wish You Were Here" runs for forty four minutes and eleven seconds, but it can run for all eternity when placed on repeat. It was the only album that didn't cause pain, so it was the only noise made to cover the silence.

The phone rang.

Before the digital tone could finish Luke had answered it.

"Hello?"

" Is Luke Edwards there please?"

"This is."

"Mr. Edwards This is Detective Angus Todd. I have a question about your daughter."

"Ok, please go ahead."

"Did she have any allergies, or conditions that required medication on a regular basis?"

The question caught him off guard. "No... No I don't think so."

"Okay then, Thanks Mr. Edwards that's all I need to know right now. Thanks for your time, we'll be in touch the first sign of anything."

"Wait..." Luke stopped him. The frustration turned to anger.

" You mean... you called me because you had one question? That's it? What do you have?!? Like ..What are your leads?"

"I'm sorry Mr. Edwards, we can't say anything right now ..."

"What the fuck! My child is gone for nine days and it's still, *I'm sorry*?!"

*The anger was roaring.*

"...You guys haven't done shit, what do you fuckin' people do anyways?! You don't care about us! Not the fuckin' regular people, NO! My wife is slaughtered and nothing happens! My child is gone and nothing happens! But if I don't pay my parking tickets, I sure as shit hear about it eh?"

*The anger had murdered all thoughts.*

"You Fucking PIGS!!!"

Luke threw the phone. He threw it at the death of his wife. He threw it at his frustration. He threw it at all the hatred for himself. He threw it at God. He threw it to get thoughts away from him. ,

The phone hit the wall and shattered into a thousand pieces. Luke broke with it, collapsing into a sobbing pile on the floor. He lay there for some time. Clawing at his face, the carpet, the world, and the pain. Time is a relative thing when you're in emotional agony.

He worked his way, sobbing, back up into his chair and within a few minutes had his breathing back under control. He sat for awhile, listening to Waters and Gilmore.

*"So, so you think you can tell Heaven from Hell, blue skies from pain. Can you tell a green field from a cold steel rail? A smile from a veil? Do you think you can tell?"* The speakers sang.

The blade fell. His mind dropped the knife on his suffering. Cutting himself free from the pain, he began to think of the positive action he could take. His mind had been pushed to the point of disparity that it had to do something in order to survive.

Luke knew all his grieving was worthless, the frustration at his helplessness was useless. What the cops were doing was one thing, but there had to be something else, something he could do. He didn't know what or how, but he knew he had to do something more productive than grieve. Nine days had been long enough, he had to start fighting for the life of his child. Sasha was gone, but Daphne hadn't been found yet. Now was the time to fight.

Susie Francis came back into his mind. The cops had said that this was a cult killing, and the kindly woman who had given him her card was a lead of his own. He went to the pile where his coat was and found the card she gave him in his pocket.

No phone.

It would have been best for him to phone first, he knew that. He couldn't let that deter him, he had to march on or the rain of depression would come again. He showered, put on some of his last clean clothes and tried not to look around the bedroom. Her smell was everywhere.

The drive was a blur. Just noise, motion and muscle memory. He managed to get out of his apartment and navigate to her office without too much problem. It was in New Westminster, and old district for North American terms, on Columbia Street. Her building was built in the twenties, when they still had character in architecture. Columbia Street was eclectic, shops that catered to all types could be found in the brickwork hovels.

He pulled into Susie's office parking lot, but his momentum was fading. But even if she wouldn't be able to see him, at least she could book a time. At least he wouldn't be at home any more. At least he was doing something.

From the outside, the building looked kind. Its four story frame stood out proudly on the street. Once upon a time, New Westminster had been the province capitol and the community still held onto that regal feel.

The brickworks and exaggerated cornered architecture gave the building a library feeling. The front doors were deep stained wood. It wasn't what Luke expected. Usually a shrinks' offices had a cold, calculating, medical look to them, this one lent itself to the holistic rather than the clinical.

Luke opened the doors and stepped inside the small foyer. The woodsy smell hit him, the slight delicate musk of old flowers, and even the air of the place was relaxing. The hardwood flooring was original, but everything else had been an addition. Looking at the registry board he could see that the buildings twelve offices were occupied by alternative health practitioners.

There were Chiropractors, Acupuncturists, Guidance Counselors, Massage Therapists, the whole building was a healing storehouse. The fourth floor was taken by Susie Francis. She wasn't listed as a counselor, but a consultant, which Luke thought odd.

She was at the station because she was an expert on these occult crimes. He thought she'd have some prestigious title. Titles usually meant bullshit, so the lack of a title was a good sign. He felt better about coming to see her. This was a positive place, and each step he took brought back his rolling conviction. There were answers here, he could feel them.

With no elevator, Luke sighed and began climbing the stairs. The beautiful oak steps almost made the labor worth it. They had been built in a time when people still cared about quality. By the time he reached the fourth floor, his recent malnutrition and weight loss were apparent. He quietly cursed at himself for letting it slip so far, but under the circumstances…No! No circumstances! He couldn't allow himself the luxury of big picture thought.

The top of the stairs had a stained glass door, the kind that Luke would have expected to see in a grand cathedral trying to look inconspicuous and leading to dark chambers. Fastened to the center of the door was a brass plaque that read:

**Susie Francis**
Consultant & Advisor

*Please come in.*

As it suggested, Luke turned the brass knob beside the plaque and let himself in.

Inside, paper shades over the windows cast a golden glow on the room. Susie had a real appreciation for antiques. The reception area of the office looked more like a library than a waiting room. Books lined the walls from floor to ceiling. A Victorian style chair sat comfortably beside a matching couch, and a woman Luke didn't recognize sat behind a dark hardwood desk. This was a safe place. The whole room had an angelic feel about it.

Luke guessed the woman behind the desk was in her late fifties, but she had a confident and kind look about her. She was at ease, wearing an olive color sleeveless blouse. She smiled as the door closed behind him. Completely unrushed, she spoke.

"Hello. Can I help you?"

Luke looked about, he wasn't really sure what to say. He pulled Susie's business card out of his pocket and walked towards her, holding it like a ticket.

"I'm Luke Edwards, Mrs. Francis told me to come by the office and talk. We met about two weeks ago. I didn't call first…Sorry.." he said.

A light of recognition. " Ah, Yes! Mr. Edwards. We've been expecting you for some time now. One moment and I'll let Susie know you're here."

She stood and Luke saw that her olive blouse was the top of an ankle length dress that ruffled like mist as she silently slipped from the room through the door behind her. Moments later she returned, Susie behind her.

Susie was wearing loose cream colored pants and an egg shell white blouse. It was the kind of thing that could be worn at the country club or around the house. She was smiling with a shade of concern floating in her eyes.

"Luke, I'm so glad you came by. Please, come into my office." Her voice had a soothing strength.

"If you're busy or anything I understand… I was just dropping by to make.." he said, already trying to run.

"Nonsense." She waved her hand. "We rarely make appointments here. Carol, could you make us some tea?"

Luke watched as the olive lady slipped through an opening in the shelves. Susan's hand was suddenly holding his own. It was a mother's touch, a comforting caress of concern. Any thought he had of protesting were vaporized as this woman led him into her office.

The room was huge, looking like a Victorian study rather than a downtown fourth floor office. The paper shades were drawn in here as well, but the windows themselves were open to let the air flow through. At the back of the room, her oak desk sat with a beautiful wingback chair behind it. Off to the left, he saw two more chairs and a table with a tea set between them basking in the golden glow of the light. All around there were small detailed trinkets amongst the floor to ceiling bookshelves.

Susie led him over to the chairs by the tea set. The chair accepted him softly as he sat down. Carol came back with herbal tea in small pastel cups. She smiled as she handed one to him, and for a moment Luke felt very small, like a child in the company of women.

The tea had a deep rich berry flavoring lying in wait for him. It washed calm warmth though him with a slight scent of frankincense. Susie settled back into her chair being at ease. This was very much her domain. Silence hung for a moment.

"Good tea." Luke said, a feeble attempt at small talk.

Susan wasn't about to let him suffer, She smiled. "Yes. Carol makes the blend herself, she is quite a holistic councilor actually. Each tea she makes tastes different for each guest, she has a feel for each person. I must admit, I'm always curious to see what she makes."

Another eternal pause.

Susie leaned forward. "How are you holding up?"

At least is wasn't 'How are you doing?' Luke hated that one.

" It's hard... It's..." Luke coughed for composure. "That's why I'm here. I'm not really here to get counseling." Luke said, feeling stronger again.

"I'm here to try and get an understanding of who it was than killed my wife. The cops said that you were an expert on the occult, a kind of specialist, right? So I wanted to know more about who was responsible."

Susan sat back in her chair. "Well, I'm more of an expert on ritual abuse and the damage that these cults do, not so much the occult itself, but my knowledge is growing."

"So why did they grab my wife and daughter, why them?"

He was cutting to the point, he had to. Susie expected it and met him in kind.

"Your wife's murder was part of ritual. In some darker cult circles, they use human sacrifices to accomplish their goals."

"Do you know why? Did the police tell you what they found out?"

"Unfortunately, there wasn't much to find out. This was the inner circle of a well organized, and devoted cult. When the police interrupted the ritual, those who didn't fight," she paused for a brief moment in a shudder, "killed themselves."

Luke was shocked. "Killed themselves?! But why? What about my daughter?" his voice got louder than he expected. He was embarrassed from the outburst, but Susan's gaze never faltered.

"You're doing very well Luke." She said.

Luke was confused again. "What?"

She went on. "I know the pain you have, the anger that's there. You are handling this better than many others would. I'll tell you all I know, from the beginning, that way you'll have all the information that I have and we can work on this together alright?"

"Yes, Please." Luke said as he settled himself back in the chair and prepared to listen. At last he was getting somewhere. Susan took another sip from her tea and cleared her throat. "You see before I can tell you what I know about your wife, I have educate you about cults themselves."

"Until recently there have been four classifications of cults, but unfortunately a fifth has been added. They are financial, sexual, esoteric, death, and most recently, the corpolitical. I classify a cult as any organization that adheres to a way of life laid out by a dogmatic doctrine, and uses its members to police themselves using psychological and physical means. To some degree, any modern church is a cult, but most do not think of it as such."

Luke was nodding as he listened, she went on.

"The United States was founded by an Egyptian cult, known today as Freemasonry, so we have cults all around us, every day. The only thing that we can do is try to eliminate the more harmful ones."

She took another sip of her tea.

"Of course that said, I think that death cult Christians have done more damage than any other group, but the others haven't had their chance."

She lost him. "Christian death cults?" He asked.

"Yes, the classification of a death cult is any organization that only gives its rewards to it's followers after their death. Christianity has two factions; there are the Christians who follow the ideas of Christ and try to live in peace with all things, this is the religious sect of Christianity. These are the ones that you never hear about, and are among the kindest and gentlest people on earth. Unfortunately there are also the Christian death cultists."

"Christian death cultists are the aggressive militant Christian's, who kill doctors and burn books. These Christians are a death cult by definition. All the rewards that they seek to obtain, they receive after death. Some sects have become so twisted that they actually want the world to end, and others plot to kill millions in the name of a loving God. This of course is not a very popular belief, but it doesn't change the fact that it's true."

"I've never really thought about it that way." Luke said.

"Most people don't." she agreed.

"It's surprising how many people will kneel before a hideously accurate depiction of a man tortured and mutilated, crucified with nails and begin to worship without actually seeing what it is that they are doing. The difference between the two sects of Christianity is the difference between dogma and ideals. To live by ideals is fine, these people are not cultists. They live peacefully and allow for cohabitation with other faiths. Those who follow dogma are cultists, and will enforce their will onto others, even if their will means death. They are destructive and evil, and unfortunately have a great deal of power in North American society."

Luke was beginning to understand, " So a cult, by definition, is any group of people who follow a belief without any concept of reality."

"Correct, or more simply, anyone who cannot grasp that they could be wrong. This is true for all cults. Another more powerful type of cult is the financial cult. These are cults that employ materialism and ideas of financial gain, usually through some self empowering means, positive outlook, that sort of thing. They can be spiritual, or corporate in how they operate, but the cult member's goal is purely financial gain."

"They usually promise wealth through devotion, or through a pyramid type scenario. But the promises are almost always empty and the victims of these cults are often left broke, humiliated, and spiritually destroyed."

All of this made sense to Luke he had seen it before with friends. Susan had given this lecture before and it showed. She paused for another sip of tea before continuing.

"Then there are sexual cults. These claim to have spiritual significance, but really are nothing more than a prevented, ritualistic form of hedonism. They were prevalent in the late 1960's and 70's, not so much any more. The free love movement is a good example.

"They don't sound so terrible as far as cults go." Luke said

"Oh no, there are many sex cults that lead to death or worse. It's important to remember that any cult can be extremely deadly. The moment that anyone believes themselves to be absolutely correct, with no chance of error, which is when the danger starts."

"The most recent addition is the corpolitical cults; these are cults that create an organization, either a government or a company, that they pledge their allegiance to and worship. They will sacrifice their own lives so that this man-made creation can continue."

"That sounds unpopular." Luke said.

"You think so? Nations are nothing more than corpolitical cults. They create imaginary borders, and in the real world a few feet make the difference from being Canadian or American. Then, somehow you are proud of the area that you were born. Armies are created for the ideals of this corpolitical cult, and the modern media glamorizes their sacrifices as *noble* and *heroic*. "

"The Nazi party was by far the most brazen corpolitical cult. It's the techniques the Nazi's created that are now used by nations all over the earth to make their own countries stronger. Anyone who speaks out against a nation is considered a traitor and is then excommunicated and punished."

Luke felt himself slump back into the chair. This whole conversation was starting to make him feel frantic. Susie waited to hear his response.

"I never thought about it that way. I mean there are so many things that are cults then! My god, Just about anything could be a cult."

"No, not everything. Just those organizations that insist on absolute obedience. It's easy to spot the tell tale signs, once you learn to recognize them."

She was concerned on how he was digesting all of this. "Perhaps we should stop…"

"No! Please! I need this, this is helping more than you know. Please go on." Luke sat forward this was healing him, her words were blades cleaving through a veil.

" All right then, where was I?" She asked

"The signs of corpolitical cults." Luke replied.

"Oh yes, I have been more concerned about them lately because certain multinational corporations are starting to use cult tactics in order to control their workers. There use phrases like *'Corporate Culture'* and play heavily on team ideas, when all they are really doing is controlling people. What's more frightening, is that this has made the cult tactics of control seem normal. It becomes dangerous when mind control techniques stop being recognized for what they are."

"The last, oldest, and probably the most dangerous of cults, are the Esoteric. The word Esoteric means *knowledge that is limited to the few*; and as we know knowledge is power."

"What kind of knowledge?" Shane asked.

"That all depends on the cult. You must understand that just as Arthur C. Clark said; any technology significantly advanced appears as magic. Advanced technology is nothing more than knowledge, and these groups go after that knowledge with a deadly ambition."

"So in essence they are scientists then, like…researchers." Luke said.

"In a sense, yes. But these esoteric groups are hoarding knowledge. Limiting it to a select few and then pursuing more, using knowledge as a reward for those they consider worthy. The darker esoteric orders, try to gain knowledge from…"

Susan paused, considering her wording. " From unrecognized means. This is the type of group that I believe is responsible for the death of your wife. I believe it was an esoteric order that were trying to gain knowledge through the summoning of some being."

She held back a little bit to see how his reception of the new information would be. Luke was only nodding his head as it was sinking in.

"So they weren't some group of lunatics? This was a planned out thing?" He asked.

"Oh yes, very much so. This is a kind of science that we do not yet understand. This was an experiment attempting to bring about contact from an out-world being."

Susan paused here again. The conversation was about to go from the disconnected realms of philosophy to hard hitting reality. These were the echoes of screams that the family never got to hear. Even those who are involved in the forensic teams remove themselves when the meat has a name they recognize. She knew what the next step would be, but would Luke be willing to take it?

Luke prepared himself, bringing himself into the mindset of the warrior. This was what he had to do for Daphne, otherwise he wouldn't be of any use to anyone, especially himself. The doors to his emotions were bolted shut. As the last one slammed into place as he blinked his eyes.

"Its okay, you can tell me. I'm ready for whatever it is." He said.

She brought out the cold clinical tone that made her work survivable. In order to maintain emotion, these safety walls were necessary.

"The nature of the cult that killed your wife is largely unknown. She was abducted along with her daughter for the purpose of a sacrifice, as to what or why, I am not entirely sure. We know Sasha was killed by using a Centodd. It is a set of ceremonial knives that that are placed into the victim at key points in the body. They believe that the Centodd allows the spirit of the victim to be released in such a way that the priest can use the energy to complete the rituals' goal."

"Why my wife? Why not some hooker, or one of their own?"

"A good question. I don't believe your wife was grabbed at random. Centodd's are very rare, and are usually used for a specific ritual, a summoning ritual. They had a reason for her specifically. It could be where they took her from, or it could be that the priest might have known her."

*What if I know the priest?* The thoughts roared in his head. The police had asked him to look at pictures of the dead cultists, he hadn't known any of them, in a flash he knew this was a dead-end thought.

"What about the rest of the cultists, wouldn't they know where Daphne would be kept?"

Susan sighed, "Yes they probably did, but they ended their own lives before they could be arrested. The police SWAT team stormed the theater after an anonymous caller phoned in the ritual. When they broke in, they spotted a man behind the alter with a blade over your wife. He was shot dead, and they moved on the rest of the room."

"There were twelve other people present at that ritual. They all slit their own throats with their ceremonial knives, and then spent their dying breaths attacking the arresting officers."

Susan's expression became distant. "The place was unbelievable. Unfortunately, during the raid the symbol scrawled on the floor was destroyed. That would have been a start, but now all we have are the tattoos."

"Tattoos?" Luke asked.

"Yes, the cult members had a variety of tattoos, which is not uncommon, but the thing is the nature of the tattoo suggests this Cult had been around for awhile." She stood and went to her desk. She reached in her drawer, pulled out a photocopy and returned to her seat.

"This symbol was tattooed on them" she said handing it to him.

79

Luke looked hard at the image, trying to make sense of it. She could see the concentration on his face and anticipated the question.

"We don't know what the symbol means, but it's very similar to angelic script."

"Angelic script? As in angels?"

"Exactly. Although the modern thoughts of angels being that they are friendly little creatures who watch over us, the tradition of angels goes back farther than the Bible does. Many Cults and secret sects have been founded around them before.

"I thought angels were supposed to be good." He said.

"Not all, remember that Satan was an angel. You see originally, according to the Jewish texts and other ancient writings, the angels were the first race created by God. Satan, who was the brightest of all the angels, wanted to be equal with God. There was a war and a great divide in the heavens. The angels who rebelled were kicked out of heaven and cast into hell, where they dwell to this day as the enemies of all things good. That is, of course, going by the legends that we are told."

Luke nodded. "But all legends have basis in truth; so you think this cult was trying to summon a fallen angel? A demon?"

"It's possible, but perhaps not a demon. Demons were the angels that swore allegiance to Satan. I think that it's possible that there were angels that became rogue. These were beings that had no allegiances to either side and now exist with their own agendas. Even if such beings exist."

"Do you believe they exist?" Luke asked.

Susan smiled, the question reminded her of something. She was looking at memories for a few moments. "Skepticism breeds madness." She said.

"What?" Luke asked.

"Its just something that an old friend used to say. He was…an investigator, after a fashion. But he always said that the more firmly you denied that something's existence, the more likely it was that you would go insane when you came across it."

"Can I keep this?" Luke asked, motioning with the photocopy.

"Yes that's fine, I have others, but why?"

Luke stood up and began preparing himself for the world beyond the walls. "I have to find my daughter."

Susan's face became severe. "Luke, I don't think you understand the depths of this cult. These are very dangerous people, in more ways than you could possibly know. If you go after them on your own, even if you find anything, you stand a very good chance of being killed, or worse.

"If my daughter is dead, then so am I. Right now she is the only thing keeping me going."

Susan shook her head but there was the light of understanding within. This was his gauntlet he had to walk, the only therapy that could heal. She wanted to say something but was hesitant. Luke reached the door before she made the decision to speak

"I may have a friend of mine contact you, if you don't mind."

Luke cocked his eyebrow. "Who? Another cop?"

"His name is …" She paused. As if uncertain how to continue. " His name isn't important right now, he's a Witch Hunter."

"A what?"

Susie smiled at how bizarre it sounded. " Yes, I know it sounds strange, but he is the most…effective person I know in these kinds of situations. He will find your daughter, I'm sure of that. He has a certain experience in these matters." She said.

Luke could see she was guarding her words. "Thanks, I can use all the help I can get right now, and thanks for the tea. I'll be in touch if I find anything."

"Please do Luke. Please do."

**Chapter 11**

"Thou shalt not suffer a witch to live."
*- Exodus 22:18*

The drive back from New Westminster was therapeutic. Driving always had a way of relaxing Luke. He was neither here or there, but going somewhere, so it gave him the feeling of function. No need to fight with thoughts, he was pleasantly distracted by the motorized hurling of steel and glass.

He didn't want to go home. There was nothing there except the same pain he left behind a couple of hours ago, and a waiting bottle.

*Not yet.* He thought to himself.

He couldn't go home just yet. He had learned more than he had expected to this trip, but it only made him aware, not proactive. He had to do more to find his daughter, but the question that mocked him was: *what?* The police were already spending time and resources using the conventional techniques, so what was left?

His attention was brought to the side of the road where quite a protest was happening. At first, he thought it was a pro-life rally, but it was far more animated. There were people shouting, waving signs, and being very careful to stay on the public sidewalk as though there was an invisible wall blocking them from a parking lot and the line of stores.

There were over twenty of them, all wearing respectable clothing, chanting the Lord 's Prayer as a victory march. Luke slowed the van and pulled into the parking lot that became the no-mans-land between the sidewalk and the stores.

"God watches", one sign said. "Cast out your devils" said another. Another sign said something about the city of Sodom . Luke couldn't see what all the fuss was about until he picked out the stained glass pentacle in one shop window.

An occult bookstore, a little shop called *"The Angels Song"* was the cause of all this. It was one of those places that the Christian cult did not approve, so the march was on. Luke sat for awhile and observed them, Susan's words about cults running through his mind.

He couldn't believe that he hadn't seen it before, the album burnings, the destruction of children's games, the book burnings. All the crimes that these so called Christians had committed against their fellow man, all in the name of purity and glory to god. There were always people holding signs on the sides of the road saying that abortion kills, and then one of there own kills a doctor to exalted cries of "Hallelujah!". Luke considered making a bumper sticker saying "Pro-life kills doctors".

His mother wasn't like this. She went to church every Sunday like clockwork, so did Sasha when she was younger, but she never waved a sign, or burned a book. Why were these followers of Christ so full of hate? It made no sense at all. This was against every ideal Christ had, but then that was the key. The ideals of Christ weren't what these bigots were about, it was the dogma, the control. Angry people seeking forgiveness for hating their own lives.

A homeless man came walking up the sidewalk carrying a sloppy piece of cardboard. It had *John 3:16* written in faded felt marker with dozens of tiny crosses circling around it. He wore rotting sneakers, greasy threadbare jeans with an old faded yellow t-shirt sporting a dense collage of stains. His hair was wild, uncut and ungroomed for some time, blending down into a large busy beard of similar hygiene. The light was far greater in his eyes than any of the others, but it all came from the same flame.

He tried to join in with the protest, but the others wouldn't have it. Two younger men met him at the edge of the group and Luke could see them pointing for him to leave. The old fellow wasn't looking like he was going to comply, until one of the two handed him some money and patted the desperate fellow on the back.

They couldn't stand to be next to a man like that, too much like a mirror. So they just gathered some cash table scraps and fed it to the dog. Extortion of the soul.

Luke pulled the photocopy of the symbol out of his pocket. If the cops were checking all the conventional means, what about the unconventional? What if you could hunt this cult in the spiritual world, as well as in the physical, beat them at their own game. Until Susie's 'Witch Hunter' friend showed, he had no other leads. He felt a rush of confidence, it wasn't much, but it was more than had a few seconds ago. He stuffed the sheet back into his coat and got out of the van.

*The angels song eh? Maybe they have something to say.* He thought.

It was a small shop, the last one on the building. Luke swung open the door and was greeted by the smell of incense. It took a few moments for his eyes to adjust, the sunlight hadn't seen much of this place.

The shop was narrow and long, with high shelves lined with books and small stands scattered about holding trinkets and charms. Couches and chairs had been strategically placed beside tea tables where people could quietly sit and read before purchasing their choice. This was hardly the kind of place one would picture being at risk for fire bombing.

It reminded him of Susan's office, but the energy here was different. At Susan's he felt calm, relaxed, serene. This place had a similar feel but it with a different taint, sweeter perhaps, more exotic. It stirred something somewhere inside him.

Luke looked around at the crystals hanging with ornate wires about the shop. They were three dimensional magic circles, wrapped around the focus of quartz. Faded rainbows moved, dancing along the book spines from the windows sunlight. The subtle sound of a babbling brook came over hidden speakers along the walls.

At most retail shops, the cashier was right by the doors. In here it was in the middle of the store against the wall where a young man sat behind the till reading a book. Luke guessed he couldn't have been more than twenty three, with a cliché goatee for a magic shop.

He looked up from his text with a slight look of mischief. "Hi there." He said.

Luke stepped forwards. With all the commotion going on outside, he thought a friendly face might be a comfort.

"Hi, I was wondering if you could help me. I have a picture of a symbol, and I need to find out what it means. I was wondering if maybe you could take a look at it."

"Sure, no problem!" The goatee said. "I'm not the best when it comes to sigils, but I'll give it a shot. You want a coffee?"

In the back corner Luke could see a courtesy coffee machine set up, hidden from view.

"I'm good thanks." He said as the clerk had already started making himself one.

Luke looked at some of the pentacle jewelry by the till. "This doesn't seem like the kind of place that should have people trying shut you down. I mean, you'd think you have dead goats and all that." He said

The clerk laughed "Yeah, I've often thought of getting a T-shirt that says "*evil one*" in big letters so they could pick me out easier. The goatee helps, but I just can't bring myself to shave my head, y'know?"

Luke smiled. "How do you guys put up with it? I mean, isn't there a law against

**84**

this sort of thing?"

"Naw, we just ignore them, that pisses them off worse than anything. Worse than hatred is indifference, they say."

The clerk handed him a brown handmade mug and perched himself back on the stool behind the counter. "So let's see what you got."

Luke pulled the paper out of his pocket and pressed it flat on the counter. The clerk looked at it for a few moments, stoking his chin.

"Hmmm." He said. "I don't think I know this one, but you might want to ask Genaya. She knows way more about this kind of stuff than I do."

"Genaya?"

"Yeah, she does all of our readings."

"So she's a psychic."

"Yeah, sorta-kinda, but that's a fairly general term. One sec, I'll see if she's got a minute."

He ducked behind a richly colored tie-dyed curtain at the back of the shop. Luke scanned the books looking for something useful, nothing jumped out at him. The clerk returned looking a little more anxious. *The coffee must be working.* Luke thought.

"She can see you now if you like." The clerk said holding the curtain aside.

Luke was led down a narrow hallway. It was a strange contrast to the rest of the shop, neglected and cracked plaster walls with no decorations of any kind. The smell of the incense was covering something here, something damp. The hallway continued on but the clerk stopped by an dark wooden door, cracked and worn from years of use. Only the brass handle shone from contact with flesh. The clerk pushed the door ajar.

"I gotta get back to the shop. She is just inside."

Luke nodded and stepped inside. The room was larger, maybe twenty feet square at a guess. It had long veils of fabric draped along the walls to hide the hallway's mirrored cracks. There were some shelves, but the trinkets on them weren't nearly as clean as the ones in the shop, they looked older. Weathered stone carved idols and strange metal disks with markings adorned hooks like tools.

A wood placard was on the wall with an intense and complex symbol burned into it. The books lining the shelves focused on something called Enochian Magic, and the works of a Dr. John Dee. At the far end of the room a doorway was covered by long hanging red veils.

A massive wooden table sat in the center of this room. It had to weigh more than five hundred pounds. Heavy set legs and thick planks roughly hewn onto the shape of a circle. On it burned a single, large kerosene lamp, bathing the room in its golden glow and placing a faded sun on the ceiling. Two heavily padded wing back chairs, covered in a deep burgundy velvet fabric sat opposing one another across the table.

This was the reading room. The feeling from the rest of the shop took another step here. Maybe it was the lamp light, but there was something primal here, something very subtly erotic.

The veil in the door was brushed aside and a woman entered. Latin, Spanish perhaps, maybe Greek. She had long jet black hair to the middle of her back, falling over tanned skin. She was shorter than Luke and with dark, beautiful features. She was wearing a long gypsy dress, sultry and smooth.

This wasn't a young awkward or playful girl, this was a woman, powerful and dangerous. She had the look of a hunter. She sized up Luke with her large deep eyes and her full lips parted as she spoke.

"Graham tells me you have some questions?" She said, nodding with an eyebrow twitch as though looking over glasses. He could feel her eyes caressing his face.

"Yes, the young fellow out front sent me back to see you, I'm trying to find some information about a symbol. Do you have a moment?"

One corner of her mouth slid into a smile. "I have many moments, I'm sure I can share one with you." Luke laughed nervously as she sat down at the table.

"Please tell me your name." She said.

"Oh, I'm sorry, I'm Luke Edwards." Luke said as he took the opposing chair. This table was the perfect sizes for two people to sit at and still touch.

"Hello Luke, My name is Genaya." She reached and Luke shook hands.

Her left hand coupled the embrace. Her touch was cool, comforting and soft. Her right hand held his in a customary fashion but he could feel the light touch of her fingers against the base of his palm, seeking through subtle creases. Her left hand caressed the outside of his fingers, it was enticing, soothing. The feeling of a curtain veil blown by the summer wind. She seeped through his whole being.

That very same moment of touch, she gasped and Luke saw her eye's flutter. The touch was not as pleasant for her as it was for himself. He tried to pull away, but she held his hand until the moment ended and she arched her back breathing a deep sigh of control. The neckline of her dress was cut deep, and her arching back thrust her chest into the light of the lamp, shielded only by the thin fabric of the dress.

Genaya relaxed her form back into the chair. The golden light played her wild hair. She opened her eyes, tears welling within them. One large drop came out and rolled over the perfect skin on her cheek.

"I can feel your pain Luke, I felt it when we touched." She said trying to control her voice. "You have suffered so!"

Luke could feel tears within his own eyes. He believed this woman had felt his pain, maybe she was the only one who could. She looked high at the oil lamp's bright spot on the ceiling regaining some composure. Luke looked down, trying to think about nothing. The tension in the moment was broken by her voice.

"I'm sorry, I should not have pried like that" she said "I always reach out to those who come to me, it helps me to get a better understanding."

Luke looked up, objective reality was cutting through the haze "Wait, you mean you just read my mind? You know about what's happened?"

"No, not specifics. I know that you have recently suffered the most painful loss that I have ever felt, and now you are searching to regain that which was taken from you. Other than that I have no details"

Luke was amazed, perhaps a little afraid. *How could she know that?*

"I'm an empath Luke, I can feel emotions and residual emotions from people, places, things. I don't know any details about the incident, but I do know your pain. What can I do to help?"

Luke shook off returning haze and brought his crumpled sheet onto the table. Her eyes widened when he pressed it down on the table.

"Where did you get this?" She said gasping.

It sounded so much like a command that Luke found himself wanting to tell her everything. He opened his mouth to speak, but something caught him. He didn't go on and didn't know why. She could see his hesitation and brought up her hands.

"Please wait a moment Luke, I want to be certain we are not interrupted".

She stood and walked by him with silent grace. As she did he found her hand on his shoulder, firm, kind, sensuous, but then gone again. She opened the door and called down the hall. "Graham, I won't be seeing anyone for awhile, and we are going to need some tea in here please."

A muffled reply was heard and she closed the door. Rather than taking her chair again she knelt by Luke's right side. For an instant she looked like a servant, an expectant slave. She reached up and took Luke's hand again, the expression of passion on her face was staggering.

"I want to help you Luke. No one should suffer the way you have, no one should have to feel that kind of pain. You are quite a man Luke Edwards. Any thing that you tell me here in this place will stay between us. There will be no charge for my services, I honestly want to help. Do you understand?"

Luke could only manage a nod, the shock of her intensity was unbalancing.

"Let me take your coat" She said.

He realized he was still wearing it. Luke shed the outer layer and Genaya hung it beside the door.

She sat back down across from him and laid out her hands beckoning for his from across the table. Luke was unsure of what to do, he looked at her soft hands like a starving man. Her flesh implied so many things.

"It's okay Luke. You don't have to be alone." He took her hand and felt the wash of her touch again.

He started from the beginning and told her everything. This was the first chance he had to relay things from his perspective. This woman was the first person who he felt may just have been able to understand, face to face. She was a stranger, and it was so much easier to share with a stranger in a time of crisis. No judgments, no haunting.

It was still the beginning of the story when Graham dropped off the tea. It was the middle before the tears started to role down Luke's face. Genaya was a mirror, focused and attuned to everything he said. Her tears fell with his and her hand was always present, lending support and comfort.

He lost all track of time, and the whole time he talked, she didn't say a word. She only nodded, watching him with a confessional intensity. He was exhausted, the emotional strain was too much to bear, but the release had taken the horrible weight away. Her touch was so very soft, he didn't want to let it go, but he knew he had to.

He used the excuse of checking his watch to release her hand. It was 4:13pm, he had been talking for more than two hours.

"Oh my god, I'm sorry I've taken so much of your time...".

"No Luke please, this is the most important thing for me, can you go on?"

Her eyes were amazing. They were broadcasting every emotion she had with the clarity of fire and the intensity of silence. He didn't know what else to say but he desperately wanted to keep talking. He remembered coming in here for information.

"So... what do you think of all this? What do you suppose this is?"

She paused for moment. "I'm glad that you told me everything Luke, because what you are saying is making sense with this symbol. This is a lesser known symbol for an Angel known as Abaddon."

Luke's mind leapt, *Progress!*

"Susan had said that it looked like angelic script, but I don't understand why a cult about an angel would want to kill my wife."

She scanned the books for a moment. "I don't know much about it, but I do recognize the symbol. I'll do some research and get back to you on it right away."

"But you know that it is this....*Abaddon* character?"

*Abaddon. That is familiar, why is that familiar?* He thought to himself.

"Yes, I'm almost sure of it." She said and approached his chair. She knelt beside him again. Luke tried not to notice how perfect she looked. Her dark eyes caught him, so did her hand.

"Thank you so much for sharing this with me." She said and he could feel something stir uncomfortably inside him. She was so kind, so passionate, she was an ocean washing away the pain that he felt inside.

"I don't think I've ever met anyone quite like you Genaya." He said it without thinking, more to himself than to her. He regretted it instantly, but her face erupted in another smile.

*Was it a blush?*

She turned as she stood up and went to the books again. "When I find out more, I'll need a way to contact you" She said turning back with a notepad and pen. "Give me your address and phone number and I'll be in touch shortly."

Luke wrote it down and stood up, suddenly her arms were around him. He couldn't remember the last time he was held this way by a woman other than Sasha. It was different, full, intoxicating. She released him before he had a chance to protest.

"We are old souls Luke, you and I. I'm happy to help, Graham will give you one of my cards on your way out. I'll see you soon."

There was an involuntary urge, suppressed even before he admitted it. Luke felt a wash of shame and looked away.

He loved Sasha with all his heart and soul, that love would burn him for thinking of this woman. The beating of guilt that was waiting for him would be merciless, the sharp shouts of his conscience were ringing in his ears now. He grabbed his coat from the wall and turned back, half of him was begging to leave, another half was begging him to stay

"Thank you Genaya. Thanks for…"

She stopped him, holding a finger gingerly up to his lips "Shhhhhh." She bowed her head looking over imaginary glasses with sensuality. "I am your servant." She said.

He would hear those words again in his dreams that night..

## Chapter 12

Something was touching Sasha. Instantly she was flailing and scurrying back through broken furniture. Her back slammed against a sideways desk. She was still in the dark place, the nightmare was still going, she was still lost. The tall lanky figure that had introduced himself in the theater was standing close by, trying to look non-threatening.

"I say, it's quite alright, really! I was rather hoping you hadn't been injured." He didn't know what else to say, so he flashed a wide smile trying to put Sasha at ease. It looked like Cheshire psychosis.

Sasha looked around, a quick check of up and down the streets. She had only run at top speed for a little while but this was no area of Vancouver she had ever seen. The way the streets moved caused her head to hurt. They were safe for now, there was nothing trying to kill them at that very moment.

"Who are you?" She asked at last.

"Ah good! I say! It seems the sickness may be starting to break. I am Clarence Winker dear lady, we met just shortly at the theater, remember?"

"Yes" She had so many questions shouting at once. She was frantic. "Where are we?"

", Yes…Umm…Rather…Well…" Winker pinched his face with strain trying to think of the best way to do this. Eventually he sighed and said " You see, you are dead, and this is Abaddon; the realm of those recently living. I am sure it has many names, but this is what I commonly refer to it as." Then he gave another Cheshire smile.

Fear was still there, but she was learning to control it. It had changed from blinding pain to a mere ache, one can function at that level. She focused her thoughts on what he was saying, trying to make sense out of them. "What did you mean when you said *the sickness was starting to break*?" she asked.

"Ah Yes, well, you see, being dead, or just recently living, its rather difficult for one accept certain truths when one arrives here."

The way he spoke he could have been an Oxford professor at talking about the history of bugs. "You see, when one dies and comes here, the first instinct is denial. This is what I've called *The Madness*. It's perfectly natural really, considering the circumstances, new arrivals panic and begin running about, totally unaware of the dangers of this place. Most Wraiths die that way don't you know."

He went on. "After the madness comes *The Sickness*. That is, the state of depression you were just in a moment ago. The 'all-hope-is-lost' mantra and what not of the wraiths"

"Wraiths?" She asked, trying to understand; focusing was hard.

"Oh yes, we are all Wraiths, my good lady. Well, at least I am for certain."

Sasha's mind flooded; Knives, the cutting blades, *her mother*.

"My mother was killed, have you seen her? Is she here?"

"Ah, I'm quite certain that you will never find her here." He said , dismissing her question without thinking and then immediately regretting it.

Her hope threads were slashed away. There was nothing for her now. This was hell.


Clarence had the most horrible expression of error on his face. He had pushed her into a relapse of the sickness. Clarence watched her tears fall as she sat.

"I say, here now…" He said and sat beside her. "None of that, it's really not good for you." He pulled an ornate handkerchief from his pocket and handed it to her. Its was lace, soft and beautiful.

Clarence tried to spur on the conversation "You know, I can't really say that you're a Wraith with certainty, you might be something else altogether. You definitely took care of that nasty Thespian without too much effort, what? So I don't think you're quite like the rest of us."

No response. He tried to think of what to say, but was coming up empty, so he sat there with her.

She cried for awhile, but after that while she glanced up to see Winkers' comical face watching her expectantly. The moment she looked at him, he flashed his nervous smile to make her feel better. She almost laughed, but it came out as a choked off chuckle that could have been mistaken for a sob. The tears stopped. She focused on her breathing, waiting for the riot in her head to stop. This was manageable, she just had to take it one step at a time.

*Keep control, get my bearings.* She thought.

"How long have you been here?" She asked.

"I say!" He said triumphantly, happy to be talking again. "The whole time thing is rather different here you know, quite different altogether. I don't really know an actual time per say."

"Where did you…Where are you from originally?" She couldn't grasp talking about death in the past tense.

" London, England. Lived there my entire life. I got rather walloped one night on my way home. Feb 11, 1858 I believe it was."

He swung the book off f his belt harness and dropped it in his lap. The loose pages that had been sticking from it were pages from the various holey texts in the street. Every square inch of the paper had been covered by handwriting with complete disregard of what had been on the pages originally. He opened his book and turned to the middle, looking to confirm the date.

Her eyes widened. "My God. You've been here.."

"Oh, I'm afraid he won't help you here." He said, still trying to confirm the date. "I have seen no evidence of him whatsoever in this place." He paused, thinking. "That is to say though that he could have existed but probably not as we know it, or maybe a God still does exist, but I certainly couldn't see him working in place like this." He made up his mind and nodded "Yes, if there is a god he has most certainly forgotten about this place."

*What a strange man.* She thought.

Now sitting here, she got a good look at him. He was dreadfully thin, hard to tell his age, maybe forty or fifty. She doubted he looked more than sixty, but age must be a relative thing here. His eyes were a stale brown and long stringy black hair hung out from under the large top hat. He was dressed as the most perfect ringmaster, every detail, right down to the handkerchief she was holding. Dirty and worn, but complete in every way. When he did smile, it was wide and full, exaggerated like a clown.

"What….. What are you?' She asked.


"I say, that's the spirit!" He was ecstatic." I, am what you would call a wraith. That is to say I am an ex-person who was snuffed out before all of his life force was used up, and consequently arrived here. I am currently compiling all the data I can in order to understand this place. But the question is dear lady; what are you?"

"What do you mean?"

He mulled it over starting to mouth words before he committed to speaking. He was having difficulty thinking of how to explain it.

"You see, whoever shows up here, is usually a wraith, just like people all over the living world are humans. But there are different species of wraiths, sort of like races of men, yes very much like that. I am a very standard wraith. Altogether nothing really special about me, but I've discovered quite a few different types of wraiths and creatures here. You are one of these different types and seem to be friendly, which is very exciting for me I must say!"

Sasha was now beating down the fear with rationality, she voiced a question softly, more to herself than to Clarence. "How did I get here?"

"I say, that's exactly what I wanted to know! How did you get here? What was the last thing that you remember, quite often that does have a lot to do with things."

Sasha was looking for answers in her memory but her mind was still reeling. She was trying to stabilize herself into understanding. She told him everything that she could remember about the evening. The pain, the knives, all of it. As he listened, Clarence sat scribbling on pieces of holey text with a long quill and inkwell he produced from his coat. She finished her story with the arrival at the theater.

"I say! That's most extraordinary! Most extraordinary indeed!" He was very excited. "Now, how did you destroy that Thespian?"

"The what?"

" The Thespian, that foul beastie that you made such short work of! Amazing really! That particular one was rather nasty altogether. So I am quite keen to know how it is that you destroyed it, what?"

"I...I don't know." She tried to remember what happened at that moment but it was all so blurred.

Clarence was disappointed, but his mind was rapidly moving on to other things. "So let me see if I have this. You were murdered in some kind of ritual, yet from your description to me it would seem that something went quite so horribly wrong with it. However, it does sound like the ritual should have consumed you entirely. Most odd altogether."

"Consumed me?" She asked.

"Yes, yes, *consumed* you see. When a person is killed quite suddenly, their essence, soul if you will, comes here. However, if the person is consumed, that is to say, their energy used up somehow, they skip this place entirely. Death is only a change, consumption is the total transformation of the essence. This spell, or ritual, or whatever it was obviously designed to use your essence, your soul as it were, to accomplish some task. Yet, the whole thing was botched somehow, and well, here you are!"

"So this is what happens to people after they die?"

"Oh most certainly not! Only to the rather unfortunate ones who get rather killed before their essence is used up."

She spoke, pondering. "People who die before their time."

"Well not, *before their time* as you say, but who have a surplus of energy." Clarence corrected her. He thought a moment longer. "I wonder why they grabbed you?"

"What do you mean?"

"This nasty bunch that killed you in that ritual, why did they grab you? What made you the subject of their sacrifice? Were you ever involved with the occult or worshiped with a group, any secret societies or that rubbish?"

"No! Not at all! I used a Ouija board with Luke the other night for the first…"

Clarence cut her off astonished, "What? You say you used Ouija and you're not occult? I say!"

She was defensive, "No, I'm not *in the occult*! It was a stupid game!"

Anger slipped into her tone. Clarence began to back away fear suddenly on his face. "No, that's not what I meant, no need to destroy me just yet, I was just rather surprised, and you're obviously telling the truth."

*This man is really afraid of me!* She realized. It was confusing to see someone afraid of her.

"It's ok…what are you afraid of?" She asked.

Clarence relaxed a little, "Ah, yes, well. You did kill that Thespian you see, and you're not too sure how you did it, so you can understand my concern, what?"

She stood up, the ground was getting uncomfortable. "What did you mean about the Ouija board?" She didn't mean to make her statement sound as much like a command as it did, but she needed answers now.

Clearance was not about to argue. "I don't know about any Ouija *Board,* I only know about Ouija systems of divination. What did it look like?"

"Its was a Ouija board, it's a game from a toy store. It was about so big." She motioned with her hands for the dimensions of the board. "And its got a bunch of numbers and letters on it. You put your hands on this thing and ask it questions, and the little pointer moves to answer the question."

Clarence had his jaw open. "I say! You mean to tell me that a Ouija is being sold in toy stores? As a game?"

"Well...Yes." Suddenly the idea seemed bizarre to her as well.

Clarence was horrified. "I say! It would be rather interesting to know how that came about! Aren't there any controlling bodies who limit the use of them?"

"No, they're a joke!" She said.

"That's rather odd don't you think? I mean, if it's just a joke there certainly wouldn't been enough of a demand to sell them would there?"

Sasha wondered whey she hadn't questioned it before. Why were they being sold as toys? Devices that could enable anyone to communicate with dimensional beings should probably be regulated, and at the very least, not sold in toy stores to children. More questions were rising.

Clarence took his large book and placed it on the ground by her. "Please watch this for a moment, will you?" He was off wandering about the cluttered street without waiting for a reply.

He located two elaborate dining room chairs. Muttering to himself about spiritual implications of children's toys, he dragged the first on back to where she stood.

It was a high back oak chair with intricate carvings of griffins on it. Two griffin heads were on the arm and the legs looked like large claws holding stone balls. On the seat was a green velvet cushion, soiled from exposure.

He dragged the second chair over and faced it to the first. This one had even a higher back with Victorian sweeping designs worked deep into the wood. There were no animal carvings on it, but there was no doubt about the hand carved effort that must have gone into it. Red leather cushions adorned this one making them an odd pair, but both works of art.

After the two chairs, he moved amongst the neighboring piles until he found a very small hand carved tea table that was still intact. He squared up the table and pulled the high back Victorian up to it. He picked up his book from beside Sasha and sat down.

She could see the other chair was for her, but still she felt hesitant. She wasn't particularly afraid of Clarence, or felt any danger at that very moment, it was the surrealistic nature, the dreamlike look of the setting. She was Alice, this was Wonderland, and the Mad Hatter had just set up for tea.

She sat down, her body was acting of its own accord, she was just along for the ride. Clarence had opened the massive book on the tea table and began shuffling through the chaos of both loose and bound pages inside. She thought it looked like some kind of journal. He finally found a piece of paper that had no writing on it and again produced an elaborate long feather quill from his pocket. Without pause, he began scribbling furious notes onto the hapless parchment. Sasha replayed their conversation in her mind. The questions were getting clear.

"What exactly is a Ouija Board?" She asked.

" What? What? What?" He looked up from his diary as if slapped. "Ah ..yes…of course….the Ouija" He leaned back in his chair tapping the long feather of the quill against his cheek

"The Ouija Board, as you call it, is a communication device. It's something that channels the essence of living beings to talk with beings in other realms." He said.

" So, its like a window."

"In a way." Clarence pinched his expression. "But it would be more accurate to call it a pipe. You see, the Ouija was originally from Egypt as I understand it. It was used there, and the knowledge came up throughout most of Europe. It is an extremely powerful ritual, but very simple to do.

Clarence leaned back in his chair waving his quill about like a conductor's wand as he spoke. "In my time, it was a bit of a party favorite among the rich. They would all gather together with cards, and write out the alphabet, numbers, hello, goodbye, yes and no on them. They would all be laid out in a circle and the pointer, as you called it, is actually a Planchete. It was usually a tall wine glass that would easily tip over if it were pushed. A minimum of two people, usually four or more were used, but a trained spiritual medium was always present to observe the rules of safety."

"Safety? Ouija boards are dangerous?"

"Oh dear me yes! Ouija is extremely dangerous! You see what happens is that you create a spiritual communication device, a type of *Phasmavigator* they are called, as I understand it. They take the essence, the life energy of those who use it and open a communication line to another world.

"This world?"

"Not necessarily. It all depends on where the board is, who's using it and with how many people, as well as a whole pack of other details. I'm not very well versed in it myself you understand, just the very basics. The danger lies if one person uses it by themselves, they open a straight conduit to the spirit world with their own essence.

Its like inviting entities and spirits to come in and corrupt your being! They can't do it if there is more than one person using it. The conscious entity can't split itself to inhabit two people, and it can't isolate the essence of a single person from the stream. As well, there is the correct way to deactivate the…"

"Abaddon!" Sasha blurted. Razor sharp memories slashed the fog in her mind.

Clarence almost jumped out of his skin, steadying his top hat from the surprise. "Yes…. Abaddon is the name of this place."

"No, who is Abaddon? When we used the Ouija board it said that I was Abaddon, does that mean anything to you?".

Winker looked perplexed. "You are Abaddon? Well it could mean the being was trying to warn you, as I understand it quite often some spirits exist outside of time…" Clarence trailed on. Sasha stopped listening. She was lost in thought. This wasn't hell, or heaven, this was another realm of existence, and if you come from earth and get here, it stood to reason……

"How do I get back?" She interrupted him again.

"I don't think you can my dear." Clarence began flipping pages in his diary. "I do believe my notes may prove useful to you here. Ah, yes! There we are! This ought to fill you in a little bit, what?" He spun the book around to face her. "Have a look then."

Sasha leaned forwards and began to read.

**Chapter 13**

Dairy Entry #66575
Sometime after death.

Dear Mr. Diary,

It would seem that I am, in fact, dead.

It has taken me quite some time to come to this conclusion, but it would seem to be so. It doesn't bother me quite so much, however, as everyone else here seems to be dead as well. What is disturbing about the whole business, is that the dead that I thought I'd be, isn't really the dead that is. That is to say, this is not nearly as I imagined death to be, Mr. Diary. Not nearly at all.

I know it must be hard to translate the last few hundred scribblings that I've put into you, but I assure you I'm feeling quite better now. Well, that's not true. Let's just say that I am feeling much better than I was a moment ago. I would give you a more accurate time frame, but I'm not to sure how exactly time frames work here. In fact, I don't think 'time frames' exist here at all.

I have been wandering about in this place for long enough to begin making some judgments about it. My information, I must confess however, comes from the other beings that I encounter. Most of them are dead (Well, in fact all of them are dead,) but you would be surprised at the stories that these pleasantly dead people (who died in not so pleasant ways) have to tell.

It is so very hard, Mr. Diary, to describe to you a world that no one has ever been able to survive in, a world that is constantly changing. I've heard many names for this place, most think it's Hell, but I disagree. I can't really say why this isn't Hell, other than if I were in Hell I don't think I would have you with me. Also there are a great many pages of bibles and other holy books littering the streets, so much so that when you are walking they are like autumn leaves rustling at your feet. But in any case I can get enough paper to write my notes, so I definitely think that this is not Hell.

I'm told this place is called Abaddon, after the Greek meaning of the word, which was the first recognized spirit world outside of Hell. Which incidentally, seems kind of handy, that "being outside Hell" bit.

Speaking of handy, I have found myself a rather interesting hiding spot. I'm really quite happy with it as there is very little chance of me getting eaten here. This I feel is a requirement for good hiding spots. It's a theatre, and it is strange that I'm safe here, as it's best to avoid theatres and other public places, but I assure you finding it was an accident. There is only one stairway down to this little room, and conversely only one stairway up. As well, there is a lot of light coming from the walls.

Oh I'm so disorganized. I'm sorry, Mr. Diary, I didn't mean to get this way. I'll tell you about my room very quickly before I get on with everything else.

I found it as I was traveling along the street. Most of the buildings are lit by the puddles of green light coming from the walls. Occasionally there are candles as well, but usually there are wraith packs that horde them, so it's not best to go near. Most wraith packs are really quite rude, and violent.

Theatres by their nature shed a lot of light, so I was drawn towards it in order to make some notes. The door on this one was in surprisingly good shape. I took off my hat and knocked but there was no answer, so I went in.

It was filled with clutter; love letters, children's toys, tattered clothes, and broken furniture. I took a side stairway which led me up to my glorious little room. I'm not sure what the room was used for, but there is a little window overlooking the stage area.

This is when I heard the Thespians moving, I still haven't ventured into the main stage area yet because of them. There's one for certain, but there may be more so I've decided to share my new home for awhile. It's really quite surprising what some well-placed smashed, and not-so-smashed bits of wood will do for a place.

It's really kind of exciting, because I don't think anyone has ever written a book about Abaddon.. Naturally I'll need a title, so I've narrowed it down to two working titles:

**The Diary of Clarence Winker;**
*"The most comprehensive and brilliant book ever written on Abaddon".*

Or perhaps:

## The Most Comprehensive and Brilliant Book Ever Written on Abaddon;
*"The Diary of Clarence Winker"*

It will take me some time to be sure, but I should try to explain what is going on here, or at least how I think it is going on, well, based on the information that I've been gathering in any case.

It's so hard to know where to start. I suppose I should change my format of how I'm doing this to see how it works, maybe if I wrote about these things in point form it will be easier to link them all together after I get them down. Very well then, perhaps we should give that a try.

### Life, Death, and Everything Else:

No wait, that's too much still. Let's try to cut that down a bit.

### Life, Death, and the Part where we go back and forth:

Yes, that's much better wouldn't you say?

It all begins with energy I suppose. Yes, that's it, energy. All things are made up of energy. The eternal questions, like who made the energy in the first place, I cannot answer. But I do know that the cosmos is like a huge ocean of energy, portioned out, poured out into vessels that are living beings.

Now here is where it gets a bit odd. You see this cosmic energy is able to coexist on many different planes of being. That is to say that the very planes of being themselves are made up of this energy. Abaddon is the realm of the dead, yet it is still made of the same energy. Am I making sense? Here, let me try it this way.

There is a vast reservoir of energy, essence if you will, that exists outside of those rather limiting things like time and space. This is where all consciousness winds up if it didn't die in nasty ways, but all energy eventually winds up there no matter what. In the tarot deck the death card means change, and the only constant I have found here is change. Life energy, essence so to speak, is the same way. It is apparently true that energy cannot be created nor destroyed, it can only be changed. (I can't remember where I read that.)

Abaddon doesn't exist separate from the world of the living, but together with it, only on a slightly different level. Before there was civilized man, this place was known to tribal societies by different names, and as civilization changed so did this place.

Think of all reality as a fabric, or as the fabric of reality. This fabric is made up of infinite materials. The world of the living exists on only a few of these materials at a time. If it were a real piece of fabric, we might say that the world of the living existed on the strands of wool, cotton, and hemp, but Abaddon exists on strands of wool, leather, and manila. Both the world's share some of the same fabric, both use wool in their make up, but each are distinctly separate, yet together.

It's a crude explanation but it's the best one I have and in all honesty, its the only one I know right now. The truly fascinating thing about this world, what ties everything together, is the life energy transformation.

Let me explain:

A woman gives birth to a child, well hopefully, but again that's another speech and I shouldn't get distracted. The child that is born is absolutely full of energy. Usually, more full than he will ever be again, but in any case, the child is positively packed.

As he grows, he expends his energy on toys, pets, and so on. Ideally, he will grow up, have experiences and build dramatic memories into his consciousness. He may then grow old and as his consciousness and essence are expelled, his body dies, and all flows back into the cosmic ocean of essence.

This is ideal however. What can happen, is that a person could be born and then murdered before all of their essence is expended. So then, since energy can not be destroyed, it switches over into the world of Abaddon, bringing the person's consciousness along for the ride.

In the world of the living, we create inanimate objects. These objects have no energy because they are not alive. As we shed essence onto an object we value and when they gather enough power, a shadow of the object is transferred to the world of Abaddon. Toys, love letters, favorite clothing, pages of sacred text, and art are all examples of objects that absorb the energy of the living, and then, even if they are destroyed, their shadow exists in the realm of Abaddon.

This is why only older buildings exist in this place. New buildings haven't existed long enough to gather the life energy of the living and appear here. This also explains how people see ghosts or Wraiths in old houses and such. As the buildings gather energy, they appear here as well as the living world, and within the building a bridge is created. The longer a building exists in the realm of the living, or the more energy is lost to it, the more solid of a bridge it is to this land of the dead, so to speak. It's really quite simple, all things considered.

Naturally, this explains certain uneasy feelings that people get in so called "haunted buildings", or when in an abandoned prison or battlefield. They often have these feelings due to their essence's natural detection of its enemies. Which unfortunately, is the rather unpleasant part of reality here, and therefore 'there ' as well. It is rather nice actually, that most people are blissfully unaware of the whole monster business.

I've always found it strange that all creatures in nature have enemies, predators if you will, except for man. Well, predators that exist in the world of the living anyway, but that's a whole other subject of which I'm still doing research on. Suffice to say that the malcuthrad, bogeymen, and slanethra are all creatures that exist to feed on man, and are only a few of many species that do so.

You see, when people die they don't always wind up here. Age, disease, spiritual parasites (I'll have to talk about them later too...) cause an entity's essence to be consumed, versus just dying. Time for a heading I think.

### *Death vs. Consumption*

Not all forms of death will send people over to Abaddon. Deaths that are consuming take the energy and transform it to their own use. Fire, for example, not only transforms the body into light and heat energy, but transforms the energy of the soul as well.

This could be why all witches and perceived demons were executed by burning, one of the ultimate deaths. In fact, it could be desirable for a devil or witch to kill themselves rather than allow themselves to be burned, if they had any knowledge of Abaddon that is.

Fire is an anomaly. Fire seems to exist in both the world of the living and the Abaddon realm at the same time. Creatures that exist here fear flame, which is why man is instinctively comforted even by a candle. (I have found that there are a series of these genetic memories that explain themselves.)

Other consuming deaths stop people from crossing over as well. Starvation, disease, being eaten etc, any death where the whole of the body is affected and consumed in some way. But what are we when we arrive here? We are no longer human as such, so what then?

We are wraiths.

Once you die and appear in Abaddon, you are a wraith; an ex-human. You are a poor etherioid and the foodstuff of most of the entities on this realm. Being as I have no method of keeping time, in fact I am not sure how time works here, I cannot tell you the average lifespan of a wraith in this place, but I promise you, it's not very long.

Quite usually, they go through the madness and the sickness (See diary entry 66560.). This causes them to act in poor judgment and they invariably become nourishment for other denizens of this place. Those who survive are the more experienced Wraiths and see so much more. It is probably best to actually be eaten in the first while you are here, if you're to be eaten at all.

I don't know who is more unfortunate, those who perish right away or those who stay around longer. We all come here to serve our time and live out the remainder of our lives and our energies, and then we simply fade away back into the great cycle. But most of us fall victim to one of the creatures here and are lost. It all seems rather morbid doesn't it? But there you are.

In any case, wraiths are not ghosts. Ghosts are a different manner of goose all together. You see a ghost is a creature that died in such distress; in such a massive burst of energy, that they can continue to create life energy to sustain themselves out of raw emotion. The unfortunate part in this (there is so much misfortune here.) is that they do not exist only here, they drift back and fourth between the land of the living and the dead.

On one hand they are not totally etherioid, which means that they cannot fall victim to most predators that live here, but they are caught in a kind of time loop, experiencing the trauma of death again and again, and losing very little life force.

This means that if a woman is tortured to death, and years after you can still hear her moaning in a dungeon, it is because she is caught in her own extra long loop of pain that will never end and she spends a dreadful amount of time screaming.

Ghosts will far outlast Wraiths in this place, and I feel that it's these unfortunate souls who are truly cursed. Many of them never know where they are, they just keep reliving those moment just before their death, feeding on their own agony.

Another thing is that the buildings and texts that were valued and yet destroyed in the realm of the living exist almost eternally in Abaddon. I've spoken with some Wraiths here who have claimed to have seen the Tower Of Babylon, as well as the Great Library of Rome! There are a lot of exceptional things here, in fact I think I take exception to this entire place!

As well, the paper and clutter here are mainly objects that people in the realm of the living placed high value on, therefore giving them substance in the realm of Abaddon. Religious texts, treasured love letters, favorite family heirlooms, dolls passed from mother to daughter, all exist here. It's no great leap to explain why sensitive individuals feel afraid over an object as simple as an old doll. It's simple, they feel its connection to the realms of the dead.

I'm not certain however how these objects release the energy given to them. They don't glow or do anything extraordinary at all, but thankfully the paper is abundant enough for me to make my notes on. As well my lovely ink bottle that never seems to be running out! I'm really very pleased about that.

What I wouldn't give to find some of the ancient texts that must be hiding in this realm. I wouldn't be surprised if the ancients had full knowledge of this place. You see, all primitive cultures; tribes that have existed for centuries with rich history's of spoken records, all have similar ideas, legends if you will. Each of these legends has identical ideas and concepts behind them.

Before the age of civilization, the natural order of things was somewhat different. According to the ancient wraiths, at that time there were no cities in the land of the dead, only mirrors of the forests and darker woods existed. These areas are the Wylds.

Plants, it seems, are able to exist on multiple realms at once. On the world we know as the realm of the living, trees are immovable defenseless things, but here it's a different story all together. Trees are able to move here, very slowly like a starfish, they worm their roots through the soil. The trees' branches are able to lash out at creatures nearby with blinding speed.

You see, just as trees are able to filter the air we breathe in the living world. They are able to filter out beings in the realms of the dead. Before civilization came to the world, man lived in harmony with nature. If one died violently by accident, he would arrive here, greeted by a twilight forest. I understand the trees here glow much brighter than the city buildings. Although I have never actually seen them myself, for reasons I will get to shortly.

Once he arrived in the forests it would be up to the relationship he held with nature as to whether or not the trees would consume, he would be "filtered" for lack of a better term. I suppose now that needs to be explained. Right then, let me try it this way.

The trees that exist within the living realm are the reflection of the trees here, not the other way around, as it is with us. The trees in the land of the living are somewhat defenseless, because this dead world is their naturally dominate realm.

Did that make sense? Right, more about the filtering. That's not a new heading, just so you know.

Supposing two male children were born in ancient times. During their lives, how they interacted with the natural environment would influence their own essence. Let's say one of the men lives his life as a shepherd, caring for animals and nature alike, living in harmony with all things.

The other brother focuses on his own life and doesn't even consider nature. He destroys forests, land, and creatures, all for his own personal gain. He claims that the shepherd brother is a fool.

Both of the brothers are marked by their karma, a term for how the essence you put forth into the world creates ripples that reflect back on to you. This Karma is taken with you no matter what happens. Now lets say that these two brothers are out for a walk one day, and they both fall off a cliff and die. They would awaken here in the Wylds, where the trees are the dominant species.

The Shepherd brother who lived in harmony with all things, his essence is clean, so the Wylds trees never notice him. Just like all the other inhabitants of the forest, he will be able to burn away his essence over time.

However, the brother who was destructive, his essence will be corrupted by the bad Karma he has gathered in life and Wylds can sense it. This then becomes a problem, because you see the trees consume corrupted essence. Roots and branches, like so many vicious tentacles, would tear the wraith apart.

Incidentally, it makes me wonder why I never noticed the tentacle type shape of plants when I was alive. It seems so obvious that those massive limbs were gripping feelers, it must be covered by the Mind Veil. (I'll talk about the Mind Veil a little later.)

Things existed this way until humanity became so disconnected from the harmony of nature, that they began to live in places totally devoid of natural life, these places were called "Cities". This *civilization* of the living realm was an extremely destructive thing to the Great Wylds.

As more forests were destroyed and value placed on the buildings and structures created by men, there was the reflection of the living essence that brought them here in a great mismatched cluster. The city now known as Abaddon began to emerge here in the lands of the dead.

There were those who opposed civilization. The Druids of ancient times had intimate knowledge of the realms of the dead, and the trees' relationship with the living realm. But their texts were scoffed and ignored by civilized science. These well-known truths, taught for thousands of years, didn't fit into the small defined boxes of understanding that "modern" science has.

There are those who still live by the natural ways and follow the old rituals. They would have no trouble venturing through the Wylds, but most modern men, people such as myself, have become so disconnected from nature that we would be gobbled up by the trees in a matter of moments.

As a note, this also explains how certain forests are considered "darker" or even "enchanted". It's because the amount of corrupted essence consumed by the trees in that region of the Wylds is greater. From that, even in the land of the living, the very feeling of evil within a forest could be detected. Its not that the forests are evil as such, they simply consume so much corruption that they become tainted. It would be as though if you ate a lot of blueberry pie, your tongue would turn purple; it's the same idea.

Now, there is a lot more to it then that, Trees do not eat corrupted wraiths only, they have a number of other parasites to feed on as well . But as man's civilization has increased, these creatures have flourished. Creatures that now have a firm grasp on our civilized world.

Everything is a cycle. This seems to be a rather universal truth that I see more as I learn about this place and in the way that out-world realms work. One of the more disturbing things that I've realized is the human races' similarity to fish.

I suppose that's going to need some clarification.

The oceans are full of fish, they are the food, the backbone that supports a large number of predators both in the sea and on the land. This is what man is: a staple.

As I learn more about the different worlds and dimensions, I find that the primary function of the human race is to act as food for so many other creatures. I must admit it's a rather discouraging concept, but I suppose it's all a matter of how you look at it. If we stop focusing on how important humans are to humans, we would realize, that we make up the diet of so many amazing predators and fantastic creatures.

If it wasn't for us they would all starve to death. There is certain nobility in that.

Now within the city of Abaddon, there are not only predators like the huge rhinoceros spiders, (I've renamed them "Wulves" by the way.) but living parasites as well. These living parasites are somewhat numerous.

Just as the phobia of spiders can be explained by the essence memory of the huge beasts here, other phobias can be explained as well. I wonder if I should use another heading here. I mean, I could, but how far down do we want to go with them? Once you start creating sub-headings it can just lead to a never ending cycle (there is that cycle thing again) of ever more specific sub-headings. I think I will just have one, just one sub-heading in depth. Yes, I think that is acceptable don't you?

### *Post-human Creatures*

That's another great heading. This is so well written! If I do say so myself. As you have probably figured out by now, everything in this realm revolves around the concept of essence, the life force that all things have.

Since the time of civilization, if people during their lives become too corrupted; that is to say their essence becomes more than just dark, when they leave the world of the living, they transform into a post- human in this place. Ghosts and wraiths could be called post-human I suppose, but we are still the shadows, the image of who we were. We still have the same consciousness but these other creatures do not.

### *Thespians.*

(I'm allowed sub headings, we already talked about this.)

Thespians are actors in the land of the living, but upon death many of them become something else. Those who give their attention and devotion to something, give part of their essence as well. This is why some folks like to be the center of attention, maybe even why some *need* to be the center of attention, and some, like myself do not. As you can imagine, anyone who acts on stage, or in front of a large audience, get a huge amounts of essence poured into them.

Often I have heard of actors saying that there is no substitute for doing a live performance. Come to think of it, I have always noticed actors, stage actors who have been in the business for years are very odd people.

If you talk to them, they seem so disjointed. Even after their careers end, they still pine for the stage like a fatigued drug addict. Now any performer runs the risk of becoming a Thespian. Singers, dancers, even politicians, anyone who is constantly in the focus of many people takes that chance.

How it happens is somewhat obvious once you see a Thespian. Lets say from a young age, a woman is trained to be a ballerina. She has talent, and her whole life becomes the training.. This in itself is not bad, the problems arise after her first performance. Before the performance she has the phenomenon of stage fright.

What is stage fright? Why is it there? Why would anyone who has trained their whole lives to do movements have stage fright? People have always said that it was nerves, but that is simply not so. Stage fright occurs because the energy that can be felt from the stage is dangerous. It is a threat to our being, our essences, and our essence tells us this through fear. Once they step out onto that stage, it is like stepping into an essence firestorm, it tears through their whole being.

So our ballerina begins performing just as she becomes an adult, not only is she good, but she is a raving success. The crowd loves her, and of course she feels it. She performs for ten years, two or three times a week basking in the massive energy of the stage.

Then tragedy, an accident. She becomes injured and can no longer dance. The lack of performing now causes her pain, actual withdrawal from being unable to get her essence fix. In a fit of despair she kills herself, and arrives here.

However, when she died, she had too much extra essence from her life as a dancer. When she arrives here, her consciousness wasn't strong enough amongst the extra power. The only thing that survives is the image the crowd saw, this sculpted, muscled, pale woman who moves with speed and grace.

She arrives naked in Abaddon and begins her dance again. She needs the essence, she craves it. She needs the energy that other wraiths possess, and since Wraiths here have no urge to come and see her, she must go and find them.

Now one might think that having a ballerina looking for you is not such a high threat, but you see she is no longer a woman. Most dancer Thespians have no face, and their bodies look like sculpted pale corpses without skin or fat. Any wraith that sees a Thespian usually has a fear response. Fear is essence, and even without a face they can smell the fear, the passion of it, and will hunt it like a child hunts candy.

Thespians tear apart other wraiths like rag dolls. They will catch a wraith, and when the fear doesn't come fast enough they begin to beat them, shake them, whip them into such a state of terror that they become completely absorbed by the Thespian. Then, never sated, the essence addict will await her next fix.

### Bogeymen

Bogeymen are creatures that can shift into the world of the living. Their whole existence is fear, particularly, intense fear, the kind of fear that only a child can create. I have heard other wraiths say that Bogeymen come from the bodies of those who have assaulted children.

In life they are abusive and take the power that children give them, either through fear or though domination. But upon death, the essence, the corrupted filth they have filled themselves with, turns these human monsters into things that prey on the children, even after death.

I myself, have never seen a bogeymen. They live within the darkest sections of this place. Their bodies are transformed, well, altered I should say. If in life one would beat children with a belt, or say cut them with knives, after death, those knives might become part of their hands, or maybe a whip would replace part of his arm. Bogeymen are a particularly loathsome thing, even for this place.

Human children are positively packed with life. They make excellent food if consumed properly. However, because a child is so powerful, creatures that try to feed on them are often destroyed by the intensity of a child's fear, an energy overload if you will.

Bogeymen are usually found, or not found as the case may be, in the dark crevices of Abaddon. They are prey for cats, wulves, chyldren and the other wraiths who hate them. The bogeymen are really quite cursed.

Most predators tend to stay in the shadows; I think that this is also where a child's natural fear of the dark comes from. Parents often tell children that their fear isn't rational, but in fact it is the most rational thing that they could have.

Usually up to the age of eight children have a lot greater memory of Abaddon, this is why their "Irrational fears" or more correctly "instincts" are so strong. As they get older they begin to forget. I think that puberty is the stage where the most changes occur in a human's essence, but I'll cover that in the next sub-section.

### Chyldren and their dogs

Human children are full of essence. They have the potential to live a very long time and are totally uncorrupted by predators or parasites. If a child dies, the body shape that arrives here is massive. In human terms your average chyld is between ten and twenty feet tall and looks like an overly muscled, featureless, monster.

You see when children die, the don't have a firm grasp on themselves, that is to say their concept of themselves. So their shapes here are somewhat formless, massive hulks of pink flesh with strange faces. They only know fear and hunger. You can see chyldren wandering the streets of Abaddon and their cry like a strange whale song can be heard echoing in the city.

Once they arrive here they instinctively look for the mother essence. Which is to say, they are looking for their mother, but since none are found there are usually are drawn to harlots. (I'll explain more about them later.)

If essence is power within this place, then chyldren are the wealthiest beings here. In fact they are the wealthiest beings on earth as well! I seem to recall a great amount of poetry and philosophy talking about the love of a child, and the power that it holds. This no doubt, is why there are so many dolls and other toys littering the streets here.

A child's love is intense, and they pour their essence into things without concern, or restraint. One of the greatest loves that some children have are their pets. I love my own cat dearly, but since he is a creature that can eat that affection, live off my essence as it were, if the feline passes on it is still part of its natural cycle. This is not true for dogs.

Animals, because of their nature, always maintain a harmony with their natural

**111**

environment. If they die and are not consumed, even if they were to die in a zoo, never having even seen the light of freedom and their natural habitat, their essence remembers and they come to the Wylds.

However, a child's pet is loved with such intensity, with such power, that if something should happen to it, that is to say it is killed suddenly, the essence the animal has absorbed transfers it to this realm of Abaddon's city. In one sense, it's rather sad that these animals will never be free because it has been domesticated, filled with the essence of humans.

The positive side is that dogs adapt quite well to this. They know the love of children in the living realm have given them, so they seek out the chyldren here. To exist in this world, is to seek distraction from pain.

Oh! I almost forgot! I never described them to you! The dogs I mean. Well they look like dogs, hair, teeth the whole bit, the only unusual thing about them, if there is anything unusual here, is that they all look the same.

No matter what species of dog they were in the realm of the living, once they arrive here they look like, well, rather large hungry wolves. I say hungry because despite their size and fur they're a little skinny, slightly emaciated perhaps. They are very protective of their chyld, and that combination makes chyldren exceptionably formidable.

What else? The dogs stay near the chyldren, the chyldren are looking for their mothers, so they try to stay near the harlots…ah yes! The harlots.

Time for another sub heading.

### Harlots

Harlots are the men and women of the evening in the living realm, and become the people of eternal night here. You see, getting back once again to the idea of essence, the act of making love is an intensely powerful, emotional thing. It is probably the single greatest expenditure of essence that a person can do. So what about these men and woman who have sex sometimes two or three times a night with different people? What about the essence they take on? The answer can be seen in their manifestation here in Abaddon.

Lets say there is a woman, who's major selling feature as a prostitute is say leather, she dresses in leather and is always playing a certain character, say Mistress

Whip, a dominatrix for her clients. (I don't frequent this type of thing myself but I have heard stories about it.)

Upon her death she will appear here not only in the clothing (or lack there of) of her character, but she (or he) will *be that character*. Now they are not predators as such, they do not feed on other wraiths. In fact, I would say that they are a type of wraith themselves, but they are still trying to "ply their wares" as it were, even though the sexual urge is the furthest thing from anyone's mind here.

The truth being told, I have heard that many wraiths will encounter the harlots and allow themselves to be seduced. But we are not human any longer, we are not living breathing beings, so neither the harlots or the other wraiths achieve any pleasure or feeling from the act of love making. There is no sensitivity, so this can lead to some dangerous results.

You see harlots are not the shadows of their living self as other wraths are, they are characters, irrational beings created for sexual exploration and exploitation; shallow, and completely hedonistic. Now they can be dangerous because they do have a tendency to gather in groups. They spend their time "being" with each other and looking for clients.

I have heard tales of harlots destroying wraiths because they get so involved with twisted sexual games that they literally tear the wraith to shreds, trying desperately to get that same living sexual sensation.

You can see them here sometimes in the streets dressed as schoolgirls, leather men, and all sorts of sultry attire. They are probably the most visually pleasing of all the wraiths. I will admit that I have spent some time in buildings watching them pass by, but I assure you it is only for research! After all we do have make sure that this manual is complete, don't we Mr. Diary?

Of course we do.

Right, now what is the relationship between the harlots and chyldren? Well you see the chyldren are seeking the mother essence, and although they do not find it, they are drawn to the next closest readily available thing, lust.

The chyldren are drawn to the harlots because somehow they can sense their lust, and although it is not love, they seem to draw some comfort. Now, the relationship that they maintain is odd to say the least. Then again, in comparison to everything else, perhaps it's not so odd. They share strange sympathies for each other

One wraith told me of how he saw a harlot get attacked by a rather large wulve (

that's what I renamed the spiders you understand.), and two chyldren came to her rescue. The two massive creatures and the twenty dogs with them, tore that wulve to shreds, throwing broken legs all over the streets. The harlots do seem to respect the chyldren, if not for what they are, then for their strength. They can always be found close to each other.

What about God? That's a big one. One might say than with all of this information, in fact the very existence if this world would disprove the Christian concept of God. It could be said that this place disproves anyone's concept of any god! I may have an explanation for this.

### The Seraphim

Although the religions of the living world cannot agree who is the one true god, or even if one true god exists. Yet every religion has the same key creatures appearing to do God's work, usually depicted by a very powerful winged being.

I am talking about angels, often called seraphim in ancient texts. Angels have always been the creatures sent by a god, because the god is too busy to go himself. As I look back at my own biblical studies, no one ever actually saw God. In fact, they only ever saw representations of God. So after doing my research dear Diary, I have begun to feel an itch on my consciousness, a tear in the mind veil that is letting an idea of truth in.

What if there is no god? What if god was something made up by another dimensional race in order to keep the sheep in line? A bedtime story that parents tell their disobedient children to ensure their obedience? I can't say that I know how life in the living realm was created, but I know how it was not created.

I think mankind was created, or came into being somehow, I'm not sure how, but we arrived on the scene. Now in the Bible, (as well as other so called "holy" texts) they make reference to a time when all people spoke that same language and demons roamed the earth. This is a relatively jaded view of how the past could be portrayed, but there it is.

Everything was in this state of chaos until the seraphim showed up, that is the "Angels of God" who proceeded to destroy everything. They destroyed our one unifying language, the language of Thesmulcar as I am led to understand, they destroyed our libraries, the great library of Babylon, also known as the tower of Babylon, and began telling mankind the "truth" about creation. The more I think about this the more I realize that this was the time in our past when the mind veil came into place.

Why is it all of the ancient libraries, even in our own recorded history, have been destroyed? Why is the library of Rome gone? Or the library of Herculaneum? Or the library of Alexander? Why is it that all these great records of our world have been destroyed? Why is everything that disagrees with the seraphim sent Bible is considered heresy?

Lets try to look at this from another perspective. Lets say there is an island. On this island there are a great many chickens. These chickens run free and are not unified, they are all wild and doing what they please. They lay eggs where they please, and roam freely.

Now, this island gets discovered by humanity, and we move in. The chickens are far too plentiful to enslave and control directly, so we must use another way to control them. We take a few chickens and feed them, treat them well, show them fire, and the chickens think we are all gods.

This doesn't work well with the idea of control, having a few hundred gods. So then, we tell the chickens that we work for "The Great Rooster". We are servants of the greatest chicken that ever was, and we are sent here to help these chickens live in the best way they can.

We teach this to several of the chickens and send them out to tell the others. These other chickens tell the flock the good news, and they all begin to worship "The Great Rooster". Of course, part of this Great Chicken worship is how they must go to areas and lay eggs in certain places that are holy to The Great Rooster. This way, we the servants of The Great Rooster can gather these eggs for him.

Then everything is wonderful. We are picking up eggs in a timely fashion and humanity flourishes. Soon, there are so many fat and well fed humans that we need to increase production of eggs on the island. We try to get the chickens to produce, but its not working. We tell them that The Great Rooster needs more eggs, but that's not working. The chickens are starting to despair, hating themselves for not doing enough.

That's when we come up with a brilliant idea. We tell the other chickens that *The Great Rooster* is going to send his favorite chicken, the holy chicken, a promised chicken that will be the one to save everyone from their sin of not laying eggs. We then go to a chicken, teach it how to use fire, and the chicken becomes worshipped as a savior; a child of The Great Rooster.

A bunch of the chickens are not buying into any of this. The whole notion of giving up their eggs is ludicrous to them. In fact, some of them know that what we as humans are trying to do, is exploit the chickens for all they are worth. We humans combat this by telling our loyal chickens that these upstarts are heretics to The Great Rooster, and that they should be killed.

These heretic chickens eventually kill the chosen "Messiah Chicken" that we created, but this was also planned. We then take the most loyal and fanatical chicken followers, and teach them how to build these intense hen houses where all the faithful chickens can gather every Sunday and to lay eggs, "on mass" one might say.

These hen houses are the answer to the human problem. Every Sunday, the chickens gather in their henhouses and focus, sometimes the whole day, almost one seventh of their life, on feeding us. This succeeds better than we had hoped, eventually making serving The Great Rooster, a lifestyle for some chickens

The problem you see, is that there is no Great Rooster, just as there is no God. Only the seraphim, the angels, who have been harvesting humanity since the time of the Mind Veil.

Instead of eggs, angels collect the essence that we humans send to them in the form of prayers. Faith healing and exorcisms are angels looking after their own food supply. Just because a farmer chases a fox out of the hen house, doesn't mean he won't have chicken for dinner.

That's about the best way to describe it I think, and I am afraid it does sound rather bleak doesn't it? I'm sure that if I was still in the land of the living, the faithful folks would declare me a heretic and I would probably be killed. It's really quite brilliant how the angels have set everything up! Once you look at the rationality of feeding creatures with essence, it seems perfectly obvious. Once again the power of the Mind Veil leaves me speechless Mr. Diary, speechless!

So the question is, what are the Seraphim? The answer is a definitive "I'm not sure", but then again I am not too sure of so many things here that it hardly seems awkward anymore. Maybe I should change the title of the completed work to

Theories of Abaddon, that way I'll never be brushed off if the truth about this place is revealed.

I lost myself again, where was I…Oh yes, the angels. You see, I think that the angels are a race of beings who are very organized. They seem to have a system of government. It's not totally unlike a group of chickens trying to understand how a structured society works. As to whether or not the seraphim are an essentially evil race, it depends.

Angels are no more evil than humans are for farming chickens. From the chicken standpoint, they could be called evil, but they do look after the animals to a large degree and keep other predators away. Therefore as to the nature of the seraphim, I'll leave that up for discussion amongst the philosophers.

They have a home dimension, or world where they used to exist as an entire race, but there was a war. The cause of the war is unknown as well as the nature of that war, but during the war the resources of the human food became a question. There were two sides, both sides wanted control of the human essence.

One of the sides won and the defeated nation of angels were kicked out of their home world. (Dimension, plane of existence, whatever you want to call it) and left them to forage on their own. This is no doubt where the legend of Satan and his minions being cast down from heaven comes from.

For the sake of keeping things clear, I think I'm going to call the original realm where the angels were from "Heaven" and the unknown world where the angels fled to "Hell". So if some angels are in Heaven, and the rest are in Hell, where do the rogue angels, that is to say; angels that don't agree with either group go? The answer is wherever they want. Some of them have come here and continue to feed on human essence. Unfortunately, they have quite a nice system worked out here as well.

In the realm of the living, there are those humans whose entire lives became a fanatical devotion to their God. There is no God, as such, so their devotion is given to the angels who harvest their essence. Now here is where things become a little strange. You see the angels do not eat the life force, that is to say the souls of humans, but they eat the byproduct of their devotion. The essence of their worship, so to speak.

Now when one of these hopelessly fanatical people die, they are so certain that they are going to go to heaven, so certain that this nonexistent God is going to take them, they in fact *will* themselves into the dead lands, into Abaddon. Once here, they become one of the most dangerous kinds of wraiths, beings known as the hallows.

### The Hallows

The more sensations that people deny themselves in the land of the living, the more essence they are able to focus on feeding the seraphim. Therefore, the seraphim took great care that the devoted worshippers denied themselves everything. This massive act of denial, lack of sex and expression, leads to a wholly unnatural build up of desires. The poor fools think that when they die, all of these desires are going to be finally sated by God.

Now, not all devoted people who die come to this place, I think that those who held onto the concepts of religion, they would pass into the natural cycle of life. However, those who are fanatical, almost to the point of self-destruction, deny themselves so much that when the die they are left holding the bag as it were. Wanting more, expecting more, and needing more, they bring themselves here, to satisfy the desires denied in the living realm.

These are extremely depraved and dangerous wraiths. They look like exaggerated forms to what they most desired in life. If they craved sex, they have exaggerated sexual organs, always ready for stimulation, weeping fluids and dragging on the ground.

If they have suppressed violence, they have horrible hooks and all manner of things that would cause pain, permanently grafted onto them. The new focus of their existence is to gain the craved sensations they left behind.

When these poor deprived souls die, cannot accept the truth, and wind up here in Abaddon, the first thing that they do is they find a church, usually a large one. I'm not entirely sure on how they know where the churches are, or how they avoid the Madness or the Sickness, but they most certainly head for a church straightaway.

Once they reach the church they invariably find other hallows in the throws of hedonism, trying to satisfy their lusts and desires. Rather than turn on each other, they are able to recognize one of their own instantly. How they do this, however, is also a mystery to me.

All hallows hunt for all manner of wraiths and satisfy their desires with whatever they find. Quite often you will get a group of hallows hunting the harlots for various pleasures, it usually kills the harlots in the process, but they will hunt wulves, bogeymen, chyldren, or anything else they can find. After they consume, they are sated for a time and await their high to wear off.

I think that's about enough for now, I should try and keep track of these creatures as I come across them. There are many more that I have no idea what to even call them. But I shall try my best to keep you informed. I'll talk to you again soon.

**Clarence Winker**
Abaddon Researcher
(I quite like the sound of that.)

**Chapter 14**

"There are enough good people doing nothing."
*-The Truth*

The relationship that had developed during the last few hours between Sasha and Clarence could be called a friendship the same way that a raft was an ocean going vessel. It wasn't ideal by any stretch, but it was the only thing she had.

Clarence tapped her on the shoulder raising her attention from his diary notes. "We should be on our way, we've been in the open far longer than we should."

Sasha was pondering. "But wait, if we die here in this world, won't we just go somewhere else?"

Winker was gathering his pages back into the book, putting his belt harness around it. "Actually, no. There is no death here as such, there is only consumption in Abaddon. Your essence is consumed by predators, parasites, other wraiths, or the city itself. There is nothing beyond here. This is it. Your consciousness ends here. "

Sasha felt frustration welling up within her. "Well, if there's is no way out, and we are all dead, and life is hopeless, then why do we even bother? Why not just let ourselves be *consumed* and end it?"

Clarence paused for a moment after slinging the book onto his back. "I say, I have often wondered that myself, I should think we should ask that of a trout."

"A trout?" She asked, shaking her head.

"Oh yes, most definitely! A trout is a beautiful creature, swimming about in lakes or streams and is usually killed and eaten by man, or some other predator.. So, I wonder why they carry on? Why don't trout everywhere just say, 'Oh bother! This is rather bally being a trout!' And fling themselves up onto the land."

Clarence leaned forwards and whispered, "I think it's because there are things that trout are not meant to know."

The two walked through the dim twisted streets examining the dark dwellings and haunted houses. Clarence would try to answer each of her questions as best as he could before she flashed a new one. Sasha was still trying to keep it all in check, trying to make sense of an insane plane of existence.

They turned a corner and a chair had been placed in the middle of the road. A symbol had been scratched into its back and it stood like a tombstone ominously facing them.

Sasha recognized it. It was the same one she saw on her apartment door. Clarence was nervous, already backing away. "I'm afraid we shan't be going down this way"

"What is it?" She asked, feeling the fear creep up again.

"It's a glyph my dear, the Danger Glyph, A warning from another wraith. There's no time, come on then." He said and broke into a careful run.

They ran for a few blocks, Clarence continuously looking for more glyphs. A waterless fountain approached them from the middle of the street. It was wide, maybe thirty feet across with four stone creatures crouched, holding a wide bowl on their back. This fountain from some European town center had seen marriage vows and a funeral procession was now a fountain of dogma, flooded with holey pages where water used to be.

Clarence stopped for a moment to catch his breath.

He puffed and sat down on the fountains' edge. "There are a series of symbols that we wraiths use in order to warn other fellows of danger. No on knows who started it, but it's carried on longer than even the ghosts can remember." He said as he scooped from the pool an Old Testament page. Bringing his quill from his coat, he began to draw. She watched the glyphs appear from the end of his feather, and their meaning became clear.

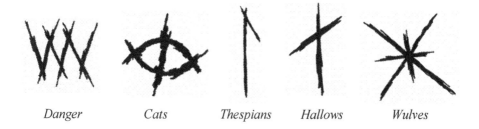

| Danger | Cats | Thespians | Hallows | Wulves |

Things that she never paid attention to, the scratching on doors now had new meaning. Each gash was trying to tell her something, if she only knew how to read it. Seeing the symbols gave her hope. Even in this place, the human will was present. These scrapings on buildings and furniture were vengeful slashes of those with nothing else to fight with.

They rested long enough for Winker to catch his breath, then carried on, going nowhere in particular but appreciating the action of movement. Clarence was still explaining in further detail his theories and ideas, feeding her illusion of progress. He explained that she shouldn't worry so, In Abaddon no matter where you were, you were lost. You got used to being lost.

The wind picked up fast. "We had better seek cover, this is going to be a storm!" Winker turned to a vacant building, a small storefront made from ancient brick. The loose holy pages in the street were spinning into devils as Winker scanned the bricks for glyphs.

"How do you know?" She called over the growing wind

"There are only storms here!" He said.

It was hard for Sasha to say what kind of building this had been. It was older, but more North American than European in design. Sasha made the general shape of the architecture out in the green gloom. It reminded her of a old western saloon. The door was only a little cracked, the lower corner on the doorknob side splintered.

They took cover inside. The empty windowpane shutters had been thoughtfully tied shut with the strings from instruments, it did the job. Peering out between the cracks to the chaos in the streets beyond, she saw papers everywhere, swirling like fish dodging sharks. Clarence took up a position so that he could peer out into the street and watch the approach of anyone or anything.

Sasha watched his poise in vigil, he was like some feral creature awaiting the shadows of beasts. With his pointed nose under his top hat, at the very least he looked distinguished and at most he looked mad.

The wind continued to build. Pressing around the outside of the dim building as though seeking shelter itself. Over the moaning came a sound, a scream. Over the rushing of the pages she heard the cry of a newborn child, so faint it was a memory. Sasha was sure she heard it.

"Did you hear that?" She said turning to Winker.

"I say, yes I most certainly did!" Clarence said, only mildly interested and still peering out the cracks "A chyld, in some distress from the sound of it."

Sasha could feel her blood hot with anger. Clarence had written about the chyldren, how strong they were, how they could look after themselves, but she didn't care. The sound of an infant in distress did something to her. She didn't know why, but right now she wasn't stopping to question it. To his surprise she walked out the door he was guarding so carefully.

"What? Where are you going?" He asked. No time to answer. She walked into the swirling papers of the street, waiting to hear the sound again.

The wind began dying down the moment she stepped outside. Within seconds, all that could be heard was the rustling of the papers as they settled. She stood, senses honed as moments passed.

A desolate wail, the sound of a chyld in fear and pain, from a street just few blocks over from where she stood. Half a heartbeat later and she was running. None of the intersections were nearby, she'd have to use the alleys to get there quickly.

Sasha's combat boots were becoming comfortable. The reassuring slam of the boots sole against the cobblestone rang out, building strength within her. A war drum against any who would harm a child, a child like her own, only damned to this place. She wasn't this child's mother, but she was someone's mother. *Enough fear*, she thought. *Build the hatred, time to learn killing. I can't let this child suffer!*

Winker was yelling from behind. "Wait!! You can't do anything, you'll just get yourself killed."

*Nothing new there,* she thought to herself and left him.

"Oh bother!" She heard him curse, then a scuffling. He was following.

Down the tight cluttered alleys she ran, towards now more frequent screams. She focused on the sound. There wasn't much room to maneuver, less than a meter in some places.

*Mother's coming.*

She was growing in power. If she had time to think, she would wonder where this building inner power was coming from. She would wonder why there was this terrible rage that had her. Its not that she wouldn't stand up to help anyone in need, most certainly she would, but this was more than just concern.

Clarence had learned long ago to avoid the alleyways, you were most certain to find a wulve den, or perhaps worse. This was far too dangerous for his liking.

A chair made an attempt to trip her up, but instead shattered on her shins. Sasha ran through it, no matter what it was. She didn't notice the chair, she had the pure conviction of a soldier flowing through her, a killer. Absolute, pure, and merciless; it was the perfect rage of a woman.

*Mother's coming!*

Sasha's legs were alive with power. One corner , another, and then another, leaping over broken piles and clutter in her way with ease. Another corner and the street came into view.

This one was a modern but cracked concrete street. The ever-present toys, papers and larger stacks of furniture were everywhere. It might have been a freeway, wide but with no paint on it. A crowd was gathered in the middle of the road.

Thirty vaguely humanoid creatures stood in a scattered circle, a large heaving, screaming mass in the center of them. The mass was a chyld, it had to be. A huge humanoid with bulging muscles, at least fifteen feet tall. It stood like an unfinished gorilla. It's swollen muscles had no definition and the whole bright pink form was as smooth as a newborn, fleshy and fresh.

The face was devoid of features and the head longer than normal, but with no mouth, nose or ears. It did have eyes however, large terrified blue eyes, the size of diner plates were staring wild as the terrors around it circled. The screams were somehow coming from its head, making it a howling drum of fear.

It was caught in a web of ropes that were wrapped around the chyld. Some around its arms, and one around its neck, the rest lashed its feet and hands out to these things that taunted.

These thirty figures were hallows. Twisted shapes of sexual torture, no two of them alike, they were everything Clarence said they would be and worse. They were demonic visions that came to masturbating perverts in sacred places.

Words are powerful, strange things. Often people forget what a word means, or worse, they will use the word without the correct respect for what it entails. It takes a situation, tailor-made for a specific word to really understand a word's full meaning. Sasha now knew the true meaning of the word "vulgar."

At first, she thought some of these things had three legs, but then she could see in the dimness that the third leg was a throbbing swollen penis that raised and lowered as the creatures screamed. Others instead of the penis had long tentacles, which they tried to reach out and touch the bound chyld. Hulking members, which they stroked and made glisten with putrid sexual juices.

Some of the female hallows had huge gaping maws of teeth, their lips exaggerated to the point where a smile would crease up to their temples. They were rubbing their exaggerated crotches so vigorously, that their hands would disappear inside of them with a wet slurp, only to be pulled out again in a sucking pop.

Their intentions were clear, they were trying to restrain the chyld, force it to the ground to extract their sick pleasures from it. They would torture, mutilate, and humiliate the chyld, then systematically rape it to death as each tried to outdo the other in a contest of depravity.

Sasha hadn't stopped running. She burst from between the buildings and turned in a wide circle like an Olympic racer towards the atrocity being committed in the street. She surveyed the situation as she ran, the realization of these creatures brought her rage to a howl. She went mad.

The largest of them was close to eight feet tall, his arms and hands were swollen and hung like ship chains down past his knees. He was wearing the robes of a catholic priest, so soiled with feces and semen that they were hardly recognizable. The crotch had been torn away and a filthy hulk of tentacles twitched where his genitals should be. The tentacles were churning with a life of their own, dropping tiny gripping feelers past his knees and reaching out expectantly. He was the leader of this pack and seeing her approach as she was riding her wave of hate, made his tendrils quiver in anticipation.

Of the thirty, there were fifteen not manning the ropes, trying to terrify the chyld into panicked compliance. The hallows heard her cry and turned expectantly to meet whatever challenge was coming. The hallowed ones saw her hate as she pumped her arms in wide powerful strides, and knew that pain was running with her. The ones not gripping the ropes began to staggering to get behind their priest, they knew he would have the lion's share of her flesh.

A hateful wraith always has the best flavor.

As the gap between them began to close and the priest thing spread wide his long arms and hooked fingers to embrace her, his gaping toothy mouth stretched into an open smile making his throat look slit. Sasha couldn't feel her arms or legs. She was a passenger now in this body that had committed to the act of violence.

She was never a violent woman, she had never been in a fight. But this rage that now governed her mind was an old one. This was a rage of blood, *a* mother's blood. All women have this rage waiting dormant within, like a firebomb waiting for a spark. Many things can happen in a woman's life, her life could be in danger, she could be victimized, and none of that will set off the bomb. But, an assault on a child, on her child and burnt flesh would be the order of the day.

Sasha had this ancient rage running within her now. The priest was fast, but he didn't expect Sasha's speed of wrath. She ran at him full force and leapt into the air at the last moment, launching herself in savage fury. She hit like a tank shell, tearing him off his feet and throwing him back through the air. She brought her knees up and caught the horror in its chest. These seconds spent in the air were stretched by the Sasha's adrenal rage.

As they flew backwards, she dug her thumbs into its eyes, stretching her fingers and gripping his skull. When they landed she felt the bone give in each socket, each thumb buried in the wet brain behind his eyes. As they landed, her body had shifted so her shin crossed his throat. She could feel the cartilage in his neck collapse and the bone break under her weight. The priest let out the painful moan of a perverts' climax, and then began the gurgling thrash of a suffocating child.

She barely had time to draw her hands up from his head when she was tackled. She was no sooner off of him than another hallow had flipped the thrashing priest over and crammed his genitals into the twitching body to feel the dying jerks on his cock.

It was a woman that tackled her, with swollen breasts like infected blisters. Sasha landed on her back with the hallowed female on top of her. She was stunned for an instant longer than she should have been. The melted flesh face of her attacker let out an ecstatic yelp, and then crammed one of her weeping breasts into Sasha's face. The runny mucus exploded into her mouth, trying to choke her, drown her in pussy juices.

Muscled limbs locked around Sasha's hips, and she could feel another fiend grabbing at her legs. She bit down, trying to sink her teeth in and tearing the breast open, but the flesh was like rubber, causing a moan of twisted pleasure from her hideous wet nurse.

Clarence wanted to help, he really did, but one does not live over a hundred years in the land of the dead by practicing heroics. There were thirty hallows, and no way that he could do anything. All he would have to do is walk out there, and he would have been destroyed as well.

It wasn't a question of cowardice that was a living trait, it was a question of survival. His shield and curse was to observe. Wraiths would help each other as much as they could, but death here truly meant forever. This woman had been able to take out the thespian in the theater, maybe she could do the same here.

…Or maybe not.

Sasha couldn't breathe. The smothering breasts of this creature filled her mouth. Her legs had been grabbed by many other hands, more still grabbed her arms.. The genitals of her smothering attacker were pumping out excretions that had coated her leather pants with a slippery ichor. This, coupled with her thrashing body, slowed the hands down from being able to get her pants off. But they were only slowed, not stopped.

She could feel herself getting weak, she couldn't breathe, the pus fluid pumped into her mouth was choking her. All around, she could hear the laughing and excited moans of hallows preparing to share her body amongst them as the chyld was still wailing, screaming in terror.

Then came another cry, more cutting than the wailing of the chyld, louder than the depraved moans, a piercing guttural scream beyond sanity. A blast of wind and Sasha's smothering attacker was gone. The other hands released her and she convulsed onto her stomach, vomiting the sickly, lumpy fluid out of her system. Though watering eyes, Sasha looked around.

The burnt flesh face of the hallowed woman who tackled her was laying on the ground a few feet away. Not the head, just the face, like some dropped rag on the street. Her body and faceless head was further away, pooling. The hallows were snarling, but not in the deviant manner that they were before, now it was anger and fear. She could see a few of them holding back from grabbing at her. They had been surprised by something.

The smell came. The thick horrid stench of wet rotting feathers filled the air. Another scream from behind her and she spun. What had been standing behind Sasha was the rotting corpse of a rooster.

Babayan stood four feet, slung low with huge talon claws, pieces of burnt face still sticking in them, scratching at the concrete street. A grapefruit size head served as hilt for a wicked hooked beak that swung back and fourth. The whole animal was filth, with feathers coming loose and falling away to its sides as it moved. This was a dead animal, its eyes glazed white, and patches of rot could be seen where feathers no longer clung.

It didn't cluck or screech as a living rooster would. Instead it swung its head low, rolling its open beak back and forth screaming like a scalded cat. The rooster didn't seem to see her, perhaps it didn't care. It stepped in a wide defensive circle around her body, begging the hallows to make a move, pleading with them to try something.

One of the hallows obliged, a second made the mistake of following. The rooster leapt into the air, fanning its wings, and caught the charging hallows' head in its claws. The head crushed like a wet sponge, forcing chunks of meat through powerful feet. The second hallow, in one instant had a throat, and before that instant could end, a beak slashed it away.

The slaughter of the two hallows would be missed if Sasha blinked. The rooster landed back on the concrete, ready for more blood leaving the two hallows kicking and thrashing as the street sucked away their essence. Babayan continued his circling around Sasha, leaving bloodied claw prints as it walked.

A hoarse whisper came bouncing off the walls from the mouth of a nearby alley. Sasha saw a tall man with a brightly colored coat and thick dreadlocks, staggering forwards.

"Gambia! Gank! Thecae!"

At first it looked as though he was injured, but then she realized this was a dance. A staggered dance that made his long coat sway, and hands tense jerk in unheard rhythm.

"Gambia! Gank! Thecae!"

His body was jerked as spasms of power caused his dreadlocks to sway with each motion, covering his face.

"Gambia! Gank! Thecae!" He chanted again.

The hallows were starting to panic, they began to howl. Sasha could see that there was some recognition here. The hallows knew this being and feared him. They let the ropes slip, at once the chyld was free, swinging its arms wildly and shaking off those that still held with powerful arms.

Its gaze caught Sasha for in instant.

*Did it pause?*

*Was it looking at her?*

She couldn't tell. The chyld vanished down a side street with surprising speed.

The other hallows were running, except for one spidery woman with stretched arms and legs, she wanted the Skatman. With wanton speed she came at him on all fours. Fluid in his staggered dance, the Skatman swung up his arms, and caught her in an invisible clutch.

She screamed, and kept screaming as she knelt on the ground and with her own hands began tearing chunks of flesh from her body. The sound of her cries cut at Sasha's soul, but the hallow's body didn't listen to itself. It tore off chunk after horrible chunk, dropped it in a splattered pile as the Skatman's dance continued. It was grabbing meat from everywhere, her legs, her breasts, her face, her stomach, all to the will of the dancer.

This creature's body was ripping itself apart. The handfuls of meat came away until finally, she reached the intestines. She pulled out the trembling wormlike organ like rope, hand over hand, eventually collapsing in a pile of her own organs.

"Gambia! Gank! Thecae!"

The hallows fled, howling down the streets. Sasha grabbed some of the ever present papers and used them to wipe away the residue on her face. The Skatman's staggered dance came to an end as he raised his hands to the black sky.

"Taly moocheda! I-YA!" He called out in prayer.

Past him, she could see Clarence sheepishly stepping out an alleyway, slowly coming down the street. Babayan saw him too and let another screech go, locking him into view.

The Skatman approached cautiously to where Sasha still crouched. She could see his stark white eyes gaping at her. He stopped just far enough away as to not seem hostile, crouching to her eye level.

He studied her intensely for a few moments and the split his mouth into a perfect pearly white smile. His voice was thick with accent.

"Moonchild, Da Skatman come be sendin' ja home, I-Ya!"

**Chapter 15**

The Internet is a good place to find information, but it's a better place to find distraction. Luke was set on gathering all the information he could find on Abaddon. What started at 3pm had eaten five hours and he was still chasing abstract thoughts. Sometime between then and now, a storm had started outside.

He was wearing loose fitting track pants and a favorite t-shirt from Floyd's *Momentary Lapse of Reason* tour. He had at one time vowed to write a letter to Gilmore personally thanking him for the album. It would be one of millions, but he needed to do it.

He had found some things in his search. Abaddon was an angel known as 'The Destroyer' according to the ancient texts. An angel more ancient than Satan, and more feared. Abaddon was associated with hideous things before the very concept of evil was born. His was a name where knowledge and madness danced. His name was the root of the word *abandon*, and all that it implies. It was the name of Abaddon that Moses invoked to slaughter the first born in Egypt. A name synonymous with forsaken, and an ancient word in the time of Christ.

Abaddon. The name was so familiar, he knew it from somewhere, but like lyrics to an old song he couldn't remember. The Internet gave answers, but none brought the realization of his own echoes. He used every search function he knew, and got a phone book of information back from each try. It was hard to sift through all the data, but at least it was some thing to do, something to keep him busy.

The rapping of a knock at the door dragged him from the screen.. Luke had no idea who it could be, and whoever it was didn't call first. The constant apologies and condolences were nice, but he was past the stage of feeling sorry for himself, and others condolences were getting dangerously close to pity.

He walked through the dark living room and went for the door. When he had crawled into his computer cave, there was daylight streaming through the windows, but that was long gone now. The streetlights through the windows made strange winking stars as the rain drops fell, and shadows of transparent eels crept down the walls.

He snapped on the room lights before looking through the doors' eyepiece. Waiting on the other side through a fisheye lens, he saw wet rumpled hair and deep eyes.

Genaya. *Oh Shit!*

The day before yesterday he was at the Angel Song. That was the day he met Genaya. Since then he had tried not to think of her. Luke had already made six trips to the guilt buffet and that was all he could handle. He shouldn't open the door, he knew that. He knew for a fact that he shouldn't let her in, but something muffled that cry and he found himself undoing the locks. With more self loathing than a catholic heroin addict, he opened the door.

A long dress stuck to her soaked supple body and a woolen shawl wrapped around her shoulders. Her hair was wild, more than if she had simply walked from a car to the curb. Luke realized she must have walked some distance in the rain. His eyes wanted to stay on her form but he pulled them back up.

"I'm sorry that I didn't call first, did I catch you at a bad time?" Her voice was everything he remembered and more.

"Uh…No." He stammered, suddenly fourteen again.

Luke backed away from the door. "Um…you look soaked…. Please come in."

She stepped through the doorway and he closed it behind her. They were close. He had to get away.

"I'll put some coffee on." He said and hurried to the kitchen. His body felt awkward..

"Did you walk all the way out here?" he called filling the pot.

"Oh no, I bussed," She said hanging her dripping shawl on a waiting hook by the door. Her tone was at ease, as though she'd been here a thousand times. "I'd rather tea if you have it, I'm not much for coffee."

Like put the kettle on to boil and retuned to the living room to find her kneeling by the coffee table looking curiously at his Ouija board. The corner of the board had crawled out from under the couch.

At that instant, he couldn't help but admire her natural grace. She was like some turn of the century painting, *"Gypsy Waiting"*. He dared not let himself stare for too long. The painting moved and he was looking into her eyes. He broke away from her gaze and sat down, trying to think of small talk.

With the tension inside of him building, that kettle wouldn't boil fast enough. He needed another excuse to get up. Perhaps she was sitting on the floor because she didn't want toe get the furniture wet.

"Don't worry about the furniture!" He said, "Please sit! Can I get you a towel?"

He was stumbling over his words. She watched smiling, amused how he was more concerned about her condition than she was.

"Its okay Luke, I'm fine. It's only little rain, rain cleanses the soul. Please relax." She whispered.

*Her voice, such a voice!*

"So... What brings you by?"

*Don't look at her neckline.*

He needed a drink. She placed her hands on the floor and slid across the hardwood, closer to his chair. She held out her hand, long and beckoning , saying nothing and waiting for him to take it. He felt like an awkward teenager again. Luke had forgotten what he just asked.

"Its okay Luke, You don't have to be afraid of me." She said, warm calm words.

He knew exactly what she meant, but he couldn't show it. She couldn't know that he saw her face in dreams for the last two nights. She mustn't know his longing for her touch.

He laughed nervously. "What makes you think I'm afraid of you?"

"I can feel it inside of you." She said, reaching for him "Please..."

Luke took her hand as though it was a joke, but as he slipped his hand into hers again he felt that rush, the joining of their souls and the flood of warmth within him. The flood was everything he and yearned for. She arched her back, twisting in a heavy gasp that made her lips quiver. The image of her made him dizzy. He felt intoxicated, light headed watching her move.

He wanted to turn away, run away, tell her to get out of the apartment. But more than this he so desperately wanted to touch her, to hide inside the drug that was this woman. As she opened her eyes from the emotional surge a tear rolled down her face. He would freeze that image forever in his mind.

"You are still in so much pain." Her voice was thick and whispered.

She broke from his grasp as though she couldn't handle his pain any longer. Suddenly Luke felt bad for suffering his own emotions. His hand hung in the air for a moment, not wanting to admit its release, then it dropped by his side.

Genaya locked on him with her eyes. He saw something there in those dark gates.

*Is that want?*

Her breath was heavy, still trying to regain control. "I came here to tell you that I know some people who may be able to help us." Her voice cracked from emotion. She cleared her throat. "I know some people who are familiar with Abaddon, and they might be able to give you some answers." She looked back to the Ouija board. "You use the Ouija?"

Luke was off balance before, he was mentally spinning out if control now. "Um...Yes. I've used the board before...." His voice trailed away and Luke remembered.

*Abaddon.*

"My god!" His words spilled out as his eyes grew wide.

"What? What is it?" Genaya could see the light of revelation.

"The night before Sasha was taken there was something on the board that called itself Abaddon..." The realization of the name brought the reality of the occult world crashing in on him.

Like so many others, Luke had been fascinated by the occult. It interested him, like a childish game, only now he could see the agony of what he had done. The entity that they spoke with, the game he had played with his wife was somehow responsible for her death. A game he *made* her play.

Genaya's voice cut into his brain like a scalpel. "Oh I see, you mean you spoke with an entity on the Ouija that identified itself as Abaddon. That must be how the followers found you, the spirit who you contacted told the cult abut her." Her voice was quiet, she was speaking out loud and to herself, the realization sinking into her as well.

Luke was crippled, falling, "You mean ...this thing ...oh my god...Sasha..."

"Not Abaddon, but the beings who worship the angel named Abaddon. That's why they took her." Genaya said, thinking he didn't understand.

But Luke did understand. The connection came like a nuclear flash blinding his senses. Now the shockwave of guilt would destroy him. If he hadn't pressured Sasha to play she would never have been known to these people. The weight of it was crushing whatever sense of self he had left.

'I didn't know ..." Tears of guilt and self loathing flooded down Luke's face. His body collapsed into the chair behind him. "Oh God..."He cried out. He couldn't go on, his arms were jerking in front of him in the chair, waving away the agony as the unbearable force built stronger. He was destroyed, his blood became the fuel to burn away his soul.

Genaya's arms were there. His cheek pressed against her chest as she wept with him. He felt her cascading around him, bathing him in her touch. She was whispering to him through his tears, but he could only hear some of her words.

" It's okay, …. I'll be here….I'm here now…..*I love you.*" She said, cooing him into oblivion.

Further and further he spun, hearing her confession of love he pushed her back as his last great act of defiance.

"What are you saying to me?" He said..

Genaya cupped his soaked face in her hands. "Luke, ever since you came into my shop, I've felt my connection with you. I have felt such strength in touching you, such strength and need." Her own tears mixed with his in starry vision. "I'm here for you Luke, I always have been. I've waited my whole life for you, to be near you. I've seen you in my dreams and I know we are meant to be together."

These things she said were his fantasies of the night before. He couldn't resist any longer. He pulled her close, returning his head to her chest in surrender. He believed in the supernatural, he knew the risks, and he brought Sasha into it anyway. It was his fault Daphne was gone. *He* had killed his wife. He needed sanctuary from all this pain.

She was whispering to him. "I know you feel the same way I do, I came here tonight not only to tell you that I have found someone to help us, but that I am yours." She kissed him gently on his forehead and stroked his hair. "I am your servant Luke. I know your pain and still I swear myself to you by all things sacred."

She lifted his face, gazing deeper into his tortured soul. "I am your servant Luke, and you have touched me in my dreams. I am yours."

She kissed him with the lust of a killer. He felt her tongue firm inside his mouth, penetrating him, lapping up any final resistance he had left inside. He was helpless, at her mercy. The tears were still rolling down his face as she lay him back in the chair. He was sobbing uncontrollably, confused , hurt desperate and ready to embraced his own death. Her body lifted and she was gone.

Luke shut his eyes, pressing himself into darkness, afraid of the things he knew. By the time he regained enough strength to open his eyes, darkness had swallowed him. The lights were out in the apartment.

"Genaya?"

Seeking in the darkness, confusion reigned his senses. Shuffling, the sound of a stove knob, she was everywhere at once. Somehow Luke stood, steadying himself with the armchair.

"I'm here." a voice came from the void and Genaya melted from the shadows into the slippery streetlight from the windows. Slowly, precisely, with each perfect calculated step, she came to him. He watched her in a trance. She slid her arms under his and engulfed him.

He should have protested, but he didn't. He should have said no, but he didn't. There was something about this woman so familiar, so close to him, and he had nothing left to fight with.

Genaya kissed him again, then as she released his lips she continued her whispers. "It's going to be fine Luke, I know the pain you feel. I've come to take it from you." Her dress was moist and warm and begging to be peeled away.

She led him to the couch. Luke responded like an compliant beast, far too broken to think for himself. He half fell onto the couch as she stood over him. She slipped off the shoulder and let her dress peel away. The wet fabric collapsed leaving her naked flesh to shimmer in the night.

Olive skin, swollen breasts and the sleek curves of a predator revealed themselves. Luke couldn't help but want her. With the balance of a spider she slid onto him, matching her hips against his own. He could feel himself swelling under the track pants. With strange strength, she reached down cradling his head and brining it up to suckle at her breast. "Taste of me Luke."

Luke opened his mouth and she thrust herself onto him. He felt her nipple against his tongue and a symphony of pleasure exploded through him. The dread, doubt and confusion numbed as he sucked, drawing solace from her.

Her back arched as she held his head firm to her breast, desperate moans escaped her lips, each more excited than the last. She pushed him down, her whispering voice echoing off the dark corners of the room

"Oh master!" Her voice was thick with reverence. "Give me your suffering." She said as her eyes shone through wild hair. She slid down his body, dragging her hands across his chest. Her fingers brushed over his shirt and his senses burned ever brighter. Her hands, a gentle grasp pressed his wrists down by his side, gently forcing him into submission.

In one savage jerk, she pulled his jogging pants down past his knees. With desperate hunger she began tonguing and kissing him. He was already firm as she slid her face under his shaft and ran her tongue up and down his full length.

She took him into her mouth and Luke exploded. His back jerked hard and he let out an involuntary scream, his mind alight with the madness of passion. When he couldn't take another stroke, she released him and slid up to straddle him. He sucked at her breasts as they pressed against his face.

Gasping, she called out, "I've always wanted this Luke! Make me your own! Claim me!" He slid inside of her with a powerful pelvic thrust and within the darkness they entwined completely.

She made him climax after a thousand years of ecstasy. Tears ran down his cheeks only to have her tongue taste the salty drops. She wanted all that he could give, and with each fluid she claimed, the more frenzied she became. He had come twice and in her merciless lust she sucked him hard again. The second climax was so intense he was screaming out unintelligible vowels, she echoed his cries with calls for more.

When two people physically mate we give it many different names. We sometimes call it making love, or having sex. In its' most selfish form it is called fucking, this was something else. This was conquest. She was on him, taking from him, stimulating him more than he ever had been before. This wasn't affection, but a raw powerful animal lust.

As he approached a third explosion, her dark whispers were still ringing in his mind. In the heat of passion she had been drifting in and out of several unintelligible tongues, all ancient and each one more guttural than the last. As he came the third time she was screaming, the pleasure turned to shock and he lost consciousness. He faded into dreams of razor wire and hideous temples, feeling her nails digging deep into his back as she eagerly sucked his essence away.

        \*                \*                \*

He awoke in his bed with Genaya's hands running through his hair. His mind didn't have time for him to get his bearings before she spoke.

"Good morning my lord." She said in a lilting voice and kissed him, flooding his senses with her warm wet flesh. She was wearing the dress from the night before, now dry and more ravishing than ever.

He couldn't do this. He had to say something, anything. As she released him from the kiss, he opened his mouth to speak but her finger was there to silence him.

"You mustn't blame yourself Luke." She said, anticipating his moves.

"What?" he asked.

"What happened between us was destiny. I am your slave now, I am the wings that you must beat to lift yourself higher." She said whispering through a knowing smile.

Luke was numb. "I don't....understand...."

Her words pounded away the voice within him. "Your wife is gone and you have suffered too greatly. The universe will not let you be alone."

"I.. I can't..." He said surrendering to the noise in his mind. After just one night, he felt out of touch with everything, lost and drifting. He wanted her touch before, but now he needed her to keep the demons away, to keep reality back.

"Don't leave me..." Was all he could say, a mad desperate cry for his own conditional salvation.

Genaya straddled him over the sheets, bringing her face so close that only their eyes existed.

"I won't leave Luke, not today, not tomorrow, not ever. I am here for you now and always. I belong to you."

He felt himself speaking. "..And I ...belong...." But he couldn't finish. Something inside him was holding his conscience hostage. There was a shade, a terrorist shadow that lurked in the occupied state of his mind. She kissed him again, washing away the uprising resistance.

Brushing her lips against his cheek she whispered. "We can be together, now and always Luke. No one can keep us apart. I'll stop anyone from hurting you, my precious master."

He felt helpless. He was the newborn child of this woman. She was his mother, lover and mistress. He wanted her, he found himself wanting to be nothing more than his slave's servant. This wasn't his house any longer, this woman had taken over his life.

Leaning back into her straddle, she touched his face in a loyal caress. "You must not allow the demons to get at your mind Luke. In loving you as I do, I love your wife unconditionally. What pleases you pleases me, what pains you pains me as well, and so I want more than anything to find your beautiful child and bring us all together."

Tears were welling in her eyes. "The future is already set Luke, I just have to prove myself worthy to you." The tears rolled down.

Luke was sheltered by the numb warmth that had taken over his life. He responded only to her stimulus. He pulled her close and put his arms around her, not knowing what to say, but knowing it must be done.

That morning, she helped him out of bed and bathed him. She picked out his clothes and helped him dress. He would be going with her into the shop today. She told him about a the group who would be willing to help them. They would try, though spiritual means, to discover the truth together.

Doing as he was told and being rewarded by her touch, Luke's mind was empty. The woman who promised herself to him as a slave was leading him by the hand out of his home. She took away his keys and the locked the apartment door behind them.

He was all hers now.

## Chapter 16

It had been two days since Susan decided to call in the Witch Hunter. She wouldn't have considered it unless a child's life was hanging in the balance.

This cult was an old one, and old cults are by far the most dangerous. When a cult is able to stay hidden for such a long time, and keep this level of bloodlust and commitment, it showed the same conviction that the Roman Catholic Church tried to burn away all those years ago.

She leaned back in the office chair taking off her glasses and let them hang on her neck rope catch. The constant outside wind running around the fourth floor office mourned the passing of time. The grandfather clock in the corner patiently ticked, bringing it's circling hands to 10:15 am.

She had the desk radio playing the CBC classical music that drove away the world's distractions. It had been nine the last time she leaned back, Carol's tea and the CBC let her focus on her work above anything.

The photos of Sasha's murder were spread on her desk. Close-ups of the cultists' faces, their markings, and pictures of the Centodd still bloody from Sasha's passing. The information was in front of her screaming answers and if she could focus on it the right way, she would hear them. But no matter how hard this was to grasp, it would be worse for Luke. What a way to have the veil of the occult ripped away, to have your family murdered for reasons you never thought possible.

These reasons were the only lead. What possible reason did they have for taking Sasha? Luke wasn't involved, his apartment only had tourist grade mystical books purchased from dime stores. Nothing real could be found in them, and certainly nothing as rare or extreme as the usage of a Centodd. On an open auction, authentic blades like the ones that killed Sasha would fetch between eighty to one hundred thousand.

Susie preferred the Wiccan faith, the old religion of the trees and the earth. The druids were amongst the first knowledgeable scientists. They had medicine even before the great Asian continent. There was no way to calculate how much knowledge was lost in the crusades holocaust, but now it was up to her and people like her to try and find that knowledge again. All seekers want power and power is knowledge. The trials and dangers come in how that ancient knowledge is used.

The ancient cults were still alive, it was all still being practiced. Some hideous rites and ceremonies worked, some didn't, but those that did brought real power from beings beyond the veil. This group was the real thing. These weren't some flesh fetish psychos, this ceremony was focused, pointed, and with purpose.

From the autopsy report she learned that each of the thirteen had fasted for two weeks before the ceremony began. The police had no leads, and she knew they wouldn't find any. The cult was too old, too practiced in the art of subterfuge. If they were able to survive in a time when criminals and creatures of darkness had no rights, today's relaxed laws would make stealth as easy as taking flesh from a child.

That's why she called him, she had to. She never agreed with the Witch Hunter's methods, but they were effective. If the child was still alive, he would find her, and the morgue would be at capacity very soon after he began to look.

If he did find her it would be a victory, but just the battle and not the war. Susan had to focus on the war, or in another three months, there would be another Sasha Edwards, and the cult would grow ever harder to find. Nightmares like this group would slip up and surfaced maybe once a century. They had to be killed before they could dive into the darkness again.

The morning cup of Carol's tea had done its job, but now the china was empty amongst the horror on her desk. Tea was an anchor, a way to keep herself rooted in this world. Without it, trying to be subjective became harder. She rubbed her eyes, it was time for a refill.

She got up from her desk and crossed the office. Carol had closed her stained glass doors so Susan would better able to concentrate. Susan turned the glass Victorian knob, opened the door and looked out into the reception.

"Carol would you be a love..." She said.

*Blood.*

Blood was everywhere. On the desk, on the hardwood floors and pooling out from where Carol's decapitated carcass sat, arms hanging limp by her sides. Susan's mind received a flash of the events that transpired.

Carol had been surprised at her desk. She was working on something at the computer. Carefully and quietly, they had come in and she greeted them with a smile. They approached her desk and swung a razor sharp blade. A heavy blade, that took her head in one swing. The blood exploded up and hit the ceiling, but the CBC and the tea had covered the sound and the splash of a few body jerks. Carol was always relaxed, her body would have barely twitched after the head was gone.

Now her headless pale corpse sat lazy in the oak office chair. That lovely tanned dress she wore was soaked and sticking to her yoga slimmed body. The slight patting sound of blood dripping from her fingers echoed, and the smell of iron flooded through the open door.

It only took a moment to perceive the scene. A moment of stark shock. A moment of hesitation, a moment before the realization that the killer was still there. A moment too late.

Susan only saw glint of steel as the long savage dagger drove through the air catching her in the left eye. The blade traveled through the eye's meat without pause, easily puncturing the orbital socket and slipping into her brain. She was aware of the hit, but then the killer twisted the blade, tilting her head down and lifting her onto her toes. Memories and life faded in a blur of damaged tissue. Another twist, and Susie's tongue fell out of her mouth, catching blood as it drained from her face.

She made a low guttural sound like a drunken whore, and was gone.

**Chapter 17**

"Who are you?" Sasha asked, wiping the Hallows' vile fluids off of her body. The Skatman was crouched in front of her, with his bright slit-throat smile. He straightened himself up but took care not to step closer.

"Dey be callin' me da Skatman, Moonchild." He said with a grandfather tone. Sasha could see war criminal light in his eyes.

"What did you call me?" She asked. Her attention was diverted by a howl from the rooster as it straddled back and forth, keeping Winker at bay.

"I say, this is quite the animal you have here sir. I don't suppose you would be so kind as to call it off? I assure you that myself and the good lady are friends."

The Skatman narrowed his eyes. "Mista Winka, I see ja be walkin' wit' da Moonchild now. Gettin' more information for da book ja always writin', always bein' a Watcha', I-Ya? "

The rooster was swaying in an intense position. The Skatman squatted beside the rotting bird. "Babayan, don't be botherin' Mista Winka, he be one of da good people."

Something passed between familiar and master. The rooster heard him and understood, but there was something else there, something whispered between words. Babayan lunged over to a pile of broken furniture, hopping with putrid wing flaps into a position of authority and surveyed down the street with a steel glare.

Clarence approached Sasha. "Are you alright?" He asked without taking his eyes from the Skatman.

"Yeah... I think so. Who is he?" She said, trying to get the taste of the Hallows from her mouth.

"The Skatman is a voodoo priest" Winker said. "A man skilled in the many ways of the occult from Haiti and the Mediterranean. One could say he was a kind of tribal mage."

He looked back at Sasha and hushed his tone "I've tried to talk to him before, but he is very dangerous."

"I-Ya! Not so Mista Winka!'" The Skatman said placing his hands on his hips. "Da Skatman never done ja harm."

Clarence was unfazed. "I've heard he is able to consume energy, eat other Wraiths."

The three now stood in a street triangle. A couple of meters between each. Sasha could feel power from this dark figure. Clarence kept an eye on the rooster, making certain if any silent commands were given he would have enough warning to flee.

A blast tore the air.

Thunder without lightning, and Sasha's ears were still ringing when the dark sky opened up and rain began to fall with an intensity beyond the living world.

Clarence darted to the side of the street and began checking for warning glyphs through the sheeted rain. Sasha was surprised by the rain, but not ungrateful. She used it to wash away the remaining vile slime covering her body.

The Skatman's expression didn't change, as though he didn't notice the sheets of falling water. He was still staring at her with his wide smile.

"I say! I think this should do the trick?" She heard Clarence yelling through the open door of what had of what had once been a dwelling. It didn't matter what it used to be, it was shelter from the onslaught. She joined Winker in the dim doorway. The Skatman stood in the sheeting water, Babayan returned to his side.

Inside the darkness of the foyer, rough furniture, broken and deranged lay scattered about on the floor. The usual compliment of broken instruments, paper and garments cluttered the darkness. Sasha was getting used to the perpetual twilight of this place.

Once inside she realized that something bizarre was happening. She wasn't wet. The rain was running off of her as if she were wax. Her clothing, hair, skin, everything had become waterproof. More than waterproof, it was immune.

Clarence noticed her bewilderment. "Ah yes, The rain. The water here is not like in the living realms. We mirror storms in the land of the living, its the only weather we have really, a total mystery to me. There is no ecosystem here as such, and nothing here gets wet."

He paused, thoughtful. "I wonder if its the water here, or if its the solid things in this realm and how they interact. If that were the case, it could be a way to see if creatures are native to this...."

"Clarence! Who is he?!" She was getting frantic, he was the only one to give her any answers and now she needed answers about their dreadlocked savior. As if strolling through the sunshine, Sasha could see the dark shape of the voodoo priest coming towards the door. He was giving her time to talk to Clarence alone.

*Maybe he is giving me time to recover, but why? What does he want?* She thought. He obviously had power, but he didn't want her to be afraid. Her confusion and fear would be usurped by curiosity.

"Ah.. yes the Skatman. He is a kind of priest as I said. You see, the native peoples of the Mediterranean have a much closer knowledge with the lands of the dead than what we would normally call civilized culture, or as I like to call it 'Civil-lied' culture. I have often wanted to talk to him here but I haven't seen him in quite some time."

Sasha remembered that quite-some-time here could be anything from a couple weeks to a couple decades. "Is he dangerous?" She asked.

"What? Oh dear me yes, I should say so. But the question is; is he dangerous to us? And I don't think so, otherwise we would in all likelihood be dead already." Clarence said twiddling the rain from his fingers.

The answer was comforting to Sasha in a bizarre way. In this place it seemed to her that there were only two kinds of beings: Ones that were trying to kill you and ones that weren't.

The Skatman brushed through the partially opened door. He paused, lettering the rain flee from his body. He didn't seem cautious, but he was taking great care as to not be rude. He took off his top hat in a most formal manor. "If it be pleasin', da Skatman be lookin' to speak wit' ja, I-Ya."

. "I say, no bother at all! Please do join us sir! It is, after all, the very least we could do after your assistance with those dreadful things, what?" Clarence was elastic, his body like a spider feeling the strands of a foreign web. This was a dangerous game.

Sasha held her tongue. She could feel something from this man, if that's what he was. He had power and purpose, he wanted something. Her instincts told her if she waited long enough, he would show it. The Skatman nodded to Winker and turned to her again, his face splitting into the same unnerving smile. The smile of a stranger offering candy.

He crouched on the floor, letting his coat drape around him like chieftains garb. His long nimble fingers turned the top hat in his hands, letting the last few drops flee from its surface. She had better chance to look at him now. His face was tight, aged and worn, framed by various trinkets weaved into his hair, each bobble with a

**144**

significance that she would never know. He was studying her with his fixed mask, reading something from the air around her.

"How long ja been here, Moonchild?" He asked.

Sasha ignored him, she had questions of her own. "What's a Moonchild?"

"Yes indeed." Clarence added, interested in his annoying way. He had found some fresh scraps of paper to take his precious notes on. "Why do you call her that?"

He smiled wider still, like a fisherman with a strong bite on his baited hook. "Da Skatman call ja Moonchild, It be, what ja be." He started nodding his head, his dreadlocks rustling the trinkets in his hair. "Da Moonchild be not like Mista Winka, not like da Skatman, ja be created out of da power, ja got life runnin' wit' ja blood"

Riddles; It was like trying to learn science from a poet. Clarence seemed to grasp what he was saying better. He took over the questions. "So then, because of the way she was killed, some essence still within her?"

"I-Ya." The Skatman continued nodding. "She be Da Moonchild, ja powa'." He laid the hat down beside him.. He opened his arms like some great perched condor, gesturing with his hooked hands.

"Ja got many questions Moonchild, ja be wantin' to know tings, I-Ya? Da Skatman tellin' ja." He glanced over at Winker with his nodding smile still in place. "Ja be getting' many notes for ja book dis day Mista Winka."

Then the Skatman spun a tale. His thick accent and whispering voice sent shivers through the dead. He said that many years ago, before the time of the great crusades, before the time of the man called Christ, there were angels.

The angles were called seraphim and they helped men, but for their own reasons and goals. It was within their best interest to keep man healthy and happy, as any good pet should be.

Lucifer was not evil, he was the target for the war winners' propaganda. Lucifer had a system that others believed in. His was a method of control that challenged the ruling hierarchy of angels. Many had their own ideas of how they should be controlled, Whether the methods were more or less savage than the angelic order of the day is a matter of viewpoint.

A political tyrant might be called evil because of the things he does, but he is not essentially evil. The same could be said for certain angels of the fallen. It was the difference between an aggressive tyrant and serial killer. A tyrant is called evil for the things he does, a serial killer does things because *he is evil.*

Yet, Before the angels rebelled and the political war with Lucifer began, there were angels who were truly tainted by darkness. Ancient before the angelic war, there was the knowledge of a being of such madness, such forsaken knowledge, that the angels themselves could only whisper his name. This was the angel Abaddon.

Evil is such an awkward word, a sorry excuse for what it truly represents. However, it is far easier to say or write this clumsy two syllable word, than to express the kind of darkness it holds. Perhaps, if a child was born into agony and his every sound were recorded through a lifetime of torment, those sounds could be scribed into a book. That book could be titled "EVIL".

The legends of Abaddon were whispered the same way we humans might speaks of war crimes. This was a creature that had no concept of boundaries in his quest for power. Not power any mortal could understand, well beyond the human realm of thought and reasoning. Murder, death, and suffering were not noteworthy sins to Abaddon, hardly even rating in his darkness.

His schemes were madness, and he knew the other seraphim would never help him, so he turned to the naïve and innocent men of earth. His power was such that earthly delights, treasures, and other materials goods were all easily attainable with so much as a thought. Humans were easily pliable with the power he could promise them, so he created a cult away from the other seraphim. A following of those who would help him, in return for their feeble scratching of power.

The legends grow mingled and faded here, the thought of being able to keep his history accurate is beyond lunacy. What is known, is that the seraphim learned of his evil plots, and Abaddon was to be destroyed. But before his destruction could take place, he used forbidden knowledge to hide himself in such a way that even the seraphim could not hunt him.

He split his essence, hiding part of it in the one place angels would never look. He placed it into his human followers.

The very thought of it was inconceivable. Even the fallen angels, the exiles would never divide themselves and trust their eternal essence to a savage race of monkeys like the mortal humans. Handing the power of a seraphim to a dangerous childlike thing such as a human is akin to letting a newborn play with a flame thrower.

At that time, the high priest had come to recognize the material possessions and sexual triumphs that Abaddon granted as the mere bobbles they were. He had the dream of gaining the forbidden knowledge and power that lay beyond the realms of man.

Through an elaborate and forbidden ritual unknown today, the angel Abaddon gave his high priest the part of his essence, and then fled into the realms of the dead. The remaining seraphim knew he had gone to this place but with his essence changed, transformed, and they could not locate him.

Once divided Abaddon, became a sickly creature, a ghost among ghost's, wretched and untraceable. He wandered through the realms and began gathering wraiths under his power. It is said than he exists now near the center of Abaddon, beyond the city and the eternal raging battlefields, waiting to be renewed.

This knowledge was never destroyed, it floated about in nameless texts and unspeakable teaching throughout out the world known only to the darkest occultists. This was how the realm became known as Abaddon. His name was used to refer to the forgotten nether realms.

But what of his high priest? His instructions were to wait until the right time, then reunite the two parts of their god. Long forgotten even by his own race, Abaddon would be able to continue his work. But until then the angel had to wait, suffering in this realms for a time until the ritual could occur and he could return to the world.

It would be a long wait.

The high priest knew that this would never occur in his lifetime, so he took special care to breed, creating a child who would understand the power of their salvation they kept within. This process was repeated within the secret cult of Abaddon for generations.

The carriers of Abaddon bore only daughters, passing the essence of their god along in blood. The Essence would only allow one child to be born to each carrier. The woman who carried Abaddon would give birth to one daughter, the daughter would only be permitted to bear one daughter herself, yet more essence for Abaddon to consume so on and so forth. If the woman was to become pregnant again, the baby would never survive. Abaddon made black eagles of men. The essence of the angel would consume the new life as it grew in their womb.

This transition carried on for centuries. Then something went wrong, somewhere along the line of passing, there was a break.

Humans have a random mutation of thought that occurs within us. The younger generation believes the methods of the older generation are corrupted, so using only core thoughts and certain facts generations tear down and rebuild their beliefs. This is mental evolution.

A woman was born and was married into the name of Sharon Catzan. She was taught the teachings of their master as all the carriers of Abaddon were, but she rejected them. While still young she escaped the clutches of the cult and fled into the darkness of obscurity.

When the news of the key's loss came to the realms of the dead, it was said that the angel went mad, slaughtering the remaining cult who allowed her unexpected flight. He killed them in dreams and brought madness to their seed. His screams echoed through the city of the damned and out into the Wylds. This was known as the great loss.

Centuries passed and madness twisted the broken seraphim Abaddon, leaving him distorted and forsaken, suffering in the dead realms of his own name. This was until the coming of one Dr. John Dee.

Dr John Dee was a mathematician and an astrologer in the late 1500's who became intensely fascinated with angelic magic, something he called Enochian Magic. At that time, he was deeply involved with a medium named Edward Kelly and the two physically conjured seraphim in order to gain knowledge. In the process of his exploration into angelic texts and knowledge, he unearthed the forbidden tomes of Abaddon.

In 1582 John Dee was coming dangerously close to being condemned for heresy by the Catholic Church. He needed to generate funds to bribe his way out of damnation and buy his absolution and salvation from the church didn't come cheap.

He had one of the largest private libraries in England and many of his texts were sold to other seekers of knowledge, whoever was willing to pay.

*Anyone.*

It was said that a secret society was created for restoring the two halves of Abaddon. The ancient texts that talked about the exiled angel desperate to be whole. Power hungry men who dreamed of vast riches knew the rewards that this damned seraphim would offer.

Through the rituals within the texts, they were able to contact the shadow spirit that was Abaddon and the cult was born again. The great search began and found nothing for hundreds of years. Women were far harder to track than men because of marriage.

But then, something happened.

There was a shift, what would have been in the last few days in the land of the living. A wraith made contact with the lost carrier of the key, the great beast Abaddon sensed her presence with the realm and sent his minions to hunt the source. One of his hallowed leaders found the wraith in contact and consumed him, but not before learning where the bridge led to in the living realm.

It led to Sasha.

She sat letting the tale drift into her consciousness. It was so fantastic, so unreal, yet somehow her blood told her it was the truth. Only the mind tried to find flaws. "So then, they've won! They killed me and their angel-god is free now right?"

"No Moonchild, sometin' go wrong. Sometin' make da dread foul."

"What?"

"He means that something happened during the ritual." Winker said. Clarence was making notes, furiously grinning the entire time. This was the new and fresh material that he had been waiting for.

She strained to remember, It was getting harder to remember her life.

"Wait a second." She said. "If my soul is part of this angel thing, why did I appear in the theater?"

Winker looked up in a puzzled state. He should have asked that question, but he was pleased she had been paying attention to his lectures. "I say, a good question indeed. Why is that?"

"The Skatman squinted his eyes looking away. He responded after moment. "Da dread 'dey workin', 'dis spell dey castin' not work da right way. So it be workin' da wrong way."

Somehow this made sense to Winker. "Yes, I would be inclined to agree I think. The ritual wasn't location specific, so when the ritual became flawed, you happened to come across into the realms as any wraith would."

Clarence explained how she was captured by the ritual, but something went wrong at the ceremony when the power of Abaddon had already started to flow. Sasha came across into these realms not as a wraith but as something else. A Moonchild, a being created from ritual power, a being created from essence.

It a was as close to a physical transition as it could be, yet her corpse remained in the living world. When the police raided the ceremony, the spell was knocked wild. Rather than bring the angel Abaddon from the lands of the dead, Sasha was dumped with the power of the forgotten god into Abaddon; the city named for him.

Sasha remembered Daphne and the truth again reared its ugly head. They had kept Daphne in case there was an error, so that would mean that she was next to die. The reserve plan.

Eyes wide with realization she spoke to the dark Houngan. "How do I get back? You said you could send me back."

The Skatman continued his nodding smile. "I-Ya."

"There are going to kill my daughter please..."

Clarence again looked up from his notes. He knew there was no way back for a wraith. Just as there is no way for a baby to be unborn, there was no way out, no way home.

*Or was there?*

The Skatman's weaved hair charms rustled in the darkness as he nodded. "Dey be openin' da gate soon , castin' dread for Abaddon, and killin' da little one."

"No! We have to stop this!" She screamed.

"She be comin' to dis place, Moonchild. But when she does, Da Skatman an' Moonchild can ride back on de other-side"

Scarring visions of her daughter.

*Daphne on that cold slab.*

*Knives slipping into her.*

Still the Skatman nodded. "No oth'a way Moonchild, Da little one will die, der is nothin' ja can do be savin' her."

Tears of rage clouded her vision "No!"

The great washing wave of nothing came for her again. There was nothing she could do to save Daphne, nothing that could be done to help Luke. Did she have the strength to scrape off her daughter and let her die? What was the point then? Why bother going back to the land of the living if she couldn't have her family? Luke no doubt has already started to move on, god only knows how much time had passed there.

The Skatman was watching Sasha as she radiated despair. He sat very still, and when he thought that she had suffered enough, he sprung the trap.

"Der may be anotha' way Moonchild. Der may be ja way be savin' da little one."

Sasha snapped out of the coma, her eyes were alive and demanding, totally fixed on the Skatman.

"Maybe, one way." He repeated.

"How?" She was desperate.

"Ja still got da powa', we be changin' da dread,"

He held up two crone fingers. "Da gate be open an two sides."

Clarence was nodding now understanding what the dark priest said. "I say, I see what you mean."

He turned to Sasha. "You see, this crossing ceremony has two parts. If we go to where the ceremony is held in this realm, then could use what essence is left within you to open the gate from this side, and then...."

Clarence stopped, turning to the dark Houngan "But if you use her essence...then she can't go back."

He saw what the old Houngan was doing ."Ah yes, of course. That's why you're here. I understand your concern now." Clarence said, his tone thick with edged venom. "The reason why the Skatman is here is because you hold the key, the essence, within you to open a physical door to the land of the living.."

The Skatman started a deep hissing chucked that rolled into a laugh. The gig was up. He would "help" her, only to help himself. She had images running through her mind. Cold calculating images, tactical images of this bargain.

"You must swear to me that you will make sure my daughter is safe, and returned to my husband Luke Edwards."

More rhythmic nodding.

"And make sure that this cult never bothers my husband and child again"

His eyes narrowed "Many t'ings Moonchild. Ja askin' many t'ings...."

"Look, you want to get back, I am your only way otherwise you wouldn't be here. That's my offer. Take it or leave it."

He was silent except for the reply of his dreadlocks. He could just betray her once through the gate, forgetting even if she had name. But The Skatman had a code, a code all men of power use if they wish to survive in the long term.

*Honor.*

These bargains spoke silently of codes and contracts. This wasn't just an agreement, this was a pact made in the lands of the dead. The Skatman looked it her and locked his nodding. His tense, almost violent voice came.

"I-Ya Moonchild, Ja family be saved."

Clarence spoke out. "I say, not to be too much bother, but it seems that in order for your little plan to work, you would need to know where the ceremony is going to be held wouldn't you? I mean, you will have to know the actual location of the new ritual in the land of the living, and then find its mirror location even if it exists ,over here. That, in of itself, is rather difficult, what?"

The Skatman ignored him. "Tell me Moonchild, tell me all ja know about da dread"

She knew he meant the ritual she was in, so she began two days before the killing. No reason to hold back now, they were a team. The roar of the rain hitting the building raised and fell as she relayed the story. Throughout he would ask the oddest questions.

*Did she see her mother die?*

*What did the circle look like?*

*Did she see her daughter at the ceremony?*

She tried to remember as much detail as she could and the Skatman captured everything, maintaining his rhythmic nodding. She finished as the storm continued its chorus outside.

"I-Ya!" He said and stood spreading his arms wide with the top hat in hand. He put his hat back on and cocked his head like a broken doll. "Don'cha worry Mista Winka, da Skatman be findin' where ja be goin.'"

His coat whirled and he vanished into the rain. His voice slithered back into the dim lit room "Da Skatman come findin' ja soon."

Then only the sizzling flesh hiss of rain.

"Well, I say!" Clarence said "Things are looking rather up, What?"

She shook her head, these were grim rules to a deadly game. Sasha didn't mind the fact that she would die, she would die a thousand times to save Daphne. She felt like she had made a pact with the prince of darkness himself. Maybe she had.

There was the chance that the Skatman could betray her. She had no way of knowing if perhaps he wasn't in league with this supposed dark angel himself. She needed more information, she needed to understand this realm. Her daughter's life depended on it.

After staring at a pool at a pool of green light on the floor, she looked up at Winker. "Could I read more of your diary?"

Clarence was overjoyed at the request. "I say! You most certainly can my dear! You most certainly can."

## Chapter 18

Dairy Entry #67973
Sometime after death.


Dear Mr. Diary


I am so very excited!! I met a Dutch fellow, a ghost actually, who was more cognitive than most. Nocolaes Dankerts, cartographer in life, a map maker, and a nice fellow I must say, once you get past all the screaming gibberish and all that.

It seems he arrived here in the late 1600's, and as I said, these poor ghosts are extremely long lived here, the poor chap. When he first arrived here, from his previous trade he was obsessed with trying to map out the realms. Of course, to map Abaddon accurately is impossible, the buildings will never sit still and there are no bearings, north or what not.

However, good old Nocolaes prevailed! He created a chart, a map you could say, that explains the general layout of the dead realms in vague terms. I have of course no way of verifying how accurate it is, but from what I have learned of Abaddon, it makes sense.

I found Dankerts hiding in a bell tower. I was going up there to get a better view, unfortunately the green mist and low light made it impossible. As it would happen however, this is where I met him. He had gone quite mad and was naked except for a leather satchel that he kept his various maps and charts in. He was impossible to speak with, (he's Dutch you know) but when he saw me writing in my diary he became very excited indeed!

He took out his charts and as best he could he explained to me how the map worked. I've very carefully copied it down and now I can explain it to you.

**The Danckerts Chart**

What a fantastic addition!

You see, the realms of the dead, well the city of it anyways, seems to be set up in rings. I was very exited to hear about this, I've felt for quite some time that I am running around in circles, because I have been running around in circles! Well the great rings of Abaddon anyways.

154

I should think that this would be the most appropriate place to go over some of the more well known glyphs, they should be quite handy for anyone unfortunate enough to come here. These symbols are a language known as Tahn'jey, Nocolaes couldn't explain it too well but it's a lost runic language, quite probably magical, for lack of a better term.

Around the outer ring of the chart there are several larger glyphs, these are the charts regional names.

**The Wylds**

The lines connecting to the Wylds across the chart show that they occupy the largest space here. The Wylds were here long before the city, but as the city grows it pushes back the Wylds. The stars at the end of the lines simply act as arrows pointing all around.

**Abaddon**

This is a massive expanse, always changing and shifting as new buildings form and old ones crumple and collapse into nothingness. This is the area that most of wraiths exist. In the chart, It has been set up in a triangle, but I'm not too sure why.

More than this, the symbols within the triangles are also something of a mystery.

From the way that Nocolaes was becoming agitated, I think that they have to do with time somehow, past present and future. I am at a loss to explain how this affects the realm, but he was very convincing that they had to stay there in my copy of the drawing. The triangles also show that the city is out of symmetry with the rest of the realm, cutting deep into the Wylds.

### The Killing Fields

The killing fields or War realm are closer to the center of this place. Open war that exists, that is a hideous and terrible thing to behold. Eternal wraiths savagely killing each other with swords, club, axes and the lot. The Vikings had legends of these fields, saying if a warrior were to die in combat he would be taken to where he would fight all day and drink all night. Well, they were half right.

The killing fields have so much essence floating around that it is impossible for the beings there to be destroyed, Yet as I understand it, they exist and feel everything just as they did in life. For those killed in the passion of war, they appear in the killing fields where the war never ends. They are constantly beating and killing others and ripping their own bodies apart only to have them reform. All the pain and suffering is theirs forever.

You must understand of course, that I have never actually been in the killing fields, dear me no! But I have looked out over them from some of the broken buildings near the inner edge of Abaddon and it's not an experience that I would care to repeat. I have heard stories of predators existing out there. There are those who say they have seen hideous *things* lurking amongst the strange clouds and perpetual war.

The fields themselves are like a massive mud bog, lined with trenches and blasted holes in the ground. Hideously loud explosions and strange clouds of gas like fog floated through the air. The screams of rage, fear, terror and agony echoing amongst the void. The smell of rotting flesh was so thick, you could taste the taint of that place.

I imagine the wars have changed since I was in the lands of the living, but the hatred and intensity of combat is always there. The wraiths that exist in the fields are called soldiers. Wraiths obsessed with combat and bloodshed, extremely dangerous and will attack anyone they see. They need the war, and have no desire to leave it. Even if soldiers maneuver into the city, its only to get a vantage point into the fields for an element of surprise. Soldiers are quite mad you know.

**The Great Darkness**

There have been very old ghosts that speak of a darkness, a place of temples at the center of this realm. They say it is something beyond human grasp, a darkness beyond darkness and a place of near infinite power. It could have been something that has existed here even before the time of man, or maybe something from our far future. There are many legends, but so few facts.

There are so many questions aren't there? So many other things that need to be asked, yet I can never sort them out in my own head, never mind trying to explain them to you, my dear Mr. Diary. I have no idea what the Tahn'jey symbols around the edge say, most likely it's an explanation of the symbols. Again, I have no way of knowing.

I have never stopped to ask how you have been handling all of this, it is quite a shock I know but I suppose we all do what we must to keep going. It's so very difficult to explain a whole world when it's constantly trying to kill you! Well, that is to kill me in a manner of speaking, consume me might be better. I'm sure you know what I mean

There is something that I have been giving much thought to in the last little bit, mind you everything is made up of little bits. What about the living concepts of communicating with the dead? That is to say, what about these Mediums?

I mean, it is quite fashionable to have séances and the like, and throughout history there have been all kinds of necromancers. That is, those who would evoke the dead. More than this, rituals having to do with the dead are all over the world! Certain Mediterranean countries I am led to understand, dedicate whole religions to the dead, getting their blessings and the like. So what of them?

The answer I find is a bit disturbing. You see, Mr. Diary, when you inhabit the city of the dead, not only do you have to worry about all the spiritual predators, parasites, wulves, and other wraiths who try to consume us, (I caught myself that time, I was much more specific), but there are those who remain in the world of the living who would enslave us as well.

Necromancy is the art of conquering and controlling the dead. It could be anything from basic Ouija, to raising an army of animated corpses; these both could be classified as Necromancy. This isn't the same as 'Conjuring' of course, since Conjuring is bringing things to the world of the living that were never there, but that's a whole other subject.

In any case, there are Necromancers of all shapes and sizes in the world of the living, from tribal Shamans who want advice, to malicious madmen who are only after twisted desires. We wraiths all run the risk of falling prey to them. Their methods will vary, but its usually a spell or an object that exists on both the realms at once, lying in wait like a fish hook. An unsuspecting wraith comes across it and Wham! They're caught in the trap.

Now like I said, not all necromancers are malicious, some are quite friendly with wraiths, but there are those who are just downright nasty, torturing wraiths to do their bidding. One would think that a living necromancer would be smarter about such things, everyone must die eventually and if he were to be unfortunate enough to come here, well I should say that there would be quite a few wraiths who might be interested to speak with him, to say the very least!

The more thought that one gives to this logic the more apparent the nature of some prominent figures in history become, John Dee, Alcazar, Solomon, and others. These were not magicians or conjurors but men who used forgotten science. Their experiments were often dangerous, and had to be conducted in secret because of the power that the seraphim had gained through the church. I wonder what we might know if the church had not been so thorough in destroying this knowledge.

It never ceases to amaze me my dear friend, how incredibly stupid humans are. I mean, of course we seem like a rather bright lot with science and all that, but we deny things that are obvious, merely because they are uncomfortable. I have spoken with a few who carry a rather unique theory. The theory of the mind veil. (Yes, I'm finally going to get around to that.)

**The Great Mind Veil**

Humans are blind to the supernaturally obvious, we have been conditioned to ignore it. The ideas of who did this are vague. Some say it was bred into us, others claim it is purely psychological. Its' purpose is to make us unaware of the creatures and beings from dimensional realms that prey upon us.

It makes a certain amount of sense I suppose, it wouldn't do to have all the cattle suddenly realize they were destined for slaughter. So instead we have this "blinder conditioning" to keep us passive.

To go with this there is rather good news, and rather bad news. The rather good news is that over time, the conditioning has become weak and once it is broken slightly, the remainder falls away very quickly. This is why there are those interested and convinced of the occult world, and yet others who are equally certain that none of it exists.

Of course there is the rather bad news as well. You see, once you break the conditioning, others (and sometimes even yourself) will have a tendency to consider you mad. When people make subtle references to the occult, they are snickered at and become the subject of jest. The stronger the reference, the stronger the reaction, to the point where if one tries to warn others of a supernatural threat, they invariably find themselves locked up in an asylum.

Once you begin to realize this Mind Veil exists, suddenly the mysterious doesn't really seem so mysterious any longer. It is amazing the degrees people will go to deny the obvious.

For example; if a man at a dinner party, without saying a word, were to, make a wine glass hover in the air three feet off the ground, others would immediately assume it's a trick and then ask how it was done.

If the man replies "It was magic." Then the group laughs out loud and then will construct a variety of wild and unlikely theories that contain the use of everything from the use of air currents to elaborate wires that are rendered invisible. They will pester and prod the magician until they divulge the secret of the trick, but if the person continues to say its magic, then they are ridiculed because of not sharing their knowledge of the "trick".

So then, if this veil is in place who is responsible for its placement? I believe it was the Seraphim, but there is certainly no shortage of creatures that feed on mankind, both living and dead, who would want us to be oblivious. I believe the seraphim are responsible simply because it would serve them most conveniently, and it seems their style. If all prisoners believe there is nothing beyond the cages, they will be easier to control.

That in essence, is The Mind Veil theory, no pun intended.

### Wulves

From what I understand, a wulve is not a pack animal, but they do have mates and offspring. A horrible family of monsters that live in dark places and attack passers by. They are not totally unlike the trapdoor spiders of the living realm, which sit and wait for their prey and then grab them with lightning speed. The major difference is in how frequent they are here.

It would be safe to say that in Abaddon, if you were to walk by twenty different alleyways, the twenty first one would most certainly contain a hungry wulve. According to some of the beings I've spoken with, wulves have been here for an extremely long time, perhaps even forever, or since the beginning in any case. This would do a lot to explain things in the living world.

Why are there such massive numbers of people terrified of spiders? They're a small creature, really quite harmless, that eat flies and other pests. But the percentage of people that feel uncomfortable around them is amazingly high! If you were to place a spider on an average persons' arm their immediate reaction would be to kill it, scream, or brush it away.

The reason for this is really quite simple. Since we know that energy can not be created or destroyed, it stands to reason that the life essence of almost all people have passed through the realm of Abaddon at some point. The fear of the spiders is a psychic memory of when they were here. The long forgotten instincts needed to stay alive in Abaddon. This supposed arachnophobia is merely a subconscious memory in our essence.

These lost thoughts and memories are so very common. Once one begins to understand and accept the concept of lost thoughts, one begins to see them far more often in memories of their life. I'm getting ahead of myself again, I'm sorry. I should finish about the wulves before I go on any further.

They are large, very ill tempered and will kill and consume the essence of any creature that is unfortunate enough to go by them. Occasionally they will hunt, but only when they are very hungry, and therefore, that's when they are the most dangerous. I don't think that there is any connection between wulves and spiders in the living world, but there is a creature able to exist and travel freely between the worlds of the living and dead.

The fact that the human race has not realized the full abilities of this creature is quite probably the strongest argument for the mind veil theory there is. It is so painfully obvious.

## Cats

Even my own beloved pet Poe, whom I cared deeply for and who I thought cared deeply for me, was one of these loathsome creatures. Now, as I have all the evidence amassed before me in heaps of tarnished and smeared paper, I wonder why I never saw this before.

You see, it is widely known that the ancient Egyptians were obsessed with death, claiming knowledge of the lands of the dead, which of course they did, only it was this place. They wrote entire libraries on the knowledge of this place, most of the teachings were kept at The Tower Of Babel and the Great Library Of Rome. This advanced culture, probably the most occult culture the world has ever seen, worshipped cats.

They even went so far to explain how it was that cats could travel between the lands of the living and the realms of the dead. But we ignored them!

I don't mean to repeat myself, and perhaps I do have a fair advantage over the average person due to my previous employment in restoration. But never the less, the implications are staggering. I have so much evidence on this subject it's hard to figure out where to begin. But before I do start, it is imperative that you forget everything that you think you know about cats, pretend as though you have never heard of them and I will explain what in fact they are.

First it must be understood that we are speaking of the domestic house cat and not the cats in the wild. Wild cats are simply animals, where as the domestic housecat is … something else. All domestic house cats come from a species of cat that was "created" in Egypt. There are no cats that are domestic that do not originally come from Egypt. Therefore all domestic cats have the same abilities.

Now it must be understood that all creatures that have consciousness can leave their body and travel to their own world, and in some cases out into others, but they can only do so for a very limited amount of time. This is what is called an 'out-of-body' experience, and is especially common amongst the more primitive people.

The concept is this; that the "Consciousness" of a living being can leave their body and while in this wraith-like state, are then able to travel. The term used for this is Astral Projection, and it is technique that people have used for thousands of years to gather knowledge.

This differs from the cats' ability, because a person's natural state is amongst others in the living realm, yet a cat's natural state is floating about in the void, existing on many different worlds at once. It's a very hard concept to grasp , but if you remember how I talked about the fabric of reality? It is the same sort of idea.

Think of the cats, the small fluffy creatures, as merely shells. Much like the "genie in the bottle" stories. Within the cat dwells the true nature of the creature that exists outside the living world. Cats can not show their true form in the land of the living. The how's and why's are a mystery even to me, but when cats leave their bodies behind in the living world, they take on a different form entirely.

It is very difficult for a human to Astral Project, and for some it's impossible. But all domestic housecats can do it on a whim simply by laying down and seeming to fall asleep. This is possible due to the Virtomic symbol the Egyptians Veraxicly placed on the bone structure of their skull.

I'm sorry. I've gotten ahead of myself again.

Right.

Virtometry was a science named in a book known as the "Ill Sanctus Ex Verax" or

" The Sacred Book Of The Flesh". I was a very fortunate to receive one of two copies discovered in Egypt in the mid 1850's. (The other book went to a German museum).

In the book it talks about how certain symbols have energy, or rather, can generate or channel energy around them, if the right dynamics are applied power can be created.

For Virtometry to work the symbols must be created with exact precision and with specific elements. Simple symbols made from simple materials can do simple things, but from the stories I've read in books long lost to the living world, a Virtomic Sorcerer (or scientist) is a powerful man indeed.

The culture to have translated the"I'll Sanctus Ex Verax" from its original dialect into Latin is unknown. In fact, it is unknown what the original dialect of the book is, but whoever translated it made reference to beings I can only call Magical.

The bible speaks of the Pharaoh's having sorcerers who used symbols for power over different creatures, and the aspect of symbol power is a recurring term in the occult. This is due entirely on the origins of Virtometry. Where the Egyptian sorcerers learned this science is vague at best, but the authors of the book did make reference to a being that taught them, but was afraid to name it.

This worried me greatly at the time, because the book had no problem mentioning the names of creatures lost and dreaming in sunken cities, or of dark creatures beyond our realms. Yet they feared to mention the name of the one who taught them of this power.

I'm on a tangent again. Back to the cats.

Apparently, the sorcerers of Egypt had knowledge that they had stolen or had given to them, to combine Virtometry ( the science of symbols) with Veraxology ( the science of working with flesh) and they placed the Virtomic symbol into the heads of the cats. If you try to find it, you can feel it on the head of every domestic housecat. It looks roughly like this:

**The Virto-Verax Feline Symbol**

Now understand that I am not well versed in Virtometry, but as I understand it, the level of intricacy needed to combine Virtomic symbols with living flesh is highly advanced. The domestic housecat was born in this way. Once we break through the Mind Veil, the reasons for creating these creatures is obvious. They were Guardians.

Cats exist on different realms then we do, so cats are able to see all manners of spirits and creatures that exist. They would then kill and consume the essence of parasites, commonly called evil spirits.

This explains why they interact with people as they do, their place in occult history as well as their habits in the family home. Witches (again another subject ) have always kept cats , and cats seem to tolerate us rather than actually care for who we are. Their aloof nature, their long hours of slumber, and their mysterious activities at night all make it clear. But the Egyptian culture is long dead, why would they stay with us?

They stay for two reasons; they need to live in the physical realm, where it's easier to be catered to, (I would like to think, few genuinely care for us) and we are *lures*. We are the gazelle in the great inter-dimensional planes. We are such easy prey for everything outside our realm, with a lure like that, any cat is guaranteed a steady steam of parasites and wyrms to feast upon. Its an uneasy partnership at best, but there it is.

Wraiths are an example of creatures that the cats would feed upon, as are ghosts and other creatures that exist purely here in this realm. We wraiths are etherioid, meaning that they exist only in the ethereal and not in the living realm. It is Etherioid creatures that the cats dine upon, and so I have no doubt that if I were to find my way back to my flat, my dear beloved Poe would swallow my soul and anyone else's who came along.

There is so much to go over it causes my head to ache. Where does one start Mr. Diary? Where indeed? It's possible for me to fill a few thousand pages with the nature habits and study of these creatures we know and love as cats, but I cannot. There is so much more that I have to cover !

What's next? It's so hard to decide.

Candles!

Candles for some reason are able to exist on multiple dimensions or planes, but again, not all of them seem to. I think I have an explanation for this! I'm very exited about having explanations for things; it makes me feel as though my research here is not totally for nothing. Of course, being dead and writing a book on the afterlife, in the afterlife, does seem rather moot.

In any case, candles! Candles are lit with intent. Humans are like powerhouses where spiritual energy is produced, we have so much of it that we give it away constantly to all of our valued possessions. One of the greatest thefts in all of history is how the seraphim have been harvesting humanity for the last three thousand years!

Fire is very easily a sacred thing. A candle here in Abaddon is visible only as a flame, we are unable to see the candle. But the light that is cast from it in this place is staggering. It's the warmth of life; it's a taste of what was.

The last time I saw a candle it was in a small hovel. I imagine it was someone's flat, but I was sitting in one of these rooms thinking. Well that a lie, I was trying not to think at all, when this bright glow dominated the room. Like an explosion of life, the room was filled with a soft warm golden glow, and a tiny beautiful flame was hovering at my chest level just out from a corner. I had to shield my eyes at first because of the light was so bright in comparison to everything else here, but I was not afraid.

It is amazing to be in Abaddon and not be afraid. It was wonderful to sit there in the light and just feel warmth, real warmth, the warmth of the living. Too soon however, the flame went out, the darkness returned, and with it the fear.

I have had an occasion to talk to other wraiths like myself, and they have told me that predators here are terrified by the candles' flame. Somehow these flames trigger an ancient response in them and they will not go near them at all!

As I understand it, fire is not totally chemical, meaning that it seems to have a life of its own. Maybe even an intelligence, but again that's something for later and I am not all that sure about it anyways.

I shall talk more later. I must keep moving for now. There is so much to do!

Clarence Winker
Abaddon Researcher

## Chapter 19

The rain stopped, choked like a gallows cry, leaving only the faint smell of wet jerking its feet in the air. The tattered coat of the Skatman brushed over the livings' wreckage that littered the streets of Abaddon.

He stalked the streets, hunting his prey, and left Babayan behind. It was his job to watch over the Moonchild, she was his skeleton key to vengeance. He had to find where the ritual would be held in the living world, and its' mirror on this plane. It was a big problem, but the Skatman had a plan, a secret. The Skatman always had a secret.

He glided over the destroyed furniture and toy shrapnel, each step carefully placed.

This street came to an end and the cross street had seen much more traffic than this one. It was almost clean , the rubbish pushed away by wind and wraiths, both searching for answers. Another wraith would be along shortly, so the Skatman hid by an awkward corner of a nearby building and waited. He was used to waiting.

The Skatman squatted in the street, his coat spreading like a blood pool. It was unfortunate that this had to come to pass. He was far beyond the concept of guilt, or even remorse, it was just that this was not the preferred way he liked to do things. Bad mojo.

Moments passed, carried by the wind, bringing with them the sounds of prey. There was screaming, confused frightened yelling for help, assistance, answers, anything. A wraith came down the street, stopping only to put his full of face into yelling. His cries were panicked and the shrill voice carried far. He was drawing so much attention it was amazing a predator hadn't found him, but then again, one had.

Wherever this man died, it was warm. He was wearing loose dress pants and an equally loose white short sleeved shirt. He had stylish sandals, the kind you wear to rich golfing lounges, or to a private spa. These were his favorite clothes, the garments he spent the most essence in. The casual style of wealth didn't suite his panicked state.

The Skatman liked the wealthy, they were useful. They believed in the lie of economic superiority, and moral virtue. It had been the Houngan's experience that a rich man will allow the most unspeakable things to happen rather than admit he was flawed. There is much profit to be had from the souls who value the lie.

**167**

The fellow hadn't seen him yet, he was to busy looking up, down, at the buildings, and everywhere else but where he should have. The dark priest cleared away some of the broken debris around him. He needed space to work.

Instants slithered past, and finally the panicked wraith saw the dark figure sweeping his feet on the corner. He could have run, he should have run, but he didn't. He saw a shape, a human shape and the madness had him in its clutches.

He started calling out as he ran, a panicked man looking for the exit. He ran at the Skatman his desperation pooling in the footsteps behind him. Perhaps he meant to tackle the Skatman, maybe he wanted to grab hold of him, to make certain he was solid, but all those questions were answered the minute he was within the Skatman's reach.

In effortless motion, the Skatman had the charging wraith by the throat and drove him into the clearing he had made at his feet. His shoulders hit first, his head followed, cracking hard against mismatched stones.

This was the most difficult part. If you throw the wraith down too hard, you could damage them. Only enough force was needed to stun, but if you didn't get them down hard enough, then they were too feisty, harder to work with. The first few were difficult to get just right, many wulves had found easy meals from crippled Wraiths in the streets, but soon he mastered this technique.

The air was shocked from the wraith's lungs and his mind was stunned. The Skatman was sitting on his chest, his knees pinning the wraith's elbows.

"What be ja name?" The Skatman asked.

" ...Mark... Mark Nociar! " The wraith answered.

The Skatman grabbed Mark's right hand and forced it back against his leg. Even if Nociar had fought it wouldn't have mattered. "Well Mista Nociar, ja be doin' da Skatman fava's now, but don' worry, Da Skatman be sending' ja away from dis place."

The Skatman felt the calluses on Mark's hands, he was right handed. He brought the right arm back pressing down on his wrist.

*Kru-Kruk!*

The bones in Mark's forearm shattered under the strain, one of them punched though the Wraiths flesh sending scarlet droplets in the air. Mark was screaming, thrashing helplessly on the ground. Confusion and terror filled his blood. The compound fracture was a mistake, but even experienced cowboys can slip up once in a while. The operation was still salvageable.

The Houngan gently laid the destroyed limb back down. "Shhhhh." He said, nodding his head like a soothing parent. There was no need to make this any more terrible than he had to, not on purpose anyways.

The Skatman's hand slipped into the patchwork of his coat, producing a long slender shard of stone. There were tiny markings over its entire black length, like some kind of pagan wand, but the ends tapered to wicked points.

He held the shard away from him so as to not let Mark's thrashing make him fumble. He reached down and brought the wraith's left hand up. The pain from his broken arm was easing his thrashing, which was the desired result. The Skatman braced the hand against his thigh, enough pressure to hold, but not enough to break it.

"No!..No!..No!" Mark was hyperventilating and begging, the wraith's terror tears streaming.

"Shhhhh." The Skatman replied again with his dark dreadlocks like tentacles over his face.

Taking one razor end of the shard, he gently slid it lengthwise between the middle knuckles, down into the palm of Mark's hand. The sickening sound of snapping cartilage echoed though the street.

Nociar never screamed so hard in all his life, only after his death did he feel enough pain to produce such a sound. The dark shaman slid the shard deeper into his hand, feeling its stony barbs click against swelling knuckles. Finally he felt the shard jolt as it reached the wrist.

Shifting weight from his knees back to his feet, the Skatman stood bringing the tortured wraith up like a dancer. Nociar screamed again. He would have collapsed if not for the Skatman's firm grip. Tears rolled down the wraith's face, the pain of movement began to shift from only blinding to pure agony. If Nociar fell now, the pain would have been unbelievable, so his body obeyed the pain and firmed his legs.

The Skatman let him stand, watching the pain drift. He was able to judge pain from people's eyes, the amount they had, and how much they could endure. A useful skill for one in his trade.

Nociar stood hunched, his limbs hanging by his sides, eyes shut, denying the reality around him. His broken arm dripping blood off of his fingers. Even the thought of running caused him pain. He was prisoner to his own suffering, bound motionless by his own nerves.

There is a knowledge called Thetachery. It involves devices gathering energy from its environment in order to perform desired tasks. An example would be those who use forked sticks to find water, commonly known as the act of dowsing.

Dowsing can be used to not only detect water, some use it to find buried wires, or even treasure. There have been those able to use bent rods or even forked sticks over maps, and been able to accurately find any number of things. They would move across the map or ground, and when held correctly, the wires would cross over the location of what it was they desired. It was only a simple matter of digging it up after that.

One of he lesser known thetacheric devices is the Hunting Shard: The shard that Mark Nociar had imbedded into his hand up to his wrist. It's difficult to make, a combination of Tahn'jey symbols on a precise piece of volcanic glass. Once imbedded in the hand, its much more accurate than a regular dowsing rod, yet the secret of it was fortunately lost in the great burnings.

But not to everyone.

The Skatman reached out and grabbed Mark's face with one hand, shaking his eyes open. "Where is da man? Where be da priest o' Abaddon?"

Nociar was shaking, trembling from shock. "I...don't know! I don't know where he is!"

"Where be de man da Skatman be after? Ja show, an Da Skatman make da pain go 'way. I-Ya!"

Nociar made the fatal flaw. He wondered where the priest this demon hunted was, and his arm was caught in claws of pain. The shard within his hand was twisting, and through the compliance of pain Mark twisted his arm with it.

If his other arm wasn't shattered, he could try and stop the shard from twisting. He could have pulled it out. But his arm was broken, now dripping fading red dots as he moved. He lifted his arm and moved as the shard demanded.

Nociar was a slave to the shard, it pulled him and he cried in fresh pain as he staggered into a run. All he could do was howl with agony and try to keep pace with the shard as it dragged him through the street.

The Skatman had made a hound, a seeker that would find who he was after. Twisting and screaming in pain, Nociar would give him what he wanted. Mark Nociar ran half a mile, and fell four times before his voice gave out, leaving only his gargled hisses to plead for mercy.

**Chapter 20**

It wasn't supposed to be like this. He was supposed to spend an eternity in the service of a forgotten God. He was to be armed with a flaming blade and fighting against the oppression of pure humanity, a predator in the predator-prey scenario.

He had risen through the sect of Abaddon, gaining authority and prestige. He had shown his dedication through spilling of blood. The inferior sheep that walked the earth had no idea the power that he held. He was a high priest of Abandon, he wasn't supposed to get shot, he wasn't supposed to be full of pain and cold, but yet he was.

James Bowman was just like anyone. He was happy in his productive, somewhat menial work as manager for local city transit. He was normal, except that he worshiped an ancient fallen angel and had killed in His name. His wife was from the sect, his children had long since been sent to his God, and it was the best thing for them.

*It wasn't supposed to be like this.*

The realm he was in now wasn't symbolic, there wasn't any room for metaphors or representation here. Here there was only darkness and fear.

They had found the woman, the one they had said was the carrier, but they had said that before! This was just another excuse to watch the light fade in another's eyes. She couldn't be the one they were after, any more than the last 6 they had ritually killed.

If it was true, the great angel would have come across and they should all have angelic powers beyond imagination. He was completing the ritual when the police showed up. He had the knife buried deep between her breasts, slipping through the ribs and releasing the energy within, but something went wrong.

*It wasn't supposed to be like this.*

He had been shot, hammering shockwaves ripping through his body. The enemies of the great angel came to destroy them, feeble men with tin badges and guns. He would never face their judgment, not from those puny men or their Jewish god. The symbols scarred into their flesh should have taken them to the realm of Abaddon, into His arms of love. They were supposed to be received as the soldiers they were, with honor and dignity.

Three shots hit him in the chest, he was certain that one tore through the tattoo, but that shouldn't have mattered. Certainly having the tattoo torn away by speeding lead wouldn't have taken away his place next to his god, he was, after all, a high priest of Abaddon, an emissary for the great angel of the beyond.

*It wasn't supposed to be like this.*

What followed was a mass of yelling and explosions, more shots and death. He remembered the bright lights and shouting. The banshee wail of an ambulance siren warbling a chorus to die by. Voices were shouting back and fourth, the last cry he heard was "I'm losing him."

But he had been lost a long time before that.

He became aware, lying on the street in his bright white robes. They were a perfect, clean, gleaming white with the scarlet crest nobly displayed. The divine set that he had worn to the orgies, the sacrifices, the beatings in the name of Abaddon.

He was lying on his back in the middle of a road. Perhaps it was the rustling of the papers around him like leaves or the forbidden sounds that echoed forever in the darkness. He was in the street, a street in a strange land where light was not a tradition.

He wandered for his own personal eternity, wondering what happened. The elders said nothing of this place, of the broken toys, the burned out buildings, and the shattered furniture. Nothing was said about the scuttling of unseen creatures echoing down alleyways and chasing the cracks in the walls.

The bullets had taken his life, but certainly by just ripping the tattoo they couldn't have taken his salvation. He had paid for that in the blood of many a sacrifice. His robes brushed over papers, catching and dragging behind him. He walked forever, and then sat forever more. Now he was back to walking again, rehashing the events.

*The madness has many forms.*

A voice called out. "James".

He looked up to see another set of white robes and a similar crest, own, standing thirty feet away. A woman that he had never met, but someone who knew him. She had shoulder length brown hair with pale stark features, her green eyes locked him in place.

"James! We have found you!" She said in a laughing smile.

*Who had found him? What did they want? Was this happening? She isn't right,*

*What is wrong with her?* Confusion roared, he wanted to say something but wound up shaking his head trying to force the words out.

She was standing at one of the many curving crossroads. Another shape moved, crawling out from behind her. Another woman, but not even vaguely like the robed figure.

She had the body of a child attached to long sultry adult legs, moving like a mismatched mannequin in a department store. The child-like head had a huge mouth and a tongue that was constantly darting out, licking her face while the heavy sound of labored snorting interrupted its breath.

There were more of these things coming from behind her as well. A total of twelve came out from the street, forming a cluster around the white robed figure. Each of them a twisted sexual creation, swarming about the priestess like a nuns' forbidden thoughts. They sprawled, gyrated and seethed out into a wide group. They had been looking, searching for something, for someone, for *him*.

He didn't know these were The Hallowed Ones, he could only recognize the wraith by the matching robes to his own. The robed woman moved forwards staggering, and the hallows parted around her like flies.

*What the hell is wrong with her legs?*

"Don't be afraid James, it's alright! We've found you, and we can take you home now! Abaddon has sent us to find you!"

"Who..." was all he could manage to jerk out.

She spoke like a puppet, happy and oblivious. "My name is Sister Tracy; I am with the order of Abaddon just as you are. The ceremony was corrupted by enemies of our cause and your sigil was damaged, your crossover to this realm was plagued, but we have found you and now you can take your place."

James watched the twisted shapes encircle him. The old man stroking his three foot penis, the gaunt woman blindfolded and gagged by tightly coiled ropes, the young boy with the razors instead of fingers wearing the uniform of the Nazi SS, and still others he didn't want to focus on. They all wanted him, to touch him, to have him for their carnal pleasures. He could feel it, but something was holding them back, something held them at bay.

"I know you don't understand James, but don't worry, once we get you back to the temple you'll understand what's happening, the time of the crossover is coming soon." She said taking another step. A mangled lump of flesh skirted out from beneath the cloak.

*My god, her body...*

Her voice like a child's. "Soon he will be able to return...."

A crash of splintering furniture and flesh hitting stone, came from the street behind James.

A hundred yards away a man stumbled out being dragged by his arm. He fell over a child's cradle, sprawling again onto the street. He crawled towards them and crawled up onto his feet, continuing his desperate footfalls, chasing his own arm.

"Stop him." Sister Tracy unleashed the hallows to do their will.

The fastest hallow had the body of an old man, but each of his arms and legs were twice as long as they should be, making him a stretched gray stickman. He ran on all fours, shimmering genitals trailing behind him like a tail as he ran.

He was upon the stumbling man in moments. Grabbing and pinning him face down to the ground with his great withered hands. The other hallows were only an instant behind him, soon their hands had added to the old spiders grip, stroking the runner with lascivious gropes. The running man still did not speak, but flailed his legs desperately still stretching his wounded hand ahead towards the two robed figures.

Sister Tracy took James's hand. Her grip was cool and dry, a numb feeling as if wearing gloves. The hallows parted as the white robes approached. James could see that one arm had been viciously broken, his other with some kind of rod jammed down into his fist. Dried, dirty blood covered his arms as he continued to flail.

Sister Tracy commanded "Roll him over. " The hallows obeyed.

Mark Nociar's eyes had rolled back in his head, Allowing the dust to clump onto the moisture of whites. He had chewed off his tongue and lips, leaving his a flesh ripped sneer around his chattering teeth. The only sound he was able to make was the throaty scratch of his breathing, and frantic thrashing controlled by the Hunting Shard biting into his flesh.

James was shaking his head, back and forth in the permanent denial of what he was seeing. His body began to tremble. She turned to him with an exaggerated concern. "No James, its okay! Everything is going to be fine" She began to lead him from the pack softly speaking to him.

Screaming.

Enraged, frantic screaming. Hateful screaming.

The two white figures turned to see the fast spider-like hallow had dislocated its jaw and was now screaming at full strength. With one powerful strike he drove his bony knuckled fist down into the face of what had once been Mark Nociar, crushing his skull like a rotting melon.

No time to react, the hallows were confused. Then the gray old hallow turned on the others. His arms launched from his side driving his fingers through the eyes of the long legged child. The subtle sound of bone giving away, then the wet slurp of fingers driving into the brain.

A bloodied fist raised up from the head of Nociar and crashed into the rope blinded hallow, snapping her neck with the impact. Its head rolled back to the center of her back, only the flesh holding it in place. A hallow with tentacles tried to grab the old spider, but the old one was too fast and whipped her with the corpse of the licking child, beating it back using the long legs like a flail. Still the howling madness came from his unhinged jaw.

"Stop!" Sister Tracy cried out, dragging James behind her. All she did was buy the spidery man more time to strike. He grabbed two more hallows and tore their heads away like a child popping flower heads. A hallowed woman with only arms to drag her swollen bloated body received a stomping blow from the gray ones foot, snapping her neck, collarbone, back and hips, in that order.

Sister Tracy could see that her power over this hallow had been lost. Its eyes were rolled back and his unhinged jaw wobbled behind each head movement like a one second shadow sidling into place. She backed away, the other hallows were fighting, out of desire or from duty, but it was no use. The spidery hallow had a strength given to him by forces unseen, and his limbs became reapers of hallowed flesh.

Some of the hallows were torn apart so rapidly, their limbs and heads were still gaping, twitching as they lay amongst forgotten clothing and splintered furniture.

The last hallow fell to the gray old thing. The stickman tore out his victim's sternum, letting lungs and intestines fall sloppy onto the ground. The cobblestone street was littered with the fleshy remains and bloodstained pages where the bodies lay.

Only the tall old hallow remained, his own flesh torn from the strength of his blows. Blood drained away showing the bare bones ripped through his hands, the force within seeking yet another victim.

Still he howled.

In a lashing desperation the spidery hallow grasped the side of its head and with a slow steady pull, ripped it free from its neck. There was a popping sound as each of the tendons gave way and finely a loud wet crack as the neck separated. The body collapsed bathed in its own geyser of blood.

James stood quite still. Sister Tracy had been within these realms awhile, enslaving hallows and continuing the work for her Seraphim Lord. She had never seen the a hallow lash out that way, not with that much power.

A whispered hiss behind them. "Where be da power now, Sista'?"

They turned behind them to see the Skatman in the middle of the street, standing straight with only his head tilted, his top hat exaggerating the angle.

"Da Skatman be havin' some questions fa da man just come. I-Ya!" He said in his whisper.

James felt the eyes of the Houngan probing him. "Dey say ja have da little one on de oth'a side. Dey say ja be killin' da little one far da crossin', I-Ya."

Sister Tracy slid her body in front of James. "Shedra M'ell Halude!" She said, extending her arm with fingers folded into an ancient sign. The motion was rehearsed and perfect, it had force. A spell, perhaps a warding to protect them. James could see the effect of it shown by Skatman's body, jerking as though startled.

The Skatman took a step back.

"You of the agents of the light will not be able to stop us! You lurk in your precious judgment, slaves to the beings who make themselves your masters."

Sister Tracy went on, hate whispered between each of her words.

"Already we have the key, and soon we will have the wraith that dwells here. We have waited too long to hear the chimes of your god! We will bring the fallen up! We will tear away the lie of you and your forgotten Christ!"

The Skatman pushed against the invisible barrier. James could almost see it as the barrier broke. He rolled his shoulders and slid one step closer. The hiss of a cobra's voice came again. "Ja be mistaken Sista'. Da god ja say, be no god to da Skatman."

Behind the shaman's voice, James could hear another voice chanting, as though his throat had second mouth that spit only forbidden curses.

"Da Skatman be no slave Sista'. No games now, time to die."

The chanting behind the shaman's voice continued and Sister Tracy began to convulse. She gave a terrific spasm, opening her mouth and vomiting her lungs, stomach and intestines in a bloodied mass. They hung out of her mouth and lay sloppy against her smeared robes. She collapsed forwards, jerking herself into a ball and holding her guts to her chest as she convulsed.

James turned and began running, hearing the screaming of his own voice. There was no dignity in this, no reserve in his motions, raw terror had him now. Any false dignity was stripped away; any pretense of trying to figure out the situation was pointless. This was terror on its home turf.

*It wasn't supposed to be like this.*

He made it almost forty feet before the Skatman was on him. He landed on James' back driving him into the littered street. He was winded for an instant, stunned, but it was long enough for the Skatman to roll him over and pin James' arms under his knees.

James saw only a flash of steel as he pulled something from his coat and drive it at his neck. James closed his eyes and heard the thunderous crack at each side of his head.

Slowly he opened his eyes. He saw the long curved blade of a sickle poised just under his chin , surrounded in his throat. The Skatman's stark face framed with dreadlocks and crowned with the dirty top hat stared down at him, wild with vengeance .

"Where be da little one?" He said.

The Skatman understood torture. He knew that torture is guaranteed to get information. It doesn't matter who you are or how much conditioning that you have. Eventually pain can strip away all of the layers and reveal whatever is contained within. But the Skatman knew the torture trick; more potent than pain, is terror. The kind of terror that can only be achieved by stripping away reality until the true nature of things is exposed. The kind of reality of having a voodoo priest holding you down after watching sexual demons tear themselves apart.

James was screaming. "At the castle! Craigdarroch Castle! That's where she is! That's where they keep her! She's at the castle!" The Skatman knew there was no way to fake this kind of fear.

"Where be dis' Castle" He whispered.

"It's in Victoria , on the island! ….. I swear to God!"

"When dey be killin da little one?"

"I don't know! Soon, I don't know when it's happening…" His psyche collapsed. The Skatman thought about it nodding his head, shaking his dreadlocks.

"Ja be keepin' da little one, ja keeping spares for da killin. Dey be killin' da little one, open da gate to Abaddon." He spoke to the mass on the ground.

"So, dey be lookin' for da Moonchild I-Ya?"

" I don't know….. Oh God I don't know.."

"I-Ya!" He said at last squinting his white eyes. James's panicked screams were halted, leaving only the gasping gurgle of an open throat. The Skatman stood, placing the bloody sickle back into the folds of the his mismatched coat.

They knew that she was here, and they were hunting her.

## Chapter 21

Luke hadn't been home in a couple of days. Since Genaya showed up on his doorstep he had become inseparable from her. She was the thing that kept the grim reality of guilt from his world. Genaya had a small apartment, sparsely furnished with various esoteric books and second hand furniture. It was so far removed from his previous world that he could forget everything there, especially himself.

During the day he stayed at the shop with Genaya in the back room reading and talking about what she called, "the truths of our world". She told him about how there really were angels, and that his wife had been murdered by those who wanted to stop the great angels return. She told him of how the great angel Abaddon would be mourning the loss of his wife, and how this fantastic angel truly loved him and wanted to help him through his time of pain.

She gave him a series of books that helped him see and understand in perfect circular logic about his essence and his wife's passage. After all of this, she told him it might be possible for him to even speak with her again. Each time she talked about his wife she was touching him, kissing him, and holding him. She was attentive and encouraged his tears against her breasts. She was his dominant slave.

Yet, the whole time, Luke could feel something within him nagging. Each moment he spent with her, he could feel this annoying voice screaming from the depths of his soul. When it was too far away, he stopped listening, but the voice didn't stop. It stayed around, just beyond his realm of hearing, a little bit farther than his conscience could call.

He tried to keep himself busy, he tried to hide from that voice, but he couldn't. As long as Genaya was there, she could keep it back, she could quell the voice within, but it was impossible to hide from himself without her as a shield.

He knew he had to get away, to sort out what he was saying to himself. There was the promise of the séance. Tonight, Genaya told him that he would be able to speak with Sasha. After this Luke vowed to take off for awhile. Just a little longer, and then he would think for himself again..

A group she worked with would be able to make contact with his wife on the other side. Then, she told him, there would be peace. In the last two days, she gave him as much peace as she could, and as often as possible. The physical sensation of their lust masked what lay beneath. The guilt that waited in Luke had grown so strong that he needed constant help to ignore it.

He was an addict now, addicted to Genaya's drug of lust and whispers. The way she moved, how she touched him, and the sensation so close to passion he could lie and say it was. He stayed with her at the shop each day until closing. Instead of leaving for food, he asked Graham to go get it and hid in the back room, denying and justifying his actions.

It was eight when the shop closed and she came back to get him with that same alluring smile. Her touch had started to lose its affect on Luke, but he still wanted it. He felt the calm hollow rise within him when she held him, and the waves of guilt after her release, yet somehow a sickness had drifted in with the calm. It was a taint of hedonism, a smear of lies.

"We will be going to the house right away, they will be waiting for us." She said.

Luke only nodded. He was torn up inside himself, constantly grasping at the threads of sanity that were becoming harder and harder to distinguish. Unthinking, everything was believable now.

*What will I tell Sasha?* He thought to himself, and the distant voice was screaming again.

"Are you okay?" Genaya asked.

"Um… I'm just feeling a bit out of it you know? Like everything is just….kinda out there right now."

"I know" She said, putting tendril arms around his waist. He could feel her breath. "It's going to be alright baby, I'm here with you."

That was the problem, and Luke was slowly admitting it to himself.

They left the shop. Genaya didn't have a car so Luke always drove. The séance was in a heritage house in New Westminster, just across the river and dangerously close to Susie's place. He made certain that his route wouldn't pass by her office, he didn't think he could handle any reminders of who he was right then.

As he drove he found his mind drifting back to leaving. The voice within him had firmly planted the seed that he had to get away for awhile, and now it had grown into a belief. He had to get his head straight , after this séance tonight, no matter what happened, he would get away from her and answer to himself.

The house was an obscure historic site, and old dwelling from the turn of the century that had been restored by the heritage society. Genaya couldn't or wouldn't answer how they were able to use the place, so Luke decided not to push it.

He found a place to park just on the side street and approached the massive home.

The house was built in the late 1800's which was old by Canadian standards. New Westminster had been the capital city of British Columbia, and this home had been built with that grandeur in mind. It was located on a corner, with a fashionable stone wall surrounding it on all sides, complete with ornate gargoyles slightly cracked and weary from their vigil.

Like other grand houses of that time, it had four floors, five if you counted the attic. A great looming box with triangular roof pieces mismatched on the top. The rooms inside were an ornate maze, each connecting to a curved hallway with narrow staircases lurking in shadows. It would be a fine house for a child to play in, taking days to discover every nook and cranny.

The river-rock walkway crossed a brief lawn to a grand set of stone steps. A wraparound porch framed the whole dwelling, with multiple doors opening to who knows where. The front entrance had two massive oak doors with a look like old bible leather, and the brass hinges and knocker had been polished to a mirror.

Luke had seen this house many times driving through New West, it wasn't hidden, but somehow he never thought to pull over and take a closer look at it. There are houses like this in every city, gothic and grand, yet no one wonders what goes on within.

Genaya had to knock loud for the sound to reach anyone inside. Within a few moment the sound of the latch echoed and the door swung open. A tall well-groomed man in his late forties with sharp features and dark hair was standing there. His well-lined face could amplify any emotion shown. Now his face was broadcasting kindness as his eyes fell on them.

"Genaya, you made it." He embraced her, the familiar greeting of the new age culture.

"And you must be Luke. Pleased to know you." He grabbed Luke's hand with both of his and shook gently.

"My name is Randolph. Please, come in out of the cold."

It wasn't that cold actually, but it seemed more of official greeting, perhaps ceremonial. Luke stopped for a second at the doorway; something wasn't right. Genaya took his hand, and led the fly into the web. He was powerless to resist once her flesh touched his.

Inside, a musty smell like spice spilled on old fur permeated everything around. Antique kerosene lamps sent dancing flame over a variety of archaic period clutter that had been laid out to show the casually curious. As they led him deeper into the house, Luke could see the usual heritage home details, brochures on the history, a guest book for visitors to sign, and of course the donation jar.

One hallway led into another, the sights became a blur. Genaya and Randolph were talking in hushed tones ahead of him. They passed by three small staircases before opening a tiny door and ascending into a much smaller passage stairway. It was only wide enough to allow one person at a time to climb it in single file. The shadows looked able to consume them at any moment. He thought perhaps this wasn't such a fantastic place for kids to play in after all

The golden glow of candles greeted him at the top of the stairs. It wasn't all that bright, but compared to the shadows in the rest of the house it was positively radiant. The walls formed an awkward polygon, the roof angles crowning them in strange ways. It could have been a bedroom at one time, or maybe a sewing room.

Sitting at an ornately carved Celtic octagon table, Luke saw three people waiting for them.

Randolph motioned to each of them in turn. Geo was a slavic fellow, younger, with long dark hair pulled back into ponytail. He was about the same size and build as Luke but something about his eyes made him more like a caged animal than a guest at a séance.

Kim was next to him, and not a day over 19. She had long straight dyed black hair, and a frame so slight she might shatter at any moment. Her skin was so fair it was almost see-through.

On the other side of Geo was an tight skinned woman in her fifties named Margaret. She was a hunter with a predatory stare and a low cut sweater that showed ample freckled cleavage. Her makeup was pristine enough to be cut from a magazine. She smiled with just a hint of hunger at them both. Luke smiled back politely at the introductions, but wasn't sure what else to do.

Randolph was to lead the ceremony, and was wearing stereotypical medium garb. A simple black turtleneck shirt and micro-weave black slacks. He motioned to the two open chairs at the one side of the table and took his place at the head. Genaya sat next to Geo, leaving Luke to sit between her and Margaret. A single candelabra sat amongst the Celtic carvings on the table throwing shadows around the barren room.

Randolph folded his hands. "Luke, Genaya told us about what had happened and that you wanted to make contact with your wife."

"Yes," Luke replied " I've never done this before and I'm not really sure…"

He thought for a second. *What am I sure of?*

He went on. "I'm not really sure what to do, or what's happening…."

That came out wrong, it sounded a little more unbalanced than he wanted it to. He felt Margaret's hand slip into his. She was looking at him with warmth, smiling and nodding. Then he felt Genaya hand on his thigh, Lending power, amongst other things. Seeing the two women's stare, he was glad others were in the room with them, but looking around the table he saw both Geo and Kim had similar expressions. A look close to compassion, but not quite.

Randolph spoke. "It's understandable Luke, Genaya has told us about the tremendous strain that you're under. You have an amazing amount of strength to have carried on through all of this." Everyone nodded in unison and murmured their agreement.

"We have assembled as a group before to help loved ones make contact with those who have crossed over. I must tell you that it can be a very…" He paused, squinting his eyes as though searching for words. "It can be a very straining experience."

Luke nodded, he should say something. "How much does this cost, I mean what do I owe you for helping me?"

Randolph smiled "There is no money here, we never charge for what we do, it's a mission of mercy for us. We just hope we can ease your pain in what has happened."

Gangly, awkward silence permeated and Luke's seat was becoming uncomfortable. "So, what we do? I mean do you need to know things about me? Should I tell you about Sasha?"

"No " Randolph replied. "It's better actually if we don't know you that well. We are all going to link hands and call out to your wife's spirit. If she answers, I will invite her into my body and then we may speak with her."

*Into your body? Is this for real?* Doubt was creeping into Luke's mind.

Randolph went on. "We should warn you, quite often spirits change when crossing into the nether realm and contact is often broken. It can be quite confusing."

"Okay." Luke replied and looked around the table. There were smiles greeting him but there was something else hiding behind those eyes.

**184**

"Let us join hands." Randolph said in his ceremonial tone. Everyone raised their arms above the table linking hands together. There was something in they way they touched him. Two days prior, something about their touch might have excited him in a strange way, but now the mixture of emotions, lust and invading feelings made him feel dirty inside, corrupted somehow. He glanced at them again and it heightened the feeling of filth within, so he stared at the table in distraction.

Randolph leaned forwards and blew out all but one of the candles. The solitary glow changed the feeling of the room. In a matter of moments it went from merely odd to completely alien. Luke always wanted to take part in a séance, but not like this, not this way. He closed his eyes and tried to lose himself in the darkness there. He tried to push all the unintelligible speech out of his mind and let it be quiet for an instant.

Randolph took a deep breath, and began.. His voice was sedated and dreamy. "Sasha Edwards. We call to you on the other side. Will you hear us?"

Echoes of silence. Randolph went on. "Sasha Edwards, We wish to speak with you, can you speak with us? Can you speak to us?"

Silence amidst the fading filth on the walls.

Luke felt a shudder run through him. *Is the room getting colder?*

Randolph's voice was monotone, hypnotic. "Sasha, we can feel you close to us. Do you wish to speak with us? Can you speak with us Sasha?" .

"Can you..."

*WAP!*

Luke felt a current pass though his body, his wrists ached from the shock. He almost let go of the others' hands but their grips were like vices .

"AAAAAIIIEEEEEGGGGHHHH!!" A woman's voice from Randolph's mouth.

A scream.

*A voice.*

Randolph's head rolled back and every muscle in his body strained. Then, all at once he relaxed and his head snapped forwards into a mindless gaze.

A woman's voice came from Randolph's lips. "Where are you Luke?" Randolph fanned his head back and fourth across the table, his eyes were unmoving, blank,. Luke wanted to speak but his mind was frozen. Genaya spoke for him.

"He is here Sasha."

Hearing his wife's name Luke snapped out of it. "Yes..... I'm here....Sasha."

It sounded foreign, weird. Randolph swung his vacant gaze back in Luke's direction, tears welling in his eyes. They spilled out and ran freely down his cheeks.

"Oh Luke!" The voice said. " I love you, I'm so sorry for leaving you." This was more than Luke could take. What started as a tremor in his guts became an explosion of emotional pain by the time it hit his face. Luke cried out in desperation as the tears came. Luke dropped his face down to his chest and let his body tremble.

"Luke," The voice went on. "I want you to know that I love you, and I want you to be happy. I want you to know that I have been watching over you and I really like Genaya, she is beautiful and very good for you...."

"Daphne" Luke interrupted weakly. "Do you know where Daphne is?"

Randolph began weeping more heavily. "Yes Luke, she's here with me on the other side."

The words came out of Randolph's mouth, fashioned themselves into a hook and tore out Luke's intestines. The words lit him on fire, they beat him, they gave him pain the likes of which a messiah couldn't take.

Luke collapsed onto the table, emotionally destroyed. A wail escaped his lips and he felt the hands of the women tighten harder upon his own. This was what he was afraid of, this is what the voices at night were saying, and only now their fears had been confirmed. All that existed now was the Celtic grooves carved into the table.

He realized the voice in Randolph was still speaking. "Luke you must go on with your life, she loves you..."

*Grinding pain.* His own cries where drowning out the voices words. "I love you...carry on....we will wait for you here...our love for you... we must go..." Then it was a blur. Somehow the séance ended and Luke was being held by Genaya.

He was beyond the realm of grief. He was trying to shake his head and scream but it was translating to trembling and a whine. There were other hands touching him, offering strength. From within that pain, he began to feel some strength coming from someplace that didn't exist, pulling himself together and pushing back from Genaya and the others. He realized that the others had surrounded him and were laying hands on him in ritualistic fashion to give him strength.

In a moment of painful clarity Genaya's sedation wore off. "I've... gotta go..." He said, surprised by his own words.

Genaya looked bewildered. "I'm here for you Luke, We are going to be together, it's all right."

It was so inviting, the thought of surrendering all reason over to Genaya, but now that he started, it had begun to gather momentum. "No!...I've got to go, I've got to think, I..."

"Its all right Genaya." Randolph said looking at a gold pocket watch. "Luke needs some time, I can give you a lift home if you like." He closed the watch and smiled at her.

Genaya's demeanor changed. "If you feel you need some time Luke, I understand, I'll be waiting for you when you're ready my love."

The change was instantaneous, only seconds prior she looked ready to destroy any resolve Luke might have in the notion of being alone. Now with Randolph's word her whole outlook had changed. She had become patient and giving, the switch only bewildered Luke more. The others moved away from him and stood by Randolph. Only Genaya remained with her sickeningly sweet eyes pumping care and compassion.

He found himself sick of others' sympathy, he was angry, sad, confused. He turned and started down the stairs as fast as he could. Genaya following behind him, another set of footsteps behind hers. Luckily the route towards the front doors was straightforward, if he had gone through too many twists and turns, he would have needed one of the others to guide him. It was all he could do not to break into a run, but he wasn't sure who or what he was running from.

Just as he reached the door Luke felt Genaya's hand on his arm.

"Luke," She said in her hypnotic tone "You've had a terrible shock, are you sure you don't want to stay with us?" Luke turned to see Genaya and the tall slender figure of Randolph behind her. He did want to stay with her. God help him, he didn't want to be away for an instant. He had to leave, his very soul was screaming an alarm in a language that he could no longer speak.

He opened the door and paused only for a moment. "No Genaya ...I ...I've gotta go, I gotta think about some things. I'll be by the shop tomorrow."

She was upon him with amazing speed, her arms tight around him and a deep kiss embracing his tongue, somehow his arms had the strength to push her back.

"Take care Luke, I'll see you tomorrow." She said.

He tried his best to smile but his mouth only twitched as he slipped away and almost ran down the steps, out into the blossoming night.

187

Randolph and Genaya watched him get into his van.

"Where will he go?" Genaya asked.

Randolph shook his head, narrowing his eyes. "It doesn't matter now."

The door closed on the heritage house, letting the street noise and traffic shroud it in invisible folds. It was just another house, on another street, in another city.

Any city.

Inside his van, Luke was on autopilot. There was nothing within him to feel an emotion. The night had been so surreal, so beyond the realm of reason. At any moment he expected to awaken.

The traffic wasn't bad that night, the drive back was a fraction of the time it had taken to arrive there. Yet it stretched on as his exhausted mind searched for answers.

He had heard a voice, *was it Sasha's?*

It seemed to be, he wanted it to be, yet the last few days were tainted. Genaya was not the answer that he wanted and he knew it.

The voice within him was growing stronger, an inner feeling of dread over the time he had spent with her. Now, away from her clutches, he could see that his time with her was wasted, it did nothing but sedate him, tying him down in knots of lust and coddling.

This wasn't the self absorbed guilt that he had felt before. This was a warning, a feeling of impending doom. He wanted to see her again, he wanted to shoot up with the ecstasy of her sex, have the high of lust, but like any junkie he knew he shouldn't, he couldn't, *he mustn't!*

He was too tired now, in the morning things would be better. In the morning he could have a coffee and make a new plan. With the ordeal he had just been through and the way his mind was trying to regain a footing, he found a new level of fatigue.

If he had not been so exhausted, he would have paid more attention on the ride home. He only wanted to get some rest, some sleep. He never noticed the long black Chrysler in the underground parking.

Had he been more awake, he would have noticed a shadowy figure lurking as he got out of his van, but the sound of shuffling footsteps couldn't draw him from his homing trance. After locking the van, he took a few steps and he felt every muscle in his body explode.

Something hit him from behind.

## Chapter 22

They waited for the Skatman.

Clarence had gone on and on, as he always did, about the different symbols on buildings and what they meant. It all just sounded like free form mishmash to Sasha. She stopped listening just after he got warmed up. She had her own thoughts to deal with.

The little saloon style building had been a shelter from the savage storm, it felt almost comfortable, but the Abaddon taint was as prevalent here as anywhere else. Winker was in depth explaining about spiritual batteries when she heard the first sounds.

She wasn't sure if she heard it but Winker paused in mid sentence, freezing himself to hear. His elflike ears were keenly listening, signifying that he had heard it as well. She was about to whisper over the bloated pause when they heard it again.

The tell tale creaking of withered boards echoed. It was a shuffling, above them on the roof. Something was up there. She looked back to Winker but he had silently shifted himself to the window. His papers already bundled under his arm, ready to bolt at any second.

He peered out of the cracks of the has-been window and began backing away. No words needed to be spoken; they were in trouble. This building had to have a back door and Clarence was heading for it.

*CRASH!*

The sound of collapsing brick and splintering wood came from the back of the building. Rending claws were tearing at the roof top and bits of dust and wood were falling as whatever it was tore through.

Before Sasha could turn her head she felt something grab her. It was Clarence half throwing, half leaping out the front window.

Clarence, through either experience or luck, had dove low through the window just as something was jumping in, passing them in mid-air. Sasha felt clutching hands miss her, then the hard crash of the ground outside. Looking around she saw the unmistakable flailing forms of the hallows. She should have been afraid, especially after the last attack had almost ended her afterlife, but instead she felt her rage returning.

Clarence was up and running like a crippled spider. A flurry of spindly legs over the street's trash. Sasha saw a group of them standing fifty feet away, they saw her and began to charge. In rage, one had to pick battles, but this battle picked her.

A wicked jerk of her arm and a hallow from the alley had grabbed her. Huge hands led to long thin arms, only to end in half a human torso and a head of a grinning drunkard. This hallow had her now, but the rage had her first, and something had awoken within.

Sasha felt a power rush and screamed at the creature. The hallow exploded backwards and away from her in a mass of clotting blood and flesh. The other hallows saw the destruction and slid to halt their attack.

There had to be at least thirty of them, but Sasha didn't care. Sasha turned to them and could feel her eyes burning with power. The hallows who paused at the front were trampled by those behind them. Sasha was hardly even in control now, her body shaking with power. The rage inside her was the will to burn the world, a hate so pure it sang.

Another blast of power came and her arms flew out from her sides, throwing energy at the approaching horde. Screaming maws and groping flesh were met with a blast of force, channeled through her body. Two hallows at the horde's front exploded backwards, sending bone shards and hulks of muscle ripping through the others.

Screams of pain and agony erupted from the wounded hallows. Six of them were killed, while ten more crumpled to the ground, wounded and ripped open. The remainder tripped and slid to a halt through the entrails of their fallen brethren. Howls of hatred and fear, were coming from the crowd. Sasha turned her attention to the figures standing behind the attacking horde.

She had not seen these white robed beings before. There were three of them, standing near an alleyway. She watched them back away as their robes reflected the dim light of the city.

More sounds behind her. Sasha spun low, arms swung wide to embrace the enemy. Another horde of the hallows were fanning out in a wide line around her. She turned again back to the blood washed remainder of the other crowd who were taking up a similar stance.

*I'm getting surrounded..*

Clarence had vanished. It was probably for the best, there was no sense in both of them getting in this predicament. She could see past the carrion that the robed ones were now coming slowly down the street. Her rage was still flowing freely, but she could sense the fatigue from the last two blasts.

She heard the sound of scuffling and the writhing forms of yet more hallows came spilling onto the street from another open alleyway. Reinforcements, the cavalry had arrived, too bad she wasn't on their side.

The hallows would rush her, that was their style. She remembered all too well their tactics from the last encounter, only now she had begun to use her power. There was more than fifty of them now, and they could feel their numbers. Each one of the seething monstrosities began to swell with the anticipation of having Sasha for their pleasure.

As sound came fast from on high, a hallow leapt from the saloon rooftop with the speed of darkness. Sasha turned, but she wasn't fast enough, its deformed body crashed into her, nailing her to the ground. If she didn't have the energy running through her it probably would have broken her body, but it didn't. Instead she was pinned under the creature's long legs. Great weeping sores covering his humanoid form opened, allowing for thrusting genitals to crawl out of each orifice like worms.

Her rage was still strong and she could have thrown it off, but it was too late. The other hallows had closed in, they were grabbing her thrashing body and draining her strength away. She could feel their fingers amongst a chorus of excited moans and cries. The hate within her wasn't enough, there were too many of them. Hands were tightening on her throat. It got harder to breathe, she could feel her self slipping into unconsciousness.

Then they were gone from around her.

A panicked Clarence pulled her to her feet.

Clarence Winker was not a heroic figure, he was not by any means dashing. He was bumbling in fact, but Abaddon was not the place for those who were dashing. Dashing wraiths drew attention, things that drew attention were consumed by the predators here. Abaddon is not about the distinctly human insanities like bravery or honor, it's about survival.

To survive in Abaddon for a long time, you live like a rat, perpetually hiding in the wreckage of the living under perpetual twilight. You had to keep to buildings that you knew were safe and forever hone your senses to danger.

Clarence Winker was a wraith who had done that. Even he didn't know how long he had been keeping notes and lurking in shadows, but he had learned a few things to be sure.

He had learned where to travel in the city, and where not to travel. He had learned some time previous that there was a large wulve den only a few blocks away. He knew that wulves could not resist a chase if tempted, especially if a wraith were to strike at them or some of their young.

Wulves loved to run down the streets of the dead city, barreling over the clutter with near blinding speed, but they can't really turn all that well. They're tenacious, and will go after you until they can no longer see you. If you duck inside a building or a small crawl space, they will sniff around and go back for easier prey. They are opportunistic hunters, so if while chasing one wraith they come across another wraith, they will just as quickly kill it as it would any other.

This was the essence of what Clarence had planned. Go bother a cluster of wulves and then run out of there, leading them back to where Sasha was surrounded; a simple plan. However, the whole thing doesn't seem so simple when you get up from being pinned by hallows, only to find three wulves tearing down the street, cascading over each other like a black hairy avalanche.

There were two smaller ones and that were only eighteen feet wide from curved leg to curved leg, but the larger one was closer to twenty five feet across. The two smaller ones had already slammed their jaws around some of the hallows and were throwing their broken bodies into buildings. The larger wulve was more experienced, it knew to step on the hallows to cripple them and come back for them later.

Sasha ran. Clarence took her off to the side towards a waiting doorway. Clarence moved as though he knew it. He jerked Sasha around the immediate stairs in the foyer and back behind them, making a makeshift barrier.

The papers were still falling back to the ground as they crouched poised and ready. Outside, they could hear the rending of hallows and screams. Sasha could see Winkers gaunt frame heaving under his coat from the intensity of running and the labor of fear.

"Thanks." She felt stupid for saying it, she owed him more than that.

He was panting hard. "I should think...that perhaps....you shouldn't...attack things...that are chasing us."

It wasn't a joke but Sasha found herself smiling. It felt foreign and strange and she stopped it immediately.

After a passing time, the sounds of the wulve frenzy was still in the street but they could tell that it wasn't at their door, as it had been only instants earlier. She stood up and slipped past Clarence, his body slowly coming under control. He touched her leg and met her eyes with implied action, she understood and nodded. The wulves were the strongest creatures that they had seen so far, she was not to do anything stupid.

The cracked tile floor scattered with papers and refuse. Ornate doors, once laden with stained glass now hung like skeletons in a slaughterhouse. Even with the noise of ripping flesh, the crinkling sounds of paper under her feet were like gunshots to Sasha. What took them mere moments to cross in terror, now loomed endlessly ahead.

She scolded herself for being too paranoid, but she realized she was weak. Destroying those hallows had taken a lot out of her, a lot more than she had thought. She had to be careful. She glanced over her shoulder to see Clarence join her in the journey to take a look outside.

"I imagine they are rather miffed, I threw a table leg at them in their den. I say, they didn't seem to like that, rather not at all"

Sasha shook her head " You could have been…"

"Consumed. Yes I know." He said. "Rather a stupid thing to do, what?"

Now Sasha trusted him.

The two of them looked out the once noble doorway into the carnage of the street. Bodies of the hallows were scattered everywhere. Wulves were scooping up bodies with their out hooked fangs and stuffing themselves, gorging on flesh. Sasha and Winker could see that some of the hallows weren't dead yet, but too crippled to get away. Sasha could not feel bad for the hallows seeing them flail futile broken limbs, there was a sense of justice here.

Winker looked down the street. "Oh dear, I've never seen those here before."

Sasha followed Winkers gaze to three trampled white figures laying in the street. They were the figures she had seen skulking only moments before the wulves had caught them.

"I saw them before, controlling the hallows." She said.

" Ah yes, well that could mean a few things." Winkers' tone was that of the professor again. "They could be mages or other practitioners, I understand that they sometimes are able to control certain creatures here…"

"There!" Sasha said, louder than she should have. "I saw one of them move. They're not dead!"

Clarence was unfazed by the discovery. "..of course if they were experienced practitioners, you would think that they would have been able to avoid the wulves, or at the very least get away. I wonder..." His voice trailed off into a ponderous mutter. Sasha was fixed on the forms in the street.

Clarence brought her attention back to the wulves. "I say! See? Yes! They are carrying the hallows back with them to their den! This is most extraordinary! They are actually hording the bodies for later, this is incredible! That shows surprising foresight don't you think?"

Sasha wondered how he could be so glib as she watched these monsters form a hallow corpse pile, grabbing three or four bodies each in their jaws. Within moments, all three lumbered out of sight down an alley. She waited until she couldn't hear them, then headed straight for the robed figures.

Walking out into the street made Sasha feel vulnerable again. The bodies of the hallows were everywhere, scattered like toys about the street. Clarence was fast behind her, also interested in the robed figures.

The three had either fallen or been piled on each other, two men and what had been a woman. The heads of the female and one of the men were gone, but the wulve had only severed an arm of the third Wraith, and his blood spilled into the street. As she looked down at him, the last of the light was fading from his eyes. Maybe he could see her, but probably not. She knelt by him.

Clarence was busy looking over the other dead ones for markings, jewelry, anything that could give him some indication on who or what they were.

"Well, I don't think they are mages, as such.." He said "But they are bearing markings that look like angelic script, I think perhaps these are some of same types of wraiths that are members of the cult that took you and your daughter."

"What? How can they be here?"

Clarence looked at her with a gentle patronization. " Oh my dear, there are many different sects that span across different worlds. Quite often groups are thought to have committed suicide when in fact they have only changed realms. If these are followers of the angel Abaddon, he must be very strong within this realm, no doubt they are part of his legion here."

Sasha took a moment. The notion seemed logical enough, simple even, but it was still something that jarred her. Things were starting to make sense, but reality had tripped again, starting to stumble. A familiar foul stench filled the air, Babayan strut from a nearby alleyway. Not far behind, the flowing figure of the Skatman came into view, stepping over the strewn bodies like a nobleman.

Sasha and Clarence rose to meet him, the rooster stayed wide ever watching. He must have run to get the Skatman as the hallows attacked. Even the mighty Babayan couldn't take on that many hallows, but she didn't believe it was capable of fear, only tactics. The Skatman had a Cheshire grin and a twinkle in his eye.

"Ja been playin' Moonchild, I-Ya!"

Clarence immediately burst into the story of the hallow attack and having the wulves follow him back. The Skatman listened, and watched Sasha wryly as the story unfolded. She was looking back at the robed corpses.

The Skatman snapped her out of darker thoughts with his husky whisper. "Ja been fighting some o' da holy demons. Ja been seein' some o' da power Moonchild."

The flux of energy that had filled her felt so natural, felt so normal that she hadn't given it any thought, but now she realized the extent of what she had done. It felt as natural as a dream, as though she had had the power her whole life and just never employed it. A long lost dance that she could still perform by instinct alone.

In life she had had many dreams of being able to fly, or being able to walk through walls. While in the dream, it didn't seem extraordinary in the least. Tearing those wraiths in half was as easy as passing the salt. The shock of it now, a wave of realization. Her eyes met the inquisitive squint of the nodding Skatman.

Clarence hadn't been there to see the damage that she had inflicted, but he wasn't surprised by it. "Oh, you've gotten a handle on your abilities have you? Jolly good! I imagine they will be quite useful indeed!"

"But how am I....How can I..."

*My god, what am I?* She thought in horror.

Still nodding, the Skatman answered her. "Da power ja keep, is da power of Abaddon. Dey be takin' da little one to da castle, Craigdarroch Castle for da crossin' "

Sasha was snapped into the present. "Daphne! They are going to take her to Craigdarroch?

"Ja be knowin' dis place?" The Skatman asked.

"Yes I do! It's in Victoria, it's a huge old mansion on a hilltop, a tourist attraction. Why would they take her there?"

Clarence cut in. "I imagine they intend on performing the same ritual on her as they did on you."

"NO!" Sasha screamed. She couldn't have it, she mustn't have her daughter suffer the same death she did. She couldn't create the image within her mind without feeling the rage begin to grow within her.

"Ah yes well.. Once we get to this castle then we can interfere with the ceremony …"

Sasha saw what he meant and remembered her deal. Suddenly she was anxious to get to the castle, anxious to die, anxious to get the Skatman back. "We have deal, that you will save my daughter correct?"

The Skatman's grim smile came into place. "I-Ya Moonchild, da promise of da Skatman."

A long pause while the Skatman watched it sink in. He had seen men shriek in terror faced with such a notion, the very sight of this world had driven men to madness in mere moments. But here this woman stood now able to grasp with cold conviction her own death. In his own dark way, the Skatman had gained respect for her.

"Not to be a bother, but there is the issue that we don't really know where this house is do we? I mean, how does one find a house like that here? Taking for granted that the house even exists within this realm." Winker said.

The Skatman's eyes were roving over the fallen hallows, movement in a building betrayed a hallow lurking within. A quick motion and Babayan released a horrific cry flying into the open doorway.

The roosters cries were mixed with the hallows as it dragged the sexually twisted form into the street. The body of a woman, gaunt and black like a shriveled corpse, except for the leather fetish attire that had been stitched into her skin.

Babayan had the hallow by the hair and she was shrieking with rage. The Skatman walked towards his familiars prey, pulling the same Thetacheric Hunting shard from his pocket once again.

"Don'cha worry Mista' Winka', Da Skatman be havin' ways o' findin' dis place."

Sasha didn't think she could feel pity for the hallows, but she was wrong.

## Chapter 23

Luke was awoken by a headache, one of those you-should-be-dead-but-you're-not headaches. The kind of headache that makes your brain rebel against the skull. His internal organs felt like they traded sleep for a few hours of continuous vomiting. Over the nausea and pain, the distinct sanitized scent of polyester filled his nostrils.

Dim light was cutting through his darkness. Transient focus formed as he looked up into a stucco ceiling. He thought about sitting up, and made a motion that way, but his body was in instant protest and he relaxed himself back down releasing an involuntary moan.

Whatever had happened to him, who ever was responsible for this pain couldn't have been completely without mercy, because the shades had been drawn in the room. He could hear rain hitting a window somewhere, and the hiss of passing tires on wet pavement.

He tried to sit up again. This time he won the battle and pushed himself into a sitting position but the movement took his focus away. Now sitting, he closed his eyes and concentrated on breathing, trying to calm himself. His organs were not at all pleased to be moving, and every muscle felt torn.

He opened his eyes again and they focused much faster. He was in a motel room, and it wasn't a good one. Cheap pattern wallpaper covered warped gyprock walls. The double bed he was sitting on took up most of the room, two cheap pressboard bedside tables were on either side of the bed and on the nearest wall was a cracked mirror closet.

The light from behind thin drawn curtains showed a soiled TV resting on a well used dresser and chair just beyond the foot of the bed. Someone was sitting in that chair.

When someone looks at a living being, there is always movement. The rise and fall of breath, slight twitches of muscles and nerves, casual drifting motions of awareness. Whoever was sitting in the chair was synthetically still, utterly devoid of lifelike traits.

Luke thought it could have been a mannequin but as he squinted he saw the head move mechanically to the right. The light seeping through the curtains silhouetted a perfect military flat top.

"You are in a motel in Surrey. You have been struck by a high voltage suppression device and then drugged. The effects should be completely gone in approximately thirty minutes. You are in no danger."

His voice was raspy with a slight southern drawl. It was the kind of voice that could carry across a parade square or a battle field effortlessly. He had anticipated Luke's first questions, waiting for a moment to see the acceptance of his answer sink in before speaking again.

"I was contacted by Susie Francis to assist in finding your daughter. Two days ago Susie Francis was murdered and I believe that you will be listed as the prime suspect. Your apartment was watched and I had to get you away without any discussion or questions."

A mechanical click sounded on the dresser and a small table lamp came to life. The sudden gust of light illuminating the room stung Luke's eyes, but it was bearable. The stranger came into view.

Clean shaven tight skin covered sharp features in artificial, military precision. His mouth was perpetually tight, as though it was a surgical slit that made him able to speak. He was older than Luke, between forty and sixty, but his highly weathered features and silvery gray hair would not reveal more accuracy than that. The man sitting across from Luke had a horror washed face, devoid of a soul.

His body was tight, lean, this was a man who had spent his life fighting, running, and moving with purpose. His clothing was simple, a plain gray T shirt and lightweight black slacks. The pants looked comfortable and loose, the shirt was tighter and showed the chiseled shape of his chest.

He wore no necklaces or jewelry of any kind except for a simple black band around his wrist; a watch worn with the face in. Along his arms he could see a mass of long faded scars, some barely visible but others looking recent.

There were no weapons. No tell tale pistol on the counter, no shotgun beside the chair, but the cold emotionless stare of this man was like a gun site keeping Luke in place. Something about this man said unarmed combat was second nature.

Things were clearing now, and the realization of being drugged and kidnapped was surfacing fast. Luke felt anger more than fear. "Who the hell are you?"

"I'm the Witch Hunter." The stranger said. "James Buchanan Wyld, You can call me Buck If you like."

Luke's memory drifted back to the last conversation with Susie. *The Witch*

*Hunter.* If these were his methods, he could see why she chose her words carefully. Still his head spun with too many questions.

Luke winced as he spoke, he was still in a dream. "Susie's dead?....How?"

"Murdered, probably by the same cult that took your daughter." Buck said. "The police won't have any leads, but it was an execution."

The anger from his quasi kidnapping was subsiding. For the first time in days the little voice that had been screaming was different. He felt like he had awakened from a deep slumber that left him neither rested or refreshed. Even though he was beaten and bruised in this bed, he felt more like his old self than he had in all the hours with Genaya.

He had every reason in the world to attack this man, to bolt out of this shabby hotel room and not look back. Yet deep inside of him, the voice had changed. That voice that had been screaming, was coaxing him on.

"Mr. Edwards," Buck leaned forwards in his seat. "I need to know what you've been doing in the last few days, I can't offer anymore of an explanation until I have all of the facts. I understand that you are afraid right now, and probably have been a victim of psychological manipulation. You must trust me."

*Trust.*

Everyone wanted Luke's trust. Genaya wanted it, Randolph at the house wanted it, and now some guy cut out of glass wanted it. Still, there was something different about this witch hunter. A clarity in how he spoke, the kind of clarity one finds in killers and children. He wanted answers and Luke was too weak to care otherwise, yet there was something else. The guilt from his affair with Genaya was welling within, and now this strange chiseled priest was here to hear his confession.

Luke exploded with information. He talked about when he last saw Susie, about the shop, how he met Genaya in and his relationship with her. He covered the days with Genaya and finally the séance the night before. He told him about Randolph and Margaret, but he couldn't remember the names of the others.

Buck sat artificially still during his tale, barely breathing and listened to him. He was unmoved as Luke burst into tears at the explanation of his affair with Genaya. He offered neither compassion or condemnation for what Luke confessed, only silent witness. It was an hour of steady monologue before Luke finally ended with the last thing he remembered; getting out of the van.

Luke sat sobbing on the bed. It was good for him to release this all finally, release it for real without the codling of vampiric, new age sedatives. He was naked on a bed covered only by a thin sheet, confessing his soul to a killer. There was a kind of absolution in that.

There was a brief silence where the Witch Hunter leaned back in his seat. It wasn't a comfortable shift, just a change of position. He reached under his chair and threw a black gym bag onto the bed.

"I'm here to solve this situation Luke. I'm here to remove the individuals who committed these crimes. You should get dressed, I had to go through your clothing to make sure you weren't bugged. You've got no affiliate markings on your body, so I believe your story. I may be able to get your daughter back alive if you're willing to help me."

Luke was startled by his cold demeanor. "But they said…"

"The séance you attended was a dupe to keep you occupied, throw you off balance. It was a good one, some parlor tricks, a shock of voltage, and it worked. You should stick with me until we sort this thing out." The Witch Hunter said.

"You think that Genaya is involved with the cult?" Luke said. " You think she's part of this somehow?"

A grim tone was in Buck's voice like a gunshot echo. " Oh, I guarantee it."

The Witch Hunter stood up and crossed to the sliding mirror. He moved it aside revealing a black hard-skinned suitcase.

Luke was busily pulling his clothes out of the gym bag. They hadn't been washed, they'd been sanitized. There was no odor on them. The clothes had obviously been worn, but there were no traces of who would have worn them.

As Luke dressed and his head started to feel vaguely human again, the questions came in, and with the questions came a strange fear. He looked up from putting on his socks to see that Buck had put on an elaborate shoulder holster and was hooking a submachine gun to it.

Luke froze on the edge of the bed watching this man gear up. He had seen these kinds of guns before in action films, but it was different seeing one casually being held by a stranger. A Heckler & Koch MP-5SD, the standard weapon of counter terrorist teams of the world, modified so that the whole barrel had become a silencer.

The collapsible stock had been snapped into the holster under his arm, and the barrel was on a breakaway system. Several long magazines hung on his other side for balance, along with a hard shell knife sheath. Buck could see his apprehensions and began sliding magazines into his concealable webbing.

"Don't worry son, if I'd wanted you dead you never would have woken up. I'm with an organization that specializes in this sort of thing."

"An organization? Like the CIA or something?"

"Let me try and clarify a few things for you." Buck said, checking each magazine; tapping the bullets to the back with a wrist jerk.

"A few decades back, the world governments became aware that the was a threat from what they called 'Outworld Regions'. At that time, they decided an organization had to be created that would be able to handle the supernatural threat."

He slid a wide blacked out blade into the Kydex sheath. "We stay out of the news for obvious reasons and we have agents who respond to situations as they occur as well as teams who monitor for events."

"And this organization, is who you work for?" Luke asked.

"No that's who I work *with,* I work *for* you."

Luke smiled, but Buck was serious. This was a man who believed he was keeping the world safe for Luke and people just like him. Buck slid on a charcoal gray blazer.

He watched Luke finish dressing. "Once you're ready, we'll go to the Angels Song and find out the location of your daughter."

"But how do you know that they're a part of it.. I mean…"

"There is a certain signature that these kinds of cults use. They will try and farm their own victims."

"Farm them?"

"Cults and groups involved with outworld entities try to select victims from within their own ranks, or they will recruit an individual and use psycho-manipulation on them until they allow themselves to be victimized. In your case they brought you closer to find out what you knew, who was leading the case, and then filled your head with the idea that your daughter was already dead so that you wouldn't be a concern."

The words slipped into Luke's consciousness. Was that what Genaya had done? She had sex with him, promising him that she would be with him always and completely dominated his mind. Was that the act of a cult member? Or was it someone who as part of the new age community was trying to reach out the only way that she knew how. It's true that he had felt himself slipping away from what he knew to be reality, but was that shock? Was it the desperate grabs of a drowning man at affection?

Luke shook his head. "So we're just going to go and ask them?"

Buck looked at him with soulless eyes. "Something like that. I've already paid for the room, as soon as you're ready, we'll get going."

*That's it? That's all this guy is going to say?* Luke thought.

Luke slipped on his shoes and within moments the two of them were walking out of the motel.

The Witch Hunter's only luggage was the hard skinned case. The most disturbing thing to Luke was how totally unremarkable he looked. Buck's charcoal blazer covered everything completely. With his features Buck looked like an intense individual, but he could have been anyone, a mailman, a car salesman, *anyone.*

Once outside, Buck walked to a dusty white Ford Taurus with a rental car sticker in the window. He put the case in the trunk and got in the drivers side unlocking the door for Luke.

Luke stood there for a moment, not sure exactly what to do. Did he get in the car with a heavily armed "Witch Hunter"? He had seen no identification, no credentials, nothing. Yet there was something to be believed here, his inner voice was leading him on. Luke opened the door and got in as Buck started the car. Within moments they were driving to the nearest gas station.

Buck looked like a machine carefully designed for whatever task was at hand. If he was walking somewhere, it was a lifetime mission realized. If still, he was a statue and while driving he had all the poise of the best Indy racers in the world. It was as though Luke wasn't even in the car, he was scanning the road and checking the mirrors with relaxed ease and readiness.

Luke watched the cement barriers and street light stream through his gaze out the side window. He felt strangely at ease in the car, a sense of being on the right track. The fog in Luke's mind was lifting. The questions began to trickle into pools and then surge into a torrent.

Buck pulled into a service station, but didn't go to the pumps, instead he parked off to the side of the lot.

"I'll be right back." He said as he got out of the car.

Luke's thoughts drifted to Susie. With Susie dead and the possibility that he might be called in as a suspect, things were not looking their best. He stared out the window watching Buck go into the service station's snack shop.

Moments later, he saw Buck walk over to the gas pumps with a shiny new bright red plastic jerry can. The kind of emergency gas can that motorists buy for too much money when they've run out of gas a few miles back. Luke watched him fill it and then nod to someone inside. He put the cap on it and then made his way to the back of the car. Luke felt the pop of the trunk, then a shuffling in the back, followed by a slam.

As Buck got back in Luke asked. "Is that just in case?"

"We'll need it." He replied and started the car.

The drive to the Angels Song was a dream. Luke was someone new, he was fresh. He wasn't the broken victim of Genaya, or the loving father that he had been only thirty days ago. He was a new person , a new alter ego that had broken from the shell.

Buck parked near the entry to the lot, backing the car in. The two sat in silence for a moment. Buck had an uncanny knack of knowing which questions were coming and when. It was the proficiency gained from experience.

"It would be best if you waited in the car." Buck said, turning his steely eyes on him.

"I want to know what's going on, I think I've got a right to know." Luke wasn't sure if this was negotiable, but he was surprised with the tone of his own voice when talking to an armed stranger.

Buck raised his eyebrows, "Well, yes sir, I guess you do."

The Witch Hunter assessed Luke for an instant, then made a silent decision "Alright then, this is what's going to happen. Once we get inside you will lock the door, and turn the open sign to closed, do you understand?"

Luke felt a sudden rush of energy, he could feel his insides shake for no reason but dared not let it show. "Sure."

"All right then," Buck's lifeless eyes blinked once. "Stay out of my way. Your little girls' life is on the line and don't you forget that."

The time for coddling and excuses had passed, now was the time for clear and concise action. The clarity was a nice change. The dream of Genaya and new age haze of his past few days evaporated.

In that crystal moment, Luke knew. The small voice inside became clear. Genaya was a drug. There was always something about her that seemed fake but he just didn't want to see it. Now he was with Buck Wyld; the Witch Hunter, and things were going to be different from here on.

He knew what that small voice was.

*Rage.*

There was still rage inside him, deep down, where all the psychosis and seductive sedation couldn't reach. In the pit of his heart, the spirit of vengeance was lurking. This was the voice that told him to get away from Genaya, and the same one that told him to trust Buck. This was the tiny piece of Luke that Buck was talking to.

Buck took out a small black cellular phone. Luke had never seen one like it before. He pressed a button on the side and held it by the windshield as though the light would power it.

Luke watched him. "What are you doing?"

Buck waited for a reading and them pressed another button to send the reading out. A short, sharp electronic beep and he put the phone away.

"Just phoning home." He said with wry smile and opened the door.

As they got out of the car, Luke felt for this first time that some real answers were coming. Buck went back and opened the trunk, pulling out the new Jerry-can. He slammed the trunk of the car and rested the can on it, then he carefully removed its lid.

Holding the open can, Buck crossed the lot towards the shop with Luke following behind.

*What is he doing with the gas?* Luke thought, but remembered the Witch Hunter's instructions to stay out of the way.

Luke tried to imagine what Buck would say once he was in the shop. What could he say? if Genaya was part of this cult, how would she be made to admit it? There were various fleeting ideas but nothing was solid. They had no leverage.

It was just after nine in the morning and the shop had just opened. It would be slow for a few hours yet. The new age crowd didn't like to get up early, the energy just wasn't right, and they might become useful with habits like that. The two of them walked through the front door striking the chimes and announcing their presence amongst the fumes of Nag-Champa incense.

In the few days that Luke helped with the daily duties of the store, he learned where the open sign was as well as the door lock. He followed Buck through the door, locking it behind him and flipping the sign beside the dream catchers on the display window.

CLOSED, *Please come again.*

Graham was crouched behind the counter putting out the new shipment of amethyst that had come in. Hearing the chimes, he stood up smiling.

"Morning Luke." He said.

Luke was about to return the greeting, but he didn't have time. With the ease of a dancer Buck slipped his hand into a hidden back belt holster under his coat and pulled a silenced Glock 45 caliber pistol. He didn't slow down, not so much as a pause in his stride, as two high pitched whispers spat out at Graham.

The first round hit Graham in the center of his forehead, the second in the cheek. Graham's head opened sideways like a coconut shell, blasting dark gray jelly and clotted meat into a wet smear on the star charts and gemstone maps behind him. His body jerked, went stiff for a moment, and then collapsed with a sound like falling logs.

Luke went into shock, everything slowed down. Buck dropped the gas can when he reached the middle of the shop. It landed on its side letting the golden pungent fluid spill out onto the floor in a great spreading pool. Still he didn't break stride. Holding his pistol by his side, he moved towards the curtained doorway in the back.

*Did that just happen? Did I just watch Graham die?*

Luke followed stumbling behind in shock and disbelief. Buck was already at the door to Genaya's back room when Luke came through the curtained entrance. He got there just in time to see Buck kick the door off of its hinges. A bizarre raspy cry came from inside.

The scream that started out as Genaya's voice, but the pitch shifted, twisting down into a guttural howl.

"Witch Hunter!" The demonic tone called.

The name cut into his Luke's mind severing all doubt, at once he knew Buck was right, about everything. *She knew him!*

Luke willed his legs faster as he chased Buck into the room. He came through the door just in time to see the reading table fly off to the side, shattering against the wall. Genaya, or what he thought was Genaya, was crouched low, swaying from side to side. Her hair was wild, shaggy like some forsaken creature.

Genaya lashed out with an unholy howl ripping from her. In that howl, Luke could hear two distinct voices, a lower one that had a snarling rage to it, and a higher more feminine voice that spit death.

Buck didn't hesitate, he dropped his aim and fired. The .45 slug hit her pelvis, shattering the bone into awkward blocks. Genaya's body crumpled to the floor. Another instant later, Buck grabbed a fistful of hair and dragged her headfirst into the center of the room.

Luke had to say something. He was about to, but he saw Genaya's face. Gone was the feminine lustful face that sold him sanctuary, it had changed from the large eyed beauty that he had made love to. Her eyes were now a wide sickeningly pus yellow, with no discernable iris or pupil. Her mouth was stretching wider and wider with each snap of her jaws, letting a tentacle tongue lash out at him like fire.

Buck dropped his knee like an anvil between the creatures' shoulder blades. Her face crashed into the floor and Luke watched her head bounce hard splintering the wood planks, yet still she was fighting. Luke was a bystander now, a face in a crowd surrounding a terrible happening. His body was paralyzed and his eyes were wide with a numb expectancy.

This thing that had once been his lover, had an unholy strength. She was writhing her arms into a position to throw Buck off of her, but he was ready. Four sputtered blasts from the Glock put single bullets through each of her elbows and shoulders.

Another terrible cry from the pinned creature. Not a cry of pain, but frustration. Both of her arms and legs were useless now, leaving only her body to rock feebly back and forth amid the choking screams.

Buck changed weapons. Swapping the pistol in his hands he pulled the large awkwardly angled knife from his shoulder rig. When it was firmly in place, pressing the blade Just under Genaya's ear, he returned his silenced pistol to the back holster with the same ease in which he drew it.

A new voice came as Buck pulled a small canister from his pocket. The voice that Genaya had coddled Luke with was gone and in its place was a lower tone of madness. Luke didn't know what language it was, but somehow he could understand it.

It was as though he were in a dream listening to the words a tree might say. After waking he couldn't repeat those words directly, but he knew exactly what the tree had meant. This was the first language, the language from before the tower of Babylon fell. The verbal telepathy of the outworld races, this was the tongue of *Thesmulcar.*

"You have come too late Witch Hunter. Soon the great crossing comes! Your kind will kneel to their master." The very tone caused Luke's hair to tingle. The words caressed his eardrums and he felt their filth swimming in his head.

"Soon, Witch Hunter, your kind will no longer be! Nothing can save you!"

Buck pressed a button on the canister gadget and small bright blue flame was conjured from its tip. It was a micro blowtorch. Luke had seen them before in magazines and specialty shops. They ran on butane and could melt a penny if held on it long enough.

Buck shoved the lighter into the base of Genaya's neck. Luke could smell the burning hair, then sizzling pork. Over the tiny torches roar he could hear the sounds of flesh burning. The voice came again, immune to the burning.

"Is this what you wanted to see Luke? Is this the love that you wanted after you have betrayed your wife and loved me? You are nothing!"

Buck made a quick glance up to see how Luke was faring. As a Witch Hunter, he was an old hand at this sort of thing, but civilians usually had a heavy reaction. Luke was still frozen in place with horror painted on his brow.

All his life Luke wanted to see some proof of the supernatural, a ghost, a creature, maybe even hear some phantom footsteps. Now seeing the face of demon on the body he had made love to, this made his mind rend into pieces, if only to spare conclusions.

Buck had to spread the pain out, he switched from burning the back of her neck to the tender flesh in the armpit. A few passes with the blue tipped paint brush and her flesh was blistering and weeping.

In less time than a knife slash, Genaya's face returned to normal. The yellow eyes were gone and the corners of her mouth were bleeding from where they had split to allow the toothy maw.

"Please! Don't kill me! I don't know what you want! Please! I'll do anything!" She was begging.

Her eyes locked on him "Luke! Please! He's killing me!"

Buck spoke, his voice was calm, commanding, and clear. "Where is the girl?"

"She's gone! She's already dead! I didn't…." Buck drew the blade back, cutting her ear off so fast that it popped off her head and landed on the floor a few inches from her face. For first time Luke heard Genaya scream in terror.

Real, life threatened fear.

Buck was in total control. "Where is the girl?" He repeated.

Genaya took a moment to catch her breath, her voice horse from the scream.

" I... I don't know!" She said rasping in agony. Her eyes fixed on the ear. "They never told me.."

"Who never told you?" Buck said, still calm.

"Randolph! He knows! He runs the Temple in New Westminster! Where we did the séance!"

Buck looked to Luke again. "Do you know where that is?"

The best Luke could manage was a frantic nod.

"Right." Buck said.

He dragged Genaya's mutilated body by the hair out the door and down the hall. It was all Luke could do to get out of his way. The store had filled with the sickeningly sweet smell of gasoline. He could hear Genaya weeping as her crippled legs flopped like severed marionette limbs.

He pulled her only as far as the gas can, then dropped her on top of the bright red plastic container and kept walking to the front door. Luke ran past Genaya who was still sobbing in agony on the floor

A bargain book display rack was at the front of the shop, Buck grabbed a text from it as he left. He didn't look at the title, that wasn't important. Calmly he unlocked the door and held it open for Luke's hasty exit, the chimes sounded as Luke fell out into the street.

Once outside Buck pulled the small micro torch from his pocket and carefully lit the open edge of the book. Luke could hear Genaya inside trying to cry out, she was begging, pleading, her words an indiscriminate mesh of "Please!" and "No!".

Luke couldn't take it any more and turned away, back to the car. Tears were running down his face, rage and sorrow were merged now. He got halfway across the parking lot and looked back. Buck waited for the edges of the book to be burning and then tossed it into the shop letting the door shut by its own return spring.

Luke would always remember the sound of those door chimes as the door closed that final time.

Buck had taken two paces when the windows exploded and flames roared out of the shop. It was an inferno spilling out the shattered windows and surrounding Buck in the flash. The Witch Hunter emerged from the orange tongues of flame and sickening smoke that belched out the windows, walking with the same calm purpose.

Something just beyond human, was screaming in the flames.

## Chapter 24

The hallow hound lurched forwards with the Hunting Shard jammed into its arm. Sasha almost felt bad for it, but she would have watched the Skatman skin the accursed thing rather than have a single scratch come to her daughter.

With Babayan sweeping behind it keeping pace, the hallow was making good speed. Clarence was not pleased about spending this much time on the streets, he had long since learned that the longer you are on the streets, the more likely you became a predator's target.

The city was immense. They had been traveling for hours, and still the city stretched without a break in the clustered buildings; a crawling chaos into and around each other.

The hallow fell again. It was happening more frequently now. The pain compliance of the shard was wearing the creatures frame. She was thankful it's voice had given away, at least she didn't have to listen to its cries with every stride. The hallow was leading them to the Craigdarroch Castle, the place of the crossing. They had to get there before the ceremony, and she hoped it wasn't much further.

One of the hardest things to deal with was the lack of time. Sasha could feel herself tire, that was her only measure of time's passage. She tried not to think about it, instead she thought of Luke and Daphne. Thoughts of her husband were becoming a half remembered dream. Small things, details were starting to slip away, becoming numb.

As they walked, she talked with Clarence about the crossover. The barrier between the two worlds had to physically be opened in order for a being to cross between. Their ethereal bodies would be made flesh by the power of the ritual. It would take a tremendous amount of power. Only beings like seraphim could attempt such a feat, and still the preparation had to be perfect in both realms. That meant her daughter would be kept safe, until the ceremony.

*But at the ceremony....*

She couldn't think about it, Daphne was the reason she kept going.

A gurgled hiss from the hallow as it fell again. The rotting Babayan was always present to slash at its back when the being faltered, taking just enough flesh away to spur it on. Behind them, the Skatman was moving with eager anticipation.

Sasha hated him. She would have to die, and this evil priest was her only hope for Daphne. She had to believe he would keep his word, or all hope would be lost.

Clarence was paying more attention to their surroundings watching for signs of danger in the area. He began muttering to himself about getting close to strange wraith pack territory. The building glyphs were telling him a story no one else could hear.

The wraith packs were the different gangs that existed within the near infinite city. A single wraith might be able to pass through these regions without suspicion, but a group this size could cause some interest, and in Abaddon, interest was always something to be avoided.

Wraith packs are unpredictable, insane, or passive depending on the gang. They were always fiercely guarding their piece of forsaken turf. They might greet a wraith and offer them sanctuary within their territory, or they might tear him to shreds, depending on their mood.

They were following their hound through the street when the Skatman jerked his head up like an animal sensing the danger. His rooster familiar immediately jumped onto the twisted hallow's back, forcing it to the ground and holding it in place.

Sasha could feel that something was different here. She could feel probing eyes, with the iron taste of imminent danger. The Skatman stood straight and still, except for the pendulum tilting of his head from left to right. The dense city was around them, the alleyways were far too close together for wulves. The buildings were all over two stories, boarding houses, family businesses, crossing Europe in architecture.

There was no clear path for something to come and attack them, but no clear path to run either. A baby's cage, broken tables and chairs, a few cabinets and wardrobes were laying about the street giving the pages a place to pile against.

Motion.

There, in the second story window.

Sasha could see a face, and then another, and another still. Faces of women, made up thick with lipstick and contrasting blushes, images of faded lust. More faces on the street level now, looking out the windows on both sides. Their expressions blank, like sculpted porcelain dolls, watching them. The first ones began slipping through the doorways revealing their bodies in the green twilight.

Harlots.

She had read about them. These were the prostitutes, women of the night. The whores of the living world often found in alleys and dumpsters, slaughtered by the men who bought their bodies. They had so much essence in them, so much conflicting sexual energy forced down their throats, that upon their death they awoke here in Abaddon with the cold dampness biting at them.

They were juicy, energy rich wraiths and prime targets for hallows, wulves, and just about any other predator. A harlot by themselves would quickly be devoured by any number of creatures, but in combined numbers, they could attack with surprising strength and speed. Even the hallows wouldn't trifle with a wraith pack of harlots.

Ahead of them, a tall woman walked out of the building. She was wearing a long white fur coat, mink probably, and loved by someone desperately. It hung open, reveling white fishnet stockings leading to soiled white silk garters and bodice. Her hair was whiter than her long coat, almost having a light of its own.

Behind her, two large naked muscular men were holding large table legs, broken in such a way to make menacing clubs. Out came more harlots with a subtle shifting in the street around them. There were more women then men, wearing provocative attire that had once accentuated their already appealing forms. There was something in the way they moved. There was no denying the sensuous nature of these beings. Something about them whispered passion, promising forbidden pleasures for the taking.

Many of them held weapons fashioned from the various trash of the living world. Sharpened stakes like daggers, some canes, and even a few whips hung by their sides. Some wore no clothing at all with their naked muscular forms glinting as if oiled in the waning light. Each harlot was synthetic perfection under their smeared colors of face paint.

A crowd of them now, all drifting about softly like snowflakes, keeping well away from Sasha's group. The Skatman was letting his head drift from side to side and shaking his dreadlocks with the slight chiming of his trinkets. Babayan had cocked its wings out, shifting his weight, barely able to control the violence within. Clarence was smiling the most friendly way he knew how, but he looked like a scared pervert on trial.

Sasha focused on the weapons instead of the wraiths, it was easier that way. More than fifty of the harlots were drifting with the subtle beauty of a fish in a tank.

Winker was never at a loss for words. Clarence took off his hat and walked past the Skatman who still stood in his tick tock fashion, stopping short behind the growling Babayan.

"I say, I hope we haven't done anything to offend you, and if we have I am most dreadfully sorry." Clarence was using his best manners, twitching his hat around in slight circles. His voice was swallowed by the harlot's silence, their bodies breaking up his words. Only the sound of gentle swishing papers at their feet as they moved.

The silence stretched onwards, Sasha could feel the tension building with each breath. She tried to focus on the energy within her, that rage that had helped her against the hallows, but the feeling here was different. She was the invader now, amongst a waltz of the desperately beautiful.

"What are you doing?" The woman in white called out. Her voice enunciated, proper.

Relieved with the dialogue, Winker was quick to answer. "We are just passing through madam, nothing more I assure you. We are most definitely not trying to upset you in any way....."

"Why do you travel with the hallow and the corpse?"

Sasha moved up beside the Skatman, the mention of Babayan froze his head in mid tick, dread locks rattling to a halt. His sudden stop rippled through the harlot crowd like a cold blood spray. Clarence was trying to keep the situation as friendly as possible.

Standing beside the Skatman, Sasha could feel the awareness heighten within his body. She never imagined seeing the Skatman concerned. The way he held himself, his mannerisms even in this place, especially in this place, made her think him unshakable. But now there was something human escaping him, an emotion, a sense of protection of his rooster familiar. He dropped his shoulders and brought slight bends to all of his joints.

Clarence went on. " Ah yes well, they are useful to us, to get where we are going, you see. They are really rather valuable to us, but if you like we will take them and leave immediately! We should have thought ahead really, frightfully sorry, What?"

Clearance's words were washing away in the crowd, no open ears for them to cling. The shaman's hands were twitching in perfect time with the fluttering of

Babayan wings. The rooster, a mountain of rotting feathers, seemed to hear, maybe even understand what was being talked about. It's actions were becoming more erratic, frantic in its clucking growl.

The white woman narrowed her eyes, hissing her judgment "You may pass, the creatures may not. They will fade here."

"They must not!" Sasha said, her voice just as commanding as the white woman's. The sound of her voice caused Clarence to rattle so badly he almost drop his hat. He turned with a mixture of surprise and fear shadowed in his face.

Sasha strode past him towards the white woman. She knew that weakness could not be shown here. She had some power of her own and was starting to get sick of all this groveling and fear. Women seemed to have authority in this wraith pack, so she had a better chance than Clarence.

The two guards moved to intercept Sasha as she approached, but the lady in white raised her fur clad arms to stop them. Sasha stopped a couple of meters short of the wraith pack queen.

"These people are traveling with me. They are helping me so that I can save my daughter in the living world. We don't have much time. Please, you must let us pass."

"I must do nothing!" The white woman answered. She dropped her shoulder forwards with visible rage at being challenged. Sasha knew she might provoke a dangerous response, but there was no time left. Her daughter's sand was falling through the hourglass and a bunch of whores were getting prissy about their little chunk of hell.

The white queen continued. "You will take your fellows and leave this place now, while you still can! Go now!"

That did it, now the rage was building. Sasha could feel the power growing within her. A thin smile creased her lips as it came. The queen sensed something and took a step back, making a move that decreed none of them were going to be leaving.

The white queen's two muscular guards stepped forwards to greet Sasha with their large clubs raised. Sasha dropped to one knee, the power in her hands giving off a slight glow before she threw the energy at her attackers. Each of them had their abdomen removed in a blast. The sound of their torn muscles and bone shrapnel mixed with the other harlots' screams of surprise and fear.

She fell back with the Skatman, Babayan and Clarence. The Skatman's long sickle had hacked out three harlots' necks. Two that came at Babayan had been disemboweled, and now the rooster stood in a pile of intestines as the crippled hallow below was whimpering in pain and fear. Clarence was crouched trying his best to put either the Skatman or Babayan between himself and the coming rush of harlots.

*The fight's on.* Sasha thought.

All attacking mobs have a pattern. The mob will gather around the target, those who have the security of the group will charge in. If those who charge in first are successful, then the victims of the attack are torn to shreds. If the first wave attackers are slaughtered however, the entire mob will push back and more carefully plan their next strike.

Sasha threw three more harlot's flesh into the air. The Skatman was a blur of color and steel, awash with the blood of his attackers. He taken four more with the whirling sickle blade, Clarence had never seen such prowess with a weapon.

Babayan killed two more harlots. They had foolishly tried to stab at the creature, only to find that once their sharpened sticks buried in his flesh, the massive beak of the rooster could snap a three inch thick oak table leg, and then take a hand as an afterthought.

From somewhere Sasha was hit in the face. It was harder than any hit in the head she had ever had, but the sting was far less than it should have been. Her sense of combat was growing along with her abilities. An animal sense of tactics had kept her alive and her hands moved with deadly results. Those not destroyed were maimed, those not maimed were bloody, those not bloody had not yet attacked.

She felt stupid for taking the hit, it could have been avoided if she had just bought her fist forward a second earlier. She was remembering something she had never known, brushing up on combat skills that she had never learned.

The Skatman was crouched low, back to back with Sasha, Babayan made the third leaf of a deadly shamrock with Clarence hiding in the center. Around them, a blossom of dead harlots with fresh wounds glistened. Sasha's hands clenched in tight fists were glowing like embers, causing the fresh blood to leave at trail of steam.

The white queen was nowhere in sight, more battle hardened harlots came to the forefront. Almost all women, but these were the weathered ones. The harlots that had been on the street before this territory had been taken.

A couple of these harlots carried ancient knives, long wicked implements of pain that they held with expert skill. Clarence knew the rarity of weapons in this place, and to see themselves surrounded by a group brandishing actual weapons was a death sentence. Thigh high boots, black leather bodices, and lace were swirling around them like insects building terror in the twilight.

A howl.

*A roar.*

The scream of a new thing tore the air, shaking the buildings around them and ripping into their minds. The harlots knew that scream well, the scream of an infant child as heard from within the womb.

Clarence knew of the harlots' strange relationship with the chyldren. The chyldren's constant search for motherhood, the source of life, had always kept them near harlots. He knew tales of chyldren coming to rescue harlots in times of distress, even taking on wulves. But this time, the harlots weren't in danger, they clearly had the upper hand, and still the chyldren were coming. Half of the harlots vanished before the howl's echoes stopped fraying the air.

The Dogs arrived. The first ones crept out into the street with their lips curled back, teeth catching the glowing green light like icicles of agony inside their gaping jaws. At least the size of lions, their hair a matted thick gray with shades of color rippling over them like water.

As a second and third hound crawled from alley. There was no difference in species here, when the fourth dog came, the last of the harlots vanished from the street. They had been helped by the chyldren in the past, but chyldren are fickle things, powerful and unpredictable and could be very cruel.

The dogs were swinging their heads, seeking danger and ignoring the cluster of blood-spattered shamrock of wraiths holding still in the street. Sasha knew they were all in plain sight, the Dogs had seen them, but didn't care.

A chyld wedged it's way out of an alley, pushing some of the loose brisk into the street. It was humanoid, in that it had two arms and legs, but like a gorilla both in body and motion. The lumbering formless creature stood over 15 feet, a monstrous bulk of sinuous muscle, terrifying and powerful.

When looking at human muscle, it has definition, finite size and shape, but this

**216**

was not so here. Huge hulking sinew had been developed giving it's shoulders muscle that ran halfway down the arms, biceps of unequal length on each. Huge abdominal muscles twisted around to the chyld's back, each so impossibly huge that they might burst.

If they had to fight it, Sasha knew they might have a chance. The Skatman had abilities that neither Clarence or herself understood, and Babayan would no doubt get at least one good strike in before being utterly pulverized. Her own abilities were getting stronger, so maybe, just maybe if the chyld decided to attack, at least one of them might be able to get out of there alive. That is, if they could get past the dogs of course.

All thoughts of survival were erased when a second and third chyld came from behind the first. Not as big, but close, lumbering like great gorillas over the mangled harlot corpses. Another chyld, then another, these silent pink behemoths were surrounding them.

No two of them were alike. Each of their muscle patterns, like markings, distinguished them as individuals, but there was no body hair, genitalia, or facial features of any kind. Vaguely round heads melted down into their vast hulks without a mouth to scream with.

They did have eyes, large and bright like a newborns, with fantastic colors showing dreams of what they could never be. Gentle eyes, expressive orbs that looked out with terror and wonder. Monstrous sculptures half finished by God.

Sasha couldn't tell how many of them there were. She counted eight of them crammed in a circle around the party, shoulder to shoulder, still leaving a twenty foot opening for them to stand. She could hear flesh scraping against brick; still more chyldren were coming. Behind the first line she could see a second wall of flesh forming.

More dogs were coming as well, impossible to tell how many. The dogs had dropped their curled lips and were cycling through the openings at the chyldren's feet, brushing against them in a reassuring fashion. They paused only for a moment to affectingly lick their gargantuan masters, then returned to their circulation like wind in a forest of legs.

Clarence was staying very still and trying not to hyperventilate. He was failing but silent as his body rose and fell with each rapid breath. The Skatman crouched with

Babayan at his feet, stroking and straightening out loose and broken feathers on the bird. His hands worked slowly and cautiously, rubbing the dead thing in slow calming motions while Babayan snarled. The trembling dread locks over the shamans face made it hard to see which way he was looking, a life learned skill to cover the whites in his eyes, but Sasha could tell he was acutely aware.

The chyldren were watching them. *No, they were all watching her!*

She could see them looking past the Skatman and Babayan, past Clarence to touch her. They were curious, wondering about her. Sasha felt emotions and thoughts outside of her body, swirling in a mass. It was like standing at a family funeral for a child she didn't know. Such sadness was waiting just beyond her reach. A thin barrier of skin, and pain reflected in their eyes.

A child is like a god in that there is no limit to what they feel. These warped reflections of young lives still had their feelings, desires, and innocence. Sasha fought back the storm around her, isolated for survival, for feeling in this place was spiritual suicide.

They parted their shoulders to allow another chyld to press through into the clearing. The group stepped back slightly to give their brother room. Sasha could see terrible rope burns around it's tree trunk wrists.

A trickle of recognition turned into a flood. This was the chyld that the hallows had captured, the one that she had helped. Its eyes were wide and wanting, moist as though ready to weep. There was no mistaking the desperate pleading within its eyes, but Sasha didn't know what it wanted.

She took a step forwards towards the scarred giant. There was no fear here, no anger or threat lurking just outside of sight. The sense of sorrow she felt went past her concern for herself, yet she knew she was safer here at this moment, than ever before. Reaching out her hand ever so gently, she touched the great column that was this chyld's arm, and her mind exploded.

Pain, loneliness, sorrow, confusion, all these emotions and their crippled kin surged through her body like voltage. She shut her eyes tight but the tears erupted down her face. She almost collapsed from the weight of it. She cried out in despair, a slur of cutting vowels explaining pain. Her cry washed over the crowd and a choir returned from them in reply.

With no mouth for voice, the noise was like a whale song, sweeping and deep, each voice circling the other in an alien melody. The circulating dogs stopped and threw back their great heads, adding their own voice to the song. They had heard her painful yell, and in their own way they were speaking, trying to comfort the chyldren.

Clarence was in awe. He had heard some wraiths refer to this as "Calling The Mourn". The woeful sound that the chyldren made, heard for impossible distances through the perpetual night. Even with as much time as he had spent wandering in the realms of the dead, he had never been this close to a pack of chyldren as they made this sound. He had a number of theories of why they did it, but the reason was so apparent now listening, seeing, and feeling it so close. It was to comfort each other.

Sasha had been many things in her life. She had been a friend, a lover, a professional, but more than any of these she had been a mother. In being a mother, she gained an intrinsic understanding of things not said, the ability to cipher chaotic emotions and stop emotional pain with subtle nuances. The greatest weapon she had in the arsenal against despair was the ability to hold. To be held was to be shielded, cleansed and healed. It was the mothers' power to refuse pain and obliterate suffering.

Now she did the only thing a mother should do, the only thing that she could do. She threw her arms around the great arm of the chyld and held it with all her might, willing peace and love, becoming a sinking sailor bailing out an ocean of pain.

The moment that Sasha put her arms around the great creature, Clarence watched its expression change. Its' eyes went wide, peaceful, relieved from the pain if only just for a moment. With Sasha firmly attached to one of the chylds' huge arms, it reached out with the other to touch its brethren.

Its fingers made contact with the closest giant. Whatever emotion Sasha had given, spread out from each one to the other. A chain of mothers' love, connected by flesh, each chyld losing the expression of pain as their mournful call faded away.

Clarence had never seen anything even close to this, but even over his awe he knew the nature of essence, the true currency of Abaddon. He was worried that these chyldren might drain her, take away every drop of her being, yet he couldn't see any signs that she was being drained. Sasha was holding the chyld as best she could, taking the pain of it and giving as much comfort as possible.

They stood there a long time before she eventually broke away, not violently but slowly, like the end of a lovers kiss. Her face was wet from tears as she looked at the forest of chyldren around them.

Something had been shared between them, some knowledge had been passed.

Sasha had felt the pain of their loneliness. She wanted to help them, heal them, take away the pain, and connected her love to them. But in doing this, the chyldren also reached inside of her, feeling her pain and thoughts.

The thoughts of her daughter were exceptionally powerful. In the desire to take the comfort from Sasha, they made her their mother, and now Daphne was their sister. Sasha's conviction to save her child, the reasons, the people who were hunting them, her experiences, everything transferred across the bridge of flesh to the chyldren, and they shared it amongst themselves.

Sasha wiped the remaining tears from her eyes and brought focus back, a merciful change from these great ones' reality. The chyldren were all looking at her with stoic, strong eyes. These were not the eyes of pain, they were eyes of rage, anger, and vengeance. The scarred chyld crouched low to meet her, warrior eyes looking out. Unsaid and unspoken, Sasha knew that the chyldren were going to help.

Daphne had become sister to the chyldren of Abaddon

## Chapter 25

This was some violent fantasy that didn't really happen. Genaya was still at the shop, Graham was still behind the till, and neither of them at this very second had their flesh searing off. Luke had been stunned, dazed as they drove. The killer who drove beside him remained silent, keeping his constant vigil. Luke dared not look at him, but thought of what had happened, what he had just seen.

"You better pull over." Luke said, and the Witch Hunter smoothly pulled the car off the road. It had just stopped when Luke opened the door and began vomiting. After the first lighter blasts of splatter passed, then the heavy heaves started to hit.

"It's a hell of a thing you just saw there Luke. A hell of a thing." Buck said.

*How the hell could he have done that, how could he have....*

" Y'know it's a funny thing..." Buck continued. "People hear about stories in the Bible and legends of Atlantis, and they have no doubt in their mind that those legends are based on fact. But you show people evidence, current reports of sightings, supernatural or outworld influence, and they will deny it until the day they die."

The drawl in Bucks' voice took off some of the edge. "What you just saw in there son, was the face of the enemy. Those are the things that have your little girl."

Luke slumped back into the seat letting the door clumsily close. He felt like two slugs moved in to where his eyes used to be. "What just happened there? What did I just see?"

Buck relaxed for a tenth of an instant, a wry smile and distant eyes made him human for the same length of time.

He took a deep breath "Well son it's like this, I don't subscribe to any particular religion, but a Christian fellow might say that woman had a demon in her. The new age crowd would say she had an angry spirit. All I know is that she had allied herself with outworld entities and was responsible for killing innocents."

"What the hell do you mean outworld entities, like that was an alien or something?" Luke didn't mean to raise his voice, but Buck didn't notice or at least never showed it.

"Don't think of the world I'm talking about here as earth, I mean the world we exist in. The moon and the other planets exist in our world, our dimension."

The slow gravel in his voice was calming, in a tombstone kind of way.

"See, if something comes from planet X to earth, they are from this world, but if some creature or being is summoned or crosses the barriers of this dimension, It's an outworld entity."

"So you're saying Genaya was from another dimension?"

Buck pulled back out onto the road continuing to New Westminster, the hum of the car and passing roads helped calm Luke's guts.

"No she wasn't, but whatever was inside of her was. There are people who think that they can gain power or wealth by letting things take over their body, harboring dangerous spirits and entities. It's up to folks like me and GOD to stop them."

Luke was almost believing him until the last part. "God?"

"Yes son, G.O.D., the Governmental Outworld Detection Agency. It's been around awhile, but we keep a low profile."

"So you're like the men in black who show up at alien crash sights."

The slightest hint of disbelief in Luke's voice, a faded echo of mental resistance. Buck gave him a quick snap in the face with his eyes and Luke remembered the lighter.

*Oh shit...*

"The guys in black suits don't exist, I do. You're already trying to forget what you saw back there."

Buck's tone wasn't angry, but cold. The same tone he used when he tortured Genaya. "That happens everyday across the world. People allow creatures from outworlds, invaders, to access our own. They've been doing it for thousands of years, but its only in the last few decades that we've been able to keep it under control."

"I'm sorry I didn't mean..."Luke said.

Buck didn't notice. "How about this; didn't you ever wonder why after hundreds of years of ghost stories and spiritualism, it all just stopped in the last seventy five years?"

Luke didn't want to make him more angry but he had to try and make sense. "It's the age of science, most of those things are myths and legends."

"Legends based in fact, not myth. The age of science that we're so proud of, is the area that we focused on openly. Back in the 30's and 40's, there was a huge interest scientifically in what they called 'Occult Studies'. People were having séances, trying to bring things across, you wouldn't believe the shit that went down. After the nazis started using outworld technology in the war, things became a lot more serious,

G.O.D. was formed and we've been going ever since."

Luke remembered the ghost stories he had read in a few of his books on World War II. It made such perfect sense. He had studied the ideas of Alistair Crowley, Madam Blavatsky, H.P. Lovecraft, and the like. All of them from the turn of the century. There was a huge occult interest in North America but nothing past the 40's.

*Why was that?*

There was no war on American soil, why would those at home give up their interests? People still had their pastimes. He had tried to find papers, articles, anything released in the respected community on the supernatural, but there was nothing.

It was as though everyone just forgot about the ideas of the occult. No more professional mediums, no more experimental research. With the end of the war everyone got back to their lives, no one noticed the shift. With the horror of war gone, the desire wasn't there.

The first World War was horrifying enough, more in many ways, yet the occult interest was still there after it ended. Why did it stop after WWII? Bucks' answers were filling in the gaps justly a little too well to be maniac rantings.

"Why are you telling me this? If you are part of some secret world government hit squad, why not just take me out as well?"

"Who says I'm not going to?" Buck grinned.

*The smile, was that a joke?*

"Relax son, you got spy syndrome. First of all, I'm not in the organization any more, and who the hell are you going to tell? The media? They'd laugh you out! Hell, you watched that woman change and you barely believe it yourself. There are no dark secrets anymore, everything is out in the open with a thousand versions of the same story mixed by crackpots everywhere. No one would know the truth now, even if they heard it. You'd scream about the GOD, and the guy next to you would scream just as loud that aliens walk among us."

Luke felt a sudden empathy for all those folks he read about in magazines, toting tales of fantastic things, trying with all their heart to warn the world about whatever. Who was right? They couldn't all be right, *could they?* He felt fear seep into him, a creeping terror like pain medication wearing off.

Luke tried to control the panic in his voice "The police are going to find the bodies at the store, they're going to come after us."

"Easy son, they're not coming after us. The proper people know what was involved there, and the whole thing is going to blow over nicely."

Luke remembered the strange cell phone call in front of the shop. "I thought you said you weren't in the organization any more."

"I'm not with the agency, but it's a little different with me now. It's best that you don't ask."

Luke took that as the conversations' end, which was all he could handle anyway. It was clear the Witch Hunter had done this for years, god knows how many people he had this conversation with, and it was perfect, rehearsed. He knew the next wave of emotions that would hit even before Luke felt it.

The car sped along the freeway up over the Port Mann Bridge. Luke was going to ask how he knew Susie, but decided against it. He had enough on his plate right now to digest. Things shifted so easily into place from here, everything was simple.

His confusion was the result of his world being dislocated from trauma, and then being put back in place. The slow rage within him securing control of all of his faculties. The cocoon that had been around him, the confusion, the pain and lust of Genaya were all kindling before the flame beginning to grow. He had been used.

They had taken his daughter, and he walked right into their hands. He gave them all the information that the police had, as well as telling them who their enemy was. Because of him Susie was dead. *No!* He couldn't heap that onto himself, he wasn't ready to take on that much pain just yet. It wasn't his fault that she was dead, *it was theirs!*

They almost had him too, how long would it have been before he would have joined them? How long before they dragged every sacred moral and sense of self from his mind, leaving him a confused slave? And slave to what? To who?

"Why are they doing this Buck? Why did they kill my wife and take my daughter?" Luke said when his thoughts couldn't spin any faster.

"Can't say for sure, but no doubt it's the usual reasons. Something told them to do it, or they think it did, and now they follow its' commands. They're cultists, probably level three at my guess, doesn't much matter I guess. Cultists are for killing."

"What do you mean by levels?"

"There are four levels of cultists; level one are groups of people who listen to rock music and screw each other claiming to worship some twisted god. They're usually run by groups of people with nothing better to do. Satanic rockers, pissed off teenagers, that kind of thing." Buck said.

"Level two cults have a leader, some charismatic person who uses drugs or charisma to gain influence and power. The leader is the heart of the cult, but his followers are deadly, and will do whatever he tells them. Charles Manson, David Koresh, that crowd.

"Level three cultists actually have rank structure and multiple locations across the country. There is one supreme leader, but he's got priests who set up churches. They're well funded and a significant threat. That's what I think we are dealing with here, an L3 cult."

Luke thought for a moment. "So what's level four?"

"L4 cults are global, they have influences in ways that affect everyone's lives. The Roman Catholic church has been a L4 cult in the past, but they're more of a religion now."

"What's the difference?"

"Between what? A religion and a cult?"

"Yeah."

"Religions are based on peace, equality and tolerance, their philosophy. Religions lead by ideals. Cults rule through dogma and force. Most of the world religions have cults within them."

Luke couldn't argue, it was simplistic clean logic. It was so simplistic that the majority of people would have a hard time accepting it.

Buck went on. "Cults throughout history were responsible for the most hideous of atrocities. The Nazis were a cult. Did they have outworld worship and control hidden in politics? It was the other way around. Cultists kill, rape, murder and molest children, all to satisfy their leader, whoever or whatever that may be. They spread their teachings like a virus, and once infected its rare that these people can be cured. Cultists are killers of the mind and body. They are the predators of our society, and there is only one way to deal with them"

"Cultists are for killing." Luke repeated.

Luke knew there would be those who would disagree with Buck, those who have never seen a child victim of ritual abuse, those who have new age ideals about peace and rehabilitation. There would be those who would call Buck's methods "barbaric" and "unjust".

Justice is a human concept, there is no justice in the wild. There is no justice for the old, sick, and young, preyed upon by wolves. There is no justice in war, death, or plague. Justice is a religious idea, a noble ideal that man tries to live up to; but it's a lie. Where was the justice for his daughter? For his wife? For him?

*Fuck justice. Cultists are for killing.*

Luke felt his illusions rot and fall away. The reality of what Buck had done was the only logical choice to get results in the fastest possible way. No time for politics now, they didn't know how much time his daughter had left and Luke was fresh out of mercy.

"I'm going to need a gun Buck."

The Witch Hunter expected that response as well. "In the glove compartment. A Glock 23, 45 Caliber, thirteen rounds and one in the pipe. Its got specialty ammo, if you need more I'll give it to you. Safety is on, just pop the lever and you're good to go."

Luke opened the glove box, amongst the new car smell and the plastic wrapped rental agreement, he found the pistol in a concealable clip-on belt holster. He pulled it out keeping low and steady, pointing the weapon at the floor of the car. He had done some shooting before, as a teenager with a few of his friends, but with nothing as serious as this weapon.

He liked his action movies as much as the next guy, but these kinds of weapons had their place, and their place, was in the movies. He pulled it from the soft leather holster. It was new, as if it came with the car. It felt heavy in his hand, the plastic handle of the weapon was thicker than he expected. It had to be to hold thirteen impartial killers.

"Don't put it on here, wait until we get to the target location." Bucks spoke casually, as if telling a child not to spoil dinner. They were in New Westminster now, not far from the house. Luke guided the last few movements of the car until they passed the previously invisible heritage building. His driving was gray and easy.

Buck turned off the main road onto a sister street, letting the car drift to a halt. The small gate was shut, an impromptu 'Closed for Renovations' sign hung over the low steel spikes. The side was slightly obscured by cherry trees but Luke could still see something odd, something was different about the house. All of the windows had been blocked. A few blinds, mostly curtains, and even cardboard had been put up to keep the light out, or perhaps the darkness in.

The house wasn't inviting anymore, like a kindly old man after his war criminal past was discovered. It stood there silently mocking him, a testament to the lie Luke had loved. He hated it.

"Weapon." Buck said, holding out his hand. Luke handed him the pistol. From a pocket inside the blazer the Witch Hunter took out a cylinder and began screwing it into the end of the pistol. A silencer.

Buck started his rapid instruction. "This is how we are going to play this. You are going to stay behind me and you are going to stay close. You do not fire at anything unless its coming at us from behind. Do not walk backwards, you will only trip. Look over your shoulders, alternating from left to right to make sure there's no blind spot. If you do engage, fire two rounds at every target. If the bullets have no effect then start yelling, other than that keep your mouth shut. If we get separated, get out of the house and go straight back to the car the same way we came in. Do not try and find me, you will only get shot. Do you understand?"

It came fast, but Luke held on to the key parts "Yes." He felt weird saying it like a new recruit trying on his voice. Buck took the strange cell phone from his pocket again, he punched a code with lightning speed and paused watching its tiny monochrome screen. One moment then another. Finally, what he waited for arrived. He hit another button brining the phone up to his ear.

"Witch Hunter, *N 49 02.028 W 123 04.68*, Large house with stone wall on corner, suspected C3, S3 to S5, twenty minutes." Then silence as he heard reply and returned the phone to his pocket.

"Leave the holster here, you won't need it." He said and got out of the car.

The two jumped the low stone wall and crossed the lawn to the house. Luke felt that same surreal feeling from the shop creeping up his spine again, he forced it down. Thoughts of Daphne and his wife kept him sharp. Buck ran casually across the lawn, like a man avoiding rain. Luke was trying as best he could to keep the cannon held by his leg, away from the street.

Buck unbuttoned his black blazer and jogged up the steps. Luke was too close, he held back a bit, feeling horribly awkward. They were almost at the top of the stairs when the fear hit, coming in shocking pulses like heart beats.

It came as questions. *What if...? Is this..? Can I..?* Buck had expected that as well, he was moving fast to beat the fear before it had a chance to build.

In all the movies Luke had seen, the police or the hero would always go up to the front door and then pause, listening inside or forming a plan. If there were two of them, they always took up positions on either sides of the door to throw around some witty banter.

This wasn't the way Buck did things. He had run across the lawn, climbed up the stairs and gathered speed as he crossed the small porch. No pause, no dialog, no waiting, he just kicked in the door. The moment his foot left the ground, there was a transformation from stern soldier to savage killer. His kick split the frame and shattered the stained glass, the door blasted open with a thunderous crash.

Buck hooked his thumb into the quick release holster under his coat, the MP5-SDK submachine gun slid out, unfolding the stock and locking into place at his shoulder. He crouched low, turning rapidly from side to side, swinging the weapon with vision fixed through his sights.

Something moved. A little old lady was standing in the hall when the door flew open, thirty feet away and caught by surprise. She was wearing a period dress matching the house, a long dark dress with a high Victorian collar with a spider web shawl draped over her shoulders.

The was the sound of slapping metal as Buck fired a three round burst into her head, smashing it and sending pieces splattering against the walls' many framed pictures.

The meeting room to the right was clear, the coat room the left as well. Luke remembered the thousands of hovels and hiding places he saw in the building. If they knew that Buck was coming they would have had a chance, but they didn't know. Buck was stepping over the old woman's body before it stopped twitching, they could hear voices from further in the house.

Further in and down.

Luke had to run to keep up. He was doing quick sweeps of the rooms after Buck, just to be certain, it felt like the right thing to do. Passing over the still twitching body of the woman he almost slipped in the growing pool of blood creeping down the hall. Doors swung open to reveal closets and storage, and then closed again. A fourth door was opened revealing a stairway straight down.

The light and voices came from below just past an angled landing. Buck broke into a rapid trot going down the stairs, the weapon in his hands, and an extension of himself. The voices below were confused.

"Did you hear that?" One voice said amongst blurred responses.

"Ingrid, what's happening?" a voice called hearing the door open.

The voice was familiar, sounded like Randolph. But he wasn't sure. Luke was close enough behind Buck to see who it was before the shooting started.

The basement was a wide open space, an amazing contrast to the network of tunnels above. Eight or nine foot ceilings and at least forty feet wide, a near perfect square. It had been converted into a dark temple, painted black with candle stands in various places to cast their light on a sprawling blasphemous symbol on the floor.

There, in various states of undress, were five men and seven women. Luke recognized Margaret from the séance, she was already undressed and laying in a half copulated pile around the now naked Randolph.

*Cultists.*

A split second freeze frame where they looked up to see a stranger with an automatic weapon previewing them through a gun site like a spurned lover. Then Buck squeezed the trigger.

Short controlled bursts, two and three rounds at a time ripped through the crowd. Buck picked his targets carefully, dropping those who were standing first. Three fell with ripped out faces in the first instant, two more the next. There was no chance to scream before corpses were piling on the floor.

The older predator Margaret was in the copulating mass, she didn't scream, but growl, a conjured sound from another being living within her. Buck fired the rest of his magazine into her body while grabbing a fresh one from his rig. Luke watched the bullets blossom red splashes as they ripped through her naked chest. Her freckled breasts rippled with each bullet, jerking her body back and then collapsing like a cut marionette.

Buck let the one magazine fall, slamming the next on into place and fanning the action to chamber the round. With the weapon loaded and Buck now off the last stair, he squeezed the trigger chopping the sexual pile laying around Randolph. Geo, the madman from the séance, was instantly on his feet and charging Buck with blurring speed

The MP5 Buck used a Brass and Glasser combination of ammo. The solid brass didn't deform, didn't change shape on impact, and didn't stop for any kind of armor. The Glasser rounds were like mini bean bags that exploded sending tiny jagged lead fragments doing hideous tissue damage.

It was a muscle spasm later, and Geo had a hole in his chest big enough to throw a cat through. Even with his chest opened, Geo tied to keep going, trying to advance without his heart or lungs. Two steps, then two more, and he crumpled as a carcass.

Randolph lost his mind, wailing and curling up in the blood spray of his brethren. Buck had changed magazines a second time before the echo of the sliding metal faded. Randolph was weeping, naked with his erection, in a pile of current and soon to be corpses. Luke felt revulsion like never before, so vile he could taste it like the floor's dried semen on the roof of his mouth. He turned away in disgust.

Buck went through the drills, by the numbers, as always. His voice solid and commanding.

"Where is the child Daphne Edwards?"

A few seconds passed. It was a few seconds longer than Buck was willing to wait.

A three round burst ripped into the Randolph's quivering shin, the leg splinter in red wet fragments. Randolph let out a scream so loud Luke was sure everyone in New Westminster must have heard it. His leg hung by smashed strands of muscle as he joined in the dying throes.

A sound from behind. Luke spun, it was another woman, Kim. She was hiding behind the altar. Her eyes locked with Luke as he looked through his gun site. Luke would have liked to demand to know why they had done this. What were they doing? Where was his daughter? But his body wasn't hearing any if it. He squeezed the trigger spitting a bullet at her with an unsatisfying burp through the silencer.

Her body was caught and thrown back against the wall. Her eyes staring wondrously wide over the fallen strands of her dark hair. Dying eyes of confusion, fear, death. She slumped down leaving a dinner plate sized red smear on the wall as she glided down.

Luke couldn't hear anything. This was the first time in his life he had ever shot anything. She was new, she couldn't have been a member for very long. Maybe she wasn't a member, maybe she was a dupe, just like he was,. Maybe he shot a person just like himself,

*Maybe… … maybe… … maybe…*

Bucks voice grabbed him off the self induced torture rack and brought him back to Randolph's sniveling wounded form. The blood from the recently living had covered the floor now, obscuring the blasphemous symbol that had been scrawled there.

"Where is Daphne Edwards?" he said.

This time Randolph didn't wait. "She's at the Craigdarroch Castle in Victoria! The ceremony is tonight! That's all I know! I swear to god that's all I know!"

*I swear to god.* Buck thought, Its funny how those caught come crawling back to thoughts of god.

"Please! Don't kill me! Please! …Please."

Luke swung the Glock back on the bleeding cultists form. Randolph could only look at Buck, he couldn't make his eyes focus on Luke. Last night made him incapable of begging from his victim. He wept pitifully, trying to stem the flow of blood from his leg.

This was the man would help his daughter die. Who spoke of help but instead brought lies and deceit. This was a man who touched his little girl, and helped those who killed his wife. This was a disgusting traitor to the beings of this world, a traitor to his own soul. This was a cultist, and cultists are for killing.

Luke pulled the trigger, a solid brass round made a small hole in just above Randolph's right temple, exiting just below his left ear not much bigger. This man was guilty, this man had to die.

No more 'maybes.

## Chapter 26

Sasha sat on the shoulders of the rope scarred chyld.

The chyld had volunteered itself to be her mount. He led the other chyldren, behind the Skatman and Babayan who kept the hallow at a good pace. The chyld shared a link with her, feeling her emotions and having constant but subtle connection to his new found mother's wishes. He would touch the other chyldren to distribute the commands, ideals, warmth and experience of being so near her. She could be named the Moon-mother now, not the Moonchild as the Skatman called her.

They followed the hallow hound through the streets of Abaddon. The chyldren swept along either side of her. They were a strong group, each one clinging to the other as family. The dogs fanned out ahead moving through the distance, gliding like sharks through the murky light.

They were moving at a much greater speed, no more dodging wulves or being afraid of other wraith packs, now she and Clarence rode like Generals on the backs of fleshy tanks into combat. Twenty feet up, the city looked different from up here.

She could see shapes and forms shifting about on the rooftop, an occasional image of a cat or a hungry bogeyman peering out into the street, not daring enough to try anything. From this height, the contours of the city appeared through the glowing mist. Like rising swells of waves, the dim ground stars showed hilly regions of the city as they traveled.

With apparent safety, not thinking was hard. The thoughts and images of the last while were taking their toll. Perhaps it would be better for her to be destroyed, or whatever it was that Clarence called it. Her life was just a dream now, the memory of her family nothing more than pain. How could she return to her husband after this, knowing what she knew now?

She didn't know where Craigdarroch Castle was in this realm, or what would the plan be once they got there. Would they just walk in and destroy the place? That wouldn't return the Skatman to the living realm or save her daughter. No, there had to be another way.

The whole purpose of this was to return the exiled angel Abaddon to the living realm, so the dark Houngan must have had a way to change the ritual, use it for his own means. The Skatman no doubt had an idea, some method of reversing the ceremony, or diverting it some how. Whatever his plan was, she could tell the voodoo priest was in this only for himself

She wondered what sins she was committing in helping the Skatman return to the living world. Man had made deals with demons to beat death since the beginning of time, the only thing that changed was the demon's name. She wondered what his story was, how he got here. It didn't much matter, as long as he could save her daughter. All things led back to Daphne.

The buildings changed as the flesh caravan traveled deeper into the city. The houses in the outlying realms were smaller, standard wraith flophouses, nothing too ornate about them. Now deeper in the city, the buildings were more grand, larger doorways with sweeping arches. Churches with tall spires reaching up into the darkness and out of sight.

The areas between the buildings were growing larger as well. Courtyards with walls of stone, and iron appeared, with tangled black vines that subtly shifted, pulsing with a life of their own.

The procession was moving out of the packed ghetto regions and approaching the higher class sections of Hell. With large stone stairways leading to foreboding manor houses, Sasha couldn't help but wonder what atrocities happened within them to bring these places across.


On these streets of nightmares there was no uniformity. Some structures were Victorian, others more colonial, others still an odd mixture of old and new style. There were more light pools here, which in turn meant more essence was involved.

Entire sections of wall would glow, rather than the tiny pools she was used to. The properties lining the streets with their broken walled borders, shattered like old slaughterhouse stocks watched the column advance. The chyldren were uneasy here. These areas were the streets closer to the Killing Fields.

The Skatman and Babayan followed behind the hallow as it stumbled. With his black dreadlocks covering his neck and that mountainous coat covering the rest of him, the Skatman looked as inhuman as the hallow that he followed.

The dark priest was feeling things much more strongly here. He wasn't as relaxed, his motions were more desperate, jerked, erratic, spurring the hallow on with increasing severity. He had taken out his sickle and was carrying it openly, ready to use it at a any instant.

The Skatman made a subtle twitch and Babayan pinned the hallow to the ground.

Having no vocal cords left it silently screamed, waving its wounded arms. The Skatman crouched low and held his hand out to stop the column.

Sensing the needs through Sasha's mount as brushing hands touched, communicating the commands the others lumbered to a halt. Chyldren, by their nature are not cautious beings. They have nothing to fear in a group so they are rarely cautious. Here they could sense the danger, they could feel it lurking unseen from attic windows and pointed spires.

With Babayan holding the hallow down, the Skatman ran off, staying near the center of the street and keeping watch on the broken walls for wulves or worse. While the buildings were not as close together, there was still as much, if not more, wreckage littering the street. The holy papers had pooled themselves thick along the courtyard walls, and most of the noble furniture in the street was still intact. This was a shunned path, not well traveled by any creature.

The extra wreckage laying about provided cover for the Skatman as his nimble bare feet carried him along. He leapt over a table with the grace of a panther and landed with deadly silence. Onward, the Skatman vanished over the rise in the road, now scouting without the use of the hallow.

"I say, we must be very close now" Clarence interrupted her thoughts from the shoulder of the next chyld. "Its very dangerous out here, we're getting much closer to the Killing Fields. Not many wraiths come this way, not many at all."

"The Killing Fields?" Sasha asked.

"Yes, the war zone of Abaddon. You see, every now and again we should be able to hear the sounds of them, gunfire carries far here indeed."

The feeling of safety had giving her a much needed pause. Sasha had been too focused on her own thought to listen to the subtle murmurs of the chyldren. Now, as they were all still, she could faintly hear the echoes of explosions, infrequent blasts like an occasional drip. The Killing Fields; perpetual war that ringed the horrors lurking at the heart of the dead realms.

The wulves, bogeymen, thespians, hallows and all the other things that Clarence wrote about, were only in the outer rings. Here, close to the Killing Fields, there was a whole new level of agony, a whole new type of darkness that waited for them.

Clarence was taking notes about everything, the walls, the layout of the ground, how the twisted black hair that could have been a living grass tangled across brief

234

courtyards. Sasha felt colder here, the dampness was deeper, more biting.

For all the ground they had covered it was only a fraction of this place. There was no way of knowing how vast this place was, no scale which to measure this place by. This wasn't a city, this wasn't a land, this was a world, a dimension. As far as terror and death can reach, those are the borders of Abaddon.

A distant blast echoed faintly, and a shape moved ahead on the road. It was the Skatman, returning at the same pace at which he left. This was a good thing, no doubt he would be returning quicker if something was giving chase.

"Please let me down." She said to her massive mount.

The chyld was reaching up to help her before she finished the sentence. It was hard for her to look in those eyes, she could only handle so much pain. The chyld set her on the ground as gently as a snowflake. Clarence was set down as well, and the chyldren were touching each other, engaged in a silent conversation amongst themselves.

Babayan maintained his post atop the writhing form of the hallow. The thetacheric shard jutting into its arm didn't understand that they had stopped. It was only seeking, bringing the compliance of its host through pain. The Skatman came close still holding his sickle low.

A quick fluid gash and he slit the throat of the hallow. The body jerked spitting its pussy ichors onto the ground. Sasha winced involuntarily as Babayan clucked happily, drinking and tearing away at the flesh. This was the moment that the rotting rooster had been waiting for, the hallow was his now. It could only writhe with decreasing strength, it still had a few good jerks left when the Skatman spoke to Sasha.

"Da Skatman be seein' da place dey be bringin' da powa', gatherin' strength for crossin'. Come now. "

Cautiously, Clarence and Sasha followed the Skatman back over the rise on the hill. They got halfway up the slight rise when she realized that the chyldren were coming along as well. They mimicked her action, each of them trying comically to crouch low and run silently. Not much chance of that, but they were trying.

She wanted to tell them to stop, but then caught herself wondering why? It's not like they couldn't protect themselves. The rope scarred one had taken over as a leader. He was the closest to Sasha, therefore he was in charge. The motley bunch crept as fast as they could over the hill. The Skatman wasn't so concerned this time, he was looking for a vantage point and found it

A few hundred feet over the rise there was a break in the buildings and walls, letting Sasha and the others look out across the churchyards and ornate garden sculptures. The dogs could sense the danger here, they stayed closer to the chyldren, not straying as far in the ruins as they had been.

The streets were still there, but they had started to blend with the concrete of walkways and the cobbled stones of church paths. These buildings, placed like fallen toys made mismatch cover, but through the opening she could see what the Skatman was pointing to, a solitary mansion sitting on a hill.

Behind it there was nothing, it looked like an end to the city. She could see the buildings continue off to the sides, but they had reached the inner edge of the city and now looked out across a great border of dark putrid mud. Gunfire rippled from deep in the mists, this was the border of the killing fields. Sasha couldn't be sure but she swore the mansions' hill was getting bigger, as though the ground had snatched this house away and carried it out into the sea of filth.

"I say!" Clarence whispered, as though afraid the mountain might hear him. "I think it growing! The hill itself is moving upwards."

The Skatman nodded. "It be growin' Mista Winka, da powa' o' Abaddon."

"I don't understand." Sasha said. "How is this hill growing out of the ground?"

The Skatman twitched his head towards her revealing his whole face, the whites of his eyes barking at her. "Abaddon be powa' Moonchild, about da gatherin' of powa', t'ings in da living world, an dead wantin' dis place to be a crossin', gateway to da otha' side."

"Ah I see." Clarence nodded. "Right now in the living world, there are people gathering power at this exact house, making it ready for the crossing so it affects the essence shadow the house casts here"

"But this never happened before Clarence, when I awoke in the theatre…"

"That was an accident, you were never supposed to be here. They're doing it differently now, making the point of crossing the site for the ceremony. It's far less likely to have an error, you see.."

He looked back at the mansion on the growing mound, he could see dark shapes going in and out, milling around it. Hallows, hundreds of them, and more were gathering. There was no mistaking their twisted forms. "I shan't think they will be taking any chances at all actually." He said with a shudder.

Sasha watched the hallows seething like rats waiting for a fresh batch of sewage. More and more were coming out from the city. Perhaps they were to witness the crossing, perhaps they would cross as well. If Abaddon wanted to conquer, maybe he needed an army. Her own death was close, she could feel it, but the thought of Daphne in the clutches of beings such as these kept her strong.

She mustered her conviction. "So what do we do now?"

" Now Moonchild," The Skatman said stroking Babayan, "Now we wait."

**Chapter 27**

Luke was silent in the car. Today he watched a woman he had made love to be burned alive. He shot a man who was begging for his life when he knew killing him wouldn't make anything better. It was a vengeful, hateful killing, but still he felt nothing.

The Craigdarroch Castle is on Vancouver Island. A tourist attraction on a hill, overlooking the city of Victoria. He and Sasha had seen the Craigdarroch house when they were last on the island, they wanted to check out the strange old place, but never got around to it.

Heritage houses close early and who knows what goes on behind those doors after dark. Buck didn't burn the house in New Westminster, they just got the information and left. But Luke felt a sense of urgency as Buck kept checking his watch, as though he placed a bomb. Since then, they drove in silence,

Luke listening to the static in his head.

*I don't feel a god damn thing.*

The made it to the ferry terminal by six. Getting lucky, they got the ferry right away. People generally didn't stay in their cars, the sailing was more than an hour. The ferries had a small café and seating upstairs to show off the ocean, and walkways for the passengers to stretch their legs.

Luke followed Buck up the metal stairways and the two made their way to a chunk of railing outside, looking out over the water. Buck stepped away for hours, Luke's perception of time was gone. When he returned he had foraged two cups of coffee and a couple of sandwiches.

"You should eat something son, you're going to need it."

Luke mumbled something like "Thanks."

He thought the coffee might be possible, but the sandwiches were a challenge. Buck devoured his sandwich in methodical rapid movements, but the coffee was a sacred thing for him. Luke forced his own sandwich down, rationalizing that he did need to keep up his strength, it was the first meal of the day after all, if one could call the ferry food 'a meal'.

The sedated roar of the water off the ship's bow and the steady distant drone of engines were comforting. The ocean, vast and deep, barely made mention that they were moving at all. The cold swells of water had no choice but to let the steel invader cut through. An occasional seal sentry could be seen in the distance watching the ferry's progress.

Luke felt small, empty. The Buddhist calm that comes after perceptions are shattered. The coffee was warm in his hands, it felt good going down. He still didn't feel alive, or even human, but after the coffee heated his guts he was a good fake.

Buck had been silent, keeping track of the time, making sure that they would reach the ferry, and therefore the island as fast as they could. The sun was setting and his daughters' chances of survival were fading with the light.

This was all a drill to him, horrendous murder, screaming victims, how many cultists would die to save an innocent? As many as he could kill, but he knew Luke was green, this would be hard for him.

"They're not like other people son" Buck said. The tone in his voice suggested that they had been involved in casual conversation, though neither spoke in two hours.

"It's not like these are folks who worked for another government, or follow a different religion. These were human beings who betrayed the human race to serve outworld creatures. You can't forget that." He watched the words fall into Luke, but didn't hear them hit bottom.

Buck continued. "Those people that we took out today were going to keep killing, keep murdering innocents, all to appease something that wasn't even part of the natural world. They weren't killing for an idea or a belief Luke, they did it just to get energy for their own selfish needs. They were traitors to all humanity."

Luke felt something inside of him agree with Buck. It's not that he felt guilt for the killings, it was that he felt nothing at all. Later, Luke knew he would be able to decide whether what he did was right or wrong, but for right now, it just was. Not everyone was going to see it like that, he had the prophesy of consequences looming.

"What is going to happen Buck? How can we cover up a basement full of dead people? The police are going to track it."

"Not so." Buck said and took the matte black cell phone from his pocket.

"I make a call with the coordinates where an operation is taking place. There are clean up crews on standby to handle these kinds of things."

That was too big, it didn't make sense.

"You mean there were people in vans waiting for your call to go carry out the bodies?"

Buck smiled, Luke's naivety was amusing him . "Again, too many spy movies. No black vans, or cleaners with bathtubs of acid. The police will show up, do an investigation, and through various means it will get explained away, or taken out if their hands. The authorities know who did the action, its just a matter of moving the case around enough to make it fade away."

"That doesn't make sense Buck."

"How so?"

"You can't just kill a room full of people and walk away.."

"Oh? Why not?"

"There's going to be news media, people will ask questions...."

"Bullshit. Hookers are stuffed in dumpsters every day by the dozen all over north America. Homeless people die in alleyways and are left for days. No one cares about what's going on, even right in front of them."

" But the news...."

"Reports what we allow them to. Its easier now than it ever was. The information age has made it possible to bury anything. You're not going to be arrested Luke, no warrants will be issued, even the local cops involved will be told this case is being taken higher. Everyone will walk away."

"Just like that?"

"Just like that."

The idea was incredulous to Luke, impossibly simple. Buck finished the last of his coffee, the wind not fazing his perfect sculpted flattop. "It's how we've operated for years Luke, And it's how we will continue to operate."

Buck turned to him now with understanding in his eyes. "There's a war going on Luke, a war that's been going on for longer than both you or I have been alive, but there's no reason to involve everyone. People don't need to know about a danger they can't prevent. Why look for a planet killing asteroid, unless you can stop it? The people on this ferry don't need to know about the things that feed on us as a race, their chances of being taken are very small."

Buck looked back out to sea. "But when it does happen, we're there to pick up the slack."

240

"How active are you guys? I mean, how often do you do these kinds of things?" Luke asked.

Buck flashed his leather smile again. "More than you can know son, but that's not important. What is important is that we're going to get your little girl back. You're going to keep living your life and pick up the pieces, because you have to." Buck took a deep breath of the air, " Let's get below deck."

A few others were milling about below, reorganizing day trip luggage or defiantly avoiding the descending crowds. Luke watched through the windshield, wondering how many massacres never made the news. Even if they did, who would care?

How many strange fires in industrial sections, or natural gas explosions were cover-ups? What about ships sinking? Or tornadoes? What if we never did go to the moon and all the crank science on the tabloids was true? What was truth? The modern media age made integrity obsolete, and disinformation the order of the day.

"Try not to think about it too much son, it won't help things. You'll have your daughter back and in three weeks all this will be a dream." Bucks words snapped him out.

"How can you be so sure? How do we even know if Daphne is still alive?"

"I know because of experience, because they took your daughter for a reason. Until tonight she's in no danger, in fact she's probably having fun, playing games with them, that sort of thing. They think she's got some kind of key, so she's very valuable. As for you, you're strong. There will be a few nightmares, a couple of panic attacks, but you'll pull through it alright."

So casual, so routine. He made it seem like the only logical thing that could happen.

"How about you Buck? What's going to happen to you after this?"

Bucks head jerked over, finally Luke asked a question he wasn't ready for. "Oh hell, this is pretty standard for me. I'll go on, doing something else, for someone else."

Luke for the first time felt an immense sense of pity for the old war dog. How long had he done this? How many had he killed? How long did he fight?

"Do you still get nightmares about this stuff?"

People were returning to their cars, oblivious, blind to everything but their own world. Buck's thin smile drifted, taking his eyes with it. For less than a moment his age showed through.

"I haven't had a dream in years, you learn not to after awhile."

It was another twenty minutes from the ferry terminal to the city itself. It was 8 pm, the sun was setting and night was almost upon them.

From the moment the ferry docked, a switch had been thrown in Buck's head. They had made it across as fast as they could, but the ferry was beyond his control. Now with the sunset, and the road before them, Buck was back in charge. Buck sped towards the city, what took twenty minutes was going to take ten.

They were five minutes from the city when Buck started his briefing.

"Ok Luke, here's the plan; we hit this house differently from the one in New West. The ceremony is most likely going to be in the basement, so that's where your girl is. I'm going in first, you will wait sixty seconds and follow me. I'll cut the power to give us cover, but its going to get hairy in there in the darkness. Your task is going to be to find your daughter and get out, that's it. I'll give you the keys to this car."

"What? How are you getting out of there?"

"Don't worry about that, I've got it covered. You hit the house and head for the basement, if your daughter isn't there, return to the car. Don't fire unless you absolutely have to. Your retrieval, leave the rest of them to me."

"What if…"

Buck cut him off. "If your daughter is not in the house, return to the car, and sit inside. I'll be interrogating for information regardless. We can deal with it from there."

"And if she's dead..?"

"If she's dead, do not touch the body and wait for me at the car. If you do find a body be sure it's your daughter, these guys might have more than one hostage."

It was a makeshift plan, fast and loose, but Buck seemed sure of it. This was it, the deadline may have already passed. "Thanks Buck, even if this doesn't…work out…"

"You're welcome son" He said.

Whatever reason Buck had for doing this, Luke's thanks were not a part of it, but he did try to be as gracious as a soldier could be. Time was fleeting, sped along by the

**242**

desperation. On the ferry Buck had grabbed a brochure that listed the whole history of the Craigdarroch Castle.

Luke had thought about if they shouldn't just call the police, let them handle it. The cultists would have prepared for that, a whole lot of gunplay and his daughter still dies in some ceremony. No win. Inside Luke's head Buck's voice was answering questions.

How about the swat team? Guys who crash houses for a living? Still, getting the police to follow a lead they got by torturing a possessed woman, he was sure the police would just love that. The reason they were so successful at the New West temple was speed and surprise. If these cultists had known a Witch Hunter was involved, they would have faded into the cracks.

Buck grilled Luke as they drove. The tension in Luke's voice was nonexistent in Buck's. Steady, firm, gravel truck questions came to make sure he knew his tasks.

"What are you doing in the house?"

"How long after me do you go in?"

"What are you looking for?"

"Where is the most likely place for the ceremony?"

"What if you don't find your daughter?"

Luke followed each with his response, and subjected to a careful polish by Buck. There was money in a case under the seat along with another gun if he needed it. Buck's briefing was comforting, secure, and confident. By the time they saw the city, there was no doubt in Luke's mind that Daphne would be in this car in less than an hour.

Luke pulled out his silenced Glock and held it the same way a child would hold a sacred toy. He could feel the power in the black polymer grips seeping up his arms, into his chest. The power of the gun, the power to kill.

He had to get Daphne back, all things led to Daphne.

Once in the city, the house was impossible to miss. The city's lights were surrounded by water and wilderness, except for one monstrous house on a hill.

It was called a castle, but in truth it was somewhere between a cathedral, a mansion, and a gigantic tombstone. The people who built it never got the chance to live there, madness and death filled its history from the start. Its' ominous, looming spires of textured stone reached to the sky like an arthritic nightmare. Flood lights shone up illuminating the walls and savage peaks.

Deep stone walls and strangely ornate peaked windows led up to turret rooftops that seemed to point power at the sky. With no symmetry to speak of, the turrets clustered around the house like a cage, with wicked points ready to impale the sky. This was a dead place, locked away on a hill and should be forgotten, yet the hand of man kept this architectural corpse from rotting.

Whoever was looking after the place had tried to make it look as appealing as possible, but it was a losing battle. Even the photographer who made up the ferry brochure could only manage a few shots that made it look gothic rather than evil. Trying to make Craigdarroch Castle look appealing was like painting a skeleton up as a clown, its smile would always be tainted with insanity.

Victoria was behind them now. The map from the ferry brochure showed them the most direct route. As they got closer the lights of the monstrous house were swallowed by thick trees on the hill. If Bucks' reactions were not honed, he never would have been able to stop for the sign.

A road closed sign came out of the darkness to greet them. A few feet behind multiple vehicles had been parked making a subtle wall. There was no way to take the car, they would have to walk from here. It was about three hundred yards to where the houses' driveway was supposed to be.

They got out of the car.

"They've set up a perimeter" Buck said " And an obvious one at that, not so good."

"Why?" Luke asked slamming the car door doing a final check, his pistol was locked and loaded.

"An obvious perimeter like this is made to keep people out, there're not worried about leaving in a hurry. They think that something is going to happen to give them power." Buck said.

The Witch Hunter opened the trunk of the car and pulled out a black SWAT-style tactical vest. It had large pockets around the front that held massive drum magazines. Luke guessed that each one had to hold more than eighty bullets. He strapped on the vest and pulled another drum magazine from the trunk, placed it in his weapon, and gently closed the trunk.

Buck fanned the action of his MP-5SD and shot Luke a glance. "I'm running ahead, by the time you hit the house I'll already be engaged. Grab your child and go. I never want to see you again son, so this is goodbye. Wait sixty seconds, then go get your daughter"

The time was at hand. He met this man less than twenty four hours previous, and in less than a day he had found his daughter's location and exposed the truth of the cult's lies. There was no way for Luke to say thank you. His feeble attempts weren't nearly good enough. A simple thank you could never make up for returning a child to their parents.

He looked back to Buck, a loss for words. Buck gave his grim smile and winked, then took off in a flat run. Luke was on his own again, with the sounds of a witch hunters rapid footfalls fading up the hill, the darkness had him.

"1, 2, 3, 4 ,5..." He counted.

Tortured with anxiety Luke began his count. With Buck gone there was so much to go wrong. The *what if's, would's, should's* and *could's* were all running round robin in his mind. What if Randolph lied? What if his child wasn't here at all and this was another decoy?

"26, 27, 28..."

*Oh god, let my baby be alive.* Luke said a silent prayer to any god who would care to listen. No parent should ever see their own child dead. Sasha's corpse almost killed him, and with a gun in his hand he didn't know what he would do if he found his little girl.

"42, 43, 44..."

*....What if she's dead?* What would be the point? Why even go back to the car? His reason for living would be gone. But living or dead, he would take back his daughter from these creatures that took her.

"57, 58, 59..."

It was go time. Luke broke into a run following Buck up the road.

His daughter was waiting for him in the hands of madmen. It was time to go get Daphne. The rage came, he channeled its power down into his legs to push them harder. He thought of hideous things, the horrible things he might find done to little Daphne, and the rage grew still. By the time he crested the hill, Luke Edwards had become someone else. Luke was now the child of vengeance, hate, and deception realized.

The spotlights on the sides of the mansion were gone. a few dying breaths sparked from a transformer almost hidden by the trees. From the brief light of raining sparks,

Luke could see tell tale wreckage of a metal twisted by gunfire. Buck probably fired the burst one handed at a full run.

Craigdarroch Castle was massive, the deception of distance had been removed and the true size of the stone fortress could be realized. The base was surrounded by a balcony, a failed attempt to make it look more inviting, but all it did was add darkness to its doorways. The rest of the gray stone was a testament to a mad architect, trying to combine Victorian and classic gothic architecture with a farmhouse feel. The spires and stretched smokestacks, coupled with deep angled rooftop points made no wall flat.

The dream of a noble home turned into a church of madness. The hill continued to climb, leaving a shifting base that elevated the house level. It had to be at least a hundred feet on each side with no less than five shifting floors.

Wide sweeping front steps, the kind graduation classes and weddings were photographed on. Luke ran for the front steps, sliding the safety off the pistol. Buildings this size would make anyone feel like a child. His legs pounded against the stone as he climbed.

The dark overhanging roof of the balcony greeted him and the massive double doors lay crippled, hanging on shot-out hinges. Buck had been here, leaving a gaping hole for him to follow, like bloody teeth under a streetlight.

The last of Luke's blood was replaced with adrenaline as he stepped through the doorway, greeting the now familiar scent of musty old books that came with these houses. The traces of cordite in the air had become Bucks tell-tale cologne. A blood soaked figure in white robes was lying a few feet into the house. He must have met Buck at the door, and probably didn't feel it.

Luke expected to see a large foyer, or a greeting room just within, but it was just a small room leading to three hallways, one on each side and one ahead.

Single candles had been lit in the house on ironwork floor stands, each one had the symbol of Abaddon, the tattooed symbol, articulately worked into iron. The small foyer candles had gone out, knocked over by Buck, but the dim flicker of others came from the halls, all three of them. With the doors' breeze, these candles cast shifting shadows everywhere.

Impasse. *Which one to take?* He trained the gun on the seeping corpse who still twitched occasionally. *Which way to go? Where was down? Where was Daphne?* Over the thunderous roar of his own breathing there was a sound. A cough, a gagging

246

sound like a man vomiting came from the hallway ahead. *Good enough*.

Luke kept his pistol low and walked down the hall. His eyes adjusted to the candle light of the house. He could see shapes, forms, shadows with golden definition, but not much else. He wasn't creeping, he wasn't running. He was walking mad, looking for a stairway.

In a dark patch, where an extinguished candle once stood, another white robed figure sprawled across the hall. Luke stepped over him going deeper still. The white robe was in his 40's with a silver Abraham Lincoln beard. He probably would have looked quite distinguished, if his throat hadn't been shot out.

A noise behind him. Luke spun to see a slight of a shape, a robed shape, which was all he needed. He fired two shots. The first caught the robed figure in the chest the second snapped back the head throwing the hood off and spinning the cultist backwards into a pile. A few jerking rustles and the body lay still.

He kept moving. Further and further in, the candles providing enough light to sense by, but not much else. Open doorways showed darkrooms where ten or twenty men could have hid, but Luke pushed through it. The only focus was to find a stairway that led down. His own footsteps were announced by the squeaking floor but the fear wasn't there for him now, he was the thing to be feared now. He was the invader, the killer, the terror in the darkness, and he had come for his little girl.

The hallway turned up ahead and a candle sat next to a ghastly woman's' portrait. Someone thought she was worth remembering, but Luke had the urge to put two rounds through it. The candle in the corner was flickering towards him, which meant another breeze. He rounded the corner to an open doorway.

A stairway leading down, *that's the ticket.*

Buck had been through here and left his crimson and cordite traces. Luke closed the door momentarily revealing a bloody white robed figure with the symbol emblazed on his chest, clutching a sword in a death grasp. No doubt a guardian to the gateway. Buck had caught him in the face with a burst.

The breeze was coming up from below. Luke wanted to break into a run down the stairs, but a tactical voice inside stopped him. Very close now, no sense screwing it up. There, deep below, he could see a light from the end of the stairs. It was a straight line down, maybe thirty feet to the candle light below, but the hallway was black. The candles, if there had been any, were extinguished in the stairway.

**247**

The crash of a falling body, not from below but from above. Buck was clearing the upstairs. Had he already been down in the cellar? Surely he couldn't have cleared it so soon. He may have left it for Luke, but he only had a pistol. It didn't matter. Luke plunged down the darkness towards the candle light. If there was someone down there with his daughter, they would die, even if he had to rip out their guts with his bare hands.

Halfway down the flight, there was something on the stairs. Something soft and wet, that was rapidly losing body heat. Luke awkwardly stepped over the carcass. Perhaps Buck had come this way, or made a casual burst down the stairs that caught this bastard by surprise. The light was getting closer. The smell hit him before he turned the corner, the sulfur sweet smell of gunfire. Buck had been down here.

There is a moment before realization that breeds fear. It starts when we are children looking at wrapped presents under the tree or perhaps waiting for a grade on project you have labored over. There was so much riding on what happened once he turned the corner, his very soul stood at the edge of the abyss.

He kept moving, he had to. All things led to Daphne.

The room was illuminated by larger ironwork candelabras like the ones upstairs, but far more elaborate. The room itself had to be more than fifty feet square, but it was hard to tell from the long sheets of black fabric hanging from the ceiling. The ceilings were high at least fifteen feet high and painted black. With the candlelight in the room it seemed like there was no house at all, only an ever expanding darkness. Above them was fabric that hid the walls and that could hide so much more.

Luke came to seek out death, he found it.

\*                                        \*                                        \*

Buck Wyld left Luke at the car and took to the darkness. The kid would be fine, he knew that. He would have some trauma but hey, don't we all? He felt the pavement hard under his feet grab at him, trying to weigh him down as he ran against gravity. How many times had he done this now? Another house, more hostages, more cultists waiting to die, so eager to greet their Outworld god.

It made him sick.

As a soldier you're supposed to be unbiased, it's a job, a profession just like any other. But after seeing too many children skinned and hung for blood, Buck began to get a little jaded. Luke's daughter might be alive, maybe he could beat them to the punch this time. The watch was saying 8:34, He knew it was likely that she'd still be alive, maybe tortured as cultists tried to get as much energy out of her tiny body as they could.

Most people who a have to deal with severe trauma in a day to day existence isolated themselves from it. They make dark jokes and become detached. Buck wasn't that way, he held it close to him. Each victim of a cult was his own child, his own wife, his own loved one. The agency set him up with a psychologist once, not a bad guy, just doing his job, following orders and all that. Buck felt bad about breaking his face when he told Buck he should release his anger.

He did release it. He was the best at what he did, you don't get this way by treating this work as a job. This was after all, a war, and innocent people like Luke's wife and daughter were dying. Buck didn't repress his emotions, he let them flow. Hate, anger and rage were a constant of being for him. These cultists wanted a god to come for them? One did. His name was Colonel James Buchanan Wyld and he was the burning voice of vengeance. The Witch Hunter. That's who he was, that's what he did.

Transformer; top right, hiding in the trees. He swung the MP5 up and fired three bursts of four rounds in a staggered pattern into the can. It roared in protest bleeding sparks, then the floodlights ahead went black. Darkness; his home.

*I'm coming for you.*

The drum magazine held a hundred rounds, he could take out an army of cultists with this mix and he had two more drums in the vest. The last light from the electric floods faded, the assault was on. Buck couldn't feel his legs as he crossed the black earth to the front door, gravity had lost its encumbrance. This was why he kept it so close to him, this was why they were all his children.

To hit as many houses as he did, to kill as many people as he had and be able to stay sharp, you needed hate. Fear makes adrenalin, but through repetition of danger one becomes accustomed to it. Buck couldn't remember what fear was, there was only the hate to give him adrenalin now. He hated this house, and everyone in it.

Speed, surprise and aggressiveness of action. He flew up the steps three at a time. As he crested the stairs the main entrance double doors came into view. The top two hinges got short bursts the bottom hinges got two more. The rasping sound of splintered wood and the reapers perfume of gun smoke filled his mind.

*I'm coming into your world now.*

No pause, no hesitation he threw his body into the doors. They screamed and fell to the inside like huge broken planks. A five point roll into the foyer and he hit something soft. A white robbed cultist was standing too close to the door. He was probably coming outside to see what the power problem was. The doors hit him and he landed on his ass. Buck rolled right on top of him practically laying on his chest.

*BRAAAPP!* The muffled slapping of gunmetal over the silencer. Buck fed him a burst. The first kill of the house, nothing to it. Into an isosceles kneeling position and another one was in the hall.

*BRAAAP! Have a face full of fuck you!*

They caught the white robed figure in the throat, good thing too, no screaming, just that gargling whisper and the body fell. There was another sound, deeper in the house. A chanting from the basement.

*"G'fawn myleh xantahedra dandrathu, dandrathus selohim Abaddon!"*

*Reap the whirl wind.*

Over the gun site, he swung left and right down the two adjoining hallways. They were lit, but god only knows why. Into the heart of darkness, straight ahead, that's where his prey was hiding.

Down the hall, the feeble bastard was still clutching his throat as Buck leapt like a panther over his body landing lightly on the other side. The gust of air from his jump blew out the iron work candle lighting the place.

A weird picture of a woman at the end of the hall almost got a burst. *No dice.* He rounded the corner and there was another white robe standing with a rune on his chest and a sword in his hands.

*"G'fawn myleh xantahedra dandrathu, dandrathus selohim Abaddon!"*

*BRAAAP!* Teeth and face sprayed along the ceiling in a wide ark.

*Fuck off. You get to lie there and twitch. Fancy costume and a sword, what do you want to guess this guy was a ceremonial guardian?* Buck thought.

Doorway to the right. The thought of throwing grenades down there was appealing, but there was one life to be spared somewhere in this house, and grenades never cared who they ripped up. He had to do it on foot.

Buck swung the guardian's door open, it made a muffled thud as it got kicked by the dying throws of the guard.

*Whatever, you weak pouge!*

**250**

A robe was halfway up the stairway, right next to a candle. He could see the wide eyes questioning.

*Who are you? What was going on? What was happening?* The eyes asked.

*I'm a Witch Hunter.*

*Everyone is dying.*

*It's your turn now.*

*BRAAAP!*

*"G'fawn myleh xantahedra dandrathu, dandrathus selohim Abaddon!"*

Red blossoms stitched his sternum from neck to crotch, his flailing hands took out the candle. He didn't quite fall fast enough to get out of Buck's way. A stomp on his chest as Buck ran over him down the stairs.. He left the robe jerking in the darkness.

*Not bad, less than a minute into the house and I'm getting into the chamber.*

He dropped to the bottom of the stars in his now instinctive combat stance. Nothing new here, big room, hung veils and a whole bunch of assholes in white robes. The standard sick scribbling on the floor, and an altar at the front. An altar with a child on it, a naked child, and no one near her.

*"G'fawn Myleh Xantahedra Dandrathu, Dandrathus ........"* They saw him and stopped in mid chant.

There it was, that permanent pause that he had expected, that beautiful moment when everyone in that room knew exactly who he was, and what he had come for. The truth of their own depravity was revealed to them in that moment.

*Caught red handed with a child on the slab. You're fucked.*

Judgment had come as Buck shouldered his weapon.


For the Witch Hunter, the systematic execution of a crowd was an art. The first instinct of a gunmen is to spray the room in fanning motions; this is wrong. It's true that you do longer bursts, eight and ten rounds rather than the usual two or three, but the crowd will try to run, take cover and escape. You have to sweep the edges of each side, keeping them in a cluster until its their turn to die. Of course there was always the fanatical ones who charge, thinking they could beat the gunman to the punch.

*Yeah right,* Buck thought, *Even with supernatural boosting you're not going to beat 1800 feet per second.*

Fire low on the ones that charge you, catching them in the hips. They drop, broken like screaming starfish, opening up the targets behind them. You want to be certain that you know where the other exits in the room are, so that the ones not so keen on dying for their master catch it next. Short burst, long burst. Left, then right, back to the chargers, Alternate your firing rate, this also saves ammo and keeps your weapon from overheating.

Watch who falls, see who catches it and where. As the crowd thins out, there are going to be those who try to hide, faking death in the pile. Buck had an old scar on the back of his leg where he fell for that trick early in his career, it's a lesson he never forgot.

The last ones who were standing out of the thirty or so when he started were behaving pretty much as expected. Screaming, crying, trying to plead for their lives as fast as they could before the flying steel ripped them up.

The last one was the best. This time it was an older man who had remained motionless throughout the entire shooting. In his hands he held a leather satchel, a set of sharp things to kill with, his robes were older, finer, with a red rune embroidered on the front.

This guy had to be the leader. He was standing there looking at Buck, quietly cursing as his brethren fell. Maybe he was trying to cast a spell, or conjure a power greater than anything Buck had ever seen. No pause for you, no quarter given. The old guys' head came off. His was the last body to fall.

He could hear the little girl softly sobbing on the altar. No blood, she was alive right now. The first drum dropped out into Buck's hand, he swapped it with one in his vest and pounded a fresh one in.

Time for a quick sweep. Everyone who doesn't have a visible wound gets one in the head. If you can only see a limb, that limb gets shot; if it moves then trace it out.

There was a woman laying untouched, Buck drilled her in the head twice. She'd been faking it, fresh spasms, you can always tell. He moved around the pile keeping his senses tuned to movement, not only on the pile but these hanging fabrics could hide a lot.

Around, up by the altar. A young girl, maybe five was strapped down. He'd seen the style before, they would have cut her up with a set of knives called a Centodd. Leaves a hell of a mess, takes awhile to die, even for a child. From under the leather blindfold he could see the steady stream of tears.

"Daphne." Buck said, as softly as he could. He saw the child tense up when she herd the name. Positive confirmation. There was another stairway going up on the other side, it was all about Luke to get his girl out now.

"Your daddy is coming to get you baby, he'll be right here."

He left the child with the blindfold still on, it was better that way. Supple straps held her in place, leather ones. He dropped the Spec-war dagger form its kydex sheath and left it on the alter, Luke could use it to cut her free. Not bad for him, not only is his daughter still alive, but he's getting a Glock with silencer and a sweet combat blade.

The odds were unlikely that any cultists would try to make it down the stairs, but Buck made damn sure that the pile in the room was really dead, no one to try and finish the ceremony. He heard the crash of a body falling by the entrance up stairs, Luke was in the house, in less than two minutes he would be down here. Things were going well, this meant no one had to be questioned. Just a straight kill zone, it was all gravy from here.

*BRAAP!* Another cloak in the stair way lost his stomach.

*BRAAP!* The one at the door lost his chest and collar bone.

*Gravy.*

**Chapter 28**

"For the Lord himself shall descend from heaven with a shout,
with the voice of the archangel,
and with the trump of God:
and the dead in Christ shall rise first."

*- 1 Thessalonians 4:15*

Here on the edge of the killing fields the sense of death seeped into Sasha's every pore. The essence of it surrounded her, soiled her in such a way so she could never be clean again.

The hallows continued to gather. They were crawling over Craigdarroch Castle, waiting on its balconies, perching themselves on the rooftops. In and out they moved, seething like bees at a hive.

Sasha wondered how long they had to wait. How long before they attack the building? There were so many hallows here now, and more were coming every moment. The Skatman crouched, watching. His body was poised, ready to leap, and he kept his familiar close.

The chyldren were all sitting away from the opening, touch talking with each other. They were near Sasha and that's all that mattered. Their dogs stayed close, keeping subtle vigil. With so many hallows, Sasha wasn't sure if the chyldren would be able to handle them.

Clarence was transfixed by the house. He was muttering softly to himself about how extraordinary it was, and never seeing the like before. The hill stopped growing and Sasha saw how bright it had become. The entire house was in iridescent glow, as though painted with the pools of light so that nothing was left uncovered..

As she watched the house sitting atop the hill like some great scab on a boil, Sasha could feel a shift in the very acrid stench of the wind. The air was becoming charred by energy, by essence. The hallows could feel it too. Their vile movements and sickened actions became more feverish, more desperate as the fogs over the fields of filth swirled. The hallows were building their mad passion, something was happening.

Sasha tried to look more at the house than at the creatures. The closest ones were more than three hundred yards away across the broken terrain, but she had seen what the hallows were like, and what they were like when they got excited. Such visions were not for eyes of the living, or even the recently dead.

It was hard to tell one from another, but she guessed at more than a hundred, maybe even more than two hundred hallows, all gathered waiting, watching, looking out into the fog of the killing fields. The forbidden ecstasy in their voices mounted each other, building into a climax of sound. A nation of more than a thousand hallows. The hallows began to moan. Their voices carrying a lewd chorus across the landscape, echoing and funneling through the streets.

Something was moving through the shroud of mists covering the field. The sounds of the gunfire, and distant explosions had died. The faucet of dripping blasts that cut the silence became less and less frequent, a momentary ceasefire in the field of eternal war. A ceasefire while all things fled.

A ceasefire brought by something terrible moving.

Sasha looked out into the shifting mists. She could see shapes billowing in the fog, great twisted worms coming out and collapsing on each other, mile wide screaming faces contorted in agony, hideous things that revealed only shades, and were gone. These were different horrors for each who looked at them, terrors revealing themselves like animals in the clouds.

One of the hallows spotted something and the wail of his brethren became a deafening drone.

That's when she saw it.

There in the distance, a small black dot emerged from the shroud. Dragging itself through the mud, a laboring single figure perceptible in the distance.

"Abaddon be comin' now." The Skatman whispered. "Abaddon gather powa', den we be takin' da crossin'."

Sasha wasn't sure what he meant so she turned to Clarence for the usual translation. Clarence was staring, his eyes wide with a fear that only deeper understanding could bring. He had realized something in its entirety, and paid for it with extra cost, his sanity.

"What is it Clarence?"

No response, he only continued to stare at the dark figure coming from the deep mists of Abaddon.

"Clarence.." She reached over and touched him. Clarence snapped his head over, turning his gaze on her.

"Ah yes well, ah…" He was flustered, even after being dead for over a hundred years, the habits of his British manners stayed strong, he composed himself as quickly as he could.

"I say! The creature that is known as Abaddon was at one time a seraphim, long before the fall of the creature that we know of as Lucifer or Satan, in the Christian dialect. That's the devil you know."

Sasha nodded, waiting for his point.

"Well, you see the hallows are coming from the city, the outer rings you see. This means that they are wraiths, or some species of wraith that inhabits the city. But you see, that thing out there…" His voice broke for a moment

"That thing is coming from a deeper core of this place, the areas beyond the killing fields, so its not just a seraphim, or a wraith, or a mage. That thing was ancient when the war in heaven took place. That is, that being would be to the devil, what the devil is to us. Do you see?"

Sasha took another look at the hobbling black shape. It was larger than a man, perhaps ten feet tall. Onward it came, drawing closer to the house. Only a few hundred yards beyond, the glowing mist behind it showed a clear profile as it moved.

It was a humanoid, tall and slender, a skeletal thin figure that took each step with labored pace. On its back hung two broken wings. What once must have spanned thirty feet or more, were mere ragged bones, barely held together and dragging limp behind this thing in the mud.

Its' approach was being celebrated by the hallows fevered pitch, some of them were throwing themselves off the top of the Craigdarroch Castle celebrating this figure by smashing their bodies into the earth.

She wondered why the hallows did not go out to greet the object of their desire, why let this thing continue its crawling pace. But the hallows themselves had no desire to go near the shape. Perhaps they all felt the power within, and none dared to approach it. The followers of this damned god were within the glowing castle, calling it on.

"Moonchild, why ja stand for Babayan?"

Sasha turned to see the Skatman's white eyes burning through his dread locks. He was still stroking Babayan, and the rooster familiar watched her in their crowded crouched position. She found it unnerving to be this close to the feathered thing, on its

256

own level.

"What are you talking about?" She asked.

The Skatman began his nodding, keeping his white orbs fixed upon her. "Da harlots. Dey say we be leavin', but Babayan and da hound be da only ones stayin'. why ja be standin' for Babayan?"

Sasha shook her head, *what was he getting at?* "We need you to open the gate, remember the deal? Without you, there's no gate."

The Skatman continued nodding "I-Ya! Ja need da Skatman for da crossin', but ja not needin' Babayan. Hound's be easy to find, Why be fightin' for Babayan?"

In truth, Sasha hadn't thought of it. She imagined that the two were somehow a team, together in some way she couldn't understand. She couldn't imagine one without the other.

"I don't know, I thought you needed that thing for your …whatever it is that you do."

This was confusing, especially now. *Why was he asking this? What did he want?*

Through his rustling dreadlocks, the Skatman split his face into his smile. His eyes were wide, Sasha felt like he was looking straight at her soul. "Ja stand for Babayan, an' da Skatman. Ja fight to keep Babayan and da Skatman one."

"You're…. welcome." She said, guessing he was saying thank you in a weird way.

He turned back to watch the black marching figure. "No one be doin Skatman fava's, not many fava's Skatman be owin'."

*What the hell does that mean?*

Slowly the broken thing began to climb the hill, the hallows were falling back from it, still droning on in their ecstasy. Sasha and the others lost sight of it for a moment, but it soon emerged in its suffering gait near the front of Craigdarroch Castle.

It stopped at the base of the huge stairs. None of the hallows were on the hilltop any longer. They had all forced themselves back, lurking and shifting around the object of their adoration. The creature itself, features made indiscernible by its charred black form, paused as though ready to make a battle speech.

Sasha watched as the creature raised its lanky black skeletal arms above its head. They looked so long and fragile, like they might snap off. The hallows were became more excited still, all of them screaming as loud as they could, stroking themselves and each other in a moving orgy around the hill.

Then Abaddon gathered his power.

Sickly yellow bolts of power leapt from the creatures hands and down into the crowds of hallows. There with the hallows still screaming, she watched the bolts jump like lightning from one hallow to the next. The bolts were sucking the life force from them, then flying back up to the forsaken being on the mount.

The hallows that the light touched could only let out a barking cry before they fell to the ground, withered husks drained of all essence. The bolts of power retuned to the creature, striking its body and a fresh bolt was emitted from its hands.

"Soon now, we go." The Skatman hissed.

Clarence was gaping at the scene. Sasha thought the hallows should have been running, they should realize that they were being fed on by this creature. Instead, they were trying to catch the yellow bolts of death as they flew between them, fighting for the privilege to be consumed by this monster.

As the infected yellow light continued throughout the crowds, the creature began to change. She could see that the arms were not as skinny as they once were, and the collapsed limp wings that hung rotting from its back began to quiver. It was still rotting, but it was taking the essence of the bloated hallows and adding it to his own.

Abaddon stopped spewing the yellow bolts and reined the last of the gathering light. What had been a seething crowd of hallows had been reduced to a scattering of moaning creatures in a field of drained shells. Only a third of the hallows remained, the rest claimed by their master. The ones left were staggering about unable to get footing on the piles of dead.

Abaddon had taken shape on the top of the mount. She could see the flesh on his bones, but the angel hadn't claimed enough souls to make himself whole. The scabbed wings were intact, spreading wide on either side with large weeping wounds and gaping holes that let the glow from the house pass through.

If he slaughtered twice as many hallows, then perhaps he would be complete, but his body was half born. Large weeping and clotting sores covered him. His skin was not yet in place and Sasha could see blood red muscles trying to function with tendons barley gripping, only the wings had the scabbed membrane of skin covering them.

A rumbling began, a storm was coming. The glowing mists of the war were beginning to swirl quicker, beginning to boil with the coming power. The time of crossing was drawing near. The creature folded its great wings and then stretched them out again, raising his arms and testing the flesh of his new form.

It howled, and the fabric of reality was ripped in half. The scream echoed inside their heads, a half born cry of agony, anger, and anguish came from this fleshy mass. This was the angel Abaddon.

The hallows that remained heard the cry of their master, and obeyed. They resumed their feverish lust, involving both the living and dead in their sexual acts and violence. They heard the echoed cry within their own shattered minds and lent their own choir to the call.

Dropping its arms, the half born Seraphim turned and began ascending the steps into Craigdarroch Castle. His wings had formed enough to fold neatly like a cape of meat, but they left a blood trail behind him as he entered the house.

The hallows were climbing over each other, snarling and moaning in what sounded like a mixture of hunger and rage. Their attention was not on the house on the hill, they looked out at the fields of the fallen, watching. They were guarding.

Their task was to not allow any creature past them. The crossing was at hand and nothing was being left to chance. Even though there was but a third of what had been amassing, there was more than three hundred of the savage abominations tearing wantonly at the earth.

The Skatman held out his hand, feeling an imaginary object in the air, sensing the texture of madness that had been brewing. His head flopped over to Sasha lazily and his eyes were wider than she had ever seen them before. He must have been closer, more sensitive to the dark powers gathering. If Sasha could sense them, then the Skatman must have the very essence of this place coursing through his veins.

"Nothin' more for you here Mista Winka, time to go."

Clarence was surprised at the Skatman's concern. "I say, well, I might rather like to see the actual ceremony, up close. It's not every day that one gets a chance to document this kind of thing, What?

Sasha felt a sudden love for the twisted old ringmaster. "He's right Clarence, there is a good chance you won't make it, there are hundreds of the hallows…"

"I think I should like to go along anyway, It's not the sort of thing that a gentleman would leave a lady alone with." Clarence cut her off and smiled in a most charming way.

Sasha realized at that moment just how much the strange old fellow had done for her. He had been her guide, if it wasn't for him she wouldn't have been able to do anything, most likely would have wound up consumed by some hateful thing. She wanted to throw her arms around him, it must have shown because Clarence actually blushed, not an easy trick for a wraith as old as he was.

She turned away from the old wraith. Sasha stayed low as she made her way back through the rubble to where they had gathered. The chyldren were still sitting, each one touching another in communicating. There was no way they would have been able to beat that many hallows, not even with the Skatman and herself using all the power at their disposal, the chyldren were vital.

The rope burned one saw Sasha coming and broke away to greet her. He came quickly but surprisingly quietly, stopping his great form only inches away from her face. It let her touch its' skin sending warmth through them both.

"We have to get into that house, the Skatman, Clarence and myself. But there are too many hallows. If we try to make it alone they will kill us. Will you help us?"

She didn't know if it could hear her, there were no ears on the child, but it big blue eyes blinked and it head moved as though it understood. The chyldren had no fear of the hallows, but they didn't want to be without the new mother they had found. At the realization she would leave, she could see and feel the sadness in its face.

"I have to go, it's my daughter, I'm sorry." Sasha wanted to speak, but found she could only whisper. Tears had begun streaming down her cheeks. These chyldren deserved better, this whole land was a horror. The cruelty of fate left nothing for them.

The chyld broke away from her and at once Sasha felt a terrible sense of loss. She didn't know if they would help. Why should they? She was abandoning them. She tried not to think that way, She had to do this, for Daphne.

The rope burned chyld slowly loped back to the others and with the speed of touch passed what it had learned from Sasha amongst them. She waited anxiously for their reaction. Then the rope burned one led the others back towards her.

There was sadness there, but when they touched, the chyldren knew Sasha's love for her daughter. That love was passed and shared between all of them, powerful and pure. They understood the love and none of them would allow Daphne to come here. The conviction in their eyes was unmistakable.

Sasha reached forward and touched the muscled arm of the chyld. She had to say thank you, she had to tell them what this meant to her. She had to tell them the storm of pain within her that came from leaving them. No words could express what she felt,. She touched them, and in touching told them with the caress of a mothers' hand.

A voice from behind. " Sasha! Now is the time! We must be off!" Clarence called.

The thought transferred instantly to the chyldren and they knew what must be done. Sasha ran back to where the Skatman and Babayan were waiting. He was standing now, no longer hiding in the shadows. His dreadlocks parted over his face with his white eyes gleaming, she caught the flash of a smile.

*Why wouldn't he smile* she thought. He had to save her daughter, yes, but after that he would be free. She hated him for it, but he would save her daughter, and that was all that mattered. After all. They had a deal. She couldn't start doubting him now.

He was a grinning reaper in the realm of death. The rooster circled anxiously at the Shamans' feet as the rising wind blew his coat about him. A crash thundered from the storm, it was building faster now.

"What now?" Sasha spoke, not looking at the Shamans' face.

"Now we go, ja be stayin' close to da Skatman, Moonchild. Mista' Winka' if ja be comin', don' get in da way." His eyes burned as he said it. There was an unspoken ultimatum there, both warning and threat.

Clarence took it in stride. "Not to worry sir."

"We go." The Skatman turned in place and ran straight towards the house. Clarence ran beside her and pulled her into motion.

"C'mon, then Tally ho!" He said with a gleam in his eyes.

For Sasha, it was so sudden. There had to be more of a plan, something more than just following him, but perhaps it would be better if she didn't know.

The field's mud would grab and pull you down if you weren't light on your feet. Sasha took three strides and began to get mired in the battle bog. The Skatman's brightly patched cloak was flapping behind him like a gypsy's cape, as his bare feet hardly sank in the muck of the field

"If you run hard you won't sink!" Clarence called to her.

Sasha started taking smaller steps, faster and so she was able to pick up speed. She would only touch the ground for an instant, just long enough to push off again. She was closing with the Skatman now. The chyldren fanning out on either side..

The chyldren lumbered into the mud, their feet sinking deep. The power of their legs tore great chunks of sticky earth as they strode. Very quickly they picked up speed with their dogs fanning out like dark ripples around them.

The sounds of the hallow's lust and the swirling mist were able to mask their sights and sounds, but wouldn't for long. The wind blowing against her, Sasha could feel the energy within begin to build and channeled it down for her legs to go faster.

With Sasha's power and the chyldren's stride, Clarence began to fall behind. A chyld scooped him up in a powerful hand and dropped him onto his shoulders. Clarence struggled for balance, nearly dropped his precious Diary, but managed to hold it.

It was then that the hallows saw the dark shape of the attacking force and a shrill scream erupted from the seething hordes of Craigdarroch Castle. Like maggots tumbling from a burst carcass they came, tumbling over one another and screaming with the vicious lust of the dead.

The chyldren fanned out making a battle line as they raced across the mud. The dogs were running ahead anticipating the hallows mangled flesh in their jaws. The hallows had no such structure. They saw the meat coming and wanted to taste it.

With the wind going against them, Sasha could smell the scent of rape as the hallows began their advance. An explosion of arms and legs, slapping leather and cutting hands, licking eyes and gazing lips held tongues swollen with desire. They would have Sasha and the chyldren, they would have them for the glory of Abaddon.

Three of the chyldren passed in front of the Skatman and Sasha forming an arrowhead of protection, a spearhead of muscle. The rope burned chyld taking up the lead swept up Sasha and dropped her onto his shoulders. She could feel the rage building further still, she would use this chyld as a firing platform for her deadly rage.

There were eternal moments that passed before the two sides collided. The forever that passed with the unbearable roar of the wind, mixed with the filth tainted howls of the hallows. Crossing the battle field towards what was her daughter, Sasha felt the power within her building to a level she had never felt before. If she unleashed a blast now, she would destroy the house, this world, this whole dimension, such power flowed within her.

She couldn't feel her own body, there was only a blur of flesh merged with the chyld. She thundered onwards leading these massive flying mountains of muscle. They would break through the hallows, Daphne was on the other side.

*The Skatman has to cross.*

The chyld that Clarence was riding took up a position behind them. Winker leaned forward over the head of his muscled steed, his top hat firmly drilled down to just over his eyebrows and his long hawk nose breaking the wind. The chyld's speed made his coat tails flap, snapping like hounds at his heels.

Only seventy five meters from the house, the two armies met. The first of the hallows who greeted their coming were the fast and nimble of their ranks. Gaunt thin shapes holding whips and rattling chains over leather and lace clad bodies.

The wave of the dogs took them. The hallows and dogs both leaping into the air, whips and jaws colliding in hate. The dogs could take three hallows at a time but there were too many. Mangled tearing and stabbing fingers frenzied in a clash of erupting filth. The front line of the hallows had been met, with the sweeping wave of chyld muscle coming up from behind

The hallows leapt high as though to clear the rushing chyldren and attack from behind. But the chyldren raised mammoth arms and slapped them from the air with sounds like cannons roar. The hallows broken bodies became a blur as they rocket down, carving out muddy graves.

The chyldren met the wave of hallows and flesh throwing bodies in all directions. The sounds of whips and chains whirling in the air and slashing at the chyldren could be heard between roars of anger. Waves of hallows crashed over each other, clawing to get a taste of flesh.

The chyldren's tactics were simple. Swat the hallows away, that which you cannot swat, *break*. That which you could not break, crush.

The lead spearhead let a couple of the more eager hallows slip through. The Skatman made sweeping motion with hooked hands like a bird spreading its wings and the hallows were fired by an invisible force under the trampling legs of the chyldren at their sides.

Babayan had moved into the forefront of the attack, ahead of the spear head. The rooster was a mass of feathered fury, perpetually screaming in the glory of combat. Babayan bathed in the chaos of death. Flapping its putrid wings, it leapt from one hallow to the next, tearing heads off in its assisted flight and leaving twisted dead to be trampled.

They were close to the front steps now, forty feet at the most. Some of the wiser hallows had waited on the roof of the house. Now they began jumping down onto them, screaming shadows against the black sky. The first ones were too eager, they were met mid air by dogs who took them from the side. Sickening crunches split the air as the hallow's spines snapped from the impact. Being so close to the house, the light it gave off gave the chyldren an edge as the hallows came down.

Two leapt straight for Sasha, another was going past her, towards Clarence.

"Clarence!" She screamed.

Sasha threw her arms into the air and a bright blast of light erupted from her fingertips. A huge cone of power, eight feet wide tore upwards catching the hallows, ripping the very flesh from their bones. The beam of power carried on and struck one of the roof peaks past them, searing a hole and blowing ash fragments into the sky.

Clarence heard the warning in time to catch the hallow as it came. He caught the being with his arms out-stretched and swept it over his head while holding onto the chyld with his legs. The hallow had nothing to grip. He tore a piece of Winker's coat and scratched his face, but tumbled into the swinging fist of the chyld running behind.

At the front steps, the spearhead formed a half circle of protection allowing for the group to climb. Winkers' mount gave him a rapid hand to the steps and he landed just behind the Skatman and Sasha as they began to climb. Babayan was furiously clearing the stairs ahead of them swinging his bloodstained body anticipating more death. The Skatman looked back. "Stay close, Moonchild!"

The steps were a blur, she could hear the sounds of ripped flesh and breaking bones behind them as they climbed. The chyldren would hold their position, they would keep killing as long as they had to. Sasha followed the Skatman and Babayan through the glowing porthole of the doorway.

It was like running into light. She heard something as she went in but her eyes couldn't adjust to the bright glowing green that now surrounded her. Over the raspy panting of Clarence behind, she heard a sound like a man vomiting and then a crash. Just past the doors a confused guardian in white robes had appeared for them, the black shamans sickle tore him open from crotch to throat.

They were in a room with an exit to either side and a hallway leading down to the front. She could see flickering tongues of candles floating in the air burning down either side. The Skatman caught sight of the blood trail made by the scabbed wings of Abaddon and knew which route to take.

*"G'fawn myleh xantahedra dandrathu, dandrathus selohim Abaddon!"*

Deep chanting came from the bowels of the house. The Skatman went further, crouched low. Over top of chanting he could hear two wraiths talking around the corner.

"This is the realms of the beyond, it must be." The calmer voice was saying.

"No we're not dead! We're not dead! Shut up I'm right here! We're still right here!" The talk of madness, wraiths not long dead.

*"G'fawn myleh xantahedra dandrathu, dandrathus selohim Abaddon!"*

The Skatman was gliding, leading Sasha and Clarence down the hall. Babayan let them pass taking up the rear of the party to slaughter any attackers from behind. As they closed around the corner, Sasha couldn't help but notice the hideous face of a woman illuminated by a floating candle flame at the end of the hall. The very essence of the picture had something about it, something she could feel.

The Skatman took the corner to see two wraiths. One was older, with a silver Abraham Lincoln beard, the other a younger, wearing a robe with a strange symbol on the front. He was looking for something, as though he had just dropped it.

They both looked up to see the long black ink dreadlocks of the Skatman, his sickle hanging by his side. An experienced wraith would have run, would have attacked, would have done something. These two were too new, they could only stare.

*"G'fawn myleh xantahedra dandrathu, dandrathus selohim Abaddon!"*

The first slash took away the old man s throat, the younger fellow tried to dodge by ducking, but instead he caught the blade in the nose, hanging himself at an awkward angle on the Skatman's hooked blade and dancing while his mind shredded. The Skatman had to put his spidery hand on his head to force the bladed back out again, cursing silently.

*"G'fawn myleh xantahedra dandrathu, dandrathus selohim Abaddon!"*

A doorway loomed, this one with a different light. All the light that Sasha had seen before, it all had the same sickly tinge of green to it, but this door was alive. It wasn't light of its own that escaped to this realm. They were looking from a green world out to natural lighting. The light that she had known in the world of the living. Beyond this door was where the crossing had to be. From below, she could hear chanting louder. The Skatman didn't hesitate, he swung open the door drifted down the stairwell.

A white robe appeared in the stairway, spilling out of the living light around them. He had just died in the living realm, and didn't have a chance to scream before the Skatman spilled his essence into this house. Again his sickle was a blur and the robes' head was removed. The Skatman held the head and guided the body onto the stairs letting the blood flow down the stairs to mark their path.

*"G'fawn myleh xantahedra dandrathu, dandrathus selohim Abaddon!"*

The Skatman began to mutter under his breath unintelligible things. He was speaking a language mankind had never known, and from its blasphemous tones, they never should. She was halfway down the steps before she realized he was casting a spell. Without pausing from his chant he reached back and grabbed Sasha's wrist.

*This was it. He was going to do it soon.*

She had been able to press it out of her mind up until this point but there was no denying it now, the Dark Houngan was going to kill her, use her energy to cross the void.

*"G'fawn myleh xantahedra dandrathu, dandrathus selohim Abaddon!"*

Clarence realized it as well, he was biting his lower lip. He wanted to say something. Behind Clarence, the wings of Babayan spread at the top of the stairs. It knew the crossing was at hand and soon it, and its master would be free of this realm. Sasha thought of Daphne, this was all to save her now.

The hallway was a mixture of the light of the living and dead as they descended. The walls were becoming more real, more alive the deeper they went. The blood running from the wraith behind them was slowing its flow, only a trickle now as they stepped. They rounded the corner amongst the chanting.

*"G'fawn myleh xantahedra dandrathu, dandrathus selohim Abaddon!"*

Thirteen white robes were standing in a circle. They all bowed their heads out of respect letting their hoods cover them, looking like perfect white pillars. Around them at their feet a massive symbol glowed in a damned red light. A pain of memory came at the sight of the symbol. She had seen it before when she was tied to a slab, a slab much like the one they had in this room at the far front.

*Was Daphne tied to that slab? Was she going to appear there in moments?*

Sasha had never thought she would want to die, or want herself to be killed, but now more than anything she wanted to feel the a bite of the shamans blade. She needed to know her daughter could be spared this place. She looked to the dark Houngan with desperation, but he was looking at something else.

*"G'fawn myleh xantahedra dandrathu, dandrathus selohim Abaddon!"*

The angel's blood trail that they had followed down the stairs passed over the glowing red sigil into the center of the white robes. There finally, up close, they could see the being that was called Abaddon.

There is no mistaking evil, no mistaking the kind of taste that rises in your mouth when you see it. Scholars and religious philosophers can bicker and feud over what they feel is holy or right, but this kind of damnation was pure, like pain. There way no denying it.

The skinless form that stood before them , huge and unfinished. A ten foot thing whose bones and tendons jutted out from uncompleted skin. The body had not had the strength to completely reform, but still large scabbed black wings hung on its back, vile and putrid reminders of what it once was. Blood forever seeped out, pumped by incomplete organs making the body shiny and wet.

*"G'fawn myleh xantahedra dandrathu, dandrathus selohim Abaddon!"*

It turned to face them showing a long deformed skull, muscles creeping onto it like mold and eyeless sockets that couldn't see, but it knew that his enemies had entered. Sasha's body surged involuntarily.

There was a part of this thing inside of her, and that part of her knew its master. She could feel the energy within wanting to get out of her wanting to return to the source. All at once, the abilities she had in this realm were disgusting. Those were not the powers of a woman, those were not the abilities given to protect herself, that was the power of Abaddon trying to return to the source.

*Kill me now.*

Before the Skatman could twitch, before Abaddon could scream, before Sasha could speak or spells be cast, something happened on the circle. It began to pulse, scream out loud in voices of the living and take on a greater light of its own.

*Daphne was dead. The gateway was opening!*

Or was it? The flashing pulses of the sigil were erratic, surging dangerously bright and then fading. The thirteen white robes within the sigil were unaware that Sasha and the others had entered but now began to look down at the unexpected surges of power.

Lives were being lost in the realm of the living. Human life force was being channeled into the circle, yet it wasn't the life of the sacrifice, it was the lives of their brethren being spilled into the sigil. Sasha's sudden loss of hope was stunted by the angel jerking left and right, there was no mistaking those movements.

*Panic!*

Something was wrong, something wasn't going as planned.

267

The howl came. The thirteen white robes broke from their chant. Their hoods sweeping back and fourth trying to get their bearings. The angel threw its skeletal form at the invaders, its eyeless sockets and gaping jaw wide, but the circle stopped him as though a sheet of glass now went from the floor to the ceiling in the room precisely at the edge of the glowing red runes.

The bloody mass of Abaddon jerked from left to right but there was nowhere to pass. The white robes inside were starting to panic themselves. Their messiah was growing more and more enraged trapped in a vortex shield they had so carefully prepared.

The inevitable happened. Abaddon turned his anger to those he could claim. Another roar from the angel and all thirteen figures collapsed to the floor. From within their robes thick chunky streams of blood and flesh flowed like tiny rivers carrying the meat from his loyal thirteen.

They weren't dead, Sasha could hear their screams even over the howl of the angel as he stripped them of form. The streams of living meat all flowed into the angels' feet running up his form and melting into his body.

He was trying to add more essence to himself for the crossing, his body was far more complete now. Outside, he slaughtered a nation of creatures to capture their essence, now his Chosen thirteen would give his body the flesh it required to make the crossing. Eyes were beginning to form and skin was growing fast.

"Now be da time." The Skatman hissed.

Sasha could feel the bite of his sickle blade already. She closed her eyes and hoped he would make it fast but the bite never came,

Sasha found herself flying through the air, the Skatman swung her hard by the arm and she didn't even touch the ground until she landed in the circle. His strength was unbelievable, the Skatman had thrown her into the runic circle before she had a chance to react.

*This was how I am to die? He is going to feed me to this thing?*

The cry of Babayan.

The rooster had worked his way around the side of the circle keeping out of the focus of the being of madness, Sasha snapped her eyes open to see the rooster fly into the circle catching the angel from behind, sinking talons deep into the forming flesh on the back of his skull.

From behind, the rooster's beak slashed around the angel's head and face, another

howl of rage came. Babayan was no match for the creature that w
For all his fury, Babayan was merely an abomination, nothir
ancient evil it attacked. But Babayan's goal wasn't to kill Abaddon, just to ——
for a severed moment. The bird was to create a window for the Skatman to strike.

The long patchwork coat became wings, as the Skatman leapt into the runic circle. The sound and fury of Babayan kept the angel busy and the Skatman's sickle caught the seraphim from the side of its throat.

It cut deep almost through its neck, but not quite. The angels' howl grew shrill, it had chosen to take a physical form and now paid the price. Babayan was at once thrown free and smashed against the invisible barrier of the circle and crumpled to the ground.

The half formed muscles that did exist snapped the creatures' head sharply to it shoulder, leaving the gaping neck wound free to shower the area with blood. Both he and the Skatman raised their arms to strike, one with an angelic fist, the other with a hooked steel razor. Their arms fell and with the power of death unleashed. There was a bright blood red flash.

The confines of two worlds were broken.

## Chapter 29

There were still bodies twitching when Luke looked into the room, sprawled in a massive bloody pile overtop the an archaic symbol that had been drawn there. The smell of blood and the stench of gun smoke mixed, stinging his senses as he viewed the carnage. Buck had just been through here, the bodies were everywhere.

There was one on the altar.

*There was a child on the altar.*

"Daphne!!!!" He shouted.

In an instant he was by her side. She was naked sprawled out across the altar, tied down with leather straps. He saw Buck's blade lying on the altar beside her.

Shaking with adrenaline, he cut the straps free and dropped the blade to the floor. Daphne didn't move, her body was only vibrating lightly under the leather blindfold. Luke stuck the pistol in the back of his pants and took off his jacket to cover his daughter. He draped it over her body and then lifted the leather mask way. Her eyes were closed tight and her face white with tension but she looked unharmed.

Luke whispered to her " Baby, it's Daddy. We're going home."

With the smell of his jacket and the sound of his voice, her eyes dared to flash open for an instant.

"Da-dey?..."She said, as if dreaming.

She was traumatized, but alive. Her arms swung up like a steel trap around his neck, desperate and firm. She was crying, her little body wracked with sobs. Luke swung her body upon to his hip and she clamped onto him.

Time to go. He was halfway across the room when the bright blood red rift opened..

Time and space ripped where the runic circle stood and the bodies were piled. The blast staggered him back a few steps, his eyes out of focus but he found the silenced Glock stuck in the back of his belt where he left it, and pointed it out ahead.

The flash faded and with Daphne on his hip he prepared to fire. Ahead of him , The bodies that piled in the circle were gone and in their place were three figures.

There was a tall man wearing a longer patchwork coat, an impossibly large rooster, and laying unconscious on the floor, a woman wearing army boots, black leather pants and a biker jacket.

*Sasha.*

*NO! Sasha is dead.* He had seen the body. She had been slashed open, cut up by the cultists. This was another trick, another ploy by these things.

The large black man with the colorful coat had a wickedly long sickle in his hands. He was covered with crusted blood, right down to his rattail dreadlocks. With Luke's eyes back in focus, he decided the one with the blade was the first to be drilled. He trained the weapon on the shambling form, but a sudden scream took away his attention.

The rooster, aside from being massive, was fast, far faster than he would have thought. Holding Daphne his balance was off and a cluster of foul feathers and flesh slammed against his wrist knocking the gun high. He fired but the muffled shot flew harmlessly into the ceiling and the Glock tumbled into the candle spared darkness.

Luke staggered but remained standing, the attacking bird stayed back keeping a distance and swinging its hideously hooked beak. Luke tried to see where the pistol fell but no sign of it. A quick shoulder check and he knew where the knife was. It wasn't much, but it was a weapon.

He glanced over his shoulder to look for the knife for a split second, but the Skatman was in front of him.

Right in front of him.

An arm of black corded muscle lashed out and grabbed his face. His spider-like fingers reaching around his head and blocking his vision.

"Be da' Watcha'!" The Skatman hissed.

A flood of images came to him. The crossing, Clarence, bogymen, hallows, cats, harlots, struck deals, tortured hounds, hideous things in the shadows of a dimly lit city, and with all of these things came understanding.

The rush was too much for him. He felt himself falling but iron arms caught him and held him up. It all came back into focus and the Skatman's burning white eyes were looking into his. His teeth gleaming in a grin. The visions were fading like a dream awoken, but understanding remained. This was his wife, brought back by this creature before him.

*There was another chance.*

" Ja must go now Luke Edwards, Ja' take da little one an' Moonchild away, leave now! Bad men be comin' soon, I-Ya!"

He didn't understand. He had his life back somehow, this was another dream. But unlike his moments with Genaya, the voice within him knew this was true. There was no time to deliberate, and he knew what had to be done. Holding his daughter he ran to where his wife lay.

"Da Skatman be payin' all fava's I-Ya!." The Skatman said, his voice laughing in his husky whisper

Sasha opened her eyes, it was the first time she had woken up for as long as she could remember. Luke was over her, tears running down his face. She was alive, or Luke was dead, but Daphne was here. The energy that was within her in Abaddon was fading fast, her body had set like concrete.

Luke helped her to her feet. With Daphne clinging to his shoulder and Sasha on his other his arm, they moved as fast as they could.

"We have to run, c'mon baby." Luke said through his tears. There was so much he didn't understand, so much that defied his logical mind, yet still he knew it was true. He couldn't prove this was his wife any more than he could prove the love of his child, but he knew it.

The Skatman was gone, vanished as though into the walls. Luke helped Sasha to her feet, and holding Daphne, stepped out of the strange circle, leaving a massive book that lay within it.

As fast as they could, Luke got his family out of the damned house. He didn't look back for Buck.

He didn't look back for the Skatman. He ran up the stairs past the blood, holding onto his wife's hand. None of this made sense, but he didn't care.

As he left the shattered front doors of Craigdarroch Castle, he heard breaking glass far above. The Witch Hunter was inside the matrix of upstairs rooms, bringing justice to any human traitors that he found.

The family ran across the dark lawn and down the gravel drive to where Luke had left the car. He put his wife and child in the back seat and ran around the outside to get in.

He had done it, he had got his daughter back and Sasha was there too. His wife was still alive.

As the car pulled away from the curb with his family inside, broken and bleeding but alive, Luks' mind was racing faster than he could ever have driven. Somehow he got it all back, somehow it was all going to be the way it was before.

As the car sped away from Craigdarroch Castle, the Witch Hunter continued his sweep as bright blues flashes of electricity erupted on the lawn.

Buck could smell the scent of ozone, and knew that the reinforcements had arrived. As always, he didn't need them.

**Chapter 30**

**Abaddon**
*The most comprehensive book ever written on the realms of the dead.*

*Volume 2*
Entry # 1

Dear Mr. Diary

Finally, I am able to report that Sasha has seemed to make it back across the void. "The Crossing" as the Skatman called it. At least I hope so, or no doubt they are somewhere else, (anywhere else actually.) But I would prefer to think that she's fine and doing well. This of course is far beyond my control, but one does what one can.

This is book two you know. My first book I had to send back across in somewhat of hurry with Sasha and the Skatman. I would have rather liked to have been able to edit it a bit more, but seize the day and all that.

I could go through a rather lengthy explanation about who I am and all that, but I'm afraid I'm not in the mood. Besides, if you want to know that history you must re-read my somewhat mammoth first diary, located I am proud to say, in the realms of the living...somewhere.

At least I think so, but I've already said that.

Oh BOTHER!

They made it into the living realm, there that's it. I'll not have any speculation about them dying or drifting about, lost in time and space. The Skatman seemed perfectly competent, and for whatever reason he didn't kill Sasha, or take her essence for the spell, a thing that I found most surprising.

I've given this much thought however, and I do feel the Skatman despite his habits is a rather noble sort. You see, in order to open the gate, the rift as it were a certain amount of energy had to be expended. The essence that was in any one of the keys of Abaddon, that is Sasha or her daughter were enough to breach the worlds, but the angel had the power too!

It would have been nothing for the Skatman to kill Sasha and lie to us all, he could have slaughtered her, opened the rift, and gone through letting Sasha's' child be damned, but he didn't.

Rather surprising, rather surprising indeed.

I myself thought for certain that we would have been destroyed by the angel, and if it wasn't for the barrier half existing. That is, locking him between worlds within that runic ward, we would all most definitely be dead, (well so to speak) but the rune held him and bought the Skatman some time.

It couldn't have been better really, his body was only forming, trapped between worlds. The Skatman knew just when to strike.

Getting out of Craigdarroch Castle was a bother, but fortunately the chyldren (Again, refer to Vol.1) managed to wait for me. I must say, I prefer riding to walking in this place, and with chyldren, one is terrifically less afraid.

I've been rather lucky in finding enough blank sheets to begin binding my new diary. (I was once a great book restorationist you know) So I'll continue my research for as long as I can. It will be rather good if someone somewhere gets a glance at my scribbling. Maybe, in my dream of dreams, they will be held with some regard.

I should go. Try to keep up, I don't have time to back track. There is still so much more here.

Yours truly,

Clarence Winker
Abaddon Researcher

## Chapter 31

Sasha sat on the couch watching the rain come down the main windows in the apartment.

Luke was back at work, finally. He just went back this week. She didn't envy him, trying to deal with questions as well as having to leave her there in the house. But he was content to phone home six or seven times over the eight hour day. The phone calls were creeping more minutes apart, the security was coming back, the pieces were being picked up.

When she walked through the door the first time, Sebastian jumped out the open window to the fire escape, and hadn't returned in the three weeks she had been back. She never liked cats much anyway.

To her, the whole thing was a dream. She spent a week lying in bed trying handle the return shock. At one moment she's running for her life from wulves, hallows, and bogeymen. The next she is trying to figure out if she can get her job back. And there were always the questions, The inevitable awkward torrent of inquisition that would come from everyone.

*"We heard you were dead...".*

The story that her and Luke were telling everyone was that she was only kidnapped and another woman had been killed. After that it was just as easy to say that she didn't want to talk about it and others would walk away with begrudging nods.

The police were surprisingly cooperative. Luke told them his wife just showed up on the doorstep one day holding her daughters' hand. There was no memory of course, that had all been blocked but Luke knew a good private therapist that could help them with their blocked memories.

Embarrassed, the police claimed the body that Luke found originally must have been Jane Doe who Luke identified due to similarities, and since there was the cremation there was no way to track the error, so it became an error that didn't exist.

It all just kind of slipped together so easily. The car Luke drove back from the island was gone the next morning, and all traces of Buck went with it. Everyone wanted this whole thing to just go away, just let it be smoothed over by a blanket of denial. The more bizarre the incident the more quickly the mind tries to save itself by changing reality.

Daphne had slept with them every night since their return. She woke up screaming the first two nights, but stopped after that. There was still damage that had to be healed. Susie was still dead, Gwen was still dead, but very slowly Daphne was returning back to being a normal little girl. This segment of her life would become a barely remembered dream. The kind of segment too many little girls already have.

Right now, Daphne way sitting quietly on the couch beside her mom. They were both enjoying hot chocolate. The flavor was amazing, the dark rich fluid warming her hands through the mug, and spilling that same warmth through her body as she drank it. They hadn't said anything for fifteen minutes. They were listening to the comfortable rhythm of the rain, swept by the melody of wind, leaving streaks down the front windows.

"Mummy?" A little voice said.

"Yes baby?"

"What happens after we die?" Daphne asked with her eyes wide.

The innocent question of a child. Met with the half truth of the uncomfortable adult. Sasha wasn't without her own scarring. She could still see the blades of the cultists, the fangs of the wulves and the clutching hands of the hallows. She still left doors open in the house and watched dark corners.

"I'll tell you when you're older sweetie, I'll tell you when you're older."

Until then, the rain swept, the window sang, and the world did turn.

Life went on.

## Chapter 32

"Nothing is so cruel as fate."

-*The Truth*

He awoke with a scream into the blackness. His own voice tearing him from the realm of dreams. He wanted to sit up but the blankets were pressed tight against him.

*No! They're holding me down!*

His old body unable to budge. Darkness all around him, and a smell. That putrid haunting smell in the room.

*Am I dreaming? Am I still dreaming?*

A sound like spit hitting pavement came from where his wife was lying beside him in the darkness. No, the smell wasn't fading, not like it had the all other times, with all the other dreams!

A single match erupted light into the into the room.

The tiny flame took away the masking darkness and showed the rooster, that same hideous rooster from that night so long ago, perched on the chest of his wife gleefully tearing strips off of her face. Most of the flesh on her head was gone now, only a crowning frame of white hair around a stripped skull, shards of meat hanging like leaches where her features used to be.

His voice couldn't scream, his throat clamped tight when he tried. Turning back, he knew who had to be holding the match. Within the darkness, the Skatman sat beside him on the bed.

"So Mista Bartlet, be takin' awhile, but da' Skatman be comin' 'round. Time ja be goin' Abaddon, I-Ya."

His scream was still choked by the terror of the vision..

"But don'cha worry Klans-mon, da little ones ja keep, an da little ones dey keep; da Skatman be sendin' all come Abaddon."

The match burned out against the Skatman's calloused fingers and darkness returned.

In the night there was pain, suffering, terror and the horrible mangling of old flesh.

The End


Sarah McLachlan:
*Building a Mystery.*

# THE SCABBED WINGS OF ABADDON

**My Dark Testament**
*By Sean Kennedy*

Many people feel that I am a fool for publishing my work on the honor system, and maybe they are right. We live in a time when honesty has become pornography, and trust has become a myth more fantastical than any of my works.

Yet I believe.

I encourage people to read my books and share them, because I believe in horror fans. Horror fans understand dark things, and are more keenly aware of the seething subtleties that others miss. The horror community celebrates their unique culture against the grain of a mediocre world. I write for the horror fan. I write for you.

Those who send what they feel this work is worth, share a sacred bond with myself and the words I write. Yet those who spread the word make a greater contribution, because they show the story to fresh eyes, and bring more people into my dark worlds.

It is more important that you share this book with someone, than it is to make a monetary donation. My stories are meant to be shared amongst friends, not bought and sold by strangers. My only request is that you replicate this book in its entirety, including this page, never sell it, and give myself the credit for penning these words.

If the fans of my work believe in me, they will support me.
I believe this, because I believe in dark powers,
I believe in the things beyond the mind veil,
I believe in the hideous strength of forgotten science,
And I believe in you.

Online contributions can be made at:

**WWW.DARKATLAS.COM**

CPSIA information can be obtained
at www.ICGtesting.com
Printed in the USA
LVHW012121201122
733657LV00001B/18

9 781430 316206